I0691778

THE WOODSTOCK PARADIGM

By Edward DeVito

Copyright © 2013 by Edward DeVito

Published by Wayward Mountain Press. All rights reserved. No part of this publication may be reproduced, or stored in a retrieval system, or transmitted in any form or by any means, mechanical, photocopying, recording or otherwise, without written permission of the Publisher, except for purposes of critical review. For information regarding permissions contact the Author at http://www.woodstockparadox.com

ISBN 978-0-9910791-1-7

V-1.4.1

First Edition printed by Odin Prints
Portland State University Bookstore
Portland, Oregon, USA

Cover execution by Bruce Spainhower

Author's Note

This novel is about time travel, family and blood, love and desire, loss and resilience, the present and future world, and another look at freedom, spirituality, and UFOs.

Edward DeVito
January 2, 2011

Thanks To:

Wayne Chadburn – for rolling with another project.

Bruce Spainhower – for ongoing technical assistance,
friendship, and encouragement.

Eadi Popick – same as above, and also for review and editing assistance.

Rod Folen and Peter Youell, reviewing and editing assistance.

Phil Manley, Master Sergeant, U.S. Army, retired – for reviewing military scenes.

Stephanie Schmidt, at The Boise Stage Stop - for reviewing the scene description
there.

Tim Werner, Principal – for sharing protocol, future plans, and logistical
information regarding the future Sandy High School.

Brogan Adams, Site Super at Hoffman Construction – for providing site elevations
and plans of Sandy High School.

Scott Maltman, from the Athletic Departmant, and Coach Matt Gist at Sandy
High School – for reviewing the basketball scene.

Sandy Hansen, Athletic Secretary, Rex Putnam High School – for reviewing
description of basketball uniforms.

Dakota, and Jake McAneny – for sharing their experience of Sandy High School.

"I wonder if Tina still has that jar of water from Filippini's Pond?" he mused. *"She told me she'd keep it and I said that was a really good idea."*

...Andy Newell

1 – Snow

A long-haired teenager leaned into the mirror, barefoot in pajamas. This sudden invasion of fine, sandy-colored fuzz actually darkened the space over his lip, invaded planes of his face and softened the outline of his chin. Hot damn! He didn't see it coming any more than the season, or for that matter, the crazy, crazy year. Good God, it wasn't even the same Century!

Even the small decision to shave it or let it alone seemed too much to deal with right now. The vivid green eyes staring back at him revealed nothing else about it. He opened the medicine cabinet. All kinds of vitamins, mouth wash, hand cream, body powder, foot powder, some pretty little boxes with Chinese characters, it was full of things like that, but nothing to dose with, nothing at all. Jesus! Andy told him there might be some herb in the house somewhere, but he said he'd been taking a break, and then months had gone by, and he didn't even know where to get some anymore. Where to get anything...

Arien was grateful for the facial fuzz. It intrigued like a tiny sparkle in his heart's deep leaden cellar.

The lights went out. It began with a subliminal pressure change, like a gust of wind that might have gone unnoticed without the sudden loss of power. Arien's inward smirk reached out with hands in the dingy room to gather his bearings. The light from the snow-splattered window required adjustment to use for navigation.

He swung the bathroom door wide open so he could see – only barely – in the hall. The dark, smooth floorboards were cool underfoot. He took short steps to avoid running into anything and then a bright shaft of light coursed up the papered wall from below to the landing off to his right.

"Are you about up there?"

"Yeah."

"I was making us breakfast."

Arien halted at the top of the stairs to look down at the old man.

"Well the stove is gas. We're good. I can broil the toast." And then he asked, "Shall I come up with the flashlight?"

"Nah, I got it." He turned away from the glow and headed for a dark patch of door to his room. It wasn't as tricky in there, dingy yes, but the broader window allowed more dim light through from outside and he saw the clothes Andy had laid out for him were neatly folded on a hope chest's lid.

Let's see... plaid boxers, a solid orange T-shirt, long-sleeved, blue cotton thermal, a long-sleeved white flannel shirt with flap pockets and a pair of blue carpenter jeans with a black web belt. The gray socks were heavy wool and a pair of Wellington boots was on the floor in front. Interesting. He has me dressing like a geezer. But everything fits, like he measured every inch of my body...

The kitchen shared its dusky light from the windows with the sharp illumination of an LED lantern. He sat at the oak table, slumping into the chair like a bag of sand. When Andy set a plate of scrambled eggs and boiled sausage links down in front of him, Arien gazed at it from his infinite distance.

The old fellow regarded the lad's face with a sad smile. "Aren't you hungry, Arien?"

"I don't know. I could eat a lot of questions, though, Dude." Arien studied the man. His etched and faded features were rounder, its angles less pronounced. He was thinner in some ways and broader in others. He looked strong, and moved easily. Andy still had the moustache! His hair used to be long and wavy; it was cut real short now, thin on top and peppered light to dark gray. But under longer, bristling brows were the same sharp, inviting brown eyes of the young man Arien knew.

"I can hardly believe you're sitting here!" Andy gasped. He set his own plate down but beheld the kid at his table like a priceless treasure, a long-lost friend, and a risen ghost with the light of deepest love and empathy. Its call echoed in the boy's hollow chambers, but he could hear it from an infinite distance. Something inside directed hand to fork and fork to a bit of egg. Once tasted, it wanted more but he wondered if it would only feed the screech in his brain.

"I saved those muddy shorts you wore," Andy said. "They're quite an item! I'm going to frame them in a glass case with some original tickets for that damned festival. You know? I got those off e-Bay a couple of years ago for a truck-load of money." He chuckled to himself.

Arien unconsciously fingered the only familiar thing on him, the silver OM Michael gave him when he, Tina, Jeff, Otter and Andy left San

Francisco. He returned a confused expression but he didn't say anything. Maybe there would be enough time to learn the language in this place but maybe not. Who the Hell knew? He swallowed a surge of grief with a mouthful of egg and sausage and chased that with a glass of canned tomato juice. "Do you have any coffee?"

"I was going to brew espresso when the lights went out." Andy hesitated and then he said, "I suppose I could boil some on the stove." He took a few quick bites of breakfast, and went over to a little gizmo on the counter to gather its dark grains and pour them in a small pot with water from the sink. "There should be enough pressure in the tank for a while," he said at the faucet.

"So what's going on around here?" Arien asked him.

"A lot of snow, for one thing, a lot, with more on top. I've never seen it like this. But it's been getting worse every year, you know." Andy's voice had lost its fullness in over forty-three years. "Everybody's stuck where they are," he continued. "This one's going to kill people, Arien. You know, I'm worried about Thomas. I can't get his cell. Remember Thomas? He was on his way here from Salamanca and should have arrived the day before yesterday. I hope he's found a warm place to wait it out."

"Where's the dog?"

"Buster? Oh, as long as it's not too cold that big fur ball would rather be outside. Ha, I knew Buster was special. He saved your life, Kid."

"Buster."

"We'll ask him if he wants to come in after breakfast, okay?"

"Sure." He drained the juice. "So, how did you find me?" Arien's hands exploded out with a pent-up curiosity that finally demanded to know something.

"Oh, Arien, after I saw you with those kids on Salmon Street – it was incredible after twenty-one years; I got all fired up. Somehow I knew I'd see you again. How else could I find you and then lose you so quickly? But you see, it wasn't sequential, you didn't know me. Ellison was still around then. I sought his advice."

"In 1990?"

"Yes, Arien. I went back to Salamanca to look him up, and Mother Shongo, too. We'd all lost touch."

Arien searched for his young friend, Andy, in the old man's face. This was very, very weird. It was like, only three days ago...

"Mother Shongo said you would come back. Oh, Hari Rama, Arien, she knew!"

3

"And?"

"Well, lucky for us your Tohono mentor out there in Arizona wrote a letter to Ellison before he died. That had to be back in the '80s sometime. Now, this is really cool stuff, Kid." Andy leaned forward from where he stood by a cooking pot of finely-ground, dark-roasted, boiling coffee that was beginning to reach into the room with its deep aroma. "He never lost touch with you! He followed you to the present, even beyond his own life, and he said you would return in the same place where you left us, so now we had it in stereo! Nobody knew exactly where that was, of course, because nobody saw you go. That's where Buster comes in, Arien. In the end it was up to Buster, it was up to a dog! But he's a good doggie. I knew he was special!"

The image of Maggie Austin, the last person he laid eyes on at Woodstock across so great a gulf of time, flashed in Arien's mind and another surge of grief leapt upward with a heaving stomach, searing his heart. This was so crazy! It was way too crazy!

He began to wail with a keening cry, yanking at his hair and Andy hurried over, pulling a chair next to him to cradle the sad, sorry boy in his arms. But Arien, his face contorted, flailing, pushed him away with such uneven force they both fell down on the floor in a thumping clatter and crash of dish and silverware and tipping chairs.

Andy held him, wrapping arms around him, locking hands together to restrain him. "No, Arien," he soothed. "No! It's alright. Please lad! Please be calm!"

Arien jerked and heaved like he'd fallen on the third rail, his body wracked in a paroxysm of grief and despair. "I want to die! Let me die!" he yelled, blending his sharp blade of voice with the dissonant, muffled concussion of a barking dog outside and the gasping, heaving breath of the old man hot against his ear. He wanted to get to the door to run outside into the snow. He wanted to lose himself in the snow.

He couldn't believe the strength in the old man who held him in a vice-like grip.

"Oh, Arien, stop it, stop it; stop it, please!"

It was an odd view from the floor. Andy was heaving and Arien gasped in quick, shallow breaths. His was a spider's eye view to an upended chair and the dark underside of the kitchen table, and a broad plain of brick-pattern linoleum with fragments of a shattered dish inches from his eyeball. "I don't want to be here," he said, going limp as he fell into himself.

It took awhile for Andy to stop panting. His face had gone pallid. "Good God, he said. "You're scaring me. I can't possibly watch you every minute of the day. Oh, Arien, you have to promise me you won't do anything stupid."

"I'm not promising anything." The teenager's voice was flat, and vacant.

Andy let go of him. "Ow, ow," he rasped, grimacing, slowly pulling himself up with the help of the table.

Arien didn't move. He stared at the gloss-white-painted, smooth-textured ceiling. The real spider was up there looking down at him. It wasn't a very large critter, but there seemed to be a tiny pinpoint of reflection from its head, from the shape of it, a gleam in its eye. And then Arien's field of view, taken like a whiskey rush, flipped past in serial staccato frames, finally settling from an absurd perspective of his giant's body splayed on the distant floor like a discarded doll, surrounded by chaotic images, a pair of chairs laying on their sides, and white porcelain fragments, and the top of the man's head making its way to the door.

This strange scene revealed itself in a cold, analytic manner with perceptive intelligence! It understood the big, shaggy creature that was invited in the room as it apprehended a spiraling turbulence of cool air around its bristling, sensitive hairs oven the splayed legs suspending its body from a seemingly infinite plain, and the concussion of opening and closing. It was far too fascinating a thing to harbor his ship of grief, so Arien's awareness slid into a detached, watchful numbness. It returned him to his own safe distance, but it was not too far for Buster, though he detoured for the splattered food as any respectable dog would do, seeming to inhale it along the way.

The dog's tongue all over his face snapped Arien back into his own body. It was too much, too wet, and a deep, still imprisoned part of him laughed. It was the irrepressible boy, pushing the slobbery, playfully intrusive, Wookie head away, and then grabbing around its neck to draw it to his heart in a hug that reminded him of their first meeting in the bitter cold snow and darkness.

"Good, good boy," Andy prayerfully said, standing off to one side. "Go save him again, Buster."

Unless a visitor already knew Buster was Andy's dog, it would have required a bit of convincing. Thereafter, Buster wouldn't let Arien out of his sight, following him everywhere, unwilling to be separated by even so much as a door.

"Arien, Buster needs to go out," Andy said. "Do you mind booting up and letting that happen?" He'd just rested a chunk of tree from a stack of them in a hamper on the coals of the Ashley woodstove in the living room.

Arien obliged. There was a nice parka hanging on a hall tree in the foyer. He put it on and the shaggy-wagging critter followed him outside into a landscape of blustering whiteness. The light was dingy here, the air crisp. It nipped his nostrils and pinched the cheeks and pressed on his scalp until Arien pulled the hood up and tied the laces at his neck. And then he had to jam his stinging fingers into the pockets. Gusts of wind whistled and fine particles of snow flew off the roof of the house in dramatic swirls that mixed with a relentless white shower from the turbulent sky. Even in the entry, snow was banked up against the walls of the house and rose up in waves, where the dog had to struggle like a dolphin through its crests.

It would be easy, Arien thought. I could just walk out into that and take off my clothes. But he could see Buster's effort to lift a leg in that stuff and the challenge of this environment began to pique his interest. To what purpose? Which triggered the memory of an acid trip that seemed so long ago, even to him, when he was sure he'd found the Beautiful Forever among a billion brilliant stars in the inky black of the deepest space and he'd heard that question, surely. He could come back after that. It was OK to return to his life because he knew in his heart of hearts that place would always be there, as it was and would be forever and ever, so what was the rush? He was still a kid!

Oh, Hell. Tears were freezing on his cheeks and sticking to his face. It had to be the coldest day he'd ever known. And the snow! He remembered snow like this on Mount Hood, in Oregon once, and how they would set up a Quonset entryway so visitors could get into Timberline Lodge through the tunnel from the parking lot with its towering frozen walls and puffy-white cartoon cars a snowman would drive.

"What?" Arien asked Andy's enigmatic smile as he stomped the snow off his boots.

"You're back."

Arien looked at him and sighed.

"Hang in there, Kid. You'll make it. Just give it some time – assuming we have any."

Arien returned the coat to its hook and followed Andy into the dusky light of the living room where the only sound was a popping fire in the

Ashley. "Do you have any tunes?" He asked, settling into a comfortable chair.

"Not without power. The portable didn't have any batteries. I forgot to get some. I could kick myself."

"So, what are we doing?"

Andy snorted. "Wait it out, I guess. We can't drive in that. I saw the plow didn't make it out here this morning. We might have to get up and shovel snow off the roof. I don't know where it'll go, though. It's up to the gutters in back."

"Do you have a car here, Andy?"

"You didn't see it when you were outside?"

"No."

A grim smile broke on Andy's face. "That's encouraging," he said.

"I asked, because the car has a radio, right?"

"Yeah, right you are."

It took almost three hours for the two of them to dig it out and open a way to the road while Buster laid himself out on a pillow of snow and watched. The first narrow passage through the drifts missed the car, but they weren't far off. After Andy went back to the steps and assessed the distance, noting a peculiar shape where it should be, they found it. Andy thought they might as well invest the time to have it ready, or take a bite out of their next effort since the flakes never stopped falling.

Arien liked the car, a dusky red, late-model Jeep Liberty. He sat in the driver's seat, settling into its luxurious cushioning and grabbed the wheel with his cold hands. Andy let the dog into the back seat. The windows were already fogging as Andy got in up front and fumbled with the keys when a motor's whine from out on the road came to their attention. It sounded like a motorcycle. Buster barked once, hurting Arien's ears. He had to swipe at the windshield to see a snowmobile stop at the border of the space they'd cleared in front. The driver looked like a snowman with goggles.

The electric window wouldn't budge so Andy had to swing his door out to speak with the fellow who approached. "Was I driving too fast Officer?"

The snowman with goggles flashed a toothy grin. "Going to a fire?" He said.

"We're taking the initiative," Andy answered. "How are you, Ralph?"

Other than having a salt and pepper moustache, it was impossible for Arien to learn anything of the man's appearance wrapped as he was in his snowsuit.

"Well, besides being holed-up at the Center, Charlie and I decided to check on the neighbors. Are you OK, Andrew?" The man's voice was deep and friendly.

"For now, thanks. We've got a good stack of wood, some food in the cupboards and enough propane for a while." Snowflakes swirled in through the open door and the dashboard already glistened.

Ralph leaned in closer. "Good," he said. "You might have company for dinner."

"Consider yourself invited. Have you heard any news?"

"It's not good," Ralph said as he lifted the goggles. "The storm came in fast enough off of Erie but now it's parked. The only way to talk to Monticello is the radio. It might as well be in Europe. The airport in Albany's closed, the Thruway's shut down with hundreds of people stranded; power's out all over the place. We might have to sit tight for a couple of days, Andrew."

"Wow."

"Yea, wow. The Apple's getting hit with another one off the Atlantic. The whole seaboard's buried from DC to Portland. No help's coming from anywhere. What a crazy year!"

"And it's not even officially winter, yet," Andy added.

Ralph chuckled. "Well, keep your house warm. I'd say, if your well's out, go ahead and collect the water you can and drain the pipes."

"Thanks, Ralph."

The man gave a quick salute and turned to stride away into the blizzard.

"Ralph works security at the Art's Center," Andy said, shutting his door.

"The Art's Center?"

"Yeah, the Bethel Woods Museum and Art's Center. It's the legacy of Woodstock, Arien. First chance we get, Kid, you'll have to take the tour." Andy chuckled.

The Legacy of Woodstock. Arien considered that. The very idea! He might have pinched himself but instead regarded an upturned hand with its ugly scar from the road trip. He'd hit it on a fence post back in Oregon, where a strand of barbed wire came around it, but rather than yanking it back he'd held it there and then twisted it until the pulsing pain practically blinded him. It took an ocean of frustration and perverted will to do that, so how could he forget? It was all real enough. But now reality was not for the timid. Everything he knew and everyone he'd come to love was gone.

Oh, there was Andy...

"You have to be here for a reason," Andy said, as if sharing his thoughts. Andy put a hand on Arien's leg, above the knee, and that was OK, but then he held it there longer than...

The feeling was similar to that screeching in his head or maybe it just got it going again. He held his breath and dropped his hand on Andy's, to stay it. The old man's eyes were lit with love and hunger. He was squeezing, inching closer.

"No, Andy!" Arien growled. "Don't even think of it!"

Andy closed his eyes and froze like something outside in the swirling snowstorm where a blanket of receding translucence again covered the windows of the car. He pulled away. "I'm so sorry," he whispered.

2 – What's the world like now?

Andy emptied the freezer in the afternoon, putting everything except the meat for the evening's dinner in a big plastic storage container that he carried to the mudroom where it would have no trouble staying cold. Neither of them spoke of the awkward moment in the car. Andy looked terribly pained and Arien couldn't help feeling it. For better or worse his sense of empathy, sharpened with every passing day on the road to Woodstock, had not been left behind. He considered how Otter would have handled it. Otter was always quick to point out, expose and refute transgressions of entitlement, self-indulgence and their various projections onto other people. Elimination, he called it. It only brought people down. Oh Otter, where are you now? A surge of panic mixed with Arien's kettle of despair but he didn't want it boiling in his chest again so soon. He'd really flipped-out in the morning and it hadn't felt good at all. In fact, it was exhausting. Sure, it simmered. There was nothing he could do about that, but losing it twice in one day... He saw the irony too, with thinking in the vernacular of the heaven he'd found. Fuckin' tears. Stop it, Bitch!

He turned his hand up to look again at the scar in his palm. "It's cool, Andy," he said. "I understand."

"Do you really? You used to love me. Can you still love me, Arien?"

"Don't go and blow it, Dude. In case you haven't noticed there's a few things that need to settle-out. But tell me about this. Is this the TV?" Arien pointed over his shoulder at the flat screen monitor that hugged the wall like a window into midnight.

"HD TV screen, yeah, Arien. That's right, you've never seen one!"

"HD?"

"High Def. It's really sharp."

"Geeze, it's huge. It'd be like going to the movies. I wish we could watch it."

"It's just as well," Andy said. "I'd want to watch the weather report and then we'd have to see the news and it's all terrible."

Arien chuckled. "So what else is new?"

And that made Andy smile just a little.

A knock at the door got the dog barking. Andy had four good-sized pork chops in the oven. He'd said the broiler would make less smoke than trying to fry them on top without an exhaust fan. Arien set down the bowl of steaming-hot instant potatoes he was whipping and went to the door. It was Ralph and another guy, Charlie, he said, introducing himself. They looked like cops under their snowsuits, with tan shirts and darker pocket flaps and official-looking security patches on their shoulders. They both wore pistols. Charlie said he'd leave the ice cream outside and Ralph carried a half-gallon bottle of whiskey in, which disarmed Arien's paranoia with pigs. They seemed like good guys. Ralph had a medium-build and graying hair, Charlie was younger, thirty-something and looked fit. They left little piles of snow in the stark light of an LED lamp at an end table in the entry, setting their bulky snowsuits on the carpet and they removed their gun belts, too.

"Don't get the wrong idea, Kid," Ralph said to Arien. "I never drink on the job, but this is a little like working a holiday, if you know what I mean."

"We almost couldn't find your house!" Charlie declared in the kitchen.

"I didn't hear you arrive," Andy said, and then, "Ralph, Charlie, this is Arien."

The guests extended hands with greetings and then stood awkwardly while Andy set a pot of canned string beans on a hot pad in the middle of the table.

"When did you get here?" Charlie asked. "I haven't seen you before."

Arien was stymied. He really didn't know. "A few days ago," he hedged.

"Arien's my friend," Andy injected. "He's visiting while he figures out what to do with his life."

Arien wondered how he would build on that if called on, though he admitted to himself it was a good way to put it. Charlie seemed to buy it and Ralph – Their eyes met and Arien could see the man's wheels turning.

"How do you like our snow?" He asked.

"It's pretty rad, Dude."

Ralph chuckled.

Then the chops came sizzling out of the oven and grabbed all the attention.

After dinner, everyone moved into the living room, warmly illuminated by a four-stick candelabrum on the coffee table, and they were reassured by the popping fire in the Ashley while gusts of wind buffeted the storm windows and rattled things outside.

"So, ah – Arien, have you dropped out?" Ralph asked, reflecting Arien's pleasantly surprised expression to see him filling all four shot glasses Andy set down.

Arien thought for a moment. "Nah, it's more like I dropped in," he said. He followed that with a silly giggle.

Ralph handed everyone a glass. When he came to the boy he said, "This isn't happening."

"Worse things haven't happened," Arien rejoined with a grateful grin.

"Well, uh, to dropping in!" Andy toasted, he winked, and all the glasses came together, clinking.

Arien imagined what wasn't happening would stop not happening after the first shot, but that isn't at all what happened. In fact, after the fourth shot and some shop, local and weather talk among the three men, he was getting a buzz, which he sorely appreciated. It began to lift him from his deep gloom. It was a challenge to not slur his words and he saw another one in meeting this moment. Who would have thought just a few days ago he would be here, drinking whiskey with a couple of rental cops and Andy, an old man...

Andy put glasses of water down for everyone and Buster came over to Arien's chair to rest a snout on a knee. "What's the world like now?" Arien asked the dog, scratching him behind the ears.

"You really want his point of view?" Charlie asked.

"What would that be?" Andy threw a smile after the question.

"Basically the same, well, maybe with a few more routines after ten or twenty thousand years.

"But, for us, in some ways it's better," Andy continued. "In other ways it's gotten worse."

"Ah, what's better?" Ralph challenged. "Damned-slick bankers only stole the country and got away with it. There hasn't been so blatant a crime since the railroads went west. And if you ask me, we'll be involved in Syria, next. Let me tell you, if that happens all bets are off. And the country's broke."

"And Obama still has to deal with Iran," Andy said.

"Another war there and gas will be too expensive for snow plows," Charlie added.

"It already is." Andy said.

"And your generation is getting stuck with the bill," Ralph enjoined, gesturing to Arien with his glass.

"Who?" Arien asked. A strange name echoed in his head.

"Who, what?" Ralph answered.

"Who's dealing with Iran?"

"Obama?"

"Like, O'Brian?"

The men paused, reflecting on that.

"The kid's a joker," Ralph said.

"It's the President, Arien," Andy helped. "President Barrack Obama. Would you believe it? It's an African name! He was first elected in 2008, and re-elected last November. He is our country's first Black President." Andy sipped with a little sparkle in his eyes.

Ralph and Charlie's eyes met, reflecting confusion.

"Mega radical," Arien said, thinking he'd heard something very unlikely but knowing anything was possible. And, if Andy was joking it was a good one. He'd felt vulnerable so far outside of his element, though drinking whiskey with these older guys was helping to reestablish a modicum of balance. The fire sliding down his throat was converted. He let himself expand, to take them in, feel them, listen to them...

Ralph began to stare. His eyes looked like balls of fat, in and out of focus, pouring another round, spilling just a few drops, he never looked away. Arien felt the man latch on to his flow of energy, like a leach. No worry. There was plenty for everyone.

"Oh, Arien, you're doing it!" Andy said, tearing up.

Charlie fidgeted. His uncertain smile lingered at the edge of his glass.

He feels guilty, Arien knew. He was actually getting better at this! And so he felt guilty, too, for allowing his depression over what was lost, and now knowing the very best may well have been saved.

"I wish Otter was here, and Tina, and Jeff and Clayboy and Aspen and Willow and Oak," Arien said, and he marveled that he was able to. But, he was determined not to forget them even as he feared conjuring them so soon would disable him with elimination. They had given him so much. And he appreciated the astonishing fact that Andy was here, where he'd waited for him on the other side in another life, as it were. This was major!

"Wow," Andy. You did it!"

Andy beamed back at Arien, raising his glass.

"You're awesome, Dude!"

"What is this?" Ralph asked carefully, like he was balancing on a railroad track. "What's the history between you two?"

"That kid saved my life, once," Andy replied.

"And now we're even," Arien said.

3 – Do they all ring like this?

The next day they battled the relentless snow. It was less of a blizzard than the previous day but the gusty wind blew it into massive drifts. The car had to be dug out again. It was completely buried on one side. Though the road was impassable, Arien considered it a worthy exercise. It felt good to be moving and have something to do. It kept his mind off the desire to venture further a field, maybe check into where the kids around here hung out and meet some people. And then it came to him that Andy struggled with a version of this, too. And he knew Andy was very worried about Thomas.

Earlier, just after breakfast, Arien heard an odd jingle, rather like a disjointed phrase from a musical number playing on a cheap little radio – Was it an orchestra, a synthesizer? Whatever it was sent Andy running. "Oh, Arien, the cell's back!" He exclaimed from the foyer.

Sell, Arien considered. Sell what? But the context Andy used... He followed the sound of Andy talking on the telephone. The telephone: It was this little black gizmo opening like a clam shell, without any chord and it fit in the palm of Andy's hand. Rad! It was a real mobile phone but it was so small! Andy chatted for a while and Arien heard his name repeated a few times.

"That was Helen," Andy said, closing the device. "We'll see her as soon as we can get out. She lives in Monticello." Then he opened it again and pecked at it, no doubt punching numbers. He listened for a while and then said, "Thomas, this is Andy, checking again to see if you're OK. Call me when you get this message." And then he closed it with an anxious look. "What do you think?" He asked Arien. "Is he alright?"

Arien's first impulse was to blow that off but he'd actually answered such questions before. He thought about it, wondering what Thomas even looked like at this point in time. He drew a blank. "I don't know," he said. "I've nothing from Thomas.

"Can I see that?"

Andy handed the cell phone to Arien who began poking buttons and checking out the various options on the screen. "Wow, Jesus, it's a camera, too! I think I just snapped a picture of my foot!"

"Yeah, kid, you've got some catching up to do."

"Shit! Does it have a manual?"

Just then it sounded off again with a likely Classical jingle. "Do they all ring like this?" He flipped it open and said, "Hello," as Andy reached for it.

"Hi! This is Helen again. You must be Arien!" It was a mature, rather grandmotherly voice. No chicks in this circle. I'm so sorry, Tina, he said to his heart.

"I'm really looking forward to meeting you, Arien. Andrew's told me so much about you!"

"He has? Like what? – It's Helen," he whispered to Andy.

"Well," she began, "Like, the last time he saw you was at Woodstock, in 1969."

"Radical!" Arien broke into a surprised grin. "He told you that?"

"Yes."

"Did he tell you I'm just a kid?"

"He said you would be a boy of about seventeen."

"And do you believe him?"

"Why, yes, I do. Of course I have questions, but what Andrew has said about your story is truly amazing and I know him and he is an amazing person who has never given me any reason to doubt him." She let that sink in and then added, "You must know he is a true Hermetic philosopher and magician."

Arien chuckled. "He knows so much about that stuff," he agreed.

"So, Arien, how are you feeling?"

He didn't expect that question. "It's been rough," he said.

"Well sit tight, Son. We've all been waiting for you, for – it seems like forever, and we're here to help you any way we can."

"Uh, wow, rad. Thank you, Ma'am."

Now Arien sweated under the parka. It was likely warmer because his breath didn't exactly freeze and fall to his feet but waited a moment before being carried away with the wind. He leaned on his shovel and chuckled to himself, thinking of the cold-intensity scale he and Andy put together shortly after stepping outside. There was VC for very cold, VDC for very damn cold, and finally VFC. That, and digging out the car, and tussling with Buster began to cover his wound like a salve. It really throbbed down there but he was feeling functional and he had some investment in the present and the puzzle it laid before him.

"I'd say it's VFC-minus, huh?"

"Yeah, plus would put it below zero, right? The outside thermometer read 4.4 degrees a little while ago," Andy said. "If you fell in the drink you'd last about a minute."

"Where is the drink, Andy? Is it nearby?"

"It's behind the house. There's some woods and then the pond. But it just looks like another buried field right now." Andy stuck the shovel in the snow and brushed powder off the windshield with his mittens.

"Did you ever go for a swim in it?"

"Yes, Arien, on Sunday afternoon, the day you disappeared. I remember it well because it was raining and there was a thunderstorm... And, I did indulge a few times since then for old time's sake." A peculiar emotion was carried in Andy's voice. It resonated with Arien's. "Ouch!" Andy said, "It hurts when your eyes water up in this.

Arien sighed. He didn't want to cry again today, either.

"You know Arien, there was a lad who was run over and killed by a tractor while he slept."

Arien crouched to listen with an arm around Buster's neck. The boy and the dog, furry tail sweeping the air, were nose-to-nose.

"It's treated like a footnote," Andy continued, "even though, for those who knew this unfortunate fellow, the name Woodstock will always bring that to mind. Hey, but would you believe it, there was a whole family of people there who may well have had the most fantastic and exalted experience of all, only to have it matched with the greatest possible disappointment."

Arien stood. Cold nipped through his parka. "Polarities, Andy. I got to know about that. What I want to know is why it isn't like that for everybody?"

A branch cracked off in the nearby woods and fell with a muffled woomph. Andy's gaze followed the sound. "Well, in one sense it is;" he answered, "we all grow old – if we're lucky." He smiled. "That being said, anybody who accomplishes anything in their life puts the polarity principle to the test, wouldn't you say? Or, maybe their opposites manifest elsewhere."

"I'm lucky you were here to catch me," Arien sincerely said.

"We make that kind of luck, Arien. It has little to do with chance. When you get the likes of Cypriano, Ellison Black Snake, Mother Shongo, and myself - if I may say, looking for you... And, to nail your question, polarity becomes exponentially acute in Magic, which you were very much engaged in. I was amazed how you took to it like a fish to water."

"I didn't have much choice."

"True, but you didn't drown, did you? On the contrary, you were anointed by your peers."

Their musings were broken by the sound of snowmobiles, at first distant, to confusing directions in the hint of primordial Ice Age terrain, and then bursting upon the visible arena from the direction of the Bethel Arts Center. Ralph and Charlie were drawing near.

Andy set mittens to hips and sighed with perceptible impatience. "They may or may not know why, but they want more. I'm afraid we drank too much last night and flapped our lips."

"Polarities, Andy, but Dude, it was perfect."

"The cavalry's making their rounds, I see!" Andy said when the motors puttered to idle.

Ralph raised his goggles. "We're headed down to White Lake to see if mail's got that far, and pick up a bit of gas and supplies. Do you guys want to come?"

"Uh, yeah!" Arien agreed happily, without even looking at Andy.

Andy must have nodded because Ralph shut off the motor. "Grab a backpack if you want to get anything and make sure you're bundled up. Put on that extra layer now, before we take off!"

Andy had a bulky sweater for Arien as well as a pair of snow pants with zippers on the legs that would go on over boots. They left Buster in the house so he wouldn't chase after them, or freeze solid if they were delayed. Arien mounted the machine with Charlie, Andy got on with Ralph, and soon they were running over the white expanse where Arien had his first sight of the Center.

A sizable installation commanded the hill on their left, maybe a hundred yards behind bits of iron pickets poking out here and there in a spindly line. It was anchored by a turreted pavilion roof looking like a giant vanilla ice cream cone from its compliment of snow. To their right was a broad flat area, where the globes of lamp posts appeared to be sinking into eternity as snowfield and sky blended together. There were large drifts on one end that barely revealed low structures in a corner of roof exposed by the wind. Arien's first impression was a lovely spot was probably ruined but allowed Andy's view that it was worth a visit, so he withheld a final judgment. The snowmobiles turned left when they reached a ribbon of unmolested white bisecting the tumble of drifts, farmhouse roofs, and winter's naked trees.

They had hardly gone a mile when the day turned grayer and then still darker with astonishing speed. Another squall of stinging snow descended with a whipping cross-wind and Ralph, who was just ahead, waved his arm out. Charlie pulled up alongside. "It's approaching white-out," Ralph shouted into the wind. "We can lose each other in this!"

Arien buried his face in the back of Charlie's parka. He could barely keep his eyes open.

"Yeah, we'd better go back," Charlie answered.

"Slow. Stay close."

"Will do!"

They turned, revving motors again, then continued on for a while until Arien could feel it with his eyes closed against the wind. Something was wrong. It came to him as confusion and concern and then a rude surprise immediately followed with an experience of crushing head and shoulder pain before the light went out. Sure enough, Charlie let up on the throttle. They stopped, listened, blinded by the howling tempest.

Arien heard Charlie faintly shout, "Where did they go?" with words whisked away in the horizontal maelstrom. There was a sudden blinking flash followed by a muffled concussion of thunder in the storm around them.

"Wow!"

Listen for them. Feel them, Arien thought.

"Damn! I don't believe it! We may have to wait 'till the wind lets up!"

"That way!" Arien urgently yelled, pointing over Charlie's shoulder.

Charlie hesitated.

"Do it! Slow! Go slow!"

Arien couldn't see the shrug but it was clear, never-the-less. The motor picked up as Charlie hunkered forward and they sallied into the blinding whiteness. Feel them. We're closing. They're closer.

"Slow! Slower – stop!"

"Good God, Kid, what the..."

But Arien had already leapt off the machine to struggle through waist-deep drifts when he practically fell on top of an upturned snowmobile, pitched down an embankment, likely stuck into something. He came upon Andy, who leaned over Ralph, splayed-out in the snow.

Charlie was right behind him.

"What happened?"

Andy was rubbing a mitten in Ralph's face. The man appeared to be unconscious. Charlie came around to nearly touch his nose to Ralph's.

"I don't know," Andy replied, "but we took off. Maybe the throttle stuck. We hit something. It threw us."

"I can't tell if he's breathing," Charlie said, loosening Ralph's top button and then the suit's zipper.

"We've got to get him indoors," Andy said.

"How the hell do we move him in this?" Charlie answered. "What if his neck is broken?"

Wind lashed them and the snow was accumulating so quickly Ralph was getting buried.

"It's got to let up," Andy said, and it almost sounded like a prayer.

Arien watched all this, feeling, listening, knowing.

"We're not too far from the house," he announced.

"Ah!" Charlie snapped. "How do you know that?"

"Because Buster is over there." Arien pointed into the void.

Charlie's impatient look repeated the question much louder than any words.

"Because I can feel him!" Arien said directly.

"Let's get to it," Andy said. "Trust me. The kid knows."

Another unusual flash of lightning and crack of thunder got Charlie moving. Arien was particularly nervous. Wasn't this impossible? How could it be here in a snowstorm? Could it be stalking him, threatening to blast him all over again to God Knows When? His confidence was about to scatter in the next gust of wind just as Charlie ordered him to hold Ralph's head, to keep it steady. Then, with Andy on one side and Charlie on the other, the three of them first pulled and lifted to lean Ralph upright against the machine, and then they began to drag him by the scruff of his coat laboriously through the ever-deepening snow.

"This is insane! I have no idea where we are!" Charlie gasped, huffing for breath.

"We're good. It's not much further." Arien told them and then they tumbled into the area he and Andy had shoveled out around the car. The storm was already beginning to fill it in.

Ralph was laid out on the couch in the living room, the warmest room in the house. He was unconscious but at least he was breathing. He'd sustained a nasty bump on his head that was worrisome because there was no way to get him to a hospital. Charlie did get Monticello on his cell phone but the call was dropped before reaching a doctor. For the moment the best that could be done was to get Ralph out of his snowsuit and to make a compress of snow in a hot water bottle.

"Okay, now you can tell me about this guy," Charlie said, motioning to Arien as Andy passed cups of herbal tea around.

Andy and Arien exchanged glances. Arien sat on the floor with Buster's head in his lap.

"What do you want to know?"

Charlie leveled his gaze at Arien. "How did you see through all that?"

"Just lucky, I guess. I don't see any better than you."

"He's got a phenomenal intuitive muscle," Andy said. "That's definitely one of his issues, isn't it, Arien?"

The boy smiled up at the security officer. "It's hard enough being a teenager," he agreed.

"Well, you've got talent, boy. I could think of plenty of agencies that could use what you did out there: the Army, the Navy, the Fire Department, and the Police, just to name a few. Jesus. The more I think of it..."

"Will he be alright?" Andy asked.

"I don't know." But Arien wondered if he could. Just maybe... He got up and went over to the couch to sit on the side. He took up Ralph's hand in both of his. Listen. Feel him, feel him.

"Arien! Arien!" He heard Andy call. Andy was cradling his head. Charlie, down on one knee, peered into his face.

"Ho, wow." Arien looked back at them, slowly integrating his consciousness with an awareness of his surroundings. He barely grasped an odd sense of falling into another, like the wisp of a dream remembered but not truly recalled. Inwardly, he studied it, attempting to follow the thread.

"Arien, are you alright?"

"Yeah, Andy." There he was, so close again. Arien struggled to sit up.

"You fainted," Andy said.

Arien waved a hand at him. He was a distraction. Both of the men moved back as he leaned against the couch from his position on the floor. He searched for words. "Not good," he said.

"What's not good?" Andy asked.

"It's swamped. Too much pressure."

Andy sat cross-legged on the floor before him and blinked. Charlie hadn't moved and simply waited. A shudder came from Ralph, stretched on the couch behind him.

"What's not good?" Andy repeated.

"His head, I guess. This dude needs a hospital. He probably won't wake up."

Charlie, suddenly very agitated, bolted to the window. "It's still blowing, but not as bad. Maybe I can try again."

"There's only one machine," Andy said. "That could be dangerous."

"This man is dying! We have to get him to a doctor!"

But Arien had already turned to look at Ralph, laid-out there as he was. "Awesome," the teenager reverently said, as he presently confronted the mystery of subtraction in the fabric of life. He'd experienced that before once, high on acid in the wilderness of Medicine Bow and he clearly recognized the oddly smooth sensation of a man's permanent withdrawal.

"It doesn't matter now. He's gone."

Of course Charlie felt Ralph's carotid pulse with Arien's announcement but he made no effort to revive him as Ralph had never regained consciousness, and the depth of their extremity was truly driven. The three of them sat in that room for a long while with their own thoughts as the day grew dark and the wind outside howled enough to buff and lean upon the house like a ravenous creature.

"The dog is hungry," Arien said, breaking into the brooding silence. He got up and Buster followed him to the kitchen where the air was dark and cold. He fumbled for the flashlight. There, he located the LED lamp and by its stark illumination found Alpo in the cupboard and kibble Andy mixed it with. It was pretty simple, he considered, with an ironic snort. The isolation, with its simple motions of survival and endurance, the oppressive storm without, the bitter cold and seeming eternity of snow so brazenly contrasted with the rain and mud and the sparkle in so many, many faces he had just barely been among. "Oh, Jimi Hendrix! I never got to see Hendrix!" He sadly whined at the dog that saved his life.

The laundry room was just off the kitchen. Andy had a rubber tub on top of the washer and dryer in there where a pair of mud-caked cut-off shorts was laid out flat. It was even cooler in this room, and though days had passed some of the mud on the shorts was still damp around the edges and no doubt, on the bottom side. Arien bent over, pressing his nose into the denim and deeply inhaled. "Oh God!" But was this elimination, too? He certainly paid for it with a wrenching, fiery pain in his chest that soundly thumped him.

His spontaneous wail arose as if vomited from the depths of his gut. He doubled over, collapsing down onto the floor into heaving sobs. Buster was there in a moment and Arien grabbed at the big furry body, pulling it to him as he had when Buster found him in the snow, smelling of ozone, half-naked and lathered from head to toe in Woodstock's holy mud.

The men were soon there, awkwardly filling the space in the little room.

"Oh, Arien, Arien," Andy soothed, reaching out to spread a hand in his hair. "Beautiful, beautiful, boy. Go to the Light, Arien. Visualize the Sacred Cup, the Vessel of Grace, the Celestial Ship, Arien. Remember how it moved us through an entire night in a matter of moments. Feel it, filled with the love and yearning of your spiritual family. You must know it was real and it was forever and we will find it again. Somehow, we'll find it again and we'll all be together again! Feel it, Arien! Believe it!"

How this poor boy's chest burned and his torso, wrung-out and quivering, struggled to help him breathe. It crowned the old, stifled pain of his boyhood and youth. I have only to give in, he thought, and I will surely die.

"I can't take it, Andy," Arien blew through a curtain of mucous. "I want to go home!" But even as he said this Andy's words began to trickle down to where he could wrap his mind around them and see them. It had been real, and for him, only very, very recent. For Andy—

"Wow, Andy," he sighed with realization and yes, empathy, "You've held that for so long!"

Now Andy wept and the poor officer who had just lost his friend and partner could only stand by and gape at these two highly irregular people.

Charlie and Andy moved Ralph's body to the mudroom off the back of the house where it would have no trouble being preserved. The outside thermometer read 7-below, and the room likely hovered around zero. Arien moved ahead of them with the flashlight to open the door and was directed to move a stack of snowshoes to clear a spot for the body on the floor where Andy laid a blanket. The floorboards dryly squeaked underfoot. Their breath extended out in clouds hanging in the still air. Charlie found reception out here and called his boss with the news, though no one answered and he was forced to leave a brief message of what happened.

"That really sucks," he said after his call, and holding the phone to his face, followed that with, "Oh, uh, Ralph happens to be dead and I'm helpless, God damn it, and I'm here with a couple of very strange people."

"Who would have thought?" Andy said.

"Do you think they'll tell his wife?" Charlie appealed with anguish. He looked like he could break something.

"Stay with us tonight. Don't even bother going back to the Center."

"Thanks, Andrew. I think I will," Charlie said.

There was a row of firewood piled against one wall in the mudroom and they all carried some inside. Back in the living room Andy stoked the fire to a rumble until the sheet-steel walls of the Ashley glowed with a dull red heart and the stovepipe pinged with expanding gasses. The fire was life. It had stopped snowing. Arien observed stars in the night sky through a slit he made in the blinds and the temperature palpably plunged further. Now it was severe cold and not wind that stalked the tinder-creaking house like a wild, hungry beast.

"Jesus," Charlie exclaimed. "With power still out this shit has got to be killing people."

Arien took a deep breath, exhaled, and visualized the countryside, as much as he knew it, and conjured the hamlet of Bethel, White Lake, and outward. Was he feeling the people and their critters hunkering down in their clapboard, snowbound bunkers for dear life or was it all in his imagination? He longed for a good hit of acid. He could do it so much better, know it and be it with such a tool. But he was exhausted and learned that even a very young man cannot cry like a baby and revive as quickly. "I'm going up to bed," he said and he carried himself up the stairs like a heavy pack after a long, sore day on the trail.

He was at Woodstock among all the people in front of the stage screaming FUCK to the top of their lungs. His heart glowed red like the Ashley, and his joy reached into forever. Such a relief! It was a terrible dream after all, and now he thought of Maggie Austin and how close she must be. He expected to lay eyes on her at any moment but then felt a sliver of apprehension before a roll of thunder and flash of lightning, and everybody was gone in an instant, as if vaporized.

The field was empty, and the grass in the bowl was a deep green like the first time he saw it. But there she was! He could see her with Hendrix, smiling down from the stage. "I'll be right back, Tina," he said to the beautiful girl standing next to him. But he couldn't move. It began to rain. His feet were stuck in the Woodstock mud and it would not let him go. Maggie was now way up on one of the towers, much further away. He struggled furiously and awakened thrashing, half-tangled in blankets on his bed in the cool room.

Arien stared up into the darkness.

"I have to admit I'm baffled by all this, Arien," Andy said over broiled toast with peanut butter and jelly. "We were having a hard winter in a place that's used to them, but..."

It didn't need saying. Arien could feel his anxiety.

"Did you see the sky last night?"

"No, Andy."

"I guess not," Andy agreed. "I was hoping you might have, later, after I'd cashed in my chips. You went down like a pile of rocks, because I wanted you to see it but you wouldn't wake up."

Arien noticed Buster's water bowl was empty. He refilled it from the cooking pot that was still half-full of snow on one of the kitchen's counters.

"You tried?" he asked.

"Yes, Arien, short of shaking you; the aurora was spectacular, like a light show at the Fillmore, kid." He spoke as if Arien understood.

Maybe he didn't. They didn't go to the Fillmore when he'd gone to the Haight with Otter, Tina, and Jeff in the spring. He'd only heard about it. And even at Woodstock, they were just out of the circle when the Airplane took the stage. There's a lot he didn't get to do. Perhaps, he thought, if he allowed himself a bit of resentment, aka elimination, it might fill the morning's vacancy. He took the pot outside and scooped it full of dry, powdery snow to bring back into the kitchen. He had to hold the door both ways for Buster.

Andy gazed back at him without revealing very much, but Arien felt cornered. He knew Andy couldn't help it; it was being stuck in the house, and the suffocating white blanket all around, like a solid ocean with its deep, frozen waves breaking on the doorstep.

"Where's Charlie?" Arien asked, passing a scrap of toast to the attentive dog.

"He was out early, just after sunup. He said he wanted to check on the Center and then take that run to White Lake we didn't get to do yesterday."

Yesterday, Arien mulled it in his mind. "That really sucks about Ralph."

"A terrible thing," Andy concurred. "He was a good fellow."

"So, now what?"

The elder took a swallow of his coffee. "Well, if it stays clear, we're likely to get some surface movement," he said. "This is an opponent, you know? I expected our window would be narrow, considering the date, but it's beginning to look like a crack in the shutters. Nobody can get here and we can't exactly go to them."

24

Arien considered the date, December, 2012. It was the first thing Andy told him when he'd awakened in this house. To him it was a terrible thing to know. He'd been abducted out of his rich dawn of a second chance at a beautiful life, and could see no solace in such a distant time. Otherwise, he'd never heard anything about it before. Oh, there was some talk among the hippies of the prophecies of Edgar Cayce and the coming earth changes, generally forecast for the 1980s. It was all mixed in the same pipe of Aquarian Age predictions, which ironically cancelled the most dreadful forecasts because they always seemed so joyous and positive. But that was all. Andy could have been killed in that accident yesterday, too! Then where would he be?

"When did you meet Helen?"

"Uh, about thirty years ago," Andy said, appearing to appreciate the question. "She was in a circle, one of several I put together to try and recreate that night at Woodstock. You know? We were never able to do it again, Arien. I'm sure it's possible because it happened once, and I think it did because you were there, but I had to try, and hitting that note, so-to-speak, just right, is surely as difficult as making gold out of lead."

"Have you ever made gold out of lead, Andy?"

Andy smiled. "In my educated opinion," he said, "Alchemy is metaphorical. Think of it: gold is associated with the sun, intelligence, brilliance and light – the nimbus lamp of kindled and expanded consciousness."

"Okay," Arien said, getting into it.

"And now you have returned to us, so..."

Arien frowned. "It wasn't just me." He got up from the table to pour more coffee in his cup from the pan on the stove. "We had Tina, we had those people in each quarter, and each one was a different race, remember? And we had the energy of half-a-million people, and let's not forget Ellison Black Snake. That dude kicked it into high gear."

Andy swayed broadly in his chair like a kid at a Heavy Metal concert. "Whoa," he said, "I was half-afraid you might disappoint but no, my liege, you do not disappoint me at all."

Arien smirked at him, barely nodding his head. "I need Otter to balance you out," he whispered.

"Oh my God, you keep hitting them out of the park!" Andy exclaimed. "I'm sure you're right!" He laughed, obviously impressed. "And you're probably right about Mother and Father and Son and Daughter in that circle at Woodstock. But Laddie, that's why... That's, well, I hadn't planned to be here alone with you."

"Right," Arien snorted.

Andy looked down. "Hey, I have no control over the winter."

There was something about the way he said that. "It beats a crowded summer though, doesn't it?"

"What?" Andy squinted. "What's that supposed to mean?"

"You had to try for a little entitlement." Arien spoke directly out of his experience of the road trip that had taught him so much – how he had grown and become transformed on that trip, perhaps molded in his fluid wanderings as it were, by this fine group of 'brothers and sisters' out of their generation's multi-layered dream! Yes, he brought it with him to 'this side,' too. He was finding once the lamp is lit it cannot be extinguished.

Andy grew introspective. "I blew it," he said, apparently coming to terms with his adept young guest. "I moved too fast. You know, Arien, even an old guy messes up sometimes. But, forgive me; the moth in me is blinded by your flame. In all those years of obsessive waiting, in and out of starved relationships, all overshadowed by your depth and your beauty..." He sighed. "Ah, to have you here close enough to touch, I feel like Bilbo with that damn ring of power in his pocket."

Arien knew nothing of the reference and didn't ask, having no desire to belabor the point. "You mentioned the note," he said. "Andy, do you have my water buffalo horn?"

"Yes," Andy said, "but if you want to see it there's a bit of a hike and lot more shoveling to do."

Carrying shovels, they trudged away on snowshoes into the woods, skirting the flat expanse of buried pond down behind the house, through an absent neighbor's back yard, and toward the crest of a broad hill that rose up south-eastward to their right. Buster labored next to them as best he could through drifts that tried to swallow him. It took longer to reach the ridge than it looked like it would. It was bitter cold but with little wind the exertion made Arien open his coat. He wore a scarf around his nose and the lower part of his face and a pair of sunglasses against the sharp dazzle.

Arien was never one to ask a lot of questions so he held his tongue, content with the physical effort and sense of mystery in their destination. There was a vaguely familiar feel to the landscape and then it came to him with a heart-pumping rush: It had to be where they'd spent Saturday night and the wee hours to daybreak of Sunday morning on August 16th and 17th, 1969.

4 – A faint vibration

Arien couldn't be sure what he was looking at. In some respects it resembled the ice cream cone the center appeared to have when he'd passed it on the snowmobile. It looked round and about as big as a two-car garage. He could see the center behind them through the barren hedgerow, across the undulating roll of topography, maybe a crow's mile or so away from the natural amphitheater where the music had been staged. The complex over there sprawled out from the main rotunda with glass-sided meeting halls shimmering like mirrors and site appendages near the rural roads that had been so jammed-up with vehicles and kids. Perhaps, turning away with a shake of his head, this structure was a large gazebo, like a picnic shelter or something. It was buried in snow along with everything else. He joined in when Andy set to digging.

"Be careful not to gouge the shutters," Andy said between heavy breaths. He dug downward and snow fell away from a door header where a pair of solid frame-and-panel shutters closed the opening. They took turns removing snow, allowing each other to pass by so it could be thrown far enough away to keep it from falling back in the trench they made.

"I didn't realize it was this deep up here," Andy said. After a while an entrance was exposed down to a granite step and some of the rough-sawn, board-and-batten walls the structure had. He grabbed a lever holding them shut and with difficulty in billowy mittens, attempted to free it. It took some wrestling and thumping with a shovel handle but at last it broke loose, and the shutters opened out to reveal a pair of natural wood mullioned doors that swung inward, hinged on each side with two rows of panes in each door that framed daylight rectangles on wide floorboards, and the burgundy edge of a Persian carpet.

"Wow!" Arien exclaimed, stepping inside of an eight-sided room with multi-paned, side-hinged windows in every section of wall, except on the opposite side where there was another set of doors. Four of the windows on the other six facing sides, in the cross-quarter directions, reached down to built-in cabinets about sixteen inches deep and three feet high, fronted with frame-and-panel doors. The exceptions were the south wall, where an ornate woodstove stood before the full-length window, its pipe running straight up through the roof, and the north wall, which was also a full-length window extending to where the kick-plate would be if it were a door.

All the windows were dark, having likewise been shuttered on the outside. The roof was framed with stout, exposed beams, set with 2 x 6 collars shaped in an eight-pointed star, its center framing the translucence of a snow-covered skylight. The more delicate framing of the skylight came together at a fixture from where an impressive iron lamp hung suspended by a chain that ran through pulleys for raising and lowering. Beneath it, totally dominating the room was a broad and sturdy round oak table, about seven feet in diameter, having thirteen oak chairs with armrests positioned around it.

Arien inspected the table. Crisply painted on its surface were white-bordered, purple runners that resembled the royal-blue bars of the British flag over quadrants colored in cobalt blue, scarlet, white and forest green. The bars of the cardinal cross terminated in four, five-pointed stars in red, yellow, white and black. Around the circumference was a white border that pulled the mandala together in a brilliant and powerful design.

"So, how does this work?" He said, resting the tips of his fingers on the table in front of him.

It's kindled, Arien, like the circle at Woodstock."

"Just like that?"

"Yes. It could use a few people," Andy said. "It is easiest to engage in multiples of four. These thirteen chairs could throw you off if you didn't know that." Andy grinned. "There's only so much I've been able to do with it, though, myself. I set it with the elemental implements and run them through the cycle of invocations to the directions. It's a powerful symbol and you know in Hermetic Tradition, the symbol is the thing. As it is, I can associate a lot of synchronistic events to it. It's helped me on my way."

Arien sat at one of the chairs, removing his mittens and splaying his hands out over the cool surface. He looked up at Andy with a surprised smile.

"This is awesome!" he cried out, seeing his breath roll away in front of him. It was a beautiful symbol, artfully rendered, and he understood enough of it to appreciate what Andy had done.

Andy's smile was gracious. Then, noticing something, he said, "Oh no! Look where you sat, Arien!"

"Where?" Arien looked at the mandala for a clue.

"Damn!" Andy scratched his chin. "You can't help it, can you?"

"This is Earth, yeah?" the young fellow said, tapping his left hand over the black star on the table. He was missing something...

"Arien, you're nearly at the end of Sagittarius, before the winter solstice! It's exactly the right time of the solar year!"

Arien's laugh bubbled out. Got-a love that. He easily recalled his duty the night of the circle at Woodstock, to perambulate the quarters with their invocations. For him, it was not so long ago.

"Oh," Andy said. Muttering something about wonders never ceasing, he went to one of the window seat cabinets and pulled out a cobalt-blue velvet bag with a solid object inside and took it over to put down in front of Arien on the table.

The lad smiled inwardly, laying his hands on it. The bag was a little worn to begin with; it looked about the same to him. He undid the bow and pulled the big, crescent-shaped horn out. "Oh, Andy... What else do you have?"

"A few things, including those muddy shorts."

Arien lowered his head. "Don't remind me," he said, and then, "How 'bout the staff?"

"It's not here. I wish it was," Andy said. He went around the table to sit on the opposite side. He folded his arms.

"What happened to it?"

"Oak took it. It was the right thing to do at the time, wouldn't you say? It belonged to them."

Arien nodded. "What's Oak doing now?"

"Good question. We lost touch years ago. If I could boot-up the laptop we could Google him."

"Google him? Help me here, Andy." Arien stuck the end of the horn in his ear.

The old man chuckled. "We could do an online search."

"Uh, yeah." Arien shook his head. "Or I could blow this horn and he'll call us on your cell phone."

"Yeah," Andy considered. He leaned back in his chair and removed the phone from the holster on his belt and flipped it open. "Still no signal," he said. "I don't get it. It's a perfectly clear day."

"What about Otter?"

"Otter, Tina and Jeff hung around for awhile. We all did, actually, but we couldn't stay here, you know? Salamanca was out. The freeway was supposed to eat the place we'd camped."

Andy pushed his chair back and returned to the cabinet where he'd retrieved the horn and took out a small brass jar about four inches high, with a loose-fitting lid. He didn't say anything but set the jar down on the table in front of Arien, who opened it right away.

The boy smiled, cheerfully dumping out about a quarter ounce of bud with a package of rolling papers and a Bic lighter, and he set to work rolling one. "It's pretty dry," he said.

"I imagine so. It's been so long I forgot where I put it," Andy now sat in the chair alongside. "I thought it was in the house." He pushed it back to look at Arien directly.

"Then what happened?"

"We moved around some, trying to keep it together. Arien, we really were lost without you. Oak was a good man and a fair leader but he didn't have Tree's gift for dreams or your really awesome, to use one of your favorite words, your perfectly awesome connection, your way with people."

Arien stuck the newly-rolled doobie in his lips and Andy picked up the lighter and lit it. Arien inhaled deeply and held his breath.

"Hawthorne had cousins in Virginia," Andy continued, "in Washington County, way west, where you can stand on a hill and see three other states. We camped in this holler that was on their land. The closest town, if you could call it that, was Coburn. A few people left, Kelsey, Cassie, Ben and Sundew... Don't know where they wound up. The rest of us spent the winter there and then... let's see, summer, 1970... Oh yeah, of course, Oak... he knew a college professor at the U of A, Pleasants, his name was, interesting guy, who had land in Vermont. It was this lovely old farm on Wheel Lock Mountain in a place called Goshen's Gorge. That's up in what they call the Northeast Kingdom. Nobody lived there, so he let us hang, or Oak rented it or something." He stopped to hit the doobie Arien passed. "Let's see, what happens when I smoke this?"

"You turn into a freak," Arien said.

"And you will freak me out."

Arien chuckled.

"Andy, give it up."

"Hope springs eternal," Andy rejoined, hitting and passing the doobie back. "A boy like you should be feeling pretty randy."

"Chill, Dude."

"I can't believe we're having this conversation," Andy added in a self-reproving tone, "or having any conversation in this space. That's not what it's for."

"We're not, Andy, you are." Arien couldn't help reflecting on the two occasions Andy had his way. Well, one occasion, because the second time Arien came away feeling like he'd asked for it. He was sure it was going to be Aspen. He was so hot and so ready that night. That had to be different. The thought of letting this old man touch his body...

"So what happened next?"

Andy returned the smoldering herb. "Vermont winters are pretty harsh," he said. "I got stir-crazy anyhow. I wanted to go as far away from cold as I could, so... I took all the money I had left and bought a one-way ticket to Honolulu." Andy's eyes broadened suddenly. "Oh, Jesus, Arien I almost forgot!" he exclaimed.

"What?"

"Oh my god!"

"What, Andy?"

"Tina bore your child!"

Arien coughed but the gritty smoke was only partly to blame. He reached down and picked up the horn there and stuck it in his ear again, as he had before, and said, "Say what?"

"Your daughter, Arienne, was born on your birthday in 1970. I remember Tina saying, any other day of the year, damn-it, and her name would have been Jane." Andy laughed deeply after saying that.

"Are you serious?"

"That girl had a terrific sense of humor."

Arien grew sad. "Did she think I died?" he asked. He missed her so much. He dreaded letting that out just now. Surely, it would set him on fire and he'd burn to death.

"A couple of times you talked about running. We wrestled with that for awhile, even though Ellison was certain you'd been snatched by lightning. You must understand people had trouble coping with that idea. So, they said, he may be a boy from the future but it would be too far-fetched to think you would just go away."

Arien, elbows on the table, buried his face in his hands. "Whoa," he sighed. Smoke from the doobie stuck in his fingers curled around his head in a spiral. Andy regarded that with a faint smile.

"God, I was so stupid, but damn it, she was right there!"

"Ellison told us you'd seen your mother."

"Yeah, Dude."

"Do you remember it?" Andy leaned forward to take the doobie, but Arien held onto it.

"No. I just remember Cypriano yelling in my head to stop. It pissed me off, Dude. I didn't listen. Oh, fuck! I didn't listen! How stupid!" Arien recalled Cypriano once said, *Treachery is everywhere, but especially hides within.* "Gag me with a snow shovel!"

"Oh, Arien." Andy put a tentative hand on his shoulder.

Arien didn't want to risk a hug, because it would have felt awfully good, and he had at least two reasons not to go there. He didn't turn away but fixed himself rigidly in his chair and allowed a barrier to drift between them. Even Buster caught it. He got up from where he'd lain looking asleep by the door, and came to Arien's side.

"Arien, I won't take this personally," Andy said, settling back. "You can't even help it. Look where you're sitting! I'm sorry for what you're going through, Young Friend. But we have to believe we can make it through this." Andy spoke sincerely.

Arien could hear Otter say that, but he would have expressed it differently. *You're eliminating on your friends* or something along those lines. The doobie had gone out. He took a hold of Buster's head and scratched him behind the ears, as much to warm his fingertips as let go a little bit. "So what happened with Tina and, and Arienne?" It was so strange to pronounce her name. "Wow," he said. "She'd be" – the fingers flailed from his hand – "forty-two, now. Holy shit! I have a daughter that's forty-two!" A flicker of childhood memory seemed to recall a young girl who had that name. He shrugged it off as unreliable.

Andy's elbows were on the armrests and he tented his hands in front of his lips. "I wonder if Tina still has that jar of water from Filippini's Pond?" he mused. "She told me she'd keep it and I said that was a really good idea."

"What happened with them? Where did they go?"

"I told you, I went to Hawaii."

"And that was it?"

"Yeah, you know, I'd had a powerful experience and it seemed nothing was going to match it, so it was time to ramble, and maybe learn more about it somewhere else. Time flies. You get a life. We lost track of each other." He shifted in his chair. "I'll hazard they returned to Oregon, though. Otter wanted to go back there."

"What happened to Clayboy?" Arien asked, growing serious.

"I think of all of us, he was the least able to cope with your disappearance. Funny, isn't it? You never can tell about people. He had a tiff with Oak that even Aspen couldn't harmonize. My bet is, some boys –

and men, too – express their grief with anger. Last I knew he split and fell in with a bad crowd from Burlington that had a dope connection in the East Village. They were into downers and smack. It wasn't pretty."

That smarted. Arien sighed. He needed to back away from the flame. It threatened to sear his heart with a mortal wound. He closed his eyes, focusing upward, freeing his breath and coming to stillness as he had learned to do until the sound of nothing, the reflections of sound in the room, Andy picking the doobie off the table, relighting it, taking a hit to the rip-stop rustle of the arm of his parka, a sliding boot sole beneath him, Buster laying at Arien's feet with a settling huff of doggie body, a sudden rushing in the silence that cascaded to a distant, ambient roar like a gust of wind in the canopy of ancient trees, and then a pounding, continuous, crashing waterfall...

Again, Arien spread his open hands on the cool surface of the painted wood. He caught the sweet, faint scent of incense in the very pores of the room, now merging with it all, and a wild sensation of flying high, soaring, and higher still to an intense glare on rolling fields of snow and the white rooftops of silent towns buried to the recesses at the back of his skull and beyond, to the arc of blue horizon, and muddled boundary of earth and sea, where snow reached over acres of shimmering, jagged floats of ice, rippling like sequins at a fashion show, and a few brave ships carved their tenuous paths through impossibly long, slushy troughs; and then the royal-blue corona of planet earth, with its cobalt sheen and fantastic, undulating curtains of aurora where invisible forces clashed amid a sprinkling of fried-satellite cadavers, and on to the dazzle of a billion stars, sharp as knives in the limitless, inky-black pool of space. He was deep, deep within himself. Oh, God, I'm going home! I'm coming home again!

But there came a flash in the corner of his field of view. It seemed to call his name, and it grabbed his attention, effectively derailing his headlong rush to the heart in the Milky Way. He turned to look as it reached out to him. It lay under him like a vast, furiously boiling cauldron with no horizon, and no shadows, only crazy leaping, splashing, churning, boiling shades of red, yellow, orange, white, and their apparently infinite range of chromatic interplay...

It was followed with a sensation of being dropped from a height without any physical sound but an internal *wee*, like a computer booting-up. It was awfully cold in that room. He folded his arms, resting his forehead on them, shoving opposing hands into the sleeves of his coat, and he watched the spread of condensation in pale, blurry flashes on the table.

"Oh Andy," he said, seeing the pulse of breath marking his words, "the sun's reaching out. I saw it. It toasted all that junk up there."

It took a while for Arien to really come back to himself, raise his head, and look at Andy. The old man's expression was hard to read.

And then he said, "I'm so proud of you."

"That pot wasn't as dry as I thought."

Andy chuckled.

"It's this space, too, Laddie, a highly charged engine, and it looks like you can drive it like a pro."

"It's amazing. When did you build it?"

"A few years ago. I may have said we had some powerful circles here."

"It feels like it."

Arien began to roll another doobie. He asked, "Dude, what do you do, or did you do for money?"

"Ah, history," Andy sighed. "Not much at first. I wandered a lot; followed the Dead and drank plenty of schroom tea in the parking lots. And, oh, the Rainbow Gatherings, they used to have some great regionals down in Arizona, too. The Gatherings were cool. I met some high people there. Some of us are still in touch." He paused, musing. "It took me about a decade to settle down."

"Rainbow Gatherings?"

"Yeah, they're like tribal conclaves from long-ago. The old ways never died, you know? It comes out of the race, I'm sure. Maybe it's in the genes of a certain segment of the population. Or, maybe we really are reincarnated and come back to another chapter in a very thick book. Free people, high people still gather and rediscover what to do, how to be, and the magick returns. Real shamans, yogis, wizards show up for these, Arien, and do their thing in plain sight. You would love it."

"Cool." Arien thought about that. He saved it to revisit later. "But what did you do to live?"

"That was the easy part. It was easy to live then, but I needed to do something more with my life so returned to college, and let me tell you, that wasn't a lark after being out so long."

"Then what?" Arien lit the joint. The smoke felt hot. It was actually pretty dry bud.

"I taught school."

Arien chuckled to himself. This was unexpected but perfect, really. Andy was a teacher – of course! "College?" he asked.

"No, high school, Arien."

"No shit! And you got rich teaching high school?" He was buzzing now. It had been a long break in that house, with its share of jonesing for a rush. Though the bud tasted stale, it still packed a punch, like alcohol on an empty stomach. He blew smoke rings out over the table of the Circle.

"I'm not rich. I have a decent retirement, maybe. Anyway, it set me up. I made some investments. There was lucky timing. I bought some houses when only a few people were thinking bubble, with very little down, and turned them before the fit hit the shan in 2008."

Arien had to stretch his brain to keep up. He was getting the gist of it, though. "Well," he said, "Dude, where does Youth Promise fit into this?"

"I was taking a break from teaching."

What would Cypriano have said now? Arien sensed discomfort in Andy's voice. He'd tensed. *Feel him.* That's what Cypriano would say. "There's more," Arien said directly. "What aren't you telling me?" He knows better than to throw bullshit.

"Oh, there's some history that really doesn't concern you."

Arian laughed. "Wow, Dude," he said, "that sounds as old as you look!" He saw that smarted but he didn't back off, and he sat more erectly in the chair. He watched as Andy caught and swallowed his next words, gazing back, looking indecisive.

"Seeing you at Youth Promise changed everything. It was all worth it. It was then I knew we were vindicated. And, most of all, it gave me hope."

Their eyes met when a faint vibration intruded from outside. Buster picked himself up off the floor with an attentive whine, his ears erect. Arien and Andy both made their way to the door and up to the surface through the snow corridor they'd dug. The sound was fresher out here. What they saw was startling and totally unexpected; a pair of black, military-style helicopters with landing skis. It was like something out of "Star Wars," dropping below the level of the trees into the open space in front of the house and the car. Their view was partially blocked by nearby trunks and bare branches of the hedgerow skirting the hilltop, but one surely landed in a fluffy cloud of prop-washed snow at the base of the bowl, roughly where the stage had been, and the other must have been set in the road in front of the house. The motors decelerated, shut down, and their whipping rotors went silent.

"They've come for us!" Arien cheered.

"Maybe, Arien, or they've come for Ralph."

"Something isn't right," Arien countered, feeling suddenly paranoid.

"Well, we're stoned. It's going to be hard to face these people. And," Andy grunted, "We have no ID for you." A moment later, watching, he noted, "They're in the house."

"I don't want to see them," Arien said.

Buster launched a rumble in this throat. Before it became a bark Arien set hand on snout. For the moment, Buster seemed to get it.

"I don't know what we can do, Arien. The country's too open, the trees are bare. They'll see our tracks. We'll just go down and greet them. We'll tell them the truth – without the spooky stuff." He smiled after saying that. "We could use a little rescue, don't you agree? And, Charlie would want them to hear our story."

"Don't you think that's a bit much?" Arien asked, indicating their direction. "Think of everything that's going on..."

"What do you mean?"

This was a struggle. Arien certainly would have liked to be rescued, but his vision in this little chapel provoked an unlikely conflict. Was he ready to be thrown in with people who didn't know him? It ran deeper: He'd only just met this amazing space.

Arien grasped for something. "How many big helicopters like that do you need to pick up Ralph? Look, Dude, there's two of them! And, check out..."

"There does seem to be a lot of them," Andy said, evidentially catching on, "and they're all dressed in white. Well, gee... Stay here. I'll go down and see what's up."

Buster growled. Off in the distance between there was a brief opening on the slope where their path wound up. Eight or ten men appeared to follow the trail Arien and Andy had left in the snow. They had snowshoes and were making steady progress.

"Andy, can't we stop them?"

"I don't know, Arien."

"I could leave my body again."

"But your body would still be here."

"Chant then, like you did in Idaho, or Wyoming, when you stopped a brawl in a greasy spoon, and like that time on the road when the pigs were about to pull us over!" Arien was growing desperate. He felt like a vise was closing around his head. It could have been the cold. After all, the hood of his parka was swept back. It was a very crisp day.

"That was different."

"Try it!"

"Arien, let's just go down and see what this is about. We haven't committed any crime."

"Believe it! They're hunters."

Andy sighed, looking at Arien. "But why? How?" he said with dismay. "I had no idea."

5 – This is amazing

There were some cool books in one of the cabinets, *The Great Book of Magical Arts*, by de Lawrence, a whole series of volumes by the Theosophical Society, *The Secret Teachings of All Ages*... Manly P. Hall... Arien pulled that one out and sat down in the chair he'd taken at the table to spread it over his lap.

"Go back inside. I'll see what I can do," Andy had said. Arien already knew.

He flipped open the cover. Reading was never easy for him. This one had pages numbered with Roman numerals. It was in a Gothic font, very mysterious.

"I hope I see you again soon, Andy," he'd said when the old fellow turned to go.

The book was really big. It was full of beautiful color illustrations. I probably have less than fifteen minutes. Wow, this book seems to be speaking to me.

The dead doobie was in the upturned lid of the brass jar. Arien relit it and had a few quick tokes. Then he swept the herb on the table back into the jar and put it away in the cabinet.

It was hard to concentrate now. Buster needed a serious admonition to be calm. Arien expected the dog would be in mortal danger if he moved to protect. He knew he would have to remain calm, himself. He had no idea how he knew, he just did. It was probably a good combination of intuition and instinct. He could feel them, single-minded, coming.

Nobody knocked. The shutters simply opened and a man in a white fatigue parka came through the double French door and stepped into the room. He actually wore an assault rifle strapped across his back.

"Be still, Buster," Arien said, remaining in the chair. He rested his hand on Buster's shoulder with enough pressure to constrain the alert and ready animal. Thank God! He obeyed.

"Are you Arien?" the man asked, eyeing the dog. A few other men clustered outside.

It took considerable effort to keep calm. Arien had to concentrate on his breath and that helped to measure his heartbeat, but he still had a stuck feeling in the throat. It took him a moment to get it out: "Yeah, Dude. I'm Arien."

"Well, this is your lucky day. I'm Captain Santorri, United States Army. We're here to take you someplace warm."

Arien had the impression they were humoring him when he was allowed to take the dog. It didn't go well at first, but when he told Captain Santorri Buster had saved his life, the officer nodded, twirled his hand in the air, and the whole troupe of soldiers divided themselves and boarded one or the other intrusive machine, hunching below the already whirling blades. Now Arien was buckled-in on a low bench seat, holding Buster tightly as instructed. Lift-off was sudden. Buster splayed his legs for balance, but otherwise maintained a stoic bearing and a soldier, sitting opposite, smiled his approval.

It was all so quick, bracing for the effects of unfamiliar motion, feeling the substance of his body flex and pull this way and that, steeling glances toward the rear and the tightly-packed row of troopers like Eskimo dolls smoking wisps of frozen breath. Who would have guessed he'd be doing this now?

"Where's Andy?" Arien had to shout above the din. Andy was not here.

"In the other bird," the captain said.

This was more than a rescue. Conversation took effort so it was easier to chase his thoughts through the racket all around. Did he see them take a body out of the house? Was Charlie even among them? Funny how the mind jumps around, he thought, looking for explanations when the obvious is too unlikely. But what did they want with him? A side of him couldn't resist being excited about it all, though. It was after all an adventure!

They were in the air less than an hour when the choppers landed on an airstrip. It was plowed and stained with salt, and bordered on one side by a pair of hangars, and on the others with high walls of displaced snow. A small passenger jet was being taxied out of the furthest hanger by a funny-looking truck without a cab. The driver wore a white parka and overalls like everybody else who was outside. Arien was very relieved to see Andy step out of the other machine and briefly wave to him.

Poor Andy, he looked sorry. His smile was winsome. Captain Santorri was talking orders to the brief company of soldiers, and then keeping just four of them, gathered them up with Andy and Arien to head for the other aircraft, which they boarded by a set of fold-down steps. The words, United States Army, was painted on the side of the little jet that otherwise looked like a small-town commuter or corporate plane.

Buster had to be coaxed to go up.

It was warm inside. The coats came off. There was an officer in desert camo, which seemed a little out-of-place in there. He was a man of about forty with thinning hair and a business-like attitude.

"This is highly irregular," he said to Santorri when Buster filled the isle with doggy. Arien stood behind him to ensure he would stay put after making an impulsive attempt to turn around.

"The dog goes with him," Santorri said.

"Oh." The officer processed that, like, *right, of course.* "Well don't we have a crate for this?"

"Sir..." the captain said, looking confused.

"Buster doesn't need a crate," Arien protested.

"You're lucky this isn't a commercial flight, Boy," the officer resolved. He introduced himself as Colonel Griffin. "We're determined to make this as pleasant as possible," he said. "We're all on the same team, got that?"

"Well, that remains to be seen," Andy said evenly from the hatchway. "There's something about all this that doesn't seem voluntary."

"You're an astute candidate," the Colonel said. He invited Andy and Arien to sit at the rear with him on a horseshoe-shaped sofa with seat belts, and fronted with a low semi-circular table. The others sat in forward-facing seats. "I want you to hug that creature when we take off," he said to Arien.

An electronic pop was followed by a voice on a two-way PA that asked, "Are we ready Colonel?"

"Yes. Get us up!"

"Where are we going," Andy asked, as they taxied forward. Then there was a roar from the twin jets on the wings, the craft shuddered and Arien felt his body slide against the restraint of seatbelt and the weight of Buster's body forced into a snuggle with his own.

"Wow!" he cried-out with an excited grin, flashing his fine set of teeth. He'd never been on a plane before. For the moment Arien's reservations went into the overhead compartment. This was really, really rad! He twisted to the window behind him and peered out with his nose pressed against it as they scurried from the landing strip to reveal a glistening white panorama. The jet quickly gained altitude to where Arien could see the curving horizon and a vast field of rippling sequins – just like he'd seen in his vision! It was almost disappointing when they climbed no higher than that, but turned into the sun, and put the great expanse of water behind them.

"Oh!" he exclaimed, "Look! You can see the aurora!" It wasn't a sharp image, but visible enough, a muddled curtain of moving color that appeared to hang ghostly in the starboard distance.

"My goodness, check that out!" Andy agreed, gazing over Arien's shoulder. "You can see it in broad daylight!"

"Indeed," the colonel said.

"They're fried, aren't they?" Arien said, pointing up.

"Yes, that's exactly what happened." Griffin folded the armrests of his center seat down and planted his elbows. He studied the boy who sat just to his right. "How did you know that?"

"Because the sun reached out and fried them," Arien said.

A bell toned to indicate the overhead seat belt light was off.

"Is that why my cell phone doesn't have a signal?" Andy asked.

"There's spotty service where towers will do, but most of the system is down. We've had to scramble AWACS to communicate, just like in the 1960s."

Arien chuckled hearing that.

"I'm curious," Andy said. "Did they find Ralph in my house?"

"Ralph?"

"Yes, the security guard from–"

"Oh, yes, uh, Ralph. A search and rescue team should be out to pick him up in a day or so, I imagine. They can't be everywhere at once."

Arien turned away from the window and fixed his attention on the man in desert fatigues with the birds on his shoulders. The obvious was becoming more likely all the time.

"You've gone through a lot of trouble for me," he said.

"Yes, Arien, and I hope it's been worth it."

They were about an hour into the flight when Andy asked, "Why did you even bother to drag me along?"

Colonel Griffin sipped a rum and coke Lieutenant Jaffrey, who was introduced as the Colonel's adjutant, had served. When Arien, practically holding his breath, told the Lieutenant he'd have the same thing it was delivered with a fleeting smile on the young officer's face. Arien was pleased to the point of giddy and ignored the wary signal Andy threw at him. "Because you go together, you have history," Griffin said. "This needn't be traumatic."

"Alright, I'll buy that," Andy answered. "But tell me how you found out about us."

Griffin pondered his question, twirling ice cubes with a finger, and said, "Let me tell you something that's as true in the military as it is for women, a little mystery goes a long way."

Andy snorted.

Arien chuckled. The dude was a hoot. How rad was this, to be going somewhere on a jet, and downing a rum and coke on top! So far the ride from Woodstock hadn't killed him. Maybe he would survive it after all.

After about two hours in the air they were told the jet would land at Fort Chaffee, Arkansas, to refuel. Arien would have liked to get off the plane to walk the dog but it didn't happen. He pissed in the jet's roomy toilet, hoping Buster would manage, and checked-out the thickening shadow on his face in the mirror. He liked the look. He couldn't be sure if it finally made him look older or merely confused the issue. He liked the alcohol rush, too. It brought a floating feeling that added to the enduring novelty of his recent experience. It was like a trip, having similarities to states of mind under the influence of LSD. The lieutenant had served him another drink. It seemed to be stronger than the last one. He could see out the window that they'd left the snow behind. The short day was darkening and looked like a clear sky was before them as well. He preferred to ignore Andy's more overt disapproval. Andy was an old man, after all, not the cool dude he used to be. Screw that. *I should be dead. I can handle this.*

Buster was lying on the carpet in front of the door. He looked up calmly at Arien; no praise or blame.

"Oh, doggie, where have you been all my life?" Arien kneeled in the isle to take the worthy creature's head in his arms, hugging him to his chest. Buster got a few licks in before Arien released him. His tail thumped on the floor.

The seat belt light came on again. "Preparing to take off," the pilot announced.

Colonel Griffin didn't respond to that. He merely held his glass and watched Arien get back into his seat to drain the drink.

"Would you like another?" he asked.

"I think the boy has had enough, don't you?"

"Oh shit, Andy, this is bitchin'. Let's party, Dude. This is so rad. Yeah, Dude. More, please!"

The jet engines outside whistled and the craft vibrated once again with forward motion. Arien looked outside to see the night close over dry stalks of tall grass and a few glowing windows from nearer buildings.

Once at altitude, the lieutenant provided a third rum and coke. He also came with an attaché case which he set on the low table.

"For the print set, Sir," he said.

"Thank you, Lieutenant," Griffin replied, motioning for Jaffrey to open it. "This is just a formality, Arien, as I have no question regarding your identity, but we need this for verification."

Jaffrey snapped-open the locks and pulled out a thin, glossy-faced tablet. It reminded Arien of a really thin Etch-a-Sketch, but larger . Very slick.

"I will take it as a personal favor if you would remove your boots and socks," Griffin requested.

Arien couldn't quite read Andy's expression here but guessed it marked some passage that was not at all unexpected. He curled his lip in a fragment of smile, shrugged, and complied. Jaffrey pointed at one and then the other foot which Arien extended over the rim of the tablet to be firmly pressed against it. It was cool to the touch. There was twice a brief flash of greenish light and next a set of perfect footprint impressions were revealed on the screen.

"These will be matched with your hospital birth record, Arien," Griffin explained, watching. "It will provide evidence that you were born in 1973 and that you are an American citizen."

"Wow, rad," Arien said, impressed with the efficiency.

"You can't beat that," Andy agreed, only now finishing his original drink and setting the glass down.

"So," Griffin asked Arien, "How many men are in the cockpit of this plane?"

"How the–" The teenager stopped himself. At this point he was rocking and rolling between his ears. What a nutty question, but... Just how much did they know about him? It was really weird. He struggled with the answer, not because he'd drawn a blank, since a number did pop up in his mind that felt totally right, but for the underlying reality of this situation. He wasn't getting too sloshed to appreciate how out-of-place he'd feel if he'd left his sense of adventure behind in New York State. He bent over to pull his socks back on, half-expecting to see ink or something on the soles of his feet, but there wasn't.

"How many?" Griffin coaxed.

"Three."

Griffin's eyes narrowed. His attention turned to Andy. "How does it work?"

"What do you mean?"

"You know perfectly well what I mean, Mister Newell."

"Bitchin'!" Arien exclaimed, clapping his hands together with a wild-eyed grin. "So, that's your last name, Andy? I never knew your last name!"

"You learn something every day, Lad."

Jaffrey held up the tablet in his hands.

"Lieutenant?"

"This is amazing, Sir." He put it on the table for Colonel Griffin to see.

Arien scooted over next to him to check it out. It was truly a marvelous thing. This was no message in green Courier type. There was no ponderous monitor. The elegant black plastic device lay on the table like a sheet of glass, and the mobeus-like, repeating image on its flat, rectangular screen was brilliant and sharp. The tiny soles of a baby's feet enlarged as the sole-prints of the full-sized versions alongside them were reduced until the dimensions were practically equal, and then coming together, the swirls on the toes and the balls of the feet, and the conformation of the heels overlapped everywhere in near-perfect alignment.

"Any coroner would testify the body had been identified," the lieutenant said. "The correlations you're seeing can only be from the same person out of six billion variations."

Griffin broke into a satisfied smile. "That will be all, Lieutenant."

Arien continued to stare at the repeating image, and take in the device, itself. His fascination giggled out of him.

By now Andy had moved to the seat on Griffin's other side and watched it, too. "Wow," he mused aloud, "to know that is one thing..."

"Indeed," Griffin answered, forcing air between his lips just shy of a whistle. "For all intents and purposes, this kid here is thirty-nine years old!"

Arien nodded, shyly smiled, knowing he covered for a deep concern and maybe even a little fear, like an experience of falling in the dark while unable to see the ground. Oh, God, he missed Tina! He needed to be with her now. He needed to snuggle in the scent of her hair, and nibble her ear... Hold on, he admonished himself. Don't cry in front of the Army! He got up and returned to the lavatory.

The kid in the mirror stared back at him with hollow eyes. Back when he was on the road with the Tree People, one of the women there, Sundew, was going on about a boss she'd had, working at A&W Root Beer on weekends when she was still in high school. Sundew said how she thought the guy was so nice for hiring her, and at first he was a righteous cat, but then he started to come on to her at work and touch her in all sorts of unwelcome ways. This got some of the other girls growling and Tina said that's what you get for trusting somebody over thirty. He wasn't sure what this had to do with anything, thinking of it now. Griffin was over thirty, Andy was too, for that matter.

Thirty-nine, what a joke! I am seventeen! I'm only seventeen years old!

Near the end of their flight, Colonel Griffin allowed his guests a confidence that would provide a rationale for the elaborate rescue. As Arien possessed considerable latitude to misrepresent his age, Griffin told him, he was invited to choose an 18th birthday in the recent past, and to strongly consider enlistment. It would be the easiest way, the colonel said.

The plane put down at an Air Force base near Tucson. Griffin called it Davis-Monthan. The temperature outside was crispy but nothing like those single-digits in New York State, so everybody left parkas and leggings on the plane. Arien couldn't see much. A pair of dark sedans picked up the passengers and took them to a matched set of stucco bungalows with porches fronting on an orderly street. The soldiers took the house on the left.

Arien wondered about that. Were they there to protect him, as he was informed, or...? Griffin actually suggested the reliability of the sources the United States (as he'd phrased it) found out about Arien, may have been compromised. Incredible! It was getting past time for a good review of all this with Andy, in private, but the opportunity was never presented.

By the end of the flight, Colonel Griffin explained their destination would be temporary. They would need a few days to debrief and work through some tests.

Arien was sure he'd connected his intention with Andy when they were in the living room, on their way to being shown their bedrooms. Arien's was on the second floor. He went over and opened the double paned, wood casement window, and saw one of the soldiers who were on the plane now posted at ease, on the lawn within sight between the two houses. This was for his protection, no doubt. Right. He wondered where he would go with an impulse to skedaddle. If Arien thought Bethel in December was a whole other world...

"I don't know," he said, sitting on the side of the bed and digging his fingers into Buster's thick fur. "They want me to join the Army. How bozo is that? Would they take you, too, Buster-Buster Dog? Is this what we need now?" He hugged the critter, resting his cheek on the back of Buster's neck. "I'm lucky to have you." He sighed, and Buster appeared to respond with a heaving breath of his own.

Buster's single bark woke him in the twilight of morning before the knock came on his door. An intense morning erection was the next assault but it partly subsided even as he grasped after the shreds of a dream. He stared at the ceiling, seeing faces in a swirl of shadows among the textures there and then listened to the sweet cacophony of mourning doves cooing from outside the window. And then that was broken with the rattling thunder of a jet engine that suddenly fell out of the sky. It seemed to pass right over the house before fading on some runway off into the broad expanse of the base.

"Yeah?" Arien responded. Now he had to piss.

"Breakfast downstairs at 0-800," a voice declared.

"Right!" Arien snorted. They're bonked, he thought, transported for a moment to the group home where he remembered this dude, Andrew, waking the boys from the hall. This wasn't Andrew, though he – or some other version of him – was in the house. Too weird.

They'd provided a set of pajamas he found folded neatly at the base of his bed, but he'd not bothered to put them on. The sheets felt good against his body. He stretched to feel the sensual tingle along the length of his limbs when the morning's erection rebounded with an earnest insistence. Oh, God, he thought, there used to be a place to put this that was far better than in his hand! And when he wanted to get stoned there was something to smoke. And there was a tribe of people who loved him.

"Oh, Tina, God, I miss you!" He cried out, to the faces in the ceiling, "Fuck!"

There used to be a place for his heart.

Arien met Andy in the open hallway when he came downstairs.

"It seems like we've got a pretty busy schedule today," Andy said.

Arien wrinkled his lip in a trace of frown. "We need to talk," he said.

"That would be nice, if we could fit it in."

"Good morning, Gentleman," Griffin greeted, stepping through the divider of dining to living room. "Come on in, sit down. Jaffrey will get something for the dog. Come, we can talk about the day ahead."

Jaffrey recited the options.

"Over easy," Arien decided, rejecting bacon, "and sausage, please."

"I'm going to be very frank," Colonel Griffin said. "We are a little unprepared because it came together so suddenly. They're letting me do it my way for now. It's not very conventional, but these are unconventional times."

"What exactly came together so suddenly?" Andy asked him. He seemed distracted, looking around the table.

"Picking you up, of course."

"Why?" Arien probed.

"Security," the colonel said, raising his coffee cup. "We expected as long as the snow was falling you wouldn't go anywhere, but when the satellites went down and communications disrupted, our percentile of certainty was greatly diminished."

"So you acted," Andy pressed.

"Exactly."

"How did you find out about me?"

"We've already been down that road, Danner."

"It's Grove."

"Excuse me?"

"My name is Arien Grove." Arien was getting irritated. This whole thing was an adventure, yes, but...

"Colonel Griffin, let me be perfectly clear," Andy interjected. "If we are going to cooperate I expect some answers. The way I see it, our predicament amounts to an abduction, plain and simple. I think it's time we're permitted to consult with a lawyer."

Jaffrey came in with three plates in his two hands, like an experienced waiter. He set them down. "I'll be right back with the toast," he said.

"Is there any cream?" Andy asked.

"I'm sorry Sir. There may be Coffee Mate in there, though. I'll see."

Griffin shook his head with a wan smile. "You can't get cream on this base and out there you'll need a cow. Lawyers are in short supply, too, like cows in Tucson." He chuckled to himself. "You'll just have to be patient, take it easy; work with me."

"And if we choose not to?" Andy probed.

"That wouldn't make any sense at all, Mr. Newell. It's in Arien's best interest to get involved with this. We can set him up for life, induction would get him an education, and we will provide him with the means to be, uh, all he can be." Griffin seemed pleased with himself. He said those last words with a flourish, raising his cup like a toast.

Colonel Griffin was good. His words flew over breakfast like a flock of birds; artfully skirting intransigence with an array of possibilities and conversational examples that touched here on the great friendships and experiences he'd had in the service of his country, and there with engaging descriptions of all the fascinating places he had been. He was at once charming and deeply interesting. Arien even entertained some admiration. He wondered if he would forget himself and who he was. Griffin went on to explore the no-man's existence Arien would likely have in the present with a patently unbelievable identity, a world of uncertainty having no movement to get caught up in, slim employment opportunity, steep inflation, escalating crime and most dire of all, a peer group that was politically fragmented and frivolously occupied. Arien had little to go on, but watching Andy, he could tell Griffin was scoring points.

But Andy was an old man...

When Griffin's cell phone jingled and he excused himself to take the call, his birds still swirled in the air.

"Oh my," Andy admitted.

Arien couldn't think of anything to say. He was so full of things to say when he came down the stairs, but now...

Andy winced, slowly, showing teeth. "Ohhhhhhhh...." he groaned. "How did this happen? This isn't what I expected at all! This isn't what I waited for all these years for – to have you taken by these people!" His complexion went white. He swooned like he would faint.

"I haven't made up my mind, Andy. Maybe I could check it out, see what this is all–"

"Arien, there's nothing provisional here. Don't you see? The moment you sign that paper you're hooked for the duration, however long it is."

"Whoa," Arien sighed. His only friend – his only human friend – was deeply distressed. This was major. "I'm confused," he allowed.

"Arien you've got to ditch this place ASAP," Andy finally declared.

"Dude," Arien said, opening his hands, "do you think they'd just let me walk away?" He'd saved a half piece of toast for Buster but now absently had a bite of it.

"God, I don't know anybody in Tucson," Andy fretted. "We need some kind of plan."

Arien snickered. He could tell it smarted.

"I can cloak you with a spell," Andy assured him. "It could get you off the base."

"Ha! You can do that, Andy?"

"Yes, I believe I can."

6 – The less we know

Arien stared up at the rock face, glinting rosy in the slanting sunlight. It was one among an egg-shaped jumble, this one split almost perfectly into two halves, one fallen over on its back, or round side, and the other revealing a quartzite pattern on its plane, web-like, natural to the stone, and over that surface were the eroded scratches and faded monochrome that had been applied by someone a long, long time ago.

Tall clumps of stiff grasses bent slightly and warbled with intermittent breezes. The air had a crisp edge. Arien buttoned the fatigue jacket he wore over the open zipper, purposely not taking its last defense though admitting to himself, perhaps, his whim might bear an uncomfortable cost.

The wide-open country here seemed like the bottom of a vast ocean that had all boiled away. There were distant, blue-grey mountains hugging one horizon; another was upstaged by a lovely peak surmounting a high range dramatically thrusting up from the desert floor. It wore a stubbly scatter of diminutive trees among turbulent folds of shadow, canyon, rock and sky. The road, about a mile behind him, bore no traffic. The last car passed at least an hour before with a distant, rushing sound, gathering echoes of itself, aching and lonesome. He snorted and shook his head. Why have I come here?

He drew his knees up to his chin, tenting the jacket over them, and clasped his hands around it. The ancient image coaxed a knowing smile from him. It first appeared spider-like, with eight zigzagging legs superimposed over the coincidental web design in the rock, a slightly oval circle having an hourglass or infinity image in the center, and a smaller circle with two leading antennas reaching out at the top. But it was also the Circle, his Circle, as it were; the plan of that transcendent ceremony with the Tree People and Ellison Black Snake that he surely anchored at Woodstock. It had to be!

The trick seemed to be this spider's "legs" did not stop at its body's circumference, but were joined together in the center. There, the infinity pattern worked like a distraction, inferring an arachnid body as it implicated something deeper and more universal. Arien stared at the creature's "head" with its two antennas. It said something he longed to grasp.

Sure, there were distractions. He struggled at first to master conflicting fusillades that would question everything, reprimand, pity, scold, jump at every impulse and unravel his mysterious purpose, if only it could. He resisted the temptation to stand and pace, to think about food, the gathering darkness, his small bottle of water, his sense of utter isolation and yes, desolation. Then, remembering something his Tohono mentor had said, *"To be master of yourself is a misleading goal."* He smiled inwardly, relaxing, allowing it all to be but not to govern him. He watched it as it tumbled away into the expanding cavern of his mind and appeared to fire impotently into churning clouds and pyrotechnic flashes.

Could Andy have deciphered this image on the rock face any better than he? He knew he'd broken through in realizing the spider's body was the mendala of the year, with its solstice and equinox axis and cross-quarters. It was the head that stumped him. Maybe it's my intention, he thought, as the sun sank still lower in the sky, and the antennas can listen both here and on the other side. Maybe it sets the direction through the web of life!

How facile the mechanism of his interpretive thoughts had become! Rad. Were it not for Andy this inquiring and understanding side of him might have lost its source of confirmation, if not its moorings. But, maybe not; his recent experience had provided proofs as solid as the rocks in this forlorn place.

Andy: There was an amazing man. They'd had a few moments together in the afternoon when the questions from a veritable committee of officers and men in suits began to wear thin and Arien concluded he could never be a soldier, whether ordinary or otherwise, and the preponderance of otherwise had nothing to do with ending wars or love for our brothers and sisters, not-to-mention "the little creatures that are just part of the Great Mystery," as Mother Shongo had said to him at a barbeque with the Seneca in New York State.

"Buster, where are you?"

The dog crept up behind him and licked the nearest ear. Arien giggled, pushing Buster back. He turned to kiss the fuzzy bridge of the doggie's nose.

"Thirsty, Boy?" The plastic liter water bottle was already half-empty. Arien unscrewed the cap, took a small sip and cupped his hand carefully to pour some, which Buster accepted. Arien felt a little guilty that his fast would be shared by his innocent companion. There hadn't been time to stop at a market on the way here. His thumb had snagged one ride after the other in quick succession from Davis-Monthan, all the way through the sprawling desert city of Tucson and beyond, after he'd nonchalantly walked the dog right off the base.

It seemed so easy and anticlimactic. Was it Andy's brief incantation or the confidence it gave to walk on like he owned the place? But no one happened to be watching the front door when he and Buster stepped out. In their hasty goodbye Andy asked Arien where he might go, and the first thing to pop into his head was to maybe find Tina and Arienne. Andy gave him forty-six dollars in cash, which is all he had in his pockets, a big hug, and a vague plan to meet a month from today at Pioneer Square in Portland, Oregon. The punch of emotion he had to absorb was not so surprising in retrospect. They both shared silent tears. There was no question about hugging the old man now. They grasped each other like life itself, and Arien was not put off by Andy's nose in his hair and the deep breath he drew there.

So, it was not so different now than it was when, on the road to Woodstock, Arien faithfully cleaved to his intuition, and stopped their caravan either here or there and it was invariably the perfect place for the Stand, the Trees and their children. Here they would camp unmolested and even await the unexpected synchronicities that had so raised his stature among them.

He knew there was no sense in returning to the road, now understanding the man who had dropped him off with raised eyebrows when impulsively ordered, "Stop! Let me out here!"

"There's nothing out here but the reservation," he'd said, adding it was unlikely anyone would pick him up after dark, except maybe, the Border Patrol. For a spell he'd stood there, bewildered, and then struck off to the south, where the sun hung south of midway in the sky, until his wanderings brought him to this unusual spot.

The temperature dropped quickly after dusk. Arien fended its effects by lying on his back with Buster on top of him. A fire would have been nice. He had no matches and there hadn't been time to look for any wood. As night closed in the dog remained near, providing him comfort and assurance. He stared up in wonder at the broad expanse of stars which were about as bright as he'd ever seen from the surface of the earth.

Buster couldn't hasten the hours that grew more tedious under the rotating dome of night. Arien slept fitfully. Buster would growl occasionally. There were yaps of coyotes in the darkness, and the plaintive call of a Poor will who spoke across the desert expanse with the tone of a mournful spirit. There was even a moment when it seemed the night would last forever that Arien was sure he'd heard voices. Buster heard it, too, but wisely didn't bark. There was no telling their distance, wafted by the wind over such a wide open space; it could have been miles away. Perhaps it came from the road.

There were a few cars when stars began to fade. Later the twilight morphed to dingy luminescence and hung there under high clouds which unexpectedly veiled the rising sun. Arien stretched and stood uncertainly, shivering. Buster stretched-out with a groaning yawn. As far as he could tell, he was the only human anywhere for miles around. There were some bird calls. This may have been a desert but it was patently alive, even in its winter drab. The lad stepped away and took a leak.

Then he noticed something he hadn't yesterday. Looking again at the face of the petroglyph, coming up to touch it, he saw the plane of the other half section of rock, which he'd assumed was blank. It was not. He now beheld another ancient image, which facing the sky in direct sunlight as it had before, rendered it invisible. Arien had to look again. It was clearly the crude outline of a man with a white head, and drawn beside him was a little four-legged creature.

"Holy fuck, Buster! Check this out!" Arien cried. Of course the dog wasn't particularly moved, but he wagged his tail and happily accepted a good rubbing. Arien was close to hyperventilation when he sat down by the stone to calm himself, and steady his breath. The whole idea presented here was mind-blowing. Words like improbable and unlikely hardly did this justice. How can it be possible? But he did come to this place. He was drawn to see it, certainly!

"Mother and Father of All Things!" the awestruck lad recited, recalling the opening invocation of the Circle he, with Cypriano, his mentor, and the Tree Family composed in Salamanca. It was the first thing that came to mind, and it felt to be spot on. "Accept me as your child, joined with you, offering myself in your service."

"To the highest and subtle One within, may I be focused in you, a living thread to which our harmony attunes."

Was there anything to hear him? Arien listened deeply within himself, and that naturally slowed the rhythm of his heart and nearly stilled his breath, and it felt like it connected him with this place. A serene sense of power filled him like the gathering wind in a broad, square sail. It was a truly beautiful moment.

Feeling a presence, but otherwise remaining very still, he was sure he saw something bright red that beckoned to his periphery. Ever so slowly he turned his head, and stopped when she was fully visible.

How? He'd heard nothing! He realized Buster was calmly watching her, too. A native woman, probably, sat pensively upon a flat stone, maybe a dozen feet away, with her profile in his line of sight. Her face was partly covered by a bright red cloak or blanket drawn tightly around her. Arien was struck by her shimmering raven hair, parted in the middle. Though so little of her features were apparent, she seemed to be youthful and vigorous. He noticed the edge of a woven grass sandal under the hem of her blanket. She was very still.

He wondered, where did she come from? How long has she been here? They sat together, as it were, Arien basking in her presence, and a perceptible contact high that surely embraced him with wonder and yes, joy. It had been a while since he'd felt that emotion. He'd begun to believe he might never feel it again, but there it was. It dawned on Arien this was no ordinary woman, but someone pretty special. If he could have mustered the word it would have been grace. He felt it in her proximity.

Arien wanted to speak to her. He searched for an opening, but couldn't bring himself to disturb the deeply reverent silence, the faint aroma of creosote bush which presently dallied at his breath, a nearby birdsong, and the barest rustle of grasses in the lightest movement of air. The color of the sky remained quite dingy and the morning was still crisp but he allowed his being to blend with it and felt no more discomfort. Maybe this was her way of speaking, and if that were so it was a marvelous conversation!

So Arien closed his eyes in silent communion, finding wonder in the moment, and feeling some restoration to his soul. He soared in that way for a long while and only opened his eyes again when pleasing warmth fell over his face as the sun broke through dissolving clouds. It painted the landscape in subtle earth colors and pastels, to the sweet k-coo of mourning doves as he'd heard at the base, and the mysterious woman was gone.

"Wow," Arien said, getting up and striding to where she'd been. The woman was nowhere to be seen in his unbroken view. Either the earth swallowed her up or she had dissolved into the very air. He giggled excitedly. Buster appeared to sniff around the rock where she was just a short time ago, then presently sat on his haunches to blankly gaze at the desert.

"God, I'm hungry," Arien said. "Let's go back to the city, Buster."

Which city? That was the question. The idea in his head on their way to the road was to check out Sells, and see what it was like. It was where Cypriano was from. Cypriano used to talk to him, set him straight. He was so wise. So Arien crossed the road to catch traffic going that way. Now only the silence greeted him, and a few passing cars.

He'd been buggin' on the cars. Leaving the base yesterday was a test of wills between keeping his head down and buggin' on the cars, or goofin' as he'd heard said among the observant Tree Clan in 1969.

The cars were really sleek, solid-colored. The bumpers were gone. Some had awesome wheels! He saw one back in Tucson that seemed to have no wheels at all, just flat little tires spinning over the road and pure air to the hub! Then it stopped at a corner and it looked like they had a solid rubber band around these weird spokes, with a pattern like you'd see on an Indian bedspread. And, there was another car that was totally quiet. He swore he heard a breeze before he saw the car. It slowed down for him where he hitched on the road from the base, but it only slowed down and then went on. It made him feel paranoid. Maybe he should have kept his head down longer. Maybe he should have waited until dark. But the urge was to get away, do it quickly, and he did just that, as luck would have it.

Now a car slowed down and stopped across the road. It was pretty cool, not because it was anything contemporary, but because it was a Suzuki Samurai, and Arien was sure he recognized the year. He'd always liked them. This one looked great with its slightly over-size tires, too. It was unfortunately headed the other way, toward Tucson.

The window rolled down and the driver leaned out. He was a young man with a lion's mane of blonde dreadlocks, a wispy, struggling beard, and ear plugs big enough to be visible from where Arien stood. "Need a ride?" he said.

"I'm going to Sells."

"I'm going to the city." He leaned an arm over the door and looked at Arien with the engine idling.

The dog barked. It was a single bark. He wagged his tail.

"Okay, Buster. I'm hungry, too," and then he said, "Wait, I changed my mind."

The driver offered a perfunctory nod when Arien got in, pushing his seat forward to let Buster in back. Arien wished it was warmer inside. His appetite, and thirst, and cold night out got in the car with him.

Soon enough Arien could smell the guy. It wasn't offensive, but constituted fresh animal body odor. It made Arien chuckle to himself, flashing on the scrubbed-shiny soldiers at the base. The guy felt real. His energy was free. Arien caught that right away.

"The name's Patrick."

Tools faintly rattled on the bare floor in the back as Buster rummaged for a comfortable spot.

"Arien."

"Cool," Patrick said, "Where you headed?"

"I don't know. Breakfast, I guess, for me and Buster."

"You're way out in the middle of nowhere. Where're you coming from?" Patrick had a rugged, handsome face. His wild, tangled dreads cascaded over the back of his seat. It must have been growing all his life, Arien thought. He wore a natural fiber, Mexican pull-over, likely layered. His loose drawstring pants were of thick, but soft cotton. His blue eyes reflected a warm light.

"I wasn't even hitchin' your way. Why'd you stop?"

"I don't know," Patrick said with a brief smile. "You looked like you needed to be somewhere and the direction wasn't relevant."

Arien laughed, sharing it a little with the driver. "Dude," he said, "I love your buggy."

"Yeah, it's cool, huh? It's as old as I am," Patrick confided.

"You were born in 1990?"

Patrick grinned. "Yeah," he confirmed. "You know 'em!"

"It's in great shape," Arien told him, admiring its silver-grey color and the clean interior.

"Thanks. Well, I built this one out of two."

The morning haze seemed to darken as they approached the city, which was still out of sight. There were some housing developments in the desert here and there. One had a forlorn, half-finished look.

"So, I'm really stopping short of town. I'll take you in, but you're welcome to come eat something with us."

Arien shivered. He worked to control it. "Uh, sure, Dude. But I need to feed the –"

"There's dogs. He can have some of their food."

"Wow, rad," Arien gratefully said.

Patrick made a left turn between a pair of slender stone columns where a narrow dirt drive wound into the desert. It passed around some rocky knobs and low hills for a ways, before a small cluster of stone cottages with red tile roofs came into view. To Arien, they looked really old, if not foreign. They blended so well with the surroundings, and it appeared no effort had ever been made to conform the perfectly lovely natural setting of burnished red-umber rocks set off with prickly pear and barrel cactus, among boulder-sized tufts of bear grass, cholla, and a few massive and tall saguaro with arms, just like on the postcards.

Three mutts came up and ran barking alongside.

"Get out of the way, dummy," the driver muttered at one. "Quit acting like dogs." He shot a grin to Arien. Buster practically danced in back and sang-out with whining vocals. He was in a big hurry to jump out when they stopped in front of one of the cottages, and immediately wolfed the attention with a set of poses, skipping legs, a negotiating nose, and his tail high in the air.

Arien appreciated that. He followed Patrick inside, unmolested by greeting dogs.

The stucco-walled interior was dingy but quaint, and mercifully warm. Charred bits of wood and ashes smoldered in the stone fireplace there. Over the mantel was a small poster of Bob Marley and a young man on the rumpled, tan-colored couch, also dreaded, with a big splash of dark brown hair, and a clean-shaven face, was coincidentally introduced as Marley. Marley had a good build under a sleeveless black T, accentuated with black, Celtic knot tattoos on both arms. He wore a ring in his nose and multiple rings bordered the rims of both of his ears. His legs filled baggy black jeans, cut off midway down the foreleg, with a fabric belt. Arien's fascinated smile was returned with a sincere greeting.

"Oh, rad! Arien declared. "I didn't expect to see that!" He pointed at a turntable on a wide set of shelves that held a good collection of vinyl 33s.

"I like 'em," Patrick responded. "I chase bands that lay their tunes in grooves."

Arien's "Groovy" won him a smirk.

"There's some old stuff there, too, '60s, '70s."

"Whoa!" Arien praised, truly impressed, and thought, Jesus, what a trip! This dude was born when I left the world I knew for... And here he is older than me! Something else began to bug him though he wasn't dizzy and sick to his stomach as he'd been the first time, and it could be said there were forty-three years and some serious history since the day it all started.

"Archetypes," he said, feeling suddenly conflicted.

"Huh?"

"You dudes remind me of friends I used to have." Arien resolved not to go any further than that.

Buster was invited in for a bowl of kibble away from the other dogs, and Arien was offered gluten-free granola with vanilla-flavored soy milk, which was readily accepted. He remembered being teased once for what he ate in the future. "Do you guys get food stamps?" he asked.

"No," Patrick told him. "I engage Babylon as little as possible." He watched as his guest slurped down breakfast at the small table in the kitchen. He asked, "Are you from around here?"

"Portland, Oregon."

"So, I'm guessing you spent the night out on the road."

"The Reservation, actually, checkin' out the rock art."

Patrick returned an attentive nod. He dipped in the open plastic bag of granola on the counter for a handful.

Marley popped his head in the doorway. "The cell's back," he announced.

"Cool. See when the girls are coming home."

"Right."

"Tonight," Arien said, before he realized what he was doing. Oh shit. He lowered his head as if to take it back.

"What's that?" Marley asked.

"Nothing."

"No," Patrick said. "I heard you say, tonight."

"I don't plan to spend tonight in the desert," Arien mumbled, crunching and swallowing. He was glad this seemed to work. Marley turned away to peck at his little phone, but Patrick's eyes seemed to linger with genuine interest. Arien pushed his empty bowl back. "Wow, thanks, Dude. That hit the spot."

"You're welcome, Brother," Patrick said. "So, what's next?"

Arien had never been far from his predicament, but the question still wasn't easy. His desert experience only opened another box. "I don't think I'm done with Sells," he ventured. "But I think I shouldn't be hanging out by the road, either."

Patrick waited, quietly probing his guest with a level gaze. He scratched an ear.

The boy from the past had to dig for suitable words. "The Pigs, well, the Military wants me for, for questioning."

"Ah," Patrick said, drawing a curious smile. "Is it serious?"

"Maybe."

"Act of terrorism?"

"I don't know," Arien mused. "I don't know what they'll say, but there'll have to be a reason, I suppose. I really don't think they'll give up." The thought chilled him. He was nobody here. He didn't even know how things worked anymore. He felt like a refugee in a foreign country. "Look, I'm not ready to talk about it. I hope that's okay."

Patrick feigned a nervous chuckle. "The less we know the better, huh?"

"You might be right about that, Brother."

"I knew there was something about you when I saw you hitchin' by the road," Patrick said. He and Arien stood by the petroglyph Arien found (or had it drawn him there?) the previous day. He'd thrown Arien a curve after breakfast by inquiring into the rock art assertion his guest had made, wanting very much to know more about it, and he pitched another by coming out with a rather large, blue-plastic bong, to Arien's utter delight. The pot was really spicy and tingly and to Arien, in his circumstantial fast for the last couple of weeks, his head rush was exceptional.

Marley squatted over the ancient image now with a little magnifying glass he carried in his pocket. "This is so sick," he said.

Arien was merely grateful he'd found it again after the first two attempts in as many hours ended in failure. He only saw it when he practically gave up and lead them in a direction he believed it wouldn't be. He was sure his credibility was on the line, and this hide-and-seek with rocks was making him feel pretty stressed and stupid. But now, vindication hung on him like the Croix de Guerre.

"Imagine finding something like this way out here! There's no fence around it. Somebody could steal it." Marley noted.

Arien considered the possibility of some connection with the woman in the red blanket that had been here with him. She'd impressed him very deeply. He wondered if perhaps they were only here now because she'd permitted them to be, and only after some due consideration. Andy used to call this "thinking magically," which always favored the most resonant mental image. God, he'd learned so much on the road to Woodstock! That amazing circle there offered another kind of vindication: the Celestial Ship! Holy shit! You can't fake that!

But catching air with this line of thinking, and association, came pre-wrapped with its own nest of coals banked against his heart, searing every beat, bellowing with every breath, and weighing upon his chest like the stack of wood that would feed it. He sank to the ground, covering his eyes. Buster came over to lie by him, resting his snout in Arien's lap, while Arien, askance, felt some of this flow into the young men who were there with him, who now grew very still and introspective.

"Wow, Brother, this is amazing," Patrick reverently said after a spell. "What a powerful place! How the heck did you find it?"

"It must have wanted me to," Arien answered, having to work at keeping his voice from cracking. God, how he missed his Stand – Tina's loving presence, Otter's willful guidance, Jeff's steady competence, Andy's marvelous occult knowledge, Clayboy's worthy, little-brother solicitude. Such a family they made! What a beautiful life that promised to be! But, was he missing something else? This one seemed more immediate, more pressing. He was still fairly ripped on Patrick's fine herb, and very in tune, and felt a wildly propitious kinship with these strange fellows in the improbable future. They seemed so similar to the people he'd known, the gentle people, the flower people, the beautiful people. He easily imagined Patrick and Marley could have been there with them, and he would be remiss to deny their medicine.

He lowered his hands to see both Patrick and Marley were silently crying. They'd also sat cross-legged on the dry, rocky ground. Surprised, he softly asked, "What are you thinking, Brothers?"

Marley balled a fist and rubbed his eyes. "My older sister came down with a fever when she was sixteen. She fell into a coma and never came out of it. My God, I loved her!"

"Wow," Arien said, but not only for Marley's sad report. His eyelids closed when Patrick spoke.

"I was thinking of this place and the native people, native people everywhere and what happened to them," he said. "I don't think I ever got it like this. I knew it before, but never like this!"

Arien stilled his breath as he'd learned to do. Maybe the stone, his high, helped. A little was going a long way with him. It packed a powerful punch. He could feel their syncopated hearts rubbing together in his own breast, along with Buster's faster beat. He smelled the creosote bush and a whiff of wild sage, and smiled inwardly as the air, too, became still, and he felt the glow of the sun on them all. It was bittersweet. It hurt so good, and he was okay with it.

He didn't object when Patrick got up and turned to go.

"Jesus," he said. "If I stay here another minute I'll cry myself to death."

"That's right, Patrick!" Marley exclaimed, jetting out of his funk with amazement on his face. "But it's totally legit! How sick is that?"

7 – Las Lomas

Arien had never heard names like Matt, Luke and Mark for dogs. That's what the mutts of Las Lomas were called. Patrick told him if Buster's name had been John, he would have left him on the highway. During the day, which hovered in the 60s from freezing at night, the dogs hung in the shade under the old, cream-colored school bus where Patrick kept his welding equipment and automotive tools. Buster didn't get into that, but preferred being Arien's shadow.

The girls that came with Patrick and Marley were Zanna and Cindy. They'd been on a trip to Phoenix where Zanna's mom lived, and they did get back that evening. If the guys made any connection with Arien's prediction they didn't say. He'd denied it, after all. But they practically begged him to stay "as long as you need," especially after appreciating how he came with only the clothes on his back, a loyal dog, and a vague desire to lay low, yet further investigate the Tohono reservation. After that, he said, he wanted to "catch up with family in Oregon."

Arien was given a small, enclosed porch with a wall of dirty windows off the west side of the cottage, barely larger than a walk-in closet, where a pile of boxes and jumble of stuff was temporarily shoved aside for a foam pad, and some spare blankets on the dark-red cement floor. He offered the forty-six dollars he had in his pocket toward the house but they told him to hold on to it for now, he needed everything, and they didn't have much, either.

That was clear. The bathroom had an old-time toilet with a tank set up high on the wall, and a grimy tub that looked like it hadn't been used very much, except maybe to clean car parts, but that was just a guess. There was no soap to be seen, or any TP for that matter, and the one towel on the rack looked like it had hung there since the Korean War and smelled like it, too. It was impossible to tell what color it was. Arien was hardly fastidious but he could have had a shower. He chuckled to himself after using the toilet, finished undressing, and squatted in the tub with the water running, which he splashed over his body with his hands. The water got cold very quickly, and considerable fortitude was required to finish the task at hand. Shivering, he finger-scraped the drops off, daubed himself dry with his T-shirt and then dressed, less the shirt. He slipped that under his belt at the seat of his pants and padded out to the living room to warm up by the fireplace.

"Did you find the soap?" Zanna asked from her seat on the couch. She was alone there, tapping on a strange device, very slim, with the proportions of a small composition book. It reminded him of the computer tablet he'd seen on the plane.

"No." Arien answered, watching her fingers sweep over its glossy, flat surface. He resisted an impulse to check it out right away.

Zanna was small and thin, but pretty, with big, brown eyes in a child-like face, a dark complexion and dark-brown hair, the house exception by not being dreaded. She had a mischievous smile, and she seemed radiant with Patrick, who shared her energy well. This night she wore a plain white cotton blouse, and a medium-length black-denim skirt. An intricate, brightly-colored tattoo design scrolled down along both her upper arms. To Arien, it made her look kind of foxy-tough. "There's a new bar in the top drawer by the sink," she said.

"Next time, thanks."

All of them had tattoos and an assortment of body piercings. When Patrick's pull-over came off in the house, Arien observed designs similar to Marley's, in wide, dark swirls circling his arms to disappear under a faded, retro-style Led Zeppelin T-shirt. Cindy's adornment favored piercings. Rings circled her lips, her tongue, and likely places that were covered by clothes. Jeweled studs sparkled in her nostrils and one speared an eyebrow as well. She came out of the kitchen with a beer mug full of black coffee and a hand-rolled cigarette dangling in her welcoming smile, her short, dreaded red hair was accented with amber bracelets that perfectly matched her hair's color, and the long, burgundy, tight-fitting dress she wore made her look like a model ready for a shoot.

She stopped by Arien to tap a forefinger on the silver Om dangling over his chest. "Ooh, where'd you get that?"

"It was a gift from a friend in the Haight."

"Sweet," she said.

Her finger dangled there, eyes sweeping around it in a little flirt. It made Arien self-conscious. He stepped back, awkwardly.

"You're a hottie," she added, "and that's a blank slate." The finger twirled over his bare chest with a languid rotation of her wrist. She winked at Zanna, whose eyes rolled up in polite concurrence.

Cindy moved away to sit in an armchair, and Arien put his shirt on, accepting dampness as the price of modesty. She'd put ink on me, he gathered. The idea did intrigue. They wouldn't have gone for that at Youth Promise. But, defying Youth Promise seemed so way moot at this point. God! Youth Promise! Ha! He added a few sticks of mesquite to the fire from a pile in a cardboard box there and sat down on the edge of the raised, Spanish-tile apron to be by Buster, who was sprawled over the painted cement floor in front. The heat spilling out of the fire felt great.

"When were you in the Haight, Arien?" Zanna asked him.

"Uh, in the spring." Arien didn't wish to lie, after all.

"Oh, wow! I was there last May; saw Crave, and got to hang with Jeff Craven, too."

"God, I was so jealous," Cindy snorted.

"That's rad, Babe," Arien said.

Zanna smiled. "So, Patrick said you're, uh, running?"

"What's that?"

"Run—?"

"Oh, yeah, that."

"From the Military?"

"Army Intelligence. They were, uh, asking questions, yeah."

Zanna leaned forward.

"And you ran?"

"Something like that."

The girls exchanged impressed glances.

"He's pretty young to be so interesting," Cindy said, aside.

Zanna nodded in agreement, and asked, "How old are you, anyway?"

"Seventeen."

"His face fuzz is pretty cute," Cindy coyly observed, between sips of coffee.

Arien reached to scratch the top of Buster's head. He easily appreciated the riddle he posed. He would love to have spilled it all out, but the often uncomfortable struggle with his friends before, suggested sitting on the lid. There had to be a better way to come to terms with reality than inviting disbelief and ridicule.

"Are you a radical Muslim?" Zanna asked.

Arien laughed to himself.

"No," he answered. "This lady, Cassie, a sister in our tribe, told me once I was a true Aquarian. I guess that's what I am."

The girls chuckled.

Arien softly sang, a bit off key, *"This is the dawning of the Age of Aquarius..."*

Zanna's jaw dropped. She threw a surprised and delighted glance to Cindy.

That felt good. Emboldened, Arien went over to check out the record albums. There were a few on top of the shelf: Strange Mercy - St Vincent, Potamento (whatever that is...) - the Drums, Crave, Bon Iver. Older stuff was below: Hendrix, (damn), The Doors, The Beatles' White Album...

"I didn't expect to see this," he confided.

"The White Album?" Zanna asked.

"No, any of them."

"That one should be locked-up," Zanna said.

"You don't like it?"

"That's not what I meant."

Arien wasn't sure what she meant. "Can I play one?"

"Go for it. I'd bet Patrick wouldn't mind, but he hates it when they're left out."

Arien tapped his forehead in an 'I got it gesture' and chose. Carefully, he turned on the amp and then found the turntable switch. It was a pretty fancy turntable. He wondered at first why the tone arm didn't drop when he let go of it, but then noticed this little lever on the side. Ah...

"You would play that!" Cindy groused.

On the other hand, Zanna allowed herself a self-satisfied smile as Jeff Craven's startling vocals outlined a complex plot in the kind of acoustic/alternative fusion that was making him famous.

Arien liked it. It was fresh. It was all so fresh. All he had to do now was catch up.

The penetrating chill had him wrapped into a ball. Half of one blanket was over the musty foam pad, and the other half over him. He'd given the second blanket to Buster to lie on. His fatigue jacket made a decent pillow and he could hug the rest, but he was still cold. His room felt like a refrigerated mausoleum. He considered taking it all into the living room, though he guessed the floor there would be cold, too.

If I can't get to sleep soon, I'll do the couch.

He didn't like sleeping with clothes on, it felt clammy, but tonight maybe he made a mistake taking them off. They were up late after pizza Patrick and Marley brought back from an afternoon run to Tucson for car parts. They drank wine, talked into the night, played records, and passed the bong. Arien noticed how the pot was measured. None of it was wasted, more like in the late '80s, before his run-in with the law effectively removed him from his life. He'd spent a lot more time in the '80s. He'd grown up there, after all. Or, he thought so once, anyway.

He'd passed tired.

It was obvious his hosts wanted to know more about him. All four of them tried various ways to get him to tell more of his story, but it didn't work. He was affable, talked about a few things, mentioned the people he'd been with and some of the things they'd done, but managed to keep it in a timeless place, like a gay man might use genderless words about his partner, so straight strangers only learn in manageable measures. Nor could he hint at the how of their separation, but that was the elephant in the room standing heavily on a coherent story.

Damn it. He rolled over. Am I dead? Is this some kind of Hell? But even here he knew when people fed off of his connection, and the yearning, the need it kindled. In fact right now somebody was up and moving around. Oh God! I'm too cold to be horny, he thought as a shiver connected the blanket to his body, and his disposition changed in an instant. Oh, the anticipation set off fireworks in his head! She was through the doorway and very close. Buster made a sound like a low-frequency whistle. Arien didn't know how he knew, but she moved like a girl. It had to be either Zanna or Cindy.

The row of windows on the outside wall must have allowed just enough moonlight for her to see. She hovered over him. The cover lifted gently. Her breath fell against his cheek. She planted a light kiss.

"Do you need a warmer, more comfortable bed?"

"That would be so rad," he heard himself say.

"Come," Cindy coaxed.

Wrapped in his blanket, he followed her through the living room to one of the two bedrooms off the hallway to the kitchen. He was so turned on it felt like he could have shot it on the way. He wondered about Marley.

"Sorry, Buster, why don't you hang-out here?"

There was a dim light on in their room. Marley was staring up at the ceiling.

Cindy said, "Get in," offering Arien the middle of the bed.

He hesitated until Marley expanded the invitation with a tap to the space beside him.

Arien slid into bed modestly, letting go of his blanket as he pulled theirs over, before being surrounded by their warmth, and their ripe animal smell. Marley pulled him close, spooning their bodies.

"You're smooth as a baby," he said, pressing their ears together and entangling their hair, "and you smell like candy."

He was certainly aroused though Arien suspected it was the energy, not his gender. How free these people were! But he could feel Cindy tremble all over as her hands discovered him and he turned to explore her. He found the rings of her mouth, and the ones through her nipples, and the ring in her navel, and several in the lips of her vagina that giddily provoked him as he slipped into her.

Oh, God, that felt so good, so warm and luscious; so damn good! Cindy swallowed his doubts along with what he gave her, and Marley was working from behind, finding his way, hugging him around the tummy, and across his chest, and holding him so tightly with all the sensual strength of an ardent young man in his prime. And so their bodies tangled into the night until satiety and exhaustion rolled Arien between beating hearts and rhythmic breath, blissful warmth and insistent sleep.

In the morning, Arien navigated the hallway wrapped in his blanket. He barely made it to the bathroom in a swirling tide of physical pleasure, on a raft of pheromones that made relieving himself highly problematic. He giggled, stepping into the bathtub where he could piss through his erection with a carefully-aimed arc to the drain. The erotic memory was overwhelming. That was so rad, he exulted. That was so fucking awesome! "Ohhhhhh..."

"Come back," Cindy whispered, when he'd clambered over her.

"Oh, yeah," he'd said, like a giddy kid. And, he was keeping his promise when he practically bumped into Zanna in the hall as he was leaving the bathroom. She was naked.

"Good morning," he said with a giggle at her startled expression.

"Oh my God!" she exclaimed.

"What?"

"Give me that blanket!"

"What? It's mine."

"But I don't have anything on!" She crossed her arms over her pelvis, sliding from surprised to looking coy.

"But then what would I have on?"

"But you're a guy!"

"I won't look," he promised.

"Oh, I will," she said, grabbing the blanket and pulling it, along with Arien, back into the bathroom where they stood for a moment, breathless. And then she took his head in her hands and kissed him. Their lips locked.

There wasn't time to think. Arien staggered back but managed lowering the toilet lid as he fell backwards onto it, his blanket falling away, and she got right on him, and rode him right there.

"What am I doing, Buster? Ohhhh..." Arien bit the edge of his fist. He was just out of sight of Las Lomas, cross legged on a broad outcrop of rock that resembled an altar to a massive, armless saguaro standing nearby. The sun was nice and warm. It sliced through a cold air front that had come through in the night with enough of a drizzle to leave pockets of ice to greet him when he found the spot. By now all the ice had turned back to water. Was he really that far from Woodstock? He'd just fucked his way through the house. Jesus! He still had to face Patrick. Zanna was wild! She just didn't care. He started to get a boner again just thinking about her.

What hot kid would not have been full of himself after all that? God! It was too much, too fast. There wasn't any guidance. Cypriano was gone. There were only his memories. Otter, what would you have said? Was there any connection to entitlement? How would this have sat with Andy? Tina (oh, wow), it was inconceivable! But, there was no going home to her – at least not as they were...

What were the kids, for want of a better word – they were all a few years older than him, after all – what were they thinking now? Should he be wary of Patrick? Would Patrick be mad, or would he want to fuck me, too? God! The thought of Marley going where he'd been while Arien was at it with his girl... But Arien had never had an orgasm like that in his life! God! Now he was hard as a rock again. "Ah!" he cried out, with hormones well beyond raging. No, it was more like rioting.

"Ohhhh... God!" Overcome by an overwhelming need for release, Arien stood, nearly ripping his fly open as his eyes swept the perimeter to be sure he was alone, and he took hold of himself in a perfect convention of Venus, Eros, and Pan, to splatter his seed over that rock, again, and again, and one more time before he could stop.

"Fuck," he panted, head swooning, dropping to the rock, closing his eyes. He opened them in time to see the dog there licking the rock. "No, Buster!" he hollered, mingling surprise with laughter. "Oh God, that's gross! Go over there and lie down! Go lie down!"

Arien owned the rock for a while longer, gently swaying with an inaudible song. He even made an effort to understand what was deeper and older than that.

"Oh shit, Dog Face, what am I going to do?" He thought about his experience with the petroglyphs, when he felt so sad that it had Patrick and Marley crying, for Heaven's sake! What the...? "This is scary shit. I'm riding a fucking rhinoceros!" He knew instinctively it could gore and trample him if he fell off.

"I'm okay. It's okay," he said, trembling, trying to calm his heart. He could feel it want to jump out of his chest. His breath came in deep drafts. "I'm a hot dude. They all want me: Andy, the new hippies, and Army Intelligence, too. Holy fuck! "Ho!" he sighed with a gulp.

The dog was good, calm; he merely listened there by the rock with Arien.

"I think if it wasn't for you I'd be dead, Buster. If all this didn't kill me, I'd do it myself." With that, a really off the wall thought came to him. It actually made him laugh: Why wait for some random thunderstorm? Maybe I could stick my finger in a light socket and blow myself out of here!

"Come on, Buster," he said, seizing on the next impulse. He got up and headed out into the desert, to make a wide arc around the stone cottages of Las Lomas. He would work his way to the road, hopefully unseen. But, when he did reach the road nearly an hour later he had a flash of paranoia. Something wasn't right along here. He could feel it. Hunting, they were hunting. Not yet. His concern with Las Lomas was a mirage compared to that. For now, he would have go back and deal with it.

Matt, Luke and Mark barked and swirled around as he approached. Arien was fairly spent, between his wild night, its desert extension, and the long walk that probably came to two or three miles. He was famished, too. He'd had nothing at all to eat yet today. It relieved him that Buster perfectly fended off the dogs.

Patrick had been standing in the doorway, no doubt alerted by the commotion, and now he came and sat on the porch steps opposite Arien, who sank wearily to lean back against a square stone column. Arien didn't say anything as Patrick studied him while the dogs revived their rituals of greeting.

The air was cooler, the sun being filtered behind high clouds in the wide-open, south-western Arizona sky. Arien snuggled into his jacket. It could have been warmer.

Oh boy, Patrick was shaking his head now. "My best friend can't look me in the eye without a stupid-face," he opened, "Cindy's been in a tizzy all day, and my girl fucked me this morning like she hasn't in a month. What the fuck did you do to them, Kid?"

"Oh, that..." Arien said, with a sly cant to his lip. "I'm sorry, Patrick. I really am."

Patrick shook his dreads again, almost ruefully. "Apology gratefully accepted," he deadpanned. "Where were you all day, anyway?"

"Sorting things out." Arien really wanted to be truthful. He hoped that said it well-enough.

"Hungry?"

"Oh, yeah, Dude. I could eat that saguaro."

8 – There was something about the eyes

Zanna said, "Patrick says you're from Portland." She held that flat, glossy little device of hers.

Cindy and Marley were rummaging in the kitchen where the hiss and tap and appealing odors of sautéed vegetables drifted out. Patrick had just gone through the front door with a stack of dog bowls for the critters in the yard, which included Buster at the moment, and Arien was following him.

"Yeah."

Zanna pecked at the screen.

Arien's curiosity won him over. Of course, he imagined it was some cool gadget, but when he came to look over her shoulder he was utterly astonished.

"What?" she said.

"That's awesome! What is it?" He couldn't help himself.

"This?" She held it up.

The graphics were as sharp as the glossiest magazine, peppered with little cartoon symbols that actually moved under her fingers and appeared to connect with various functions of the thing. When he'd first looked, there was certainly a keyboard there, but now it was gone! "I'm sorry," he said, "I've been away for a while."

"You don't know what this is." She didn't phrase it like a question; it was more like she was telling herself something in order to properly absorb it.

Arien shifted self-consciously.

"You've never seen an I-pad?"

"No, never. What does it do?"

"My God!" Zanna held it up, seeming to show him the back of it.

In retrospect, Arien made the connection when a twist of her wrist flaunted his image on the screen! "Wow! You got my picture!"

Now Zanna's fingers flew over the surface and various fields came and went. "Ta!" she said, with a final peck. "Now you're my guest on Facebook!"

"Oh wow!" Arien exclaimed, hunkering over her shoulder. "That is so rad, Babe! Can I see your...?" He didn't want to ask what Facebook was, and imagined he could figure it out with a closer look.

"Scroll like this," she said, and with her close proximity, the scent of her hair took him back to the morning with her in the bathroom. It made her seem to grow bigger, with the expanding pupils of her eyes.

That was awkward. "Ummmm..." It was an effort to look at the screen. He scrolled with his finger. There were lots of photos, little boxes of conversation and announcements, a column of advertising, some of it flickering for attention.

It was cool to see his image there. He saw a section on the top left side that noted Zanna had 137 friends. That's an impossible lot of friends, he thought.

Zanna retrieved the I-pad and flipped through a short cascade of screens, pressed a symbol and a long list came up. "What do you want to hear?" she asked.

"Do you have any U2?"

She smiled. "Yeah, let's see..." she pecked, "Boy, War, whatever."

"Boy" was Arien's request. She tapped it again and the album began to play.

"That was old when... I always liked U2," he corrected. And when he looked at her again her face had blushed, he was sure like his own.

"God, you were a great fuck," she reported, with a deep breath. "I wanted more and gave it to Patrick."

"He told me," Arien said, getting turned-on.

She reached to place four fingers over his mouth. He moved to bite them, but she tapped his lips and yanked them away. "I can't be going there," she said, as much to herself as to him. "I love Patrick. This is too crazy."

"It's crazy," he agreed.

"Look at you! You're so young!" She pushed him back so he would stand further away. "I don't know what got over me."

"You're not sorry, are you?"

"Not yet," she said, with a little wink.

The young Bono sang, ...You *let me go-o-oh...*

Cindy poked her head in. "Dinner's ready!" she announced. "Arien, tell Patrick!"

The dining room was essentially a large booth, with a wooden bench around three sides. The table was made of four wide boards about four inches thick, like a picnic table in a park, clear-coated with a thick urethane. It was yellowed with age. Arien got on an end sitting next to Patrick, which probably made it a bit easier to eat, for the sake of his personal space. Steaming jumbles of veggies were in a large, stainless frying pan. It was set on a pad in the middle of the table. A big ceramic bowl was heaped with a yellowish grain Arien wasn't familiar with.

"You don't use chop sticks?" Arien asked generally.

Marley chuckled. "My grandfather uses them," he said. "My grandfather's weird. There's some in the drawer under the toaster."

Arien had left-over pizza earlier but he was hungry again by now and dug in, trying to balance the rather intense energy in the small space. He was the new guy in the mix who had set off a bomb, after all. He asked Patrick if he had Blind Faith on vinyl.

"Yeah, Arien. Holy shit, that's good. It's cool you like the records."

Somebody's toes found Arien's ankle. It had to be Cindy, sitting across from him, though her face revealed nothing. He pushed against them. They held and pushed back. He chuckled. "I do," he said. "I knew a guy in Portland who had a totally rad collection. You would have loved it."

"This is good." He pointed at the grain on his plate. "What is this?"

"Quinoa," Marley answered, admiring the heap of it balanced on Arien's utensils. "It's staying on your chop sticks, too."

Arien nodded while toes caressed his ankle. One of the boots he wore, courtesy of the U.S. Army, was loose enough and he worked it off. He wasn't wearing socks. He'd rinsed his only pair and they were drying by the fireplace. He could now engage the foot under the table with his own so, when Patrick asked Arien to get him another microbrew, he had to stalk to the refrigerator with only one foot in a shoe. He got himself another one, too, and was still goofing on having to use an opener. But it was well worth the trouble. The beer they were drinking tasted terrific.

"Was your grandfather a hippie?" Arien asked when he returned.

"'Fraid so," Marley said with a grin.

"Well, Ha! Look at you! And you don't think your grandpa would take *you* for weird?" Arien rolled-out a good laugh.

Marley responded with a defiant grin and a flicking middle finger.

"Now Children," Patrick admonished.

"Does he live in Tucson?" Arien asked.

"My grandfather?"

"Yeah."

"Over on the north side of town, by Sabino Canyon." Marley had a sip off his bottle. "He visits now n' then. You might get to meet him."

"Rad. I like hippies."

"You're weird," Cindy told Arien with a smirk.

Arien flashed his middle finger with a wink at her, when toenails suddenly raked over his bare foot. "Ow!" he cried, jerking it away, and thumping it hard against the bench. "Ow!"

She smiled and winked back.

Zanna had to lean past Patrick. "What are you kids doing?" she scolded in a teasing tone.

"It's your damn cat," Arien said. "I think I need a tetanus shot."

Patrick said, "Rub some salt in it; kills the tetanus."

"Salt's right here," Cindy agreed, pointing at the shaker on the table.

She really did rake him. He looked down at it. "Fuck," he said, under his breath.

At this point Cindy swayed in her seat to have a gander, but he was already pushing it back into the shoe. "Aw," she soothed, her expression changing. "I'm sorry. Is it okay?"

"It's fine." He reached for another helping of veggies. He either had to push himself to do something constructive or get up from the table, which didn't seem like a good option.

"I'll have more, too," Marley said.

After a pause, Cindy asked, "Do you do Facebook, Arien?"

"Nah. I don't, uh, have an I-pad."

"It's not a good idea, anyway," Patrick said.

"Why not?"

"Because he's running from the man, Cindy. He doesn't need to advertise where he is."

"Oh," Zanna blurted, growing introspective.

"How's that?" Arien followed.

"Facial recognition tech," Patrick explained. "If they're looking for you, one of the places they check is social networking sites. C'mon. You know that!" He moved towards Arien. "Excuse me," he said.

Arien didn't move right away. He'd locked eyes with Zanna.

"Let me out. I got-a pee."

"Oh God," Zanna sighed. "Patrick..." She got up, too.

"What?"

As Zanna headed for the living room, Patrick looked to Arien for an explanation. He drained his beer and set the bottle down.

"She put my picture on her, uh, Facebook," Arien volunteered. He was growing concerned.

"You posted his picture?" Patrick hollered, as Cindy wagged a finger at Marley and Marley shrugged.

"Yes! Yes, I'm sorry. I'm deleting it right now!"

"Jesus, Arien. I hope that was quick enough," Patrick said, on his way to the bathroom.

"Can they really do that? There must be millions of –"

"Yes! It happens all the time. Last summer, at the Rainbow Council, Larry Crow said a friend of his was busted when they picked up the license number of the guy's car from a picture taken at Larry's farm, in Tennessee." Patrick said, stopped in the hallway. "It came up in a discussion about privacy and security on the net. The net's great for keeping everybody connected, but it has a really dark side we need to be aware of."

Arien couldn't imagine how any of this was possible, but this was the future, after all, and he recognized a great deal must have happened. He'd had twenty-one years on his friends at Woodstock and that provided considerable perspective; he could only imagine what another twenty-two could have gotten past him. It was mind-boggling. All he could do was take Patrick's words at face value. His heart began to thump. He didn't particularly want to see Colonel Griffin again, especially after the poke in the eye that dude must have taken. Wow. He was beginning to feel as helpless as a cat on the expressway.

Restlessness came on Arien fast. His guard was posted and ordered to stay awake. The world was a more sinister place. It should have been no surprise that everyone in the house became wary with him. They were all in the living room with a warm fire in the hearth, and Buster was there, too, watching Arien pace.

"Look, maybe it's nothing," Patrick said, "but I'd feel better if you had another place to stay for a while, at least until we can be sure that post didn't light a fire."

Arien closed his eyes. "I tried to hit the road," he said. "I'm afraid of being picked-up."

"We don't want you to go," Zanna said emphatically. "It's just that, that we don't want you to get caught."

"Arien, tell me," Patrick pleaded, "are we in deep shit for harboring you?"

"I don't think so. I didn't do anything. I didn't break any laws, except maybe natural laws." Whoa. I shouldn't have said that!

"Fuck!" Marley guffawed. "This is bullshit."

Arien ignored that. He sat on the edge of the threshold, close to the fire, staring at his clenched hands.

"Come on, we need ideas," Patrick said.

"Can we post something, like how our visitor has moved on?" Cindy asked.

And Zanna said, "Maybe one of us knows somebody who could put you up?"

"Oh, this is so bozo," Arien lamented. "Thanks, Brothers n' Sisters. I'll just split town. I got places to go."

"No, no," Patrick said. "You just told us, you might get picked-up. That's not an option, Arien, unless they were breaking the door down."

Arien had to wonder about such loyalty achieved in a very short time. As yet, he'd revealed so little, and most of that was with his erotic body, as distinct from the mental or spiritual, and he was as much affected as anyone. Arien remembered traces of one of those late-night rap sessions he had during his days with the Tree Clan. Somebody stated the very common belief that everything happens for a reason. Andy, always coming off the wall, suggested things happen in your rhythm and you make the reason. Arien had to think about that then and it seemed relevant now, as though he was closer to understanding it. We are all sons of God, Andy said. For our "short stack of decades," we all take part in the ongoing creation of the Universe. To know that was one of Andy's pillars of enlightenment. The other was recognizing your oneness with all life, and everything that is. It was heady stuff for a kid.

"My grandfather," Marley thought aloud. "I'll bet, my grandfather would put him up."

The view from Craycroft Drive cascaded down and away in a sparkling blanket of lights, and blended with the curtain of night in the distant south, where it fused again into the enormous upended bowl of Heaven. The stars were fewer and less dazzling here than out Ajo Way and on into the shadow of the reservation, but it was still magnificent. Arien was impressed by the rather palatial houses in the Santa Catalina foothills, revealed though they were by modest lighting, in deference to the famous observatory to the west from where they'd come, though some were already framed or pulsed with Christmas Holiday lights.

Marley's grandfather's house was much more modest, but it had been there a very long time. It was up a gravel road off of Craycroft, backed against a fold of Ventana Canyon, a really terrific location. The house had thick adobe walls surfaced in the ubiquitous sunrise pink, Sonora stucco. The windows were deeply set and their way to the door, likewise, affected to approach the portcullis of a fort. A tile walkway, illuminated by an iron wall lamp, wound to it from the gravel drive.

Patrick parked his Samurai right there in front.

"Thanks for letting me ride shotgun," Arien told Marley, who had scrunched in the back with Buster.

"No problem."

The three of them approached the primitive ranch-style door and Marley rapped a knocker that was surrounded with a Christmas wreath. An old fellow, easily in his sixties, opened up. Arien noted the butt of a six-shooter in his belt.

"Yes? Oh! Oh, for goodness... Marley! My God, Marley, couldn't you call?" He hugged his grandson, and stood aside to let the three of them and the dog into the house, muttering that Grandma might object to the dog.

"Hello, Patrick."

"Hello Jason," Patrick greeted.

It was nice in there. The house had a large front room with worn, but inviting, iconic cowboy furniture. It had a log-beamed ceiling and timber lintels over the doorways. Colorful Native American rugs partly covered the glossy, dark-brown Spanish tiles on the floor. Thematic Southwestern artwork hung all over the walls. Arien took to a rather ornate dream catcher hanging in front of a mirror that was set off with tasteful holiday decorations.

"So why didn't you give a little jingle? We weren't expecting you, Son!" Jason's tone didn't scold, but it did imply acceptance of a sensible answer.

"Patrick didn't think it was a good idea, at least not right away," Marley told him.

A woman's voice called from the back of the house, "Who is that, Jason?"

"It's your grandson, with Patrick, and –"

"Arien," Marley introduced.

"Your grandson, with Patrick, and Arien!" he shouted.

"Who?"

"Sit down everybody," he said, motioning to the furniture. "Do you want anything to drink?"

Marley said, "I'll have a beer, Grandpa."

"Patrick? You, too? And, uh, Arien... You look too young to drink beer!" And then he said, "Who is this young fellow, Patrick? Did you pick up another Fourth Avenue runaway?" He smiled at Arien. "He's always picking people up on the road and sometimes he brings them home."

"It's like you say, Sir. He picked me up on the road."

"See!" he cried triumphantly. "You see? I know this guy!"

Patrick grinned.

"And, you needn't call me Sir. My name is Jason."

Arien nodded, then looked up to see an elderly lady with a kindly face come into the room from a hallway. She was medium-height, with gray hair woven to a single braid down her back. She wore a modest house dress, and her feet were in white sox and sandals.

"Who did you say–?" She stopped in mid-sentence and stared. It seemed a bit off, goofy, rude, even.

"Well, what's the matter with you, Cassie? Cat got your tongue?"

Marley looked surprised by his grandmother's behavior. He glanced at Patrick, who caught it and squinted at her.

"Oh my God!" she blurted, with hands framing her cheeks, and her eyes seeming to behold the asteroid that would wipe out all life on earth.

There was something about the eyes that connected with her name. And then Arien recognized her. Tears immediately began to run on his face. He stood and nearly staggered over to her, where they embraced and Arien cried, "Cassie! Cassie" with great heaving sobs, and she kept saying, "Oh my God! Oh my God! Oh, my God!"

It was obvious Patrick, Marley and Jason could hardly believe what they were seeing. Jaws were practically in laps. Marley's grandmother and Arien had sunk together to the floor. Her hands now framed the face of the boy before her and appeared to gather the wet of his tears on her fingers and kiss them with her lips. And then they embraced even tighter to rock together while the hapless onlookers stared in astonishment.

At one point, Jason said, 'What in God's name?!" but it didn't stop the mesmerizing demonstration, and all anyone could do was wait for it to pass.

It was a long time before anyone spoke. The old woman and the boy simply stared into one another's eyes as both became radiant. To Arien, it felt like the warm sun after a heavy spring shower.

He finally asked, "Is Wally his father?"

Instead of answering, Cassie pointed at the dream catcher in front of the mirror.

"Kelsey made that dream catcher with Wally," she recounted, intently staring into Arien's eyes. "I remember the day like it happened this morning. She said it would help bring you back someday. It would catch you in its web. Hawthorne dusted it with ash from our fire at Woodstock, Ellison Black Snake blew his smoke from the Tuscarora tobacco through its strands, and he had it blessed by Mother Shongo, too. And, you know, she kept it for three days! We kept that fire burning in Bethel for a few weeks after that, too, Arien. We couldn't help but hope you were just lost, or off on one of your mysterious adventures. Oh, Arien! My God! She said it would bring you back!"

"Cassie, you got so freekin' old." Arien whispered, his heart breaking. He needed to blow his nose. Cassie's husband grabbed a box of tissues off an end table to deliver it in the nick of time. Both Cassie and Arien took some.

She chuckled.

"We all do, *Dude*." She laid emphasis on that word. "Maybe you will, too, if you're lucky."

"I hope I die before I get old," Arien said, over bittersweet laughter.

Marley came over to kneel by the two of them. It had to be evident to him, to Patrick, and Jason, that Grandma not only knew Arien but knew him rather well. "Did I hear you say, Woodstock, Grandma?"

9 – How the heck did they find you

The jingle on Patrick's cell phone seemed an unwelcome intrusion. A few hours had passed since the guys' arrival at Jason and Cassie DeGrazia's. The animation, the personal radiance among the residents and visitors did not broach interruption. Patrick kept raising his eyebrows and shaking his dreads, turning a bottle of Pacifico in his hands, as if giddily at war with belief. Marley patiently waited, and intently listened like a child to a bed-time story for any scrap of history to be revealed, and his Grandpa did the same. For them all, nothing less than a life-changing rend in their fabric of reality was contemplated. Cassie and Arien sat together on the couch holding hands.

Patrick glanced at the phone before putting it to his ear. "Hello, Zanna." He listened. "Oh, wow. No kidding? Shit! That was really fast. Holy shit! Well. I'll be there as soon as I can. Maybe you and Cindy should get out. Go hide in the... No. Don't do that. We don't want it to look like we know anything at all. Just be cool. Call again. Let me know what's going on as soon as you can." He looked up at concerned faces. "She's freaked. A bunch of cars have pulled into Las Lomas. The dogs are going nuts. I could hear them over the phone!"

"What's all this? Cassie asked.

"Somehow these Army spooks found out about me," Arien said. "Andy and I got rescued from all the snow up in Bethel and they brought us here. They were trying to get me to join the Army. Can you believe that? Ha!" His smile was ironic. "We were at Davis-Monthan when I took the dog for a walk. Andy's probably still there." Arien was particularly worried about Andy now. He didn't believe they'd just let him go.

"Andy Newell?"

"Yeah."

"*The* Andy Newell?"

"Yes, *the* Andy Newell. But I never knew his last name until recently."

"Oh, will wonders never cease! I haven't seen him for..."

"So they're looking for you now? Is that why you brought him here, Marley?"

"Yeah, Grandpa."

"And, how long have they been looking for you?"

"I walked off the base the day before yesterday. Or, maybe it was the day before that." Arien said.

"Wow. How the heck did they find you so fast?" Jason was incredulous.

"Patrick's stupid bitch posted his picture on Facebook," Marley said. Patrick shot him an irritated look.

"Oh, Marley, come on, it was a simple mistake. How was she to know?"

"Yeah, cut her some slack," Arien agreed. "These guys are really, really good. I can't imagine how they found me in Bethel, to begin with. I'm still trying to figure that out."

"Why do they want you, Arien?" Cassie asked.

"You got three guesses, Babe."

"Oh my, yes," Jason concurred. "This is major. If it's true that you knew this boy over forty years ago, Cassie... He's probably more valuable to the government than all the UFOs at Roswell."

"It's true," she flatly affirmed.

"Oh, Jesus," Arien said. "Have you seen Tina since...?"

Cassie smoothed-out the lap of her house dress. "Jason and I went on a vacation up to the Pacific Northwest about ten years ago and I looked her up. And, I met –" her expression grew both kindly and serious, "— you had a daughter with her, you know."

"Yes. I know."

"Well, we met Arienne, her husband, Brett, and her young son, uh, Danner, I think it is."

"No kidding!" Jason bellowed. "Do you mean to say this *old friend* of yours, we visited in Portland, knew this boy, too?"

"Yes, Dear."

"Danner," Arien repeated to himself.

"Well, I didn't know... Why didn't you tell me? How could you keep such a big secret from me?" Jason was practically indignant.

"What was there to tell, Jason? Who knew he would actually ever come back?"

"Oh. Of course. I'm sorry."

"Don't be," she giggled. "It's beyond all that."

Everybody chuckled at this.

"Say, guys," Patrick interjected, "I don't want to flood our parade, but if those spooks are as good as they've already been, they'll be here next."

Arien felt a lump in his throat. It was like a nightmare where you can't run fast enough, and the monster is getting closer with each leaden step. *I am the cause of all this!* His mind raced to take charge of the situation. He was growing more worried for his new friends as well as for himself.

"Yeah, your stupid bitch just called here," Marley threw that at Patrick while a middle finger scratched his temple.

"Marley!" Grandma scolded. "Your mouth has gone rogue."

Arien laughed nervously.

"Even if she didn't, it seems they'll check-out everybody you know. They can tap your Facebook, right?"

"You're probably right, Arien," Patrick agreed, with a thin smile at Marley, and a suggestive lick of his tongue to the tip of his own middle finger.

"Some *free country*," Marley sneered."

"Free to choose between VISA and Master Card," Jason said. "So, we've got to get you out of here – now."

"Can we get him to Portland?" Cassie wondered.

How perfect! Arien liked that idea a lot. It was on his agenda, after all. But before he could say anything he felt the hairs tingle on the back of his neck. "I smell hunters. They're on their way," he abruptly announced.

The decision regarding who would "get him out of Dodge," as Jason framed it, fell heavily on Arien, as he knew success or failure, whatever that turned out to be, could be determined by the person or persons he was with. There were so many variables to consider. Patrick's car got excellent gas mileage, but might well be marked by law enforcement. Likewise, both Patrick and Marley, through their association with Zanna, could be sought for questioning. Cassie offered to go as a non-descript old lady, but again, another association, easily cross-checked, might put her picture out on the highway as well. The nature of the trip and the likely need for youthful flexibility argued against it, too. Another consideration would be getting hold of enough cash since using a credit card was out-of-the-question, as was even using a phone. This would not be an easy thing at all.

Meanwhile, Arien's view of the time-piece ticking on the DeGrazia's wall was a minute hand that would glow red if it moved any faster.

"Okay," Patrick announced. "I'm taking him to River's."

"Hmmm," Marley considered. "That might work."

"Where's that, Son?"

"River's near the U, in a house down on Second Street," Grandma.

"And what does that accomplish?" the old fellow asked.

"River *is* Rainbow Central, Jason," Patrick explained. "He's been doing the invocations at the Cochise Stronghold equinox gatherings for a few years now. I'd trust him with my life," he added, looking at Arien.

"If you need a ride all the way to Portland you'll have to have money," Jason said. "I don't have that kind of cash. I'll have to get to an ATM in the morning. That could be tricky. I could be followed..."

"Oh fuck. I'm so sorry. I have to go *now*," Arien declared.

Now the clock could have stopped. There was no way to tell who thought of it, first, but both Arien and Cassie stretched-out to take the nearest hand, and together they made a circle in that room.

"Oh, Arien, Arien. This is too quick. It's way too quick! I can't believe we have to let you go, already!" Cassie held herself erect, bravely facing him. She obviously couldn't stop her tears but never lost her poise.

Arien said, "In the words of our Brother, Andy, Om shri Ram jai Ram, jai jai Ram." When he repeated that the others joined in, and by the third recitation it had blended to one voice.

He rushed to embrace Cassie, kissed her on the forehead, and turned away blinking. He was barely able to see for all the water in his eyes.

"Jason, I'm sorry if I brought you any trouble."

The old fellow shook his hand vigorously.

"If they shoot us, I think it would still have been worth it."

Before going out the door, Arien went over to the mirror and laid both his hands on the dream catcher. "Thanks, Kelsey," he told it.

"Tell Wally I said hello."

"He probably doesn't remember you, Arien," Cassie ruefully said.

Buster made the rounds, too, seeming to know what was happening in his doggie way. The whole time they were there he'd been rather unobtrusive, lying on the floor, only occasionally visiting with someone, but it was noted that his most fervent connection was with Cassie, and he had never seen her before. Arien had to call him to follow.

When they were in the car Jason hurried out as Arien rolled the window down.

"Here! It's not much, Son, but every little bit helps." He passed Arien a small roll of bills.

"Thank you, Sir." He stuffed it into his pocket.

"And the name's Jason, not Sir."

"Oh, Right."

"Buckle up," Patrick ordered as they slowly moved away.

Patrick shot straight across Sunrise onto Kolb road. As the light changed behind him, Arien caught him squinting at the rear-view mirror.

"There's headlights turning into your Grandpa's drive, Marley," Arien said.

"Shit! You're right, Arien," Marley agreed, peering through the plastic window at the rear.

"Fuckin' close!" Patrick marveled.

"They went the wrong way, first," Arien said. "Ha!" He laughed. "That bought us our last minute."

"Oh shit!" Patrick exclaimed.

"What?" Marley asked.

"You got your cell phone?"

"No, I left it home."

"Well, I didn't!" Patrick fumbled with his phone and passed it over. "Turn it off, Arien."

Arien held it but drew a blank in the darkness. "I don't know how," he said.

"Marley reached from behind. "Give it here, Arien. I can't believe you don't know how to turn off a cell phone."

"Marley, my good brother, I think you're forgetting something," Patrick said.

"What's that?" Marley asked, over an electronic beep from the back.

"This dude was with your Grandma at Woodstock! They didn't have cell phones in 1969!"

Arien chuckled.

"And they were as big as a quart of milk in 1990," he recalled.

River's house on Second Street was up about a half-block from the park. River was a clean-shaven, tall, thin man, about thirty. His long, dark hair was parted in the middle and pulled-back in a pony tail. He was barefoot, and requested his visitors remove their shoes. Inside was Wendy, River's wife, who was about her husband's age, and a daughter, introduced as Free. Wendy was a good-looking woman with dark hair braided about her head in an old-time style. Free looked to be about nine or ten. She had lovely, sparkly, big brown eyes. Set up on a small table was this crazy, dried-out tumbleweed that was being decorated with origami, paper chains, and crystals shimmering with the vibrant colors of a strand of twinkling LED lights. Arien admired the effect. It was pretty.

"Don't ask me why we're bothering," River snickered, as he waved at their tumbleweed Christmas tree. "It all ends before Christmas Day, right?"

Patrick and Marley nodded and chuckled.

"Stop it, Daddy," Free protested. "Mommy says the world isn't going to end!"

"That's right, Honey," Wendy agreed. "Your Daddy had *better* stop it or something he *likes* will end." She winked at their visitors. "I don't know you," she added.

"Arien." He reached to shake her hand, but she welcomed him with a hug, instead.

"Hi, Arien!" Free greeted. She obviously saw something worthy of approval, revealing a bright, beautiful smile. She liked Buster right away, too, petting him on the head when he came over to greet her before acknowledging anyone else.

"I'm River," thir host said, offering his hand to Arien. He seemed pleased with his daughter's reaction. "So what brings you guys here at this hour?"

Arien realized it was pretty late, which had him wondering how the kid was doing.

"We got a serious favor to ask you," Patrick opened. Free returned to hanging a paper bird on the expansive bush, but as River and Wendy went all ears he continued, though first looking to Arien and Marley for support. Their gesture was to stand a little closer together.

"Arien here is wanted by the military. He needs to go underground, fast. Ideally he needs to get out-a town."

"Hum, okay," River considered with raised eyebrows. "What can we do?"

"Well, River," Marley threw in, "they're at my grandfather's house right now. They were right behind us!"

"And they hit Las Lomas a couple of hours before that," Patrick added.

"Wait a minute, wait a minute. So, you brought this guy here?" River shrugged incredulously at Wendy who rolled her eyes.

"We fucked-up," Patrick went on. "Zanna posted Arien's picture on Facebook, not realizing what a hot item he is. Then, we dashed off to Marley's grandparent's house. I never turned my phone off and Zanna called me there when they showed-up at our place. They must have been scanning us or something with all that high-tech shit."

"What did you do, Arien? What do they want you for?"

"It's – it's classified," Marley blurted out.

"What?" River clapped his hands as he laughed. "You guys got into some kind-a mushroom!"

But then Patrick said, "River, he's an eco-raider, like Earth First. Nah, beyond Earth First! He makes them look wimpy. He's true, River. He's legit. They got him on a terrorist list. They want to throw him in a hole forever for fighting for our planet!"

His appeal must have found the button because River said, "Wow," and grew serious. "Why didn't you say that to begin with?"

"Mommy, what's Earth First?"

"They're like soldiers, Honey, fighting the corporate bullies, and they have to be very brave to do that, anymore."

"And it's long-past time you were in bed, Free," River informed her. "Just because there's no school tomorrow, it's no reason for you to be up all night."

"Ohhhhh, but the tree, Daddy."

"The tree's just about done, Sweets. Let's do bed now. We can finish it in the morning, okay?"

"I'll get her in," Wendy told River. "You guys figure it out."

But before Free left the room, she came up to Arien and opened her arms wide for his hug.

"Thanks," she said, "for helping save our planet!"

"You're very welcome, Free," Arien responded, locking with her eyes, and he planted a kiss on her forehead.

After Mom and Daughter were gone, River offered the visitors a cup of herbal tea, and they moved to the kitchen table.

"I'm real curious," River said, pouring the brew through a bamboo sieve into cups, "What did you do, Arien?"

Arien had already been given an answer to that question. "The less you know the better," he cautioned, with a glimmer of smile to Patrick.

River chuckled. "So, ah, let's see if I have this right, you need asylum in the Rainbow Nation?"

"That's about it, and uh, transportation, if at all possible," Arien posed.

"Can you help with gas?"

Arien pulled-out the money in his pocket. The roll of bills he got from Jason amounted to three-hundred and twenty-five dollars, making three-hundred, seventy-one dollars with Andy's contribution. "That's it," he said.

"I'm thinking we can take up a collection in the community," Patrick proposed, "but after tonight we'll probably be followed. We'll need to come up with a way to communicate privately."

River sighed. "That's a regular art-form these days," he said.

"Wait," Arien said, "three-hundred and seventy-one won't do it?"

"That would buy gas for a bicycle to Salt Lake City if you peddled it there, yourself," River cracked.

"Holy shit!" Arien exclaimed.

"He's exaggerating, Arien, but not that much," Patrick responded.

"Yeah, Arien, money don't buy much these days," Marley added, "unless it's stuff. Stuff is dirt cheap."

The lad contemplated that. It was hard to make sense of it, but delving deeper into the subject might seem out of place. River appeared bemused, already. Then River asked what Arien had with him, to go ahead and bring it in the house.

"I don't have anything," Arien answered. "Just the clothes I'm wearing."

"I've known a lot of people in the underground..." River began, but he didn't finish the thought.

Marley picked it up. "Arien's a fucking fugitive," he said with a clubby grin.

River said, "Well, you won't need a lot to get by. I can fix you up with a change of clothes, a washcloth, we can get you a toothbrush, and there's a spare sleeping bag around here someplace. You should have your own portable bed if you're crashing with people."

"We're mighty grateful, River," Patrick told him. "I knew you were the man."

"De nada." River went off into the house and returned with a fairly nice day pack. "That's a good place to start. Everything except your sleeping bag can go in it."

"Rad, Dude! I owe you big," Arien said.

"No, you don't owe me anything. Just pass it forward, Brother." River resumed his place at the table to take a few sips of his tea. "So, where do you need to go?"

"Portland."

"Ah, Arien," Marley asked, "Grandma said she saw that lady you'd mentioned, what, 10 years ago?"

"Tina?" Arien guessed where this was going but was already making up his mind about it.

"Yeah, I think that's who you said. Well, um, do you think it's a good idea to go there? Wouldn't they be watched?"

"He has a good point," Patrick agreed.

Arien said, "You know, they might give Portland a shot because they know I came from there and may have connections, but unless somebody barfs-up everything, Griffin likely doesn't know where the folks I'd be looking for are," *Any more than I do*, he thought.

"Griffin?"

"Colonel Griffin."

"Oh." Patrick said, exchanging glances with Marley and River. The elements of mystery, risk, excitement and curiosity were so thick at this point Arien thought, with a little concentration, it would be visible to the naked eye. Strange to discover, a side of him was beginning to get a kick out of it. What good was fearing it, anyhow? That could cripple him. Yes, Griffin may have had awesome resources at his disposal, but Arien had something there was no reason what-so-ever to reject perfect faith in – his sense of rhythm. It was magical thinking, wasn't it? He knew it had to be outside the proverbial box, because Griffin already owned the box and the game on his terms would certainly be lost. Wow: He'd fallen right into Kelsey's beautifully-crafted net! To think of it sent a tingle up his spine. How totally, mega-radical was that?

"Wow. I kind-a hate to leave you now, Bro," Patrick said, obviously speaking for the three of them when it was time to go. They'd drained their tea, River was yawning, and by now Arien fully-felt the effects of an amazing day. He needed to crash and picked-up on River's suggestion with a wide yawn of his own.

"I'll second that emotion," Marley concurred. He'd unselfconsciously stared at Arien for the longest time, while tugging on a tendril of dreaded hair with a twirling finger. "I s'pose I'll have Cindy all to myself again," he added, with a languid, double-eyed wink.

"Dude, that was awesome," Arien admitted.

Patrick took a deep breath. "I'm not going there," he chided.

Arien said, "Marley, if there's any way you can get Tina's address or phone number from Cassie – um, your grandmother, I'd be obliged."

"I'll see what I can do, Arien."

"Well, I'm thinking we'll get him out of here, quick," River said. "I can drive you to Phoenix, Arien, where Eddie Jay can take over, and maybe Eddie can get you to Flagstaff, where my good Brothers, Connor, and Joey

Montana can trip you to Vegas, and so on, with brothers and sisters they know. So, Patrick, don't worry about getting back here. I don't think you'll need to do that and risk bringing the heat down." River considered further. On the table was a little note pad and a pencil stub. He tore a leaf out and jotted down a number, handing it to Marley. "Memorize that number," he instructed. "It's Joey's. Tell your grandma to call him with whatever she has on that lady for Arien. That should work, huh?"

"Oh, yeah," Arien applauded. "Cool plan, Dude."

"And don't worry about money. You probably have enough to help out where needed. The Family's got your back, Bro."

Patrick and Marley concurred, though both expressed regret at maybe not seeing Arien again after tonight. "And that probably speaks for Cindy and Zanna, too," Patrick added.

It was a sad parting. Arien had only known these guys a couple of days, but they were a couple of days none of them were ever likely to forget.

They hugged on the steps of River's house. "Shit! There's sooooo much I wanted to ask you about," Marley pined.

"I'll second that emotion," Patrick echoed. "Godspeed," he wished, looking into Arien's eyes. "And safe travels, Bro."

And Arien said, "Blessings Be! You've done so much. I sure hope we see each other again!"

River, standing in the doorway said, "Maybe we'll all meet at the Gathering next year – That's if the world doesn't end before Christmas Day!" He chuckled to himself.

"Goodbye, Buster," Marley said to Arien's dog-friend. Buster moved his tail with that as he stood smartly to Arien's side.

Arien sat in River and Wendy's living room in a straight-backed chair right next to the Christmas tumbleweed. River unplugged it shortly before going to bed, so its inherent cheer and the lovely colored shadows it put on the wall were all gone. The room was quietly steeped in a dim red twilight from the charging beacon of a mobile phone and a feebly shining nightlight in the adjacent family office where Arien's sleeping bag was rolled-out on the floor. Buster was in there, whistling from somewhere in the prehistoric canine subconscious.

Arien tried sleeping. It hadn't been uncomfortable. The thin, back-packing air mattress felt pretty good under him, too, but the turning wheels in his head barred the gate of dreams. When he retrieved a string of conversation he'd had with River a little earlier, it led back out to this chair.

At the moment his heart was a fulcrum where the balance between so much loss and considerable, though mysterious promise rested. The hints from the world around him were making inroads. It was at least enough to have moved him from despair to melancholy, and he recognized that. Intellectually, he could talk with it, but not move it just because he might want to. It could only move with his body, and the body had to allow it. Simply knowing was too weak by itself to push that big a thing.

It was so weird. His eyelids were heavy with tearing, not enough to run over but it kept his sinuses all stuffed where he had to breathe with his mouth open. Some of this wellspring was rooted in awe and joy, while other sources brought memories that battled and blended before flooding his eyes. Along with this was the excitement, the sheer adrenaline rush coming from being one step ahead of the chase. What a trip! The whip was a-crackin'. He wondered how it would end.

And that led to the next thing banging around in his head. "River," he'd called, as his host aimed for the back of the house. "What's this about the end of the world?"

"December 21st is the last day of the ancient Mayan calendar, Bro. It's the end of a cycle that's taken five-thousand, one-hundred twenty-five years. It's funny, I've been focused on that for ever, so it still has some pull over me, but now that I have a kid and all..."

"So, what's the big deal?"

"Well, the predictions call for earth changes, all kinds of shit. I don't know. Maybe it's really about transformation. That's more positive, anyway. But, you have to admit things are pretty fucked-up." Strange coincidence, but the lights flickered when River said that. Then the house went all dark and quiet, and it was ten or fifteen minutes before they came on again. River chuckled, said goodnight, and felt his way on. Arien could make out the refrigerator motor starting up, and other buzzes and noises come through the house when the power was restored.

...Things happen in your rhythm and you make the reason. Well, why can't December 21st go with that? I'll tell River in the morning...

10 – Their secret was locked away

"Arien, come quick!" It was Wendy from the back of the house. He barely got out of the bathroom and dashed down the hall in time to see his picture, the very picture Zanna posted on Facebook fade from a TV morning news segment in time for a commercial. It was a small flat-screen monitor on the dresser in River and Wendy's bedroom. Again, Arien was fascinated by the clarity of the thing. His picture looked just like it did on Zanna's I-pad, only bigger.

"Holy fuck! What did they say?" he breathlessly asked.

"You're an Amber Alert, Bro," River said. He sat cross-legged in skivvies and a rumpled T-shirt on the unmade bed, nursing a cup of coffee with his back against the board. "They said you're a sixteen year-old whose gone missing and foul-play may have been involved; that you're a possible abductee, since a ransom note was found!"

"Oh, no! That's so bogus!" Arien cried.

"Well, that's better than saying you're a terrorist," Wendy said. She'd been standing there topless, and only now began to put on the garment she was holding.

Arien got a look at her as the dress went over her head. Nice. But the news item was wider than the view. "Did they say anything else?"

"Arien Grove," River repeated flatly. "They said if you're seen, to report it to the police immediately. It's possible you may be in fear for your life or your parent's lives." He took a sip of his coffee. "Your parents are worried sick about you."

"My parents! My parents are dead!"

Arien watched River level his gaze with a subtle tilt to the head, and it came to him how very clever this was. He would have to prove himself constantly. People would be inclined to believe he was a pathological runaway, and even more underage that he actually was! Wow!

"It's not true, River! It's all a lie. Think of it. As a terrorist I'll have friends."

"I think I believe you, Arien," River thoughtfully said, "because Patrick and Marley sure do, but a weak link might snap your chain to the Great Northwest."

Arien sat on a corner of the bed. "Yeah," he agreed.

"Would you like a cup of coffee, Arien?"

"Yeah, Wendy. Thanks."

River wasn't much help beyond his initial plan. Could Arien disguise himself, cut his hair? Wendy had a plausible suggestion – he could dress as a girl.

"No," Arien said. "Nice try." The idea wasn't so bad, actually. It was the thought of maybe getting caught like that.

"How about dying it?" Wendy pressed.

Arien's eyes fell on the pull-over River was wearing. "I'll go with a hoodie," he said.

It took about four hours to get up to the north end of Phoenix in River and Wendy's 2002 Toyota SUV. That included an exit for the Casa Grande National Monument and a gas stop that seemed to Arien like a shakedown.

The Casa Grande visitor center was closed when their car pulled into the parking lot, a few miles east of I-10. Arien had an impulse to see it that was strong enough to parlay a measure of the goodwill he travelled with. River didn't want to stop, worrying someone recognizing Arien might bring his family to an unnecessary situation. Arien practically had to plead and the impasse was broken when Wendy said she needed a pit stop. Everyone got out anyway, and Arien walked up to a middle-aged Indian in Cargills who was collecting trash near the imposing structure's melting adobe walls to ask why it was closed in the middle of the day.

"It's only open on weekends now," the man said.

"Can I walk around and have a look?"

The pre-Columbian ruin was covered over with a towering, rectangular roof, supported on four, splayed steel poles to protect it from weather. Arien didn't wait for an answer but walked towards it while the man quietly returned to his task.

It was fairly warm, in surprising contrast with the chilly morning they'd left behind in Tucson. Arien removed the fatigue jacket he wore over his hoodie, and would have taken that off, too, but didn't want to risk a row with River, who appeared to be easing off the ants and getting into the stop. River walked hand-in-hand with his daughter while Mom went out of sight behind the center where the restrooms were and Arien continued until he saw Buster freeze, looking intently at something around the corner.

"What is it, Boy?"

Buster displayed no sign that anything was amiss, but neither did he move, except to acknowledge Arien's question with the subtlest flick of his tail. Arien became both alert and quiet. He crept forward to peer around the corner and was surprised, and even a little frightened, to see her for the second time! There, on the structure's other side, sitting calmly in the sunshine against the adobe wall was the mysterious young woman he saw on the reservation by the petroglyphs! As before, the bright red blanket was drawn snugly about her. Again, Arien couldn't see her face, or any part of her anatomy but for a shimmer of her raven hair and a bit of woven grass sandal under the hem of the blanket.

Transfixed, Arien moved forward just enough to sit down on the ground by the dog to simply be there with her. After a while, Free came around the corner calling and talking to Arien, then stopping in the middle of her sentence on seeing the woman. She, too, sat by Arien and Buster.

"Who is the lady?" Free whispered.

"I don't know her name," Arien answered.

"She's pretty!"

"Yes, Free. She is."

Arien saw the posted prices at the Union 76 off the Santan Freeway exit to Chandler, and wondered aloud how people could afford to go anywhere and River told him they couldn't, "though it would help if they could find jobs." There were still more cars on the road than Arien expected to see, though some probes into the conversation suggested his country had fallen on hard times. He hadn't noticed it before in what little he'd seen of the world since waking up in a bed at Andy's snow-bound house in Bethel. He was further impressed by the number of boarded-up businesses and vacant malls in Phoenix. River informed him the epic dust storms of the last few summers had clobbered the city with enough frequency, and problems with drinking water were beginning to drive the more agile inhabitants away.

"I never liked it up here, anyway," he groused. "This many people shouldn't live in the desert."

That made perfect sense. In retrospect, another thing did, too. When they'd left the native ruins of Casa Grande in the rear-view mirror, Wendy asked, "What was the name of the tribe of those people?"

River said. "They don't know. They call them the Hohokam, the Lost Ones, or something like that."

"Tohono," Arien said.

"No, Arien, the Hohokam. The Tohono are out there where you were with Patrick and Marley."

"The Tohono. They are the Lost Ones. Trust me." He knew that. He didn't know how. It was a gut-feeling. Maybe the woman in the red blanket held a sign he could read.

Back there, when the energy was flowing away, Wendy drifted over almost absently to retrieve her daughter, but stopped because something had gotten into her eye. Arien was pulled out of his meditation to look at her, and Free was saying, "Look Mom," pointing at the pretty lady, but she was already gone. It obviously impressed the child as much as Arien, all the more for it being the second time. Their eyes met, child and lad, and without speaking, their secret was locked away in each-other's hearts.

"What, Free?" Wendy asked.

Free looked up at Arien and smiled with a sweet sparkle she bore, "Oh, I forgot, Mom. It's nothing."

Arien watched the signs as they went this way and that, but it all began to blur after they exited the Pima Highway in Tempe. They drove for awhile, making several more turns. He knew there was no way he could have found his way through this maze of look-alike neighborhoods again, when River pulled past the driveway of a rather beaten-looking stucco-walled ranch house. It had a gravel yard and a sorry nest of barrel cactus that had scraps of paper stuck in its thorns. Three cars packed the driveway. One of them was up on blocks with its wheels off. The windows had drawn curtains, except for a prominent bay window that was covered on the inside with the silver reflection of a space blanket.

"We're here," River announced. "Eddie said he'd be home, but I'll go check. Wait here."

"Sorry we didn't get to know you better," Wendy told Arien as they sat in the car.

"Me, too," Free agreed.

"Yeah." Arien smiled, but he was already feeling for vibes. No hunters. It was strange, though. The trip from Tucson was disorienting. He'd fallen in with these people and turned himself over to them. The dog was his only constant though it gave him something to worry about. Buster might make things harder. He couldn't be sure. Anyhow, the thought of leaving him with somebody was met with a visceral resistance that surprised him. He was sure walking with Buster helped him get off the base back there. Scratch one for Buster. And then there was the simple fact that he loved the critter. Scratch one apiece.

But now he confronted reality in the rhythm of things, with River coming to the car after being in the house for only a few minutes. He sat back in the driver's seat and let out a long, slow exhale.

"What?"

"I'm standing in the living room talking to Eddie and the TV's on and there's that picture of you, and another one of you with the dog on the front steps of your house in Tucson. It's a big house in the foothills, too. And these scared, anxious folks are pleading with your kidnappers not to harm you, and to let you go and let you come home." River said this looking all the while through the windshield, not making eye contact. "Jesus. What am I supposed to tell Eddie?"

Arien swallowed. "Do you believe that, River?"

"I don't know what to believe."

"Oh, fuck! I am so fucked." Arien covered his brow with a hand. "River, it's not what it seems. Get me to that guy, Joey, Joey..."

"Montana. Joey Montana."

"Yeah. Maybe you'll believe me if Cassie called him."

"Oh, God!" River exclaimed. "I've got my family in this car! Why did I bring them along?"

Wendy didn't answer that.

Free assumed a highly-focused look, like a kid studying a wild animal, or fascinated by a war of ants. One hand was over the back seat where Buster's snout rested. She scratched his ear.

Arien was very confused. How was it possible to put him in a picture with the dog in front of a house in Tucson? Who were these *parents*? He thought back. Sure, he remembered that captain who was on the plane took a picture of Buster, but did he take a picture of them together? It didn't make any sense.

"Leave us here, Daddy," Free abruptly said. "Then you can take him to Joey's. We've been there before. It's not far."

River let out a weak laugh, like only half a haw. "You don't remember, Honey. It's a long way. It's further than we've already come. I'd have to come back tomorrow." It was like River was thinking out loud. "Besides, this is no place for you to stay."

"Take me to the freeway, Dude. I'll hitch," Arien said.

"You don't know where you're going, Arien," River answered.

"Give me his address. I'll find it."

Wendy's face looked pained.

"No Daddy, they'll catch him!"

"Everybody doesn't watch the news, right? I'll get lucky."

"Oh, Arien, you don't know. Eddie Jay doesn't watch the news. It's all propaganda. Nobody watches that shit. They must have your face plastered all over the menu, though. It's like a big deal, Bro, an Amber Alert. You're fucked, just like you said."

This is crazy Arien thought, struggling, but the impulse was strong to cast his die on a very long shot. With a racing heart, sufficiently frightened, and his mouth going dry he ordered, "Dude, drop me off at the nearest on ramp now, or I swear, I'll get out right here and start walking."

"Well, I don't want that on me," River said, turning the key. He made a K-turn in the street as the door to the house opened.

"River! Where you going, Bro? Aren't you coming in?" a shirtless guy in the doorway yelled, as the Toyota rolled away.

Wow. The freeway entrance seemed so destitute. It was getting near dark-thirty with a chill, damp wind blustering around his buttoned fatigue jacket, and a grizzled man in an overcoat who had been standing there with a cardboard sign appeared to be leaving. Arien was sure he did the right thing when, seeing River begin to fight with himself, considering heading on to Flag, Arien took his hand in both of his and sincerely thanked him. "No," he'd insisted. "Drop us right here and go home." The child actually cried and that was cool. The love of a child is a blessing, indeed. Arien couldn't remember where he'd heard that. It didn't matter. Maybe he'd made it up. He could see that Wendy was relieved. That was empowering. There was no need to venture into entitlement because results gained that way were not trustworthy, right? This was a brief but wrenching struggle, until he'd decided. Had going with his gut ever let him down?

His hoodie was up, but he showed enough face so drivers could see he had one.

A low growl from Buster announced the man who was here before hadn't really gone.

"Where ya headed, Kid?" The guy scratched his salt and pepper-whiskered chin and fumbled with the sign as a gust of wind threatened to carry it away.

Arien held Buster's leash in one hand and the sleeping bag in the other. He felt safer with the dog. The man's vacant stare was unsettling.

"North."

"Well, Hell, I can see that. This way's north. Where, north?" He eyed the dog.

"Flagstaff would be a good start," Arien said, walking away. The first car turned onto the ramp and went by.

The man followed.

"Why not spend the night? I got a warm place we could be."

Arien kept walking. He said, "No thanks."

"Aw, c'mon, Kid. It's gettin' dark. No one's stopping. Let's go." He began to reach out when Buster's growl bid him do otherwise.

"Call that dog off or I'll fuckin' crush his skull," the man cursed. His eyes grew wild. He reached under his coat, pulling out a tire iron.

That was so quick. Arien was about to say Back off, Asshole, but switched gears at the last minute. "Om shri Ram, jai Ram, jai jai Ram," he warily chanted, with all he could muster, seeing Buster threatened. The man settled down, listening, blinking at him, and holding the tire iron ready. Arien backed away, facing him, like the guy was a cougar ready to pounce.

"Buster," Arien quietly ordered, "let's go." He had to jerk the leash. "Put it away, Dude. Go home. I got miles ahead."

The man now assumed a faraway, almost yearning look. He stuck the iron back into his coat and turned away but didn't otherwise move.

The dude's a nut cake. Arien and Buster went about halfway up the ramp and sat on the guardrail. Then the guy with the sign began to inch backwards, drawing closer! Another car got on the ramp and slowed down as Arien raised his thumb, but the man turned, moved still closer, and the car drove off.

Arien's heartbeat picked up. Buster growled again, with the hair stiffening on the back of his neck. Arien got it. The guy was a vamp! He drew energy and liked it, but he gave nothing back. He wanted more, not like a thirsty soul but rather like a thief. It was pretty creepy.

"Please go home," Arien said.

"No one will stop for us, will they? Hehe..." the fellow taunted, coming still closer, to sit on the guardrail about seven feet away. When another car came by he held up his sign. The car continued onto the highway with a cool rush of wind, its headlights throwing a glare. When Buster rumbled louder Arien could see a hand go under the coat.

Arien cursed under his breath. The impasse begged for speedy resolution for a number of reasons. He expected walking on the freeway asked for a ride to Colonel Griffin, and the next on ramp might be a very long way off. This guy was a serious obstacle! What should I do?

The man moved closer. Buster barked at him. "Come on, Doggie, come to Papa," the fellow whispered, pulling the iron out again and tapping it menacingly on the rail as he sat, inching yet closer.

Arien stood, wiggled out of his day pack, held the sleeping bag by the string of its stuff sack and let go of the leash, holding his arms out wide. The man rose to face him with a fearsome grin, but began backing up. Arien and Buster sprang at the same time. As the iron swung to the dog's flank the sleeping bag came between, still throwing Buster down with the force of the blunted swing. The man stumbled as Buster rolled with the bag, allowing Arien's fist to find that leering face just as Buster recovered, to spring at the arm holding the tire iron with a fearsome set of teeth. It was very quick. Arien was on him with a fury, punching and kicking at him, blending their pain and anger with grunting and cursing. At one point a well-placed leg nearly threw Arien down but he grabbed an ear with one hand while pushing with the flat of the other on the man's forehead, and the motion of his whole body behind it, to fling the guy's head back, BAM, against the guardrail, once, twice, BAM, again and again – until he slipped, limply down, to lay quiet in a very long moment where time seemed to slow, and then stop.

Arien hunkered over him, huffing, and in a sudden rush of adrenaline and pristine clarity, he raised the limp body up over the guardrail to roll it over the other side, where it slid down an embankment into the shadow of twilight. A breeze caught the cardboard sign and it whirled and skittered away in a flash.

"Oh, Buster," Arien gasped, hunkering on his knees, feeling suddenly dizzy. "Did we kill him?"

Buster already sat on his haunches, but stretched forward to get a lick at Arien's face.

Arien's breath came in short gasps. He felt clammy and caught a whiff of himself. His wrist reported a sharp, hot twang along the forearm's sinews, up to the elbow. Wow. Arien hadn't been in a rumble since he lived on the streets in Portland. He was pretty young then, but he'd been fearless, with so much pent-up anger and resentment that word got around not to mess with him.

He didn't like it though. It shattered his peace, especially now. It pained him that love had failed and that he'd put himself and his furry companion in this situation. "God, I might have killed him!" he cried, "And, he might have killed you!" The very thought was perfectly awful.

Buster's low whine and expressive whip of tongue around the lips indicated disagreement with this line of thought. Arien got that as sure as if the critter could speak, but he stared back blankly. "Come on, Buster," he said, rallying as the headlights from another car briefly revealed a smatter of blood, flesh and hair on the guardrail. But by the time Arien had reassumed his baggage and could raise his thumb, the next car, a shiny 1970's Pontiac, stopped and scooped them up. It was like a dream. Arien mechanically opened the wide back door to let Buster in, and then he got in up front with the driver.

"Hola," the driver said, with a thick accent. "My name is Ruiz." He reached out a hand and had a gander at his passenger as they passed under a streetlamp. Ruiz was heavy-set. He looked to be in his thirties. He wore an open sweatshirt with a zippered front. His hand felt rough and leathery. Arien's wrist fired a salvo of pain.

"Arien," he answered through gritting teeth.

"And the perro?"

"Huh?"

"The dog," he corrected.

"Oh, that's Buster." The lad worked to calm himself. It didn't help that the man stole another look at him, but it felt really, really good to be moving away from that on ramp.

"I stop for el perro, not for you." Ruiz didn't wink but he may as well have. "Are you okay, Amigo?"

"Oh, uh, yeah, I'm fine."

"Well, you bloody on the face. You were in a fight, maybe, huh?"

Arien touched his face. Yeah, it was damp. Yeah, it was blood. His initial reaction was to deny a fight, and for a very good reason, but his intuition suggested otherwise. "Yes. Yes, we were attacked by a bum back there. He wanted to kill my dog." He tried massaging the throbbing wrist. The pain was beginning to immobilize his hand.

"Oh, muy malo, señor joven. No bueno," he said. "No good."

"Exactly. The guy was, uh, is a crazy fuck."

Ruiz chuckled. "Did he keel you, or you keel him?" he asked seriously.

"Maybe," Arien said flatly.

"Oh!" Ruiz banged merrily on the wheel. His burst of laughter was infectious and Arien began to chuckle at first, and then laughed along. It felt really good to do that, but it didn't last. Hey, I'm just a kid, he told himself. This is funny! But it was laughter in a hollow chamber. His bell was clapped back there on the freeway entrance, and still rang.

"Where are you going, Arien?" Ruiz asked, chuckling. He pronounced it more like, "Arieen."

"I'm supposed to meet a friend in Flagstaff."

"Oh, muy interesante," Ruiz said. "Sedona. That get you close by. Sedona es muy bonita, mi amigo. You been?"

He guessed at the meaning. "No, never been."

Arien's hair was getting long enough to tie back in a pony tail, so he did, with a meaty rubber band he found on the trail. At least it might make him look a little different from the picture on television. The bangs in front didn't quite reach the back and blew out a little over his ears, so he parted it in the middle as best he could without a comb or a mirror. Along similar lines, Buster wore a T-shirt, though the temperature was only in the forties. He stood on a knoll in a fantastic location. This place was amazing! It had to be the most magnificent scenery ever, for its variety, contrast, and stunning colors that could touch his core even through a drab winter day with a washed-out sky.

He was sad again, not sure if it was coming from inside or mingled with the space, invested as it was in Creation's highest artistry. He missed Tina. He imagined holding her hand here by the twisted ironwood, and tall, gray stamens of oversize grasses, and the scrubby, blue-gray juniper, and blood-hued, rock outcrops sculpted by the ages, recapitulating their wild, iconic theme over and beyond again, to the distant mesas.

At his feet in the clearing was a wide circle of gray-white rocks that contrasted with the red-umber slab of geologic crust they rested on. They were obviously carried here by people and maintained, for the ring was perfect, devoid of debris, and the rocks were evenly spaced to a radius of about twelve feet, and the circle was bisected by two intersecting lines, laying out the four directions.

He imagined Andy here, too, the young Andy, dark, handsome, in that sometimes intense, bitter-sweet mood of his, and they would be getting stoned and delving deeply into some profound metaphysical question. Getting stoned, boy, that would be nice! Wasn't this a form of entitlement – feeling sorry for yourself?

"Okay, Buster, I know you must be ready," he said. The dog was staring. Arien pulled a can of dog food out of his day pack and slowly, carefully opened it, along with jabs of wrist-pain, using the flimsy tool he'd bought at a gas station-food mart Ruiz stopped at the night before. Not long after that, they'd arrived at Ruiz's Boynton Canyon turn-off. Ruiz didn't invite Arien to come along, though Arien could tell he'd felt guilty depositing his passenger on the highway in the dark. The guy was likely dealing with other issues. It felt right, though. Arien thanked him, and tracked off into a wash down from the road, guided by the dog, until they came to a place to roll out his bag. The thought he'd awakened in Heaven got him up. After that, Arien followed an overriding impulse to explore this incredibly beautiful place until coming upon this stone circle in the mid-afternoon.

He dug out a small bottled-water and a ham sandwich. It was wrapped in bar-coded cellophane. He wished he'd thought to grab a few packages of mustard and mayonnaise. "Let's see," he said between bland bites, slowly walking around the stone circumference. "Where are we?" He stopped at the top of the north-south axis, partly informed by his place at Andy's ceremonial table in Bethel, and partly by what felt right. He sat down there, cross-legged on the ground, facing into the center.

He tried to calm himself to meditate but his wrist throbbed and looked puffy. Arien wondered if he'd broken it. If he had, it wasn't too bad because everything felt like it was in the right place. He could move the fingers. It hurt most to bend it. Ah, well, that crazy dude was a serious threat. The fact that Arien was safe for the moment supported his dealing with the matter as he had. Arien felt fortunate no one came by during the fight or its immediate aftermath. His instinct, his timing was good. He told himself the guy would be alright and maybe will have learned a lesson, though there lingered an uncomfortable doubt.

"Gee," Arien said, when Buster came over to lie by him, "We might have killed that dude."

He made another effort at meditation. This had to be the perfect place. He considered if the stone circle wasn't here, this spot would still have drawn him. It was so beautiful. But the attempt was short, not for his throbbing wrist, but a sense that someone – or a few more than one – approached. He picked it up before Buster did, before the dog raised his nose to sniff the air. Arien pulled his head back in the hood as far as it would go, and looked down into the circle, hearing voices that told him they were already in sight.

They hushed as they approached, evidently not wishing to disturb the person they found here. There was a tall, thin, older man, with medium-length gray hair and a rather substantial silver and turquoise necklace, a man and woman, in the forty-something range, looking fairly conservative and a teenage girl about Arien's age. She was pretty, but all the girls were pretty to Arien unless, of course, they decidedly weren't. His dog barked once, and then otherwise watched as Arien put an arm over Buster's shoulders, while the visitors quietly sat down together around the perimeter of the circle. He noticed some brought small cushions and the girl had a roll of carpet to sit on.

Arien greeted with a bit of smile and a nod, which was returned. He was reasonably confident if anyone had either seen his picture or was yet to, he wouldn't be recognized by the narrow view of his face. He relaxed. These folks were here for the space just as he was.

Soon others arrived, some couples in their twenties, looking hipper, and then even more who ranged through early to later middle age, and the air became busy with the vibes of all these people who now arranged themselves around the circle. Arien made eye contact with a few, and all simply accepted him as one of their party.

The elder man with the turquoise necklace assumed a meditative pose with palms facing up as the others followed suit. "Mother Earth, Father Sky," he announced, breaking the studied silence among them, "we have come on this special day to your temple place of healing and wisdom to mark the death and certain resurrection of the sun." Briefly, he let his words settle before going on. "The tortured land stumbles and groans beneath the weight of abuses of our race and we are here, on this, the shortest day, to dedicate ourselves to the healing, to the rebalancing of our way, and for the courage we will need to endure the dark times that are coming."

As a backdrop, the dingy sky happened to break into more turbulent formations of clouds, now clashing in shades of rose and gray as the low sun began to break through here and there in brilliant shafts of golden light. It brought out the dazzling, Technicolor reds of the landscape, and everyone was obviously caught by nature's timely and spectacular show.

Wow! This is *way* cool! Arien thought, with tingling goose bumps. The likelihood he would run into anything like this! Fantastic! He'd have pinched himself but the ache in his wrist accomplished that well-enough. The only thing missing were the colored pennants of the quarters, and the four races in their proper place, though he imagined them to be there now. Why not? If I hold them in my mind's eye... He visualized Ellison Black

Snake blessing the group with a dusting of his Carolina tobacco. He could hear Andy's invocations in his head, and the drum of the African woman. He could almost smell Hawthorne's smudge of sage...

The elder was looking at him with an inquiring smile. Arien hardly realized how he wept now, and this must have caught the man's attention, even past the narrow view permitted by the hoodie. A beam of sunshine slipped through to sparkle in the well of his eyes. It became difficult to see. He felt more watching him. The moment was his.

"In the circle, it's like, it's like, I'm home again," Arien softly told his listeners, his youthful voice deep with emotion. "It doesn't matter where, it doesn't matter when, it doesn't matter who, but I'm here and that's all that matters." He audibly sobbed, yet keenly he felt the connection and sudden, surprised, and curiously tantalized sense of empathy from these strangers. He'd drifted to a garden island in an unknown, glowering sea, a land where the citizens were his friends and his family. He merely had to learn their names.

Arien began an Om. He could practically hear it. It was only a matter of tuning in with the note. The others took it up. Their voices blended into a single sound.

Arien fell into himself as his awareness and sense of being rapidly expanded to the sound of an inner squeal, and a rush of immeasurable bliss. He could feel the swoon pass through the others as he came out to meet them, easily detecting the syncing rhythm in their hearts and the sensual, even erotic pleasure in the effect. A steady breeze came up, dropping the temperature. Arien met that, too, as it came upon him, and allowed it, adjusting, feeling his way. And then he sensed another thing, lives, other beings, a small herd of feral goats had materialized, already standing around the circle watching, like a stand of guardians, by the time participants realized in wide-eyed recognition these creatures had come. Arien never imagined such a thing could happen! They simply watched. They were there.

"In this Word is Life," he said, certainly. "And the life is our Light and the Light shines in the Darkness and the Darkness comprehends it not."

Arien looked up. His hoodie fell back. His mouth dropped open in awe as an instantaneous flash of brilliant light shot horizontally, at eye level, in the near distance over where the topography dropped away into a very broad, scenic canyon. All the way behind the hurtling ball of the most intense light stretched a diminishing tail, like a thin band of white-hot plasma through a tunnel of turbulence, a vapor trail, but it was dense, iridescent, from brilliant white to copy-screen-green, and at its edges churning, boiling, with traces like the glimmer of silver and gold on storm clouds at a post card sunset. It moved incomprehensibly fast, covering a few hundred yards in a fraction of the blink of an eye, leaving a momentarily solid effect that instantly extended from one end of the near horizon to the other. And it was followed by a rolling sound, a compressed, explosive vibration, very similar to a crack of thunder but above the range of normal hearing, and likewise, it pushed a shock wave so fine it blew through thoughts and emotions with a sudden, shuddering rack of chills – and it was already gone.

Arien eyes met the elder's, his *'Did you see what I saw?'* expression, beset with wonder and astonishment. It was evident most of the other's had missed the phenomenon. The teenage girl certainly saw it, one of the young men and an older woman likely caught it, too, but the others better expressed a missed sense of, *'Yes, what?'*

"I think I know what that is!" Arien exclaimed, trembling with excitement. He lit up all over, struggling to wrap words around it, but he knew it. He was sure.

"My god!" the elder said. "A meteor?"

"It has something to do with consciousness," Arien hastened to explain, "and maybe riders of the Celestial Ship. It's the workings in the mind out there," he continued, waving his hands, "a picture of thought as it connects with this." He pointed at his temple. "It's knowing itself."

Arien's description appeared to sit well with those who hadn't caught the sight of the thing. Perhaps they accepted he was channeling a type of koan. Arien guessed their bodies knew something happened and informed them through feeling. Those who did see it were only the more deeply intrigued, both with what just happened and with the young stranger. Arien accepted his words, and perhaps words generally, were incapable of a direct description, but could only skitter about the edges like trying to explain the smell and taste of an orange to a person who'd never seen one, or conveying the validity of a divine experience on LSD; its integrated, holistic reality with its own set of rules, instinctually known from what was safely dormant, like a genetic disposition, until the light switches on.

If they only knew, Arien thought, flashing on Colonel Griffin. Well, maybe they do!

That was an unpleasant thought. Oh, how it raised the stakes! Later, he thought. I'll pass on that now.

For the moment, he freely dove into the ocean of himself; eyes rolling back into his head, yet feeling the focus of everyone's eyes tapping on his body's most subtle, sensitive surface like the press of extended fingers. And then he sensed the prayers of the older man lapping at his shore as the sounds of language obliquely translated to a sensual nest of nouns, verbs, adverbs, consonants, vowels... He'd tuned hearing words out; shut it right down, switching and channeling power from his normal senses and then even the unconscious bodily functions, one-by-one, to feed his expanding personal nimbus.

I am this, I am that, I am the Life within you and without you.

Are you me? a small, skeptical side of him asked. And he knew the answer hung in the mystery of All that Is.

When Arien opened his eyes everyone was sitting around him. The girl held his hand, her legs folded under her. She had a dark complexion with piercing, dark-brown eyes. The elder man offered a canteen, which Arien accepted with a general, "Hey," in greeting.

Greetings were returned in happy laughs, smiles, nods, and some relief.

Buster came to lick Arien's ear. Arien giggled, pushing him back with a kiss to his snout.

"You look familiar," one of the young men observed.

There was a call of crows. The goats were gone. The sky's brilliance had faded to pastel patches of color now merely accenting, rather than glorifying the majestic terrain.

"Yeah, I'm one of the twelve people in the world," Arien replied, recalling something he remembered Andy said once. It was beginning to seem like a long time ago, probably more for having it ripped away and the emotional yo-yo of the repercussions than the actual time elapsed, a lot like seeing it just across the street, but having inched to the other side on his belly over pieces of broken glass.

The elder regarded Arien with a complexity of bemusement and reverence. Maybe it was love, a vicarious, fatherly affinity and recognition. Arien knew it could happen like that. He rode the nuances though its vocabulary was a bit ahead of him. "What?" he asked, still grounding.

"You make me feel like a sanyasin," the elder told him. "Where did you learn how to do that? At first I thought it was the vortex until I realized it was you!"

"Exactly," one of the older men, the girl's likely dad, said. He wore a sweater, sport jacket, and slacks with a good pair of trail shoes. His hair was dark, without a hint of gray. Arien saw some of his features in the girl. "I haven't felt like that since my rave days in the '90s."

"Extacy," the woman alongside of him agreed, with a mischievous smile."

Arien squeezed the girl's hand. "What's your name?"

"Farah," she said. "And you?"

"Andy," Arien replied, "Andy Thomas." It was the first thing to enter his head. *Maybe they'll help me get through this, wherever they are...*

"I had some good teachers," Arien answered the elder, returning to his question. "I learned so much from them."

"And I'll bet they learned something from you," he said.

11 – God works in mysterious ways

Arien had the best dinner he'd eaten in quite a while at the rustic cabin Dr. Joseph Blake was renting in Oak Creek Canyon. He didn't care to call attention to his wrist and managed to get through it by switching his knife hand and very careful use of the fork. Blake still wore the turquoise necklace. Arien admired the silver backings and finely-worked links, and the glow of its rich aquamarine color in the candlelight. It terminated with a little silver turtle, its four-quartered oval shell divided in four colors, white, black, red and yellow. Arien wondered how he missed that. He'd seen the turtle before, but somehow missed the colors in its shell. This was major!

In response to Arien's stare, Dr. Blake took it off, set it on the dark wood table, and pushed it over the surface to his guest. "The inlay is opal, onyx, garnet, and chrysoberyl," he said. "Beautiful work, don't you think?"

"Oh, Dude. It's awesome. It's the four races in the Circle of the Tohono!" Arien's excitement fetched Buster over from the braided rug he'd claimed in front of the glass-faced wood heater. Arien obliged him with the worked-over T-bone off his plate. Buster was very pleased with that, and trotted back to the rug with it.

"That's very interesting, Andy. I never saw it like... I've thought of it as an elemental thing, directions, times of the year. The artist is Navaho." Dr. Blake poured more cabernet in their glasses.

"Well, there it is," Arien said, pointing at it. "It's a powerful archetype of the perfect Circle." He knew what he was talking about. He'd been in discussions about archetypes, and the Circle at Woodstock was like that. They were there... "Black Mother, Red Father, Yellow Son and White Daughter," he recited, almost to himself.

"Hm." Blake sipped his wine. "I have a good friend you should meet. I think you would blow him away."

"Cool."

"Farah was attracted to you," Dr. Blake said.

Arien smiled. "Yeah."

"In fact, I'd say everybody was."

"Yeah," Arien agreed.

"You're a good-looking kid," Blake drove on, "but that isn't it. There are lots of good-looking kids. Heck, by the time you're my age, everybody's good-looking." He chuckled to himself.

Arien didn't respond to that. He gazed into his glass, swirled its contents and sniffed at it. He'd had wine before, but it was cheap wine to get drunk with. This was something else, rather like a revelation, riding on his breath with a complexity of earthy, woodsy, fruity essences of surprising, evocative depth, perfectly complementing a most satisfying dinner. So, this is what all the fuss is about!

"Why, Andy, I couldn't say if you know about it, but in the old days we called it a contact high."

The young guest spit out a little laugh, recovered himself and lifted his glass. "This stuff is awesome," he confided.

"Yes, it's a damn good thirty-dollar bottle."

A phone jingled. It was a real phone with a wire attached to it, sitting on an end table by a suede couch in the living area. Blake waved his hand in a polite gesture. "I wonder who that could be, calling now."

Arien sipped at his flavorful beverage. He rolled his tongue through it. Yum, so rad. Then he got up and gathered their empty plates to take to the sink.

"Whoa, hello there, Thorne! My goodness, I was just talking about you! There's somebody staying with me here in the Canyon tonight I'd like you to meet, that's if he'll... ... Oh? ... Uh huh. ... So, who is it? ... Oh, Thorne, that's pretty far-fetched. ... So, tell me who it is? ... Well, what's his name? ... Crazy. ... Did you say, thirty thousand dollars? ... Wow. ... Yeah. ... So, you want to get together tomorrow? ... Okay. Well, the Goose? ... Good. Look – then come here, first. ... Yes, noonish? ... Okay, see you then."

Arien was running water over the plates.

"Oh, Andy, you don't have to do that. You're my guest."

"I needed to stand up or crash at the table, Dude. It's been an awesome day."

"That was the damnedest thing!"

"What?"

"Well, Thorne's the guy I thought would like to meet you. That was him!"

"Cool. I love that stuff."

"Yes, synchronicity, yes, but he was going on about something awfully far-fetched." Dr. Blake came over to the sink. "Go ahead, sit down, Andy. I'll do that. Here's another bone. He can have this one, too."

"Thanks, I'll give it to him, tomorrow. What about?" Arien headed for the couch. He stopped to pick up his glass off the table.

"He wouldn't tell me all that much." Blake stood at the sink, staring beyond the boy he spoke to. "He just said the police are looking for an alleged kidnap victim who's the clone-copy of someone he knew over forty years ago. Speaking of synchronicity, this is the real punch: he said even the kid's name is the same, which of course is so unlikely, and there's a thirty thousand dollar reward for information leading to his safe return."

"What's the kid's name?" Arien asked evenly, noting the higher figure.

"He wouldn't say, Andy. He just said he was so freaked-out, to use his words, he had to see me as soon as possible. It's the darnedest thing. You can meet him tomorrow, if you don't mind. He lives in Jerome. It's not that far from here."

Arien asked, "Uh, is Thorne short for Hawthorne, by any chance?"

"Why, yes, that's right. That's his full name..." Dr. Blake said, his expression already questioning. He waited, perhaps responding to his guest's sudden, intense focus.

Arien's heart could have leapt out of his body. He began pacing. Buster watched him, tilting his doggie head. "Fuckin' Griffin!" the teenager blurted out. "I'll bet Yasgur's Farm you didn't think of that, Dude! Ha!"

The sound of the dog smacking and grunting, licking his paws, was annoying. "Cool it, Buster!" Arien ordered into the darkness, though he knew it wasn't Buster that kept him awake, more the thoughts rattling in his head. Arien did square with his host before retiring to the bedroom he was graciously offered, confiding his real name, apologizing for lying, explaining little and asking for patience. Blake was good about it, evidently appreciating a profound connection with his friend, Thorne's strange phone call, and no doubt riding on the afterglow of the solstice circle and the naturally, really high kid who was spending the night.

Arien turned, thrusting legs restlessly between fresh, crispy sheets. He reviewed his serendipitous meeting with Dr. Blake at the vortex, he'd called it. Arien had never known a college professor before. Blake taught Psychology at NAU, now shut down for winter break. The professor said at dinner "the New Age thing" had always fascinated him, and when he became a focalizer for an experimental circle of friends and people of like interest, he'd found it blended well with his profession and philosophical pursuits. Being recently separated from his second wife, he preferred spending the holiday alone. That seemed strange. Surely he had somebody. Blake had known Thorn for at least twenty years. That seemed like such a long time!

Thorn. Wow. Dr. Blake told Arien, Thorne used to own a New Age bookstore in San Diego where the two of them met while Blake was on a speaking tour. The bookstore closed a few years ago when Thorne moved to Jerome. He still carried a fairly good business online, had written a few books, and occasionally guest-lectured at Dr. Blake's classes. It was all he could say. He didn't know a lot about Thorne's earlier history, and said he was surprised to realize that.

"Buster! Please!" That brought Buster to the bedside to bury his nose in Arien's hair, sniffing and snuffing. It tickled. "Ah!" Arien, squealed, pulling the covers over his head while Buster forcefully nosed for an opening.

Thorn. Oh Tina, I wish I could tell you about all this. So weird. What's it all about? I love you, Girl! What's it all for? But Buster wouldn't let him wallow there.

"I had a difficult time getting to sleep last night," Blake said. He just set a box of Toasted Os next to a bowl and a quart of 2% milk on the round oak table in front of Arien.

"Me, too."

"Don't eat too much of that. Thorne will be here in about an hour, and we're going out to lunch shortly after, probably the Golden Goose. They're good. You'll want to go with an appetite."

"Thanks, Dude." Arien didn't expect a bit of cereal would do any damage. Even with the dinner he'd had yesterday, maybe because of it, he started the new day feeling famished.

He was grateful someone had taken charge. It felt right to delay consideration of his next move, which entailed locating Connor and Joey in Flagstaff. Hopefully, Joey would have received Tina's address in Oregon, but it could wait. Seeing a sister Tree, and now the prospect of a brother in such a short time after coming to Arizona was nothing less than Providential. On one level, it was inexplicable, yet sensible in the mysterious inner arrangement of the progression of things. On another, it was following a thread, or maybe the thread was tugging him along, possibly a bit of both. What had LSD taught him? They were the *same thing*! The mechanism shares the same consciousness, like different parts of a brain underlying the mind it hosts! So, it certainly wasn't chance. But to think it pre-determined missed the mark as well.

To Arien, the phenomena had more to do with the idea, and its rhythm and focus. Focus steers the ship constructed by an idea. Rhythm fills its sails with the right amount of force for the perfect speed. It follows that people and events find each other through a power of attraction, operating both horizontally and vertically. A religious person might say God works in mysterious ways, but Arien was way beyond that, and he knew it. He knew it when the kids from Oregon, who hoped to find him at Woodstock, stumbled upon his caravan encamped in central Illinois. And, he knew it when he met Ellison Black Snake, the essential catalyst for what was born in Salamanca, New York, and ultimately shared at Woodstock.

"Coffee, Andy – uh, Arien?"

"Love it."

Blake filled clear mugs from a glass cylinder that pressed the grounds through kettle-hot water which ended up on top as coffee. Arien thought the stuff was really good. It was dark and rich, like the coffee Andy made on the stovetop, only without the grounds in it.

"So, Arien, can I assume you haven't really been abducted?" Blake asked as he added half and half from a plastic quart bottle.

"Yup. It's a lie, Dr. Blake. I ran from them."

"A rather elaborate lie, I should think. Thirty thousand dollars is a handsome reward."

"They want me pretty bad, I guess," he said, through a mouthful of Toasted Os.

"Have they abused you?"

"Who?"

"Your parents."

"They're not my parents. The whole thing is totally made-up."

"And, um, have you and Thorne already met?"

"It looks that way."

"I can't bring myself to ask the next question."

"Yeah, Dude," Arien agreed with a chuckle. "You'll just have to be patient, like I said last night."

Hawthorne used to be a tall, long, dark-haired young man with a full, ragged beard. The tall, erect fellow Arien regarded in the doorway now still had hair, though it was evenly buzzed and gray. The facial hair remained there, too, though it was more of a trimmed goatee. He carried a bottle of wine into the cabin, and concentrated on Dr. Blake with a warm greeting that appeared not to see the boy who came out of the bathroom with a toothbrush in his face.

"I know what you're going to say, Joe, but hear me out," Thorn abruptly said. "This whole thing is too heavy for me alone. When I saw that kid on TV... I lost it."

"Come on in, Thorne. Come in," Blake said, taking the bottle while the visitor removed his coat.

Arien swallowed the toothpaste in his mouth, injecting a minty rush into his involuntary gulp of breath, and mechanically stuck the business end of the brush in his pocket. Be cool. Be cool, he told himself.

Thorne had been reaching to a row of pegs on the wall but managed to drop the coat on the floor when his eyes finally connected with Arien's. His hands came together in a ball under his chin. His eyes widened. His chest heaved.

Dr. Blake watched him with keen curiosity and wonder.

"Hey Dude," Arien said.

"Oh.............." Hawthorne uttered, drawing out the syllable like the opening note of a song. He seemed to momentarily hyperventilate, as if fearing what he beheld, but then appeared to get a hold of himself. "It's true then. It *is* you, Arien Grove!" he said with words like drawn gasps.

Hawthorne appeared to be stuck in place, so Arien forced himself to move, crossing the distance in an elongated moment, his energy and awareness expanding to the walls like a sudden change of air pressure before a storm's onrushing curtain.

Buster, attentively sitting, emitted a sentient whine. It was very strange. And Dr. Blake wore astonishment beyond whatever his expectations for this meeting might have been, especially so when the visitor sank to his knees.

But Arien took the man's shoulders when he got there, raising him up, and they embraced. He could feel warm tears on his cheek, and the tap of his heart. They swayed slightly, like exhausted marathon dancers keeping each other standing.

"Whoa!" Thorne declared when they finally let go. "I need to sit down, Brother Grove. We need to open that wine. I need to drink it myself."

Dr. Blake rummaged a corkscrew out of a kitchen drawer, but before touching the bottle with it he asked if gin or vodka would be preferred.

"Let's start with the wine," Thorne said, sitting at the oak table in the open kitchen, not taking his eyes off of Arien. "Christ, I can't believe it. I can't believe it. You haven't changed at all. You're still a fresh, squeaky kid!"

Blake had emptied the bottle into three tumblers. Nice touch, Arien thought, even seeing the glass set before him had the least. Age before beauty came to mind.

"You're old," Arien said, "but you still look like Hawthorne. Your eyes... They're the same." Hawthorne's eyes were dark brown, but it wasn't their color, it was the light in them.

"Um, I'm sorry Friends, but exactly when did you know each other?"

Thorne took a few thirsty gulps. "Joe," he advised, "don't ask that question."

Blake laughed. "Come on," he said. "I'm intrigued."

"Let's put it this way, we're deep in the Twilight Zone," Thorne said. He looked intently at the boy across the table. "Arien, How? Where did you go? Christ, you couldn't have been gone very long!"

"Dude, I think it was the storm, the lightening. Mother Shongo warned me at the picnic. I didn't get it, but that had to be it. And, it must have been something like that to begin with." The drink was pretty good, flavorful, and aromatic. He allowed his nose to linger over the glass. "There was a hippie wizard in the Haight who told me it doesn't happen very much, maybe once every five thousand years, or so..."

"Mother Shongo. Oh my God! I forgot about her. That was such a long time ago!"

"Arien, what is he talking about? Maybe you can tell me."

"That was in Salamanca," Arien told Blake.

"Salamanca?"

"New York," Thorne added, "New York State."

"You knew each-other there? Hm. I'm getting more confused, not less."

"Holy Mother of..." Thorne said, taking another gulp of his wine. "I just can't believe this is happening!"

"I'm having a hard time, myself," Arien said, looking into his glass. Buster came over and pushed his wet nose at Arien's hand. Arien tickled a furry ear. "Buster here, he saved my life."

"Oh, my!" Thorne said, extending his hand out on the table.

Arien was grateful Thorn seemed to get it. He reached out, too. Their fingers touched. He allowed some of himself to pour through the connection. The old man began to tremble and tears ran down his cheeks.

"It's so wonderful, and so sad, and so wonderful," he said softly, over a sniffle. "I can only imagine how difficult..."

Arien silently cried, but he knew it was wonderful, too. Buster grew more insistent. Maybe I can help, he seemed to say.

"This pup's so cool, he's so hip to my vibes," the boy said, in the archaic vernacular he'd picked up with people like Hawthorne, when he was young. This was so very, very weird.

Arien could see Dr. Blake wasn't getting it. How could he? He saw Blake sit back with a bemused smile, waiting for the explanation that was surely there, if he was patient.

"Ho! Gods and goddesses!" Thorn abruptly declared. "I can remember your debut with the Tree Family! My, that was something, Arien. You hit old Tree like an avatar out of India and swept everybody up with your brand of sparkle and mystique. Why, those people you travelled with... Otter, wow, what a high fellow, and I loved that Andy guy! He really knew a lot. We hit it off. I got to know him pretty well in Salamanca, and we kept in touch off and on over the years. The last I knew he was either still in Bethel, or returned there. Something about finding you, he told me in a letter, but I took it for finding you like a spiritual thing, you know, because you were one high kid. That circle we did was fantastic.

"Joe, this kid and the people he attracted like a holy magnet, they made a circle for magic that would have blown your skull away. I'd never seen anything like it. Shit! There was a Native American guy, uh..."

"Ellison," Arien helped.

"Yeah, he was Seneca, a medicine man. He was the real thing, Joe."

"Wow," Dr. Blake said. "I'm impressed. And I wanted to tell you about this boy at our circle yesterday at the vortex. He's a natural. I can see that, Thorne. But now I'm really confused. We've known each other at least twenty years and I can't recall if you've ever said anything about this."

Thorn drained his glass and wiped at tears with the back of his hand. "I kept you in my heart," he said to the boy, sniffling.

"And this brings us back to the question..." Blake said in an affably ponderous manner.

That got Thorne to start laughing and Arien chuckled, too.

"We all went to Woodstock, didn't we?" Thorne said.

"You what? That commercial lollapalooza in the 90s?" Blake snorted. "Well that's impossible. Do you mean the town in New York State?"

"No, Woodstock, Dude, Richie Havens, Swami Satchidananda, Sweetwater, Bert Sommer, Santana..." Oh, that's when I saw her, but he didn't mention it. "The Airplane was playing when the Circle ended," Arien recalled. "Damn! I missed Hendrix, though." Arien felt burned about that, no doubt, but he realized it could have been worse. He really should have died there.

Dr, Blake took a long breath that ended with a whistle. "I see," he said. "Right, Woodstock, of course!"

12 – It's the work of the devil

"How do you expect me to believe this?" Blake said, as they turned into the parking area.

Arien was scrunched in the small back seat of Thorne's vintage Karmann Ghia. He'd insisted they take it. It was too cool, even having to ride in the back with Buster over his lap, stretched from one side to the other of the car like a big, living, shaggy lap robe. Buster loved it. Getting out was suited to a teenager, too. Piece of cake. He walked to the rim by an outcrop and looked over the side, down into the broad draw, where a little further along the place he and Buster spent the night before last was.

"Don't you see why they're making such an effort to find him?" Thorne argued.

This was a familiar place. It was where he and Blake and the others came out from the trail yesterday, the day of the winter solstice. Nice. The world was still here. Ha! And the reward today for information leading to his rescue was up by another twenty thousand. Jesus. Yesterday, he'd looked over the panoramic landscape as the sun settled to the horizon, making long shadows blend red mountains to purple, and the ripple of the highest clouds glow a golden, luminous rose with tails of feather-gray. That girl, Farah, took his hand. He winced because it still really hurt. The wrist was swollen but not visible in the sleeve of his fatigue coat. He let her have it, internalizing the pain. He could tell she made a bold gesture, a gamble. It made him flash with heat, an unexpected rush he had to dampen, because he knew he could have her, and blow her mind on the way. But then her parents called from their car. They'd turned down Dr. Blake's discrete dinner invitation on the trail out, due to another engagement. Too bad, Arien would have enjoyed more time with this girl. A dance had already begun. It was a shame to have to stop it. But then, was he prepared to hurt her?

"Will I see you again?" she'd asked.

"I don't know."

Oh, God, I could live for that alone, he thought, standing there again. It seemed so right when it was offered on a platter like that. But he'd lost so much, already. I'm not going to let it happen again!

Thorne rested a hand on Arien's shoulder. "Beautiful place," he said.

"It's unsettling to think we're driving around with such a hot commodity," Blake fended. He got out of the car and opened the trunk in front for the lunches he picked up at the Golden Goose. "Look," he said, "I can see you two have a connection, and you agree on the story, which is phenomenal in itself. I don't doubt your sincerity, just your reality. It's crazy. Don't you agree? Come on," he added. "I know a good spot a short way down the trail. We don't have to go all the way to the circle. It's too far and the Rubens will be stone cold."

It was a good spot. It had a big flat rock like a low table. They merely had to sit around it and enjoy the view.

"It's cold today, but I'm glad you wanted to come here," Thorne said to Arien.

"It wasn't my idea."

"It was," Blake said. "You wanted to come back here."

Arien's intention was to revisit the circle. "Wow! The sandwich is good! What did you call it?"

"A Reuben," Blake answered. "Never had one, huh?"

"No."

"It's not hippie food," Thorne said, taking a long glance at the boy.

Arien smirked. He remembered what it was like to get a burger with Otter and the others around. It took either being sneaky or open defiance. Of course he could do whatever he wanted. Nobody would stop him, but he did fall in more with the program as time went on, and bore it in comfort with his surrogate family. Oh, how he loved being in the middle of all that. He watched Buster wolf the ample burger and fries that Blake bought for him.

"Arien, tell me everything."

"About what, Hawthorne?"

"Since you've been here, in 2012."

"Oh, yes, I would very much like to hear that, too!" Blake eagerly agreed, passing a plastic bottle of water.

Arien obliged. He recounted the time with Andy, in Bethel, the death of the security guard, and the vision he had at the chapel Andy had built on the site of the Circle they did at Woodstock. Hawthorne was fascinated. He asked a lot of questions about Andy which Arien answered as best he could. When he recounted his 'rescue' out of the snow Blake grew especially interested, probing for ideas over how the military could have known about him.

He pondered the question long enough to nurse a last bite of sandwich, and a fat sweet potato fry. "I can't imagine."

"Well, think, who besides Andy knew you were there?"

"Those two security guards," he pondered. "One finally got out, Hawthorne, but..."

"No one else?"

"Hmmmm... Wait a minute. There was a lady."

"What lady?"

Arien had to dig to remember her name. "She called Andy's cell. He said she lived in Monticello. When she called back I answered and she already knew me. She knew all about me, Hawthorne. Helen! That's her name. Do you know her?"

"No, Arien."

"It could have been her," Dr. Blake said.

"I don't know. She was a friend of Andy's. She told me they'd all been waiting for me. Andy told a bunch of people, I guess. He wanted to do another Circle, like the one we did, Hawthorne. His dream has been to make that Ship again."

"Oh my! The Celestial Ship!"

"Yeah." Their eyes locked in reverent remembrance.

And then Hawthorne said, "Well, the leak must have been there someplace, if not her, it was someone else in that group."

"Okay. That's something," Arien agreed.

"What's this ship?"

"Oh, God, what a dazzle, Joe; it was fantastic, like something out of science fiction."

"Excuse me, Thorne. I'd say the two of you are out of science fiction." A chuckle went around. "But tell me more," he probed.

Arien smiled. His sandy hair had a rusty-golden cast in the slanting sunlight, which lent an already favored appearance another gift as he waxed with the memory. "It was made of light, bridges, beams of light. It surrounded us. It heard us, like a living thing, but it was a machine, and it transported us to the morning, didn't it, Hawthorne?"

Hawthorne's eyes already welled with tears.

Arien thought that was beautiful. His old brother was right there.

"It was faceted," Hawthorne added, "so complex, brilliant, like being inside a kaleidoscope, and we could hear ourselves inside of it, not in the same way as the cathedral, because it absorbed as much as it reflected."

"The cathedral?"

"Yes, Joe. Before we manifested the ship, we conjured a cathedral with our voices together in the misty air. It was massive, a great gothic edifice all around us, and when somebody spoke, we could hear their echo inside!" Thorn wore a beatific face.

"Wow, that's quite a story! Were you all on drugs? You know, I have to ask you that."

Arien laughed. "I'd been doing Otter's peyote tea," he admitted. "And I don't know about the others, but not everybody was high. Ellison, Thomas, Oak. I doubt they were high."

"A mass hallucination," Blake speculated.

"It was there," Thorne objected, "just like we're here now."

"Yep," Arien added.

"And when was this?"

"At Woodstock, in 1969, Joe," Thorne answered, leveling his gaze.

Arien chuckled. "And that was no hallucination, either. I was just there a few weeks ago, and this dude was still a young guy."

"Good God," Blake exclaimed, shaking his head. "I think I believe you two. But it's positively insane."

"C'mon," Arien said, not up to wallowing in proofs, "let's go on to the – What did you call it, the vortex?"

They followed the trail to descend downward in a dry wash and up again on the other side. There were places where their way grew narrow and seemed to disappear over the red rock surface and others that were wide and worn. Buster and Arien worked their way out ahead. Arien was fascinated by the astonishing beauty of this place. He would close his eyes to open them at a new direction, and another perfect garden arrangement of prickly pear, or yucca and grasses, the magnificent stalk of a century plant, the red, red rock, mummified trees in their twisted tangles, bunches of juniper or cedar, ironwood, or scrub oak, and always the weathered backdrop of ridges and canyons that etched their ancient seasons across the ridges of his thirsty brain. My God, he thought, I could be here forever! And then he came upon the special place smack into befuddlement. What he saw – or didn't see – was so unexpected; he stared at it blankly, and for the tiniest moment sucked his breath in like a traumatized veteran, transported, as it were, to his newest, deepest dread.

But there was no reason, no lightening to blast him away, and Buster was still there, following the aberration at first with his nose, and then moving on to the area's edge where he raised his leg at a large rock. Whew! This was no other time but the day after yesterday in the normal progression of things.

Arien scratched the back of his neck. "Who did that?" In place of the circle of rocks and its axes was a large cross. It lay on the ground at his feet as if someone had been buried there.

Hawthorne and Dr. Blake drew up now to stand quietly on each side of him.

"What is this? How bogus!" Arien protested.

"Oh my," Blake sighed. "The Fundies beat us here today."

"Fundies?"

"Yes, Arien," Thorne rued, that was a Pagan Circle, you know. It's the work of the devil." He pulled at the end of his goatee.

"That's stupid! That was our Circle!"

"Well, this is their cross." Thorne added, with a wistful grin. "Cross covers Circle."

"And foot smashes it," Arien angrily added. He took several quick steps to where the arms of the cross came together at the trunk, soundly kicking into the rocks. They flew in various directions. "Stupid bozo jerks!"

"He has a temper," Dr. Blake observed.

Thorne's grin grew wider. "He's still a kid, Joe."

"But he kicks for the two of us," Blake asserted.

Arien looked at the elder men. It was his turn to smile now. He raised a balled fist in the air. "Yeah!" he exclaimed triumphantly. But then he winced as pain shot down his arm. It was the sore wrist.
"Ow!"

"What's that, Arien?"

He was tired of hiding it. It was taking too long to feel better. "I think I busted my wrist the other day, or almost did," he said, wrapping his free hand around the pulsing thing. "I just tweaked it again."

"Hm, I saw you favoring that last night," Dr, Blake said. "Maybe you should have it checked-out."

"Oh no," Arien answered with a smirk. "You might as well drive me back to Davis-Monthan."

"He's probably right, Joe," Thorne agreed.

"Look, it's not too bad. I just need to keep it still."

"We can pick up an Ace bandage on the way back," Blake offered.

"How'd it happen, Arien?" Thorne came over to take the forearm in both his hands for a close inspection. He pushed the sleeve up. The area at the pivot of his hand was red and swollen.

"It's okay."

"You may have a fracture."

Arien shook his head, no. "I just need to keep it still for a while."

He sat down and regarded the panorama on the rock Buster had used. "When we were still at Medicine Bow," he began, gently massaging the wrist in his lap, "Andy told me LSD altered his understanding of what it is to be spiritual. That's the way he said it. Looking at it that way, he said the Bible took a wrong turn right away. I think I know what he meant."

"Oh now, you have to be fair. There's more than one way to take it," Thorne replied.

"Opiate of the people," Dr, Blake asserted.

"So, Joe, what is it that you were doing up here only yesterday?"

"Ambrosia, Thorne, not opium. There's a difference."

Arien laughed. He didn't know what ambrosia was but he got it was something different. He had to ask what it was.

"It was the food of the Olympian Gods, Arien. They ate ambrosia and drank nectar."

"Oh, I like that! It's rad."

"They liked it, too."

"No, I mean, what you said. You know what you're doing and you're still doing it, because it works. It's not just dope you're shooting to stay safe, or something you believe because that's what everybody believes and you're supposed to. It's something you know. If I got anything from Andy, and the Circle we did at Woodstock, I got that."

"That's good, Arien," Blake said, with an admiring nod to his friend.

"They kill it," Arien said, turning to look over his shoulder at the cross. "It's dead. It lies there like a grave. It's in your face. It doesn't do anything but insult you. It stops the conversation."

"The conversation?" Blake prodded.

"Yeah, with that." Arien waved a finger at the view.

"Oh, that's even better!" Blake declared.

"No doubt, he's got it," Thorne agreed.

Hawthorne stayed over at his friend, Joe's Oak Creek Canyon cabin that night. He couldn't let go, which added to Dr. Blake's fascination with the unfolding story of these two and its outrageous implications. Blake kept the proceedings well lubricated from an impressive pantry-turned wine closet, and he jotted notes in a memo pad. Hawthorne wanted to hear all about Arien's recent experience of another time that had been locked in his own personal, iconic memory, and history's divergent interpretations. He remarked how so much of it was like hearing it for the first time, as some parts coincided well with his recollections, and other parts did not.

Arien got a kick out of it, though it was not so easy to say, "No, Hawthorne, Willow and Laurel were over it by then. It started when Nita got pregnant." He didn't dwell on Laurel's tragic drowning, either. That was not fun and still raw. What would make Hawthorne forget how that went down, he wondered. So Arien pushed away from it, and relaxed instead into the gregarious buzz while regaining his delight in the taste of an excellent wine.

Friends, such as they were, had always been much closer to his own age. When this came to include the sisters and brothers in their twenties, as it had on the road, it filled him with pride. Now, he knew he charmed these older men, and he also felt privileged to be engaged with them as an equal. This was another new experience. In a way, he appreciated how youth enhanced his adaptability. Attachment was a very painful snare, its wound stabbing deep into his soul. The elders seemed to have so much more invested in the present than he. He wondered how they would have managed if the situation were reversed.

Wow, he thought. Maybe this wine carried his head here. He longed for the Mary Jane. She could take him further. Ha! Always more! Was it ever perfect?

"Is it selfish to want more?" he asked.

"It depends what it is," Hawthorne answered.

"Maybe it doesn't matter."

"Oh, it matters."

"Then I want more wine." He scratched the top of Buster's head, there in his lap, where he sat on the rug by the fire.

Dr. Blake laughed, and passed the boy the copper-tinted vintage he just un-corked. "They would drum me out of the university if it were known I got a kid drunk," he observed.

"Dude, do you have any weed?" Arien refilled his glass to the brim.

"No, Arien," Blake said with a sigh, shaking his head slightly.

"Oh, I have a little bag at home," Hawthorne asserted. "It's for medicine. I didn't think to bring it."

"This is rad, too," Arien said, after tasting the complex, yet perfect balance of flavor and delicacy in his glass. He smacked his lips, guiding his senses to engulf its spicy hints and velvet feeling. Wow.

"It's an Oregon wine, from an Italian pinot gris, pinot grigio. The Oregon pinots are notable."

"That's where I'm going."

"Why, Arien?" Hawthorne asked him.

"I want to see Tina."

"Oh my God!"

"Who's that?"

"Tina was his girlfriend, Joe. He left her behind at Woodstock."

"No kidding? Well, she'd, she'd be..."

"Exactly," Hawthorne affirmed.

"I don't care. I want to see her. I want to see her so bad." Tears came easily, silently running over his cheeks. He guessed wine helped that happen, too. He held his expression rigid, though.

"Arien, I would give that serious consideration," Dr. Blake said. "It might be disappointing."

"Do you know she bore your daughter?" Hawthorne asked.

"Yeah, Dude, I know. And Arienne had a kid, too. I'm a grandfather." Arien said that evenly, blowing a teardrop off his upper lip that splashed in his glass.

"Oh, I didn't know that."

"Wow!" Blake exclaimed. "Can you imagine?"

Arien insisted Hawthorne use his bed in the guestroom, he would roll out the sleeping bag on the floor; it was no problem. And, even with Buster being playful, having Arien down at his level, it wasn't a problem at all.

13 – A pretty creepy place

In the dream, he sat in a finely-crafted wooden canoe at the edge of a bowl of deep snow covering the pond that had to be crossed. On the far side beckoned his destination's flickering light. It sparkled and shimmered while pulsing with changing hues and singing tones. He knew it in his bones, like the feel of his body, its structure, harmonies, and interdependencies. It awaited him with a yearning that matched his own. As it reached to him and he to it, he could hear a deep rumble and crackling of breaking ice and observe the settling, imploding blanket of white before him.

Wow. He blinked, staring up at the log beams in the cabin's vaulted ceiling. He had to push Buster's nose out of his face. "Buster Dog!" he greeted. And he listened to the phone ring, the rising and falling cadences of a one-sided conversation, and then faint voices filtering through the bedroom door.

He waited before getting up, and would have lingered but the dog wanted out. Buster's vocalizations were somewhere between whine and bark, a clear message in articulate Doglish: "Let's go! I need to go!" The dream was slipping away. Where was it going? Was a path for him about to open or would it be blocked? It was encouraging, anyway.

He woke up hard, too, as he often did, especially when out of a dream. He felt himself, pushing it down, just so, to crack it like a popping knuckle. He loved that. It sent a delicious, erotic shiver all through him. "Oh Buster, why couldn't you be Zanna or Cindy for a little while?" The idea brought a smile, but Buster didn't get it. "Okay, damn it, okay."

Reluctantly, he got up and pulled his pants on, carefully. "Ohhhhh....," he groaned, telling himself he had to pee, anyway. He reached for his T-shirt but changed his mind. I really got spoiled, he thought. There was no Myrtle around to keep him and Tina in clean clothes. What was that, anyway? Was it entitlement, too? He eventually tried to stop it because it seemed kind-a weird, but Myrtle wouldn't have it. *It's the least I can do*, she'd insisted. *It serves us all.*

He met the smell of fresh coffee and sizzling bacon outside the bedroom door. Hawthorne greeted him from the kitchen, raising a mug.

"I was just going to bring it to you," he announced. "You like it with cream, and sweet, right?"

Arien was impressed. "You remembered!"

"It's not raw sugar," Hawthorne said, bringing it.

"Ah, it all tastes the same. Thanks, Hawthorne!" That was really impressive.

"Good morning, Arien," Dr. Blake called from the stove.

Arien raised his mug and padded over to open the door to let doggie out, but Buster hung there, waiting. "Just go, Buster," Arien whined. "He wants me to go with him."

"It's nippy this morning. You'll need more than pants."

"Yeah, Dr. Blake," Arien agreed. He stood uncertain.

"Yes?" Blake asked. "Is there something?"

"I'd be obliged if I could borrow a fresh T and unders. My uh, socks are pretty stale, too, Sir."

Blake smiled. "Certainly, Arien, I can fix you up."

"I'm going to take a shower, first, okay? – As soon as we get back."

"Go for it. Fresh towels are in the bureau there. Don't dally, though, or cold breakfast."

Arien knew he was pushing it when he heard the door open.

"Five minutes."

"I'm done!" Reluctantly, he shut it off. It had been hot as he could stand it, and it felt wonderful. The room was all steamy. Rad: A black T-shirt, white briefs and a pair of black wool socks waited on the edge of the bureau. I could get used to this, he thought.

"You look nice and shiny," Blake said when Arien got to the table.

Hawthorne poured more coffee in Arien's mug while Blake served over-easy eggs from the pan. Arien's plate was already heaped with several thick slices of bacon and a pile of friend potatoes.

"Oh, this is awesome," he said, digging in. "The shower was awesome, too. It's been a long time."

"Since you had a shower?" Dr. Blake asked.

"No hot showers, Dude. At Andy's we had to heat water on the stove for a sponge. There was no power. I did have one at the base, but it was a quickie." He thought about Las Lomas and laughed. "And the only shower at Woodstock was rain." He winked at Hawthorne, who seemed unable to move his eyes away.

"There was a phone call for you this morning," Blake said.

"Huh?" Arien held a piece of toast like his picture was being taken.

"It was Farah, asking after you."

"Oh wow," Arien said. He didn't see that coming at all. "She called me, here?"

"Her dad's on the faculty. We're good friends. I've known Farah since the day she came into the world. She was wondering what became of that boy, Andy Thomas, she met at the Circle."

"Andy Thomas?" Hawthorne asked.

"Yeah, I was afraid to use my real name. What did you tell her?"

"That you had gone on your way." Blake's expression was serious, and kindly, too.

"Oh. Yeah. Right." Damn. He knew it was the right thing to say, but it still smarted.

The phone in the living room rang again. Blake just sat there.

"Aren't you going to answer it?"

Dr. Blake shook his head, no, but it kept ringing. He shrugged, pushed his chair back, and then took his time to go over and pick it up. "Hello?" The caller was still on the line because Blake listened for a while. "Oh, really! ... No. ... Oh, I don't think so. ... Well, it couldn't have been. That boy, Andy Thomas was obviously not being held for ransom, you have to be mistaken. ... The dog, too? ... That's got to be a coincidence. ... Yes. ... No. ... Ah, I don't think so. ... No, that's not his name. ... Well, it's moot, anyway. He's gone. ... Yes. ... He drove off. ... I don't know. He got in a car and drove away. ... Yes, we talked for awhile in the parking lot and then he drove off. ... By himself. ... Well, you are mistaken, Ivan. ... No, don't do that. ... Because. ... Because you would be making a mistake. They'd ask all kind of questions. Our Circle is sacred. Besides, it would be a royal pain in the ass. ... Right! That kid was fantastic. ... Yes, he contributed a lot. ... Well, I hope we see him again. ... Ivan, don't. ... Yes. ... I'm sure, yes. ... Well, thanks for calling me, but I really don't think so. ... That's right. ... Okay, goodbye. ... Bye now, I'll be in touch."

Dr. Blake set the phone back in the receiver and stood there looking at Arien and Hawthorne who had been hanging on every word.

"God," Arien said. "They're using all this high-tech shit and they're really serious. They want me so bad, Dr. Blake. I better not stay here and get you in trouble."

"Oh, I could say you told me your name was Andy."

Arien tapped his fork in his fried potatoes. "That guy was on it, huh?"

"I'm just glad Ivan called here, first. He was primed to call the police."

"Your caller mentioned Arien's name to you, didn't he?" Hawthorne asked.

"Yes. Why?"

"I'll take him to Oregon right after breakfast, Joe," Hawthorne asserted, looking resolutely at Arien.

Blake's retort was, "Not unless I go with you."

"You don't have to do this, you know." Arien said, staring out over the Subaru's metallic-gray hood to the scenic, winding road beyond. He was finding it difficult to wrap his head around the fact that pursuers could actually be listening in to millions of conversations with a mainframe computer that spotted key words, and narrowed the search by a series of logical steps like the game, Twenty Questions, all in a fairly short time. He regarded both Hawthorne and Dr. Blake with considerable respect and gratitude. The old dudes were really putting themselves out. Hawthorne cancelled a Christmas Eve flight to Denver to be with his daughter for a few days. On the other hand, it appeared Blake had second thoughts about spending the semester break alone, even though he'd planned to do some research for an article he said he was working on. Arien told them what he wanted to do was get to Flagstaff, next. He was confident that would be enough. Hawthorne was concerned anything Cassie was likely to do would be watched, it was safer to assume the worst.

"I know. I could turn you in, instead, and collect all that money for a more respectable vacation." Hawthorne said from the back seat with a wily smile.

"Wow, you're perfect," Arien said. "I feel sooooo lucky!" He switched on the radio. 88.1 played a Christmas carol. It wasn't because the radio/CD player in the Subaru was all that special, considering the item it was connected to, nestled there in the console. Dr, Blake called it an I-pod. That thing was fantastic! It totally blew the Walkman away. If every inch of the car was packed with cassettes it couldn't hold so much music! But he was curious about what was going on in the world.

Children singing, *Oh Come All Ye Faithful* sounded sappy. 88.7 had news. Something different was going on. He listened. A kid froze to death on the National Mall while protesting the war in Afghanistan. How could that happen? Arien noted Hawthorne's rueful snap of the tongue.

"What's this Occupy thing I heard about?"

"Oh, it's a movement, Arien, or was. It's still the first serious resistance since the times you recently visited. It began with a big camp-in in a park near Wall Street, in the fall last year, and then it spread to other cities all over the country. We're the ninety-nine percent."

"You said, *we?*"

"Sure, Dude." Hawthorne grinned when he said that. "I went to several marches."

"What's it about?"

"A bunch of issues, Arien: Basically, the top one percent has been scoring all the gains. The wealth-gap is so wide the movie would be, *Revenge of the Robber Barons*. A lot of people have been falling behind, going deeper in debt, out of work, losing their homes, facing impossible medical bills, food prices – Put your hoodie up!"

Arien complied, noticing a traffic accident up ahead with a couple of very banged-up vehicles on the side of the road, and some policemen standing around, looking into cars as they slowed down.

"Anyway," Hawthorne continued, "Occupy had to cause some serious disruptions in the name of Free Speech to keep itself in the news. The camps were eventually driven out by a combination of tactical mistakes and community pressure. Typical reasons were concern for safety, law and order, and such. No surprises there. I don't know where it's going. I think it should get more political. I can't say it had an influence on the last election. Obama had more support the first time around."

Hawthorne adjusted a car blanket covering Buster on the seat beside him. "I'd like to see flash-mob gatherings at corporate HQs, banks and government buildings," he mused, "mixing 60's sit-ins with last-minute texting, to beat the barricades. "Sit-ins at wealthy neighborhoods might be effective, too. Get them shut down for the day with thousands of people converging on a place. It needs a new direction."

"What's last-minute texting?"

"Oh, people type-out short messages, heavy on the abbreviation, and send it out to a hundred friends on everyone's phone, then they text everybody on their list. The Arab Spring went down that way."

"You might add the Tea Party to the mix, Thorne."

"Well, yeah, Joe, but they got caught-up with the social-issue fundie crowd, and they let themselves get thrown in the blender with Republican Conservatives. They'll blast the bailout but won't tackle a bank, and the Pentagon is invisible, too. I won't bother."

They inched through the bottleneck now. Arien tinkered with the radio to give his face a reason not to be in a window. It seemed to work-out well enough. He didn't get a focused hunter vibe, though it was a little like riding a rag top through a game park, and having to slow down for the hungry lions in the way.

Hawthorne sped up when they were past it. "That looked nasty," he said.

"You didn't want us to leave Sedona, did you, Dr. Blake?"

"No. I would like to have returned to the vortex with some select people."

"So now you can imagine what I've been dealing with all these years," Hawthorne added. "But it's too risky, right here, right now."

"Yes, Thorne. Unfortunately, yes." Blake guided the car to the Interstate's entrance, and began to pick up speed. "You know, Arien," he continued, "it's frightening to think about what you're mixed up in, but I've hardly been more excited to be with anyone I've met in my life."

Arien switched the sound back to the I-pod. Sarah McLachlan began singing *Angel.* "This is amazing," he said, finding his way through the menu to a list of thousands of songs. The good doctor's musical taste was all over the charts. There was a lot of classical, pop, rock, folk, a bzillion groups Arien had never heard of. He wondered why Andy didn't have one of these in Bethel.

It was turned up fairly loud. Blake snorted.

"Do you know what's happening with Andy?" Hawthorne asked. He had to speak up.

"Sorry, dudes, I'm buggin' on this thing." He stopped at an album title that caught his attention. "Uh, no, Hawthorne, I don't have anything from him. I've been thinking about him, though. He said he would meet me in Portland. I sure hope he can."

"Ah," Hawthorne said with a gleam, "this could be perfect."

"When?"

"About a month, Dr. Blake."

Blake clicked his tongue. "I have to be back at school, then."

The lay of the land changed after coming up out of Oak Creek Canyon. It broadened to a high-desert vista with a thin blanket of snow. It was like this right into Flagstaff. It reminded Arien a little of eastern Oregon, in its open, semi-arid country. The city, like the surrounding territory, was spread-out with broad streets under a big sky. Christmas motifs were everywhere.

Christmas is in two days. Big fucking deal, Arien thought, with a little sting in it. Overlooking the city to the north was a majestic, gleaming-white range of mountains.

"So, dudes, let's keep going." Up until this moment, it wasn't what Arien expected to say. He said it almost involuntarily, like he'd been holding his breath and his body took over, defying his will. He looked over his shoulder to see Buster's fuzzy head poking from the blanket, tongue out, and cheeks pulled back in a doggie smile. He had a paw over Hawthorne's hand there on the seat. It was kind-a cute. But when he thought about looking up those guys, Connor and Joey, Arien got a bad feeling. The creepy vibe returned. He fumbled with the ace bandage he wore now. It kept his wrist more rigid. When he bumped it, which seemed to happen way too often, it didn't tweak as bad. And a couple of Ibuprofens Dr. Blake gave him before they left Sedona made it almost feel right.

"On to Portland?" Dr. Blake asked.

"Yeah, Dude."

"How is that going to work?"

"What do you mean?"

"How will you find the people you're looking for? Portland's a big city."

"He's got a nose, Joe that will blow you away. Let's just take him where he says to go."

"Well," Dr. Blake answered, we can take I-40 west, or 89 north."

"Do you have a map?"

"The Garmin's in the glove box." Blake said.

Arien dropped the door down. "The what?"

"The Garmin, the black thing."

"Okay," Arien said, perplexed. He reached for a slim item resting on top of stuff in there. It had a flat screen that was a bit bigger than the I-pod's. "This?" Uncertainly, he handed it over.

Blake took it, and stuck it over a wide suction cup in the middle of the dashboard. He aimed it for his eyes, and pressed a button. Then, after tapping the screen, a colorful map of major roads in northern Arizona came up.

"Wow! Rad!"

"Cool, yeah?"

"Awesome."

"Last week, it wasn't working. Phones were down everywhere, too. It really screwed things up. We've become so dependent on our technology..."

"I know. I saw it happen."

"What, Arien?"

"I saw an explosion on the sun that reached out and fried a bunch of the technology."

Blake looked at him, soberly.

Arien watched a smile creep across Hawthorne's face. He met it with one of his own.

"Go north," he instructed.

"Okay. Eighty-nine it is."

"Um, Arien, Have you seen the Grand Canyon?" Hawthorne interjected.

"No, Dude."

"Oh, my," Dr. Blake said. "I can tell already what this trip is going to be like. Scratch eighty-nine. The way is one-eighty." He tapped at the Garmin and a woman's voice shortly intoned, *One hour, thirty-five minutes.*

Arien dangled his forelegs in Best Western's indoor pool. Buster was beside him at the rim. He didn't see a sign saying, no pets in the pool area. Maybe he hadn't looked. It was after closing time, but since they were the only guests in the water and they weren't raising a fuss, nobody bothered them. Hawthorne and Dr. Blake were still lolling in the Jacuzzi. It was hot enough to make a cool water pool plunge feel absolutely delicious. The wrist was a little stiff but getting better. It must have been the fantastic sight of a mile-deep chasm that had gouged its geologic way across the brow of Arizona and variously, the soul of its witnesses. This absolutely magnificent, gaping vista happened to be dusted with a few inches of fresh sparkling snow, coaxing his delighted eye through descending scales of flame-red outcrops to a delicate, flashing-silvery thread in its cellar that certainly healed him. It surely had. It was numbing-cold, and he shivered the whole time, but it didn't matter. He didn't want to get back in the car.

He laughed to himself with the consideration, legs scissor-sloshing the water. Arien was so moved on the South Rim he'd taken that wash of energy like an infusion to his veins, where it flowed to the extremities and yes, beyond, into the Mystery. And coincidentally, intuitively, he could bend his wrist further than before. It's funny how things can come together like that. And then the dog took off after a rabbit and while they waited for him to return, Arien got to stay there a little longer.

Now he examined the smooth, vaguely star-shaped, red scar on the edge of his palm, and the way it contrasted so vividly with pale, water-wrinkled flesh. He reviewed how he'd earned it early on the road trip to Woodstock, hammering into barbed wire with a bare fist. Things like that are forgotten to notice after a while, especially to bury torment, but over in the Jacuzzi Hawthorne took his hand to stare at it, and ask about it. It had happened only a few days before they met at the Tree Family camp in the Medicine Bow. Ha! How small and inconsequential his burst of mutilating fury seemed now! Though he blanched when memory was about to awaken the reason. Better not to think about it. Better to look away. But how he struggled with himself then! And here he was in this mind-boggling arrangement and a pair of the oldest dudes he had ever gone anywhere with, ever. He only wanted to see Tina. It kept returning to that.

Sure they vamped off his energy a little, but it felt benign and natural enough. He was being helped on his way. Yes, they might be expecting to gain something marvelous and they saw him as a key or breakthrough of sorts, but not at his expense. They didn't maneuver to own him and use him like the Army. What they wanted was his goal, too, wasn't it?

I don't know, he mused.

What would she be like? She'd be an old lady, too. Oh God! How fucked-up is that? Was this a good idea? It didn't matter, did it? The depths of his heart burned for the lack of her, his first love, yes, his sweet babe. He would find her. She would understand. That's all he cared about now.

Arien's companions offered to sleep together so he could have the other broad, double bed for himself, but he declined, grabbing a pillow off one and rolling his bag out on the floor where Buster could lie by him. Dr. Blake turned a news channel on that ran though a litany of panic, murder and mayhem. Guns were a big topic. It was perforated with interminable ads for every imaginable sickness, with smiling old people playing tennis or running on the beach with their grandchildren. What a load of shit, he thought, seeing nothing whatever useful there. All in all, the future was working out to be a pretty creepy place, even with its marvels. He was quite content to borrow the I-pod and surf tunes with a pair of ear buds. A lot of the music was stuff he would not normally listen to.

He didn't relate to classical. Opera was way out there. He did however find U2 among the amazing list of unknowns. U2 sported a number of titles that hadn't existed before. Wow. Awesome! *Pop* was strange, evolved, maybe, but strange. Sadly, one of his favorite bands was getting old, like watching the pretty girl from Shangri La wither before his eyes. Well, he thought, I can always come back to it later. Maybe I just don't get it.

He happened on another classical piece, Delius' Florida Suite. It sucked him in. It was so beautiful. Wow, describing a wondrous landscape like places he'd recently been. Words alone couldn't do that. He marveled at how the music played his feelings.

"Arien! Arien!" His name being called intruded. He pulled-out the ear buds.

"Look!"

There he was on TV again. A talking head on CNN was considering the possibility Arien was being won over by his abductors, like Patty Hearst, as there were unsubstantiated reports he had been seen in the Sedona area. One proposal floated implicated radical environmentalists; another speculated it was a Mexican drug cartel. The reward for leading to his recovery now surpassed fifty thousand dollars with an anonymous ante of twenty-five thousand by a group of "Grove family friends."

"This is so..." His jaw dropped.

Hawthorne roused himself enough from slumber to say staying at a hotel might have been too risky.

"I kept my head down."

"Lucky nobody else used the pool." Dr. Blake considered.

"At least Buster wasn't in the news spot," Hawthorne said.

"When was the last time you heard of such a large reward being offered in a case like this?" the moderator asked.

"Well, the United States Government offered a million to get Osama," the analyst replied.

"You wonder why they just don't pay the ransom," the moderator added.

"Nobody's saying," the analyst said. *"There's speculation a time limit may have elapsed."*

"Thank you, John! In other news, concern over the fiscal cliff may have severe repercussions in the financial sector. We'll just have to see when the markets open for business tomorrow. The President is expected to endorse a last-minute bi-partisan..." Dr. Blake turned it off.

"I need to blow through a little time," Arien said. He stared up at the ceiling, hands behind his head on the pillow.

"I've got a contact at PSU. She's a friend and former classmate." Dr. Blake offered. "Maybe she can help us out when we reach Portland."

"In the morning, I'll bring the dog out before we have breakfast," Hawthorne said. "You can wear your hoodie up, and tie-back the hair. It makes it look different than the TV spot."

Everyone fell silent and into their own thoughts after that. Then the lamp between the beds was turned off.

Arien missed Andy. What could be happening with him? The I-pod flashed its stark white light in the darkness as he chose *shuffle songs* from the menu. He worked the buds back into his ears to hear the haunting solo, *Today* from *Surrealistic Pillow,* of all things.

"Goodnight, Tina," he whispered.

Hawthorne and Buster were already out of the room when Arien opened his eyes. Dr. Blake was getting dressed. He told him the weather report warned Southwest Idaho would be slammed by snow sometime during the day. It was going to be a white Christmas all over the region, and expected to be a nightmare for Holiday travelers.

"I know you wanted to keep to the back roads, Arien, but Thorne and I agree staying with I-84 out of Ogden makes more sense, especially now."

Arien admired the running shoes Dr, Blake was slipping into. Nothing like a high-top, it sported fluting on the sides in tones of tan and brown, and the wavy, tan sole was formed up over the toe and likewise, reached up behind the heel. They looked really cool. "I don't know," he said, with a yawn.

"It's about twelve hours on the freeway to Portland, if we can beat the snow. Otherwise, we had better know where to stop and dig in. A lot of towns out here will be buttoned-down tomorrow. It might not be pretty."

"We could have driven straight through," Arien said. "I could have helped with the driving."

"We all wanted to stop."

"The pool was rad."

"Yes. It was perfect, and we had it to ourselves." Blake headed to the door with the small suitcase he'd taken from home. "I'll see you downstairs. There's complimentary waffles, muffins, fruit and stuff. Be sure you have everything from the room, and wear your hoodie. Thorn will be waiting for us in the car."

"Okay. Be right down."

Blake was halfway though a waffle when Arien reached the serving area, adjacent to the lobby. A generic Holiday melody played from speakers in the wall. Arien helped himself to the coffee first, and then grabbed a fat blueberry muffin, and a pat of butter he'd inserted with the help of a plastic knife. He stuck it into the microwave. The metal box version used at Youth

Promise had a dial that was twisted to turn it on and set the time. The digital buttons on this thing were easy to figure out, though.

While the muffin heated he scoped the room. A man and woman with two little kids sat at one of the round tables. At another table a guy in a suit sipped coffee and read a newspaper. A pair of elderly ladies chatted over fruit and toast over by the windowed outside wall, and that was it. He felt fairly safe, even though the older of the kids, a boy of about seven, kept stealing glances. Arien knew it wasn't recognition but curiosity drawing his attention.

"Children are fascinated by teenagers," Blake observed when Arien sat down.

Arien smiled. "If I make eye contact they'll be over here." He took a bite of his muffin. Some of it crumbled into the paper plate.

"Then don't."

"I can prove it."

"I'm sure you can," Blake quietly agreed. "And you might prove what a hot commodity you are, too. But I'd rather not get carted off to questioning, Thanks."

"I won't let that happen." The muffin wasn't enough. Arien got up and went over to the counter with the waffle iron. He was reading the instructions when that curious little boy came over to stand there with him. His head was about even with the counter top.

"Put the batter in it and flip it," the boy said.

Arien did what he was told. "Do you want some?"

The kid shook his head, no. He stood there looking up, simply studying Arien's face. "Where are you going?" he asked.

"Where are *you* going?"

"I asked you, first."

"Oregon."

"I'm going to Grandma's for Christmas." The boy's hands were on the edge of the counter now. He was looking at the bananas stacked in front of him. Arien handed him one. The boy took it without missing a beat.

"Oh yeah? What's her name?" That just came out, making conversation, Arien thought.

"Myrtle. That's a tree."

Arien giggled with surprise and delight. The name was coincidence enough, but to have it defined like that! The Universe is talking to me, he mused. What if she really were...? He bent down a little for effect. "Can you do me a favor?"

The boy nodded.

"When you see Grandma Myrtle, tell her Arien said, Hello."

The boy looked up and blinked.

"Can you do that?"

He nodded.

"Tell her *Arien* said, Hello," he repeated. "And can you keep it a secret, not tell anybody else?"

The boy nodded again, with a flicker of conspiratorial smile.

Arien winked at him. It would be so mega rad if she really was *the* Tree-Tribe Myrtle! Probably not, but... How many people have that name, anyway? Then he spied a pen at the edge of the counter and it was just a short jump from there to a paper napkin. "Give her this, okay?" he said, scratching a few words on the napkin. He folded it and handed it to the boy.

They stood there for a bit, feeling each-other. It was so neat when that happened: This little kid, a complete stranger, the bright eyes, the pure natural force and certainty of connection, of brotherhood, that "I know you," déjà-vu-like feeling.

A little *ding* sounded from the waffle iron, and an amber light came on.

"It's ready," the boy said.

Snow held back until they passed Mountain Home on I-89 in Idaho. The temperature dropped sharply, reducing its first big, fluffy flakes to icy sparkles in the noon-hour headlights. It swirled over the highway's glossy surface in diaphanous banks of glitter caught in the frontal wake of the vehicle.

Dr. Blake let up on the peddle. "This car has excellent traction, but I still have to be able to stop it."

Arien looked up from his lap where he was fiddling with the I-pod. The professor was on it, breaking gently, turning into the skid. Auto emergency lights strobed up ahead. They were close and got closer extremely fast. "Turn into the median," Arien said, feeling the recoil of hair at the back of his neck.

"There's plenty of time to stop, Arien."

"Turn into the median, now!"

"Do it, Joe!"

"We might get stuck," Blake protested, but he steered to the center as ordered.

It was almost too late. A tractor-trailer rig came up so fast and was already skidding sideways, its container taking both lanes and the shoulder, flying like a battleaxe as it bore-down upon them. Arien could see the professor's expression change when he glanced at the rear-view mirror. He gunned it, and their wheels whined as the car fishtailed, throwing bits of grass, dirt, and powdery snow, thumping, strafing and scudding under them. The hurtling metal box swept ferociously upon them to barely tap the corner of the rear bumper, ever so lightly as it whipped past, but the smash of its concussion with the cars stopped in the road, maybe twenty feet ahead was tremendous. And then there was a great roar and flash of bright yellow and orange blowing up the dingy mid-day scene in a garish exposition of fire and muffled screams.

Blake threw it in reverse now, circling away from the tortured conflagration, well into the center of the median. But Arien didn't see the livid panorama splayed before them through the windshield, dappling their faces with its hellish red-orange glow. He glanced at it from the inside, with that runaway trailer, just flicking the bumper. He saw the terror, and the rendered flesh, and shattered bone, and searing, impossible pain, horror, and dismay. And so it blew him completely out of there, to where he was high above a river, looking down as if with the eye of a soaring bird.

The air rubbed across his ears with a faint roar, like a great wave that had come so far over the curve of the world to pounce upon the shore with its cathartic roll into the ultimate exhale, as from the very breath of God over the surface of the waters.

Blissfully he soared. A broad river shimmered below. There were a few boats, some little ones, aluminum, parked bobbing off a bit from the shore, and a barge heaping with black gold off the single-minded, driving nose of a stout little tug. And on the north side of the river an impossibly long, seeming H-O scale freight train blended its clatter with the wind, and highways on either side of the liquid ribbon threw flashing sun beams off the metal and glass of moving traffic.

He simply had to be actually seeing this! But his excitement was deeply internalized and as distant as the wind's buffeting roar. He'd left the horror far behind.

There, he recognized the Bridge of the Gods! Below him was the mighty Columbia! To the south, the awesome mountain hung ghostly in a misty shroud where delicate silver ribbons peeked-out, glinting, flashing, and then disappearing into the thick mass of green canyons, to reappear as falling gossamer veils against the rippling curtains of basalt. He recognized the one with its iconic bridge, and maybe another where once, not really *that* long ago, he'd found a Swiss Army knife on the trail there, and he was with Andy when Andy was still a dude in his forties.

And then he came to a tributary's mouth, a good-sized river that wound all the way back again to the mountain. His eye, hanging beneath black, outstretched wings riding the currents of air, followed its branching way under bridges bordered by bluffs and woodland, and a patchwork of fields, and the roofs of barns, greenhouses, and clusters of buildings along the roads, to a town that was bigger than its nearest neighbors. It was clustered around parallel sections of the highway to northwest Oregon's iconic volcano.

"Arien! Arien! Can you hear me?" It was Hawthorne, his mouth caressed in puffs of visible breath from the cold, damp air. He was reaching through the open window with a hand over Arien's heart, rubbing the thermal shirt under his jacket. Hawthorne's voice sounded off to the side, as if a ventriloquist had been projecting the words.

Arien focused. It was blurry.

"Whew! You went catatonic, Arien."

Now he could hear the screaming sirens, a wailing voice, and the staccato chopping of a helicopter. It reminded him of the riot in Berkeley. Was it a riot?

"I remember when something like this happened before," Hawthorne said, with deep concern. "Good God, Arien, it was like you'd died!"

"Where am I?"

"Idaho, Arien, somewhere between Mountain Home and Boise. It appears we got stopped by the weather."

"Oh. Yeah. Wow. Are we, are we okay?"

"I hope so."

"Where's Buster?"

"He's here, in the back seat."

"Where's..."

"Joe went to see what he could do to help."

"Ohhhhh..." Arien groaned through his teeth. "An old couple, a girl, and... They were probably her grandparents... And a kid, and a man, and another..." He grimaced painfully. "And a few people are hurt bad."

"You saved our lives," Hawthorne said.

"I was worried about Buster."

Arien's sudden, nearly subliminal smile was caught and reflected in Hawthorne's respectful nod. "You're stronger than I remember. The last time you went out like that you were gone for a few days." Hawthorne rested his forearms on the window sill. "I'll never forget how worried everybody was."

"Oh, Laurel, yes." Arien's heart sank with the recollection.

"I'm sorry, I shouldn't–"

"It's okay," Arien said, collecting himself. "I went on a trip."

"Huh?"

"I guess I was a bird. I flew over the Columbia. I recognized it. And I followed another river that led me to... What's its name? I should know it."

"Why?"

"Is everything alright here?" Arien could see a section of smoky hat on a tall trooper who had come up behind Hawthorne. He wore ear muffs and an overcoat with a badge over the left breast.

"Yes, we're fine, officer. We got out of the way just in time." Hawthorne turned, blocking Arien's view.

"Are you ready to move this?"

"There are three of us. Dr. Blake is helping the victims."

"Oh, good, glad to have a doctor on the scene. Terrible thing, Christmas Eve and all," he added sadly. "Which way are you headed?"

"West."

"Well, not now. The road's closed for awhile. In fact, the whole area's roads are being shut down for lack of visibility and treacherous conditions. The Boise Stage Stop is only about a mile back at the interchange." The trooper indicated the eastbound lanes with his gloved hand. "When you're ready to move, drive slow," he added.

The Boise Stage Stop was already crowded when the three travelers pulled in. The police had set up a barrier at the exit there to keep people from coming on to the accident scene about a mile further west. They used a military-style truck with big tires to shuttle people whose cars had been damaged but were otherwise unhurt. Arien got out of the car for a stretch with Buster, while Dr. Blake, with somebody's blood on the sleeve of his coat, nudged for gas into a line under the Sinclair dinosaur. He made a quick decision to top it off so they could run the motor as needed through the night to keep warm, and still be ready to move when the highway was reopened. The Stop was a great spot for truckers. It could serve a lot of people, having amenities like a comfortable TV lounge, a decent restaurant, great big bathrooms, and shower stalls, but no rooms. Blake refused the money Arien offered to help pay for the gas.

A bit later, Arien felt good about using the facilities and buying a cheese Danish from the food and beverage mart, though all agreed it was likely a prudent idea for him to avoid hanging-out inside. Then he noticed some kids his age in there. There was a guy and a girl that looked like stoners. They sat in a booth just past an antique sleigh like one that could be on a Christmas card. It was filled with presents wrapped in colored foils and ribbons, and festooned with green garlands and twinkling LED lights.

He and the dude made simultaneous eye contact over some forty feet, and then the girl turned her head. Her glance was not unlike the little boy's had been back there in Ogden, only her body language conveyed broader interests. Some things don't change at all, Arien realized, glad he was young. There was something special going on in his wavelength which seemed to accumulate static around older people. It was as if they forgot. But how could they? And then, just as well they didn't remember. Ha!

Arien went directly to their booth. It felt like the perfect thing to do. Standing there a matter of seconds he began to say, "Mind if I...?" while at the same instant the boy said, "Would you like to...?" as the girl was moving over to make space.

All three of them laughed.

"Denver Roundtree," the boy said, extending his hand over the table. His dark hair was nearly as long as Arien's, though most of it was covered with a blue-black stocking cap. He had high cheekbones, soft features and deep, dark eyes. He wore a classic Navy pea coat like a lot of the hippies wore in San Francisco. Cool.

"Arien," their visitor answered, slipping and catching himself, and splitting the difference in the same nanosecond, "Arien Danner." Oh, Hell. I like my name, anyway. He really didn't want to be anyone else. It was hard enough to lose the Grove. Before Arien could grip it, the other fellow's hand slipped backwards across his palm, and then made a fist. Arien reflexively balled his hand, too, in time for their knuckles to punch lightly together. "Cool!" he said, nodding, smiling.

The boy smirked a little; catching Arien's unaccustomed process, but it was friendly and reeled out some line.

"Bonnie McCloud," the girl joined. Bonnie's nice smile was framed with straight brown hair falling from under a more elaborate, bright green stocking cap with white reindeer that had little red noses, and continued under an open, puffy-down jacket with a faux-fur lined hood. She'd been nursing a bowl of chili buried under crushed saltines. She took a spoonful, and pushed it across to her companion.

Arien tore open the Danish. "Want some?"

Bonnie said, "Nah"

"I'm okay," Denver added.

But Arien knew a weak refusal. He broke a chunk of the pastry off and offered it, and the fellow accepted, putting it all in his mouth at once.

"Roundtree..." Arien mused aloud. He watched Denver swallow his portion of the Danish, take another spoonful of chili, and chase that with a gulp of water. It put a grin on Arien's face.

Denver wiped at his lips with a paper napkin and smiled. "My dad's half Cherokee," he said, taking a breath, "and Mom is Wasco. Welcome to my country." He smiled, spreading his hands.

"The trees are coming out of the forest," Arien replied, more to himself than the people he sat with. It recharged his excitement to something more substantial than merely being hunted. He caught a stare from the entry, and twisted his head as Bonnie had for him to see Dr. Blake back there. Blake weakly nodded, turned and went outside.

"Who's that?" Denver asked.

"One of the dudes I'm traveling with."

"Ya have to go?"

"No. We're not going anywhere 'till they open the road."

"Oh?" Bonnie said, retrieving the chili bowl.

"You don't know about the accident on the road?"

"Whoa, I wondered why the place filled-up all of a sudden." Denver blinked intimately at the girl who returned the gesture as she tore open the last package of crackers in the caddy on the table.

"You're burying that stuff," Arien observed.

She looked away briefly. It was coy. It had to be about something she didn't want to say.

Denver stretched in his seat. "Hey, ah, Bro, can you spare a few bucks?"

"Order whatever you want," Arien said. "It's on me."

A waitress materialized so fast it crossed Arien's mind their table was wired. The trim, sharp-eyed middle-aged lady in cowboy shirt and jeans returned his wary snicker with a confused look. "What?" she probed.

"Uh, nothing."

"Would you like to order?"

"I know what I'd like," Denver interrupted with a grateful smile. "I want a mushroom and cheese burger with fries."

"Same here," Arien joined, deciding he was hungry.

Bonnie poked at the chili in front of her. "I'll get more of this," she said, giggling. "I put in too many crackers, and a side salad, too, okay?"

The conversation Arien interrupted at the Subaru several hours later continued a running debate between two old friends that had been batted around almost from the outset. Arien's interest oscillated, since on one hand the significance of Woodstock and its historical role had genuine bearing on his own recent experience, while on the other, it offered little relevance to his current circumstance. Hawthorne's opinion that it was a pivotal, mythic event of enduring value clashed with Dr. Blake's view the drug-culture was a dead-end that shot its own ideals in the foot, and while Joe Blake acknowledged a certain debt to LSD for opening the New Age hope chest, his Devil seemed to harden to a more polarized advocate the more they hashed it.

"The very source of the stuff has documented links to the military and the CIA," Blake said when Arien got in the back seat with Buster, who happily greeted him. The motor was running. Joe and Thorne each held a paper cup of coffee and the remains of dinner rested in Styrofoam on their laps.

An intense expression Hawthorne wore relaxed when he looked at Arien. "Did you make some friends?" he asked.

"Not a good idea," Dr. Blake said, with a note of irritation. "There's too much at stake."

"Oh no, they're cool." He was practically in heaven and a wet towel wasn't about to dampen it. His smile must have given it away, because Hawthorne feigned sniffing, and threw a knowing smirk his way.

"Yeah," Arien grinned. "God, I was so ready!"

"Oh boy, I can smell that," Dr. Blake said.

Arien shook his head in wonder. "Den and Bonnie turned me on to some bowls out back. They told me it's medical. Jesus, who'd have known!" He smacked his lips, and reached for the water bottle on the floor.

Buster was getting sir-crazy. He stood up on the seat, wagging his tail, and pushed his nose into Arien's face. Arien opened the door.

"Where you going now?"

"Take him for a walk, Dr. Blake."

"Why not let one of us do—"

"Nah, I got it."

How am I going to tell them, he wondered, clipping Buster's leash, and shutting the car door behind them. He cinched the hoodie tight and buttoned his jacket. It was a few degrees above freezing, bone-chilling, with a gusty breeze that blew wet snow crystals into the air over the parking lot, to pulse in ephemeral, swirling cones under the light poles.

He made his way to a corner of the lot behind a long row of grumbling diesel rigs to an old, medium-sized extended pickup with steamy windows. A tap on one got it cleaned enough for the girl inside to see who it was. Bonnie waved and shortly the rear passenger door opened for Buster and Arien to get in.

"You got your stuff?" Denver asked

"Not yet. I'm procrastinating." It was about the biggest word Arien could comfortably use. The cab went to twilight when he pulled the door shut after himself with Buster climbing half on top of him.

"So, you changed your mind?"

"No way, Dude. No rush though. They won't open the highway until morning."

"Nice dog!" Both Denver and Bonnie shared a moment with him in the space between the front seats.

"Yeah, Buster's so rad."

"Thanks again, for offering to buy our gas," Denver said.

"So, what were you guys going to do if I hadn't come along?"

"Bonnie was going to blow some truckers." Denver said with a chuckle.

"I was not!"

"Alright, fuck them and blow them." There was a thwack in the dimness up front. "Ow, bitch!" Denver laughed.

Arien whispered, "Shit!" to himself. That exchange made him think of Tina, and how they used to banter like that. Damn.

"Shall we get gas now?"

"I best get my stuff," Arien answered. "The dudes need to know what's up so they can turn around, and get a room for tonight."

Going back was even harder the second time. He actually considered just skipping; it was all for the best because they had so much to lose if they were pulled over, right? But belaboring that idea scratched his conscience. They had been very kind to him, and Hawthorne, after all, was pretty special. Then again, he still had stuff in the Subaru.

He met with silence in the car, and he felt boxed-in with a bit of pot paranoia. Yet another bowl with his new friends had really baked him. That shit rocked! He couldn't find the words to meet his obligation.

"Where's the dog?" Dr. Blake asked.

"He's with Denver and Bonnie."

That met with more silence. Then Hawthorne got out of the car. He came around to the back door by Arien, and opened it. He just stood there, looking.

That was so much better than words. "You're awesome, Dude!" Arien praised, getting out and hugging him.

"Look who's talking!"

"Oh no..." Dr. Blake sighed, also getting out.

Arien gave him a hug next. It was awkward at first, but the man finally relaxed into it.

"It's best," Arien said, finding his voice. "I won't stand-out with kids."

"Will we–"

"Why not?" Arien stepped back to regard them both. "I'm supposed to look for Andy at Pioneer Square in Portland about three weeks from now. It'll be good to see Andy, huh?"

"Yeah, it sure will," Hawthorne said.

"Jesus. I, I had no idea," Dr. Blake stammered. "It's, it's really hard to just give you up like this. I don't know if we should."

"You and Colonel Griffin ought to get together," Arien said with a chuckle.

Hawthorne wiped a tear off his cheek. Arien smiled, went around to the back, and pulled-out his day pack and sleeping bag. "Later, Dudes," he said.

14 – It crept up on him from behind

The sound of air brakes and revving motors woke them up. Arien blinked under his jacket and pulled it away to greet early-morning light in a cold, damp cab with frosted windows. Denver started the engine and turned the blower up. Bonnie groaned. It sounded sexy to Arien. "They've opened the road," he said, with equal parts anticipation and anxiety. The fact that his ride was aiming for a certain town in north-western Oregon, not thirty miles east of downtown Portland, imposed its synchronicity with the swing of a splitting mall. It *had* to be the very town the tributary river in his vision led him to! He would know for sure when they arrived, but he already knew, like the guy whose bags were packed before buying the winning lottery ticket. He'd known since yesterday at the restaurant meal where the conversation established that marvelous fact, and plainly informed him his trip with Hawthorne and Dr. Blake had come to an end.

They all got out of the pickup to use the restrooms. Bonnie hung outside with Buster while the guys went in. Afterwards, Denver walked around the Stage Stop with Arien to take Buster out by the edge of the parking lot. Arien was pleasantly surprised with their easy flow. When a suspicious car with a wrong vibe slowly cruised by them, Denver unconsciously exchanged places with him by the curb to effectively block the stalker's view of Arien. That was amazing!

It had to be a cop. But were they really looking for him here? He couldn't be sure. They were always looking, anyway. That was their vibe. It was hunting; it was examining the everyday world with eyes that don't see like everyone else's.

He got down on one knee to fiddle with Buster's collar.

"Hey, Buster: How ya doing, Pup?" He was sure he could see the connection of amber fire in the critter's brown eyes, this loyal, devoted being that seemed to know something nobody ever taught him, and he was right there with it and everything else that he had.

"Lucky," Denver said. "I almost pulled out my pipe."

"Yup, we got-a stay alert." Arien got it: cops were the same as ever, especially if you were a kid without any ID. Even so small a moment and

Denver's response revealed it all. This was a good thing. Like those brothers n' sisters back in Tucson, Denver and Bonnie were on the same page. How lucky was that?

"Do you believe in luck?" Arien asked. He watched as Bonnie found them, and made her way across the parking lot.

"Sure, that was lucky."

"Yea, maybe, but it was you listening to yourself."

"You think so?"

"Can I borrow six bucks?" Bonnie asked, drawing up to them.

Arien reached into his pocket and pealed-off a ten from the roll of bills he had. "Keep it all," he said, "Merry Christmas."

She flashed a sultry smile, took the bill and turned away.

"We'll see you back at the truck," Denver called after her. "Shit, that's right. It's Christmas."

In some sense revisiting the flat, rolling country of south-western Idaho did not sit well. Arien had braced himself with the idea of more than a two score gap in his personal experience during four fantastic months of his seventeenth year, but as they progressed on through Boise, and approached the Oregon line, the internal pressure gradually increased. Even then, seeing the sign for Huntington unexpectedly tore into Arien's breast like the vengeful eagle of Zeus.

"What just happened?" Denver cried. The car veered to the side as if he were on the verge of losing control. It made Bonnie, who had exchanged places before leaving Idaho, push herself forward to see the guys up front, and Buster's canine vocalization added critter to the moment as well.

Arien regarded the unfamiliar overlap of I-84 and SR-30 with a drawn face he didn't want to share. His mind re-visited Clark's Café that advertised "A Good Place to Eat" right on the exterior brick wall. But other implications were suggested by the line above it, proclaiming "All White Help."

"I'm back in Texas," Jeff had said, early in that once-upon-a-trip to Woodstock, and to his credit he was offended. Andy, the much younger version, followed that with sneering something about "red neck bastards," and they decided not to eat there, so they put together sandwiches and snacks they bought at the Jiffy Market, instead. They ate it a couple of miles down the steep grade to Farewell Bend, where Jeff parked Van Gogh at a lovely spot by the river, Otter prepared doobies for the road, and Arien made-out some with Tina.

Arien pushed through his pain and yes, his confusion. What the...? I'm not going to let it eat me.

"Let's revisit Huntington!" he said, taking charge of his reckless emotion. The dark vibe in the truck evaporated, leaving Denver leaning on the steering wheel, stopped over the shoulder of the highway with beads of sweat on his brow.

"That's got-t be thought-control shit!" Bonnie declared. "We all felt that, right?"

"A good guess, but it's not what it was," Arien said.

"What was it, then?" Bonnie struggled nervously with a cigarette, finally getting it lit.

Gazing out, he said, "More like a contact high."

They both looked at him.

"What are you on, Bro?" Denver softly asked.

"I don't know. But it's like, it's coming from the center of everything."

Denver laughed. His eyes lit up, while Bonnie sat back quietly, taking two rapid fire puffs off her smoke. Buster sat up next to her like any other attentive passenger, though he snorted into the bad air she made.

Acceptance was all there was to do. Arien relaxed into it, rolling his shoulders – revisiting how rather spontaneous it used to be, working his awareness into LSD. His body's memory was keen.

"You don't have to," he said.

"I don't have to what?"

"Go into Huntington." Now, Arien laughed. He realized something that had been bothering him at the restaurant. At the time, he couldn't figure out what it was, like a missing object. Another puff of tobacco from the back seat and he nailed it, an environmental contrast with any restaurant in 1969. How fascinating!

Denver lowered his window to look out. There were no cars. He began to back-up on the shoulder to the exit they'd already passed.

Arien could hardly keep awestruck fascination to himself. A familiar space was transformed in a way implying near-liquid motion to the material face of the world, a study in entropy, impermanence, presenting other ramifications to his friend, and brother, and mentor, Otter's assertion that, "It's all Maya. It's not real." Huntington had been transformed!

"Look!" he cried, "The railroad sheds are all gone!" The station was closed up, windows papered over, and the siding needed paint. Clark's Café was a beer hall now, though the faded advertisement was still legible on the wall. A lot of the town was just gone. At least some of the buildings were still there. "That was the Jiffy Market," he pointed as they drove by Candy's Corner. He would have stopped there if everything hadn't been buttoned down for Christmas.

Denver drove on because Arien didn't say to turn around. Farewell Bend was where he'd expected it would be but it wasn't the same. The spot by the river where Van Gogh stopped was off to the left someplace around here. It was still open, unspoiled...

He wasn't sure. Today he saw a thin scattering of snow in the grass. It was blown into wavelets like beach sand. The trees were all bare. When they reached the state park he said it was time to go back.

"When were you here last?"

"Late May or, early June."

"You must have been pretty ripped."

"I must have."

"I'd go west from here but the pass is probably closed." Denver said when they reached I-84 again.

"You know it pretty-well."

"Well yeah, he grew up in Madras," Bonnie informed him.

"We could go through the John Day from North Powder, but 224 after La Grande will certainly be clear and we can drop back down to 26. It's a little out of the way but..." Denver didn't finish. It was as if he were talking to himself.

Arien had no objection other than to question why not stay with 84.

"We can stop and see my mom in Madras for Christmas. Maybe we can be there this afternoon."

It was getting dark when Denver guided his truck to a stop in front of a modest ranch house on a neighborhood street. Arien admired the silvery icicle lights dangling along the gutters. He'd never seen these before, or the flickering riot of LEDs all over the house across from Roundtree's. The snow here was light, but there was enough of it to accent to the decorations. The sky was hazy, seeming reflectively luminous. Buster jumped out to run his nose over the low surfaces and enthusiastically left his mark here and there. Arien hesitated.

"Come on," Denver said, waving. "Bring your stuff." Both he and Bonnie approached the front door without anything in their hands. It made Arien feel awkward, like he was moving in without even knowing these people. But inside was a nice lady with glasses that hung on a lanyard around her neck. She appeared forty-something, medium-height, perhaps a little heavy for her frame. Her black hair was tied back in a very-long pony tail. She hugged her boy and kissed him, gave Bonnie a hug, and welcomed Arien warmly, pointing to a room where he could put his things, through a sudden cacophony of three barking little dachshunds.

Arien had to grab Buster's collar. For a moment he looked like he would rip those little critters right up. Denver's mom's eyes widened, but she laughed, guiding the racket to the back of the house.

"We can re-introduce them later, when things settle down," she said. "He's so nice!" She rubbed Buster like she meant it. "What's his name?"

"Buster, Ma'am."

"He looks like a briard," she affectionately said, and Buster obviously liked her also.

"I don't know. He never said." Arien shook the lady's hand as Denver introduced. His mom's name was Alice.

A boy of fourteen or fifteen then came into the room to stand by the Christmas tree in there. It was all lit up to where his dark eyes and the smooth sheen of his face reflected its colors. His sleek and abundant, very long hair was tied back in a pony tail. Otherwise, he resembled Denver. He smiled his gladness at greeting him, moving his upper body and head in primal physical language.

"Lil' Bro, this is my friend, Arien."

"Hello, I'm Salem," he said. He reached out his hand.

"Would you kids like to eat?" Alice invited. "Dinner isn't all put away, and we can heat it up for you."

"Where's Dad?"

"He's at the station tonight, Honey."

"The station?" Arien asked.

"He's a fireman," Alice said.

"Oh."

Arien had to fight the sadness. It crept up to ambush and out-flank him, to wrap its hollow, demon arms around him, and steal him away yet again to the dark, empty nothing. How he hated that place! Why? What could have set it off this time? He reached for it with a flash of simple reason and courage. A veritable banquet of succulent salmon, baked potatoes and gravy, a festive, live tree with its twinkling lights, garlands, and shimmering balls, the happy faces, a few boxes of gifts for the returned son and his girl, and between the brothers, the son and his mother, and a phone call to their father... It could have been any one of these things or maybe all of them together. Though he saw himself struggle with what they had, Arien didn't want to ruin it for them. He could practically hear Otter's stern reprimand slam the door at his back before he could even walk through it, *"You're eliminating! Stop bringing us down!"*

Leave me alone, Otter! You're not even here anymore.

He made for the outside, saying he needed some air, and Buster who had actually come to a state of truce with three imperious little dogs in their own cozy den, rousted himself to follow with his most serious devoted intensity, his ears erect for any nuance of vibration, his focused eyes and lowered head poised to jump into a run if required to keep up. So insistent he was the two of them could barely exit together at the same time in the entryway, the boy hitting the jamb while the dog slid against the door, throwing it wider on their way through.

Arien heard the yapping little dogs and surprises behind him. The people weren't loud but he could hear them well enough with his body if not through his ears. He hoped the solid door would shut them away or better, protect them from him. "Oh, Buster," he said to the cold air, pulling his hoodie up on his head, feeling the ominous tug of the emotional whirlpool. "You should have stayed inside."

It was so quiet on the street that a corner of him could hear his silence fill it up as he crept into it to peal against the walls of the houses up and down. And deeply he knew his loneliness and sorrow fell at the temple of other's loved ones who would have to do without so much! Nothing could ever fill the big black hole in this long winter night, now and forevermore, packaged though it was in embossed foils with bows and twinkling lights for Baby Jesus, or Santa Claus, or Kwanza, or whatever.

He sat on the curb with its thin cover of frosty snow. "Should I be ashamed?" he whispered, wrapping his arm around Buster's neck. "Those people in the accident – they're not home tonight, either. They didn't make it home."

The front door of the house opened. Arien felt somebody waver, deciding.

"Ohhhhhhh...." Arien sighed.

Buster growled, but it wasn't menacing.

Tenuous footsteps approached. It had to be Denver. He hunkered at the shoulder opposite the dog, and pressed the tips of fingers against it, pushing slightly, like testing to see if it were alive.

"Are you okay, Bro?"

"I'm groovy," Arien sniffed, to the curb.

"What's up?"

"Why did she need six dollars?"

"Huh?" Denver sat down next to him.

"What was it with that? Cigarettes? A pack of cigarettes?"

"Who? Bonnie?"

"Yeah."

"Probably, yeah," Denver uncertainly answered, "or five-fifty or so."

"Fuckin' A. They're like, thirty - forty cents in 1969!"

"Okay..." There was a moment's silence. "I guess you haven't smoked them in awhile," Denver said with a chuckle.

"I haven't."

"You want one? I'll tell Bonnie to give you one."

"No. I quit, a long, long time ago."

"It's cold, Bro. Let's go back inside. We'll snatch a couple of Dad's beers."

The beers did help. They drank them in the finished basement where a new-looking 1950s-style refrigerator stock-full of bottles and cans provided a handy supply. After Denver passed one to Arien and Bonnie, Brother Salem helped himself to another, giving his older brother a look to say it was happening.

Denver merely picked up a remote to fill their comfortable array around a pair of facing couches with a lively country fiddle sound.

The label on his bottle read, *Dos Equis.* Arien noted the bottles had to be opened with an opener. Crazy. *Product of Mexico.* He took a sip of the amber stuff in a green bottle. It was light, crisp and cold. It'll do. "Who's playing?" he asked.

"Uncle Earle," Salem said. "Dad likes it. Well, me, too," he considered.

"It's rad," Arien agreed.

Buster curled-up on the floor at Arien's feet. Though Alice stayed upstairs Arien felt her thoughts there, also, like knowing someone who can't be seen is looking after him.

"Alice told Denver to go after you," Bonnie said, contemplating her bottle.

"Goin' to the country to meet some friends of mine..." the lyrics told.

He wondered what made her say that, especially then.

"No, it was my idea," Denver said.

Bonnie shrugged. "He just sat there," she explained.

Arien nodded, smiled.

"I was just going to give you a little more time."

"So, how soon are we leaving?"

"There's no hurry. You're cool to hang with us. I have to visit with the little brother and see Dad before we go."

Salem raised his bottle in a fraternal salute.

"Are you in a rush?"

"No. Where did you say we were going?"

"Sandy," Denver said. "It's on the other side of the mountain, on the way to Portland."

"That must be it," Arien mused. "That's where I'm going."

Denver and Bonnie exchanged glances. "Aren't you meeting people in Portland?" Bonnie asked.

"What's happening in Sandy?" Arien asked.

"I go back to school on the third," Bonnie told him. "We should do New Year's in Portland," she suggested to Denver.

"You're in high school?"

"Yeah, and I'll get to graduate in June." She said, slyly smiling.

"That's right. The world didn't end the other day," Denver said with a chuckle.

"I'm glad," Salem, added.

Arien laughed. It seemed everybody was on that one, seeing the evident hype in the rear-view mirror. He realized he'd already returned to himself, just a kid drinking beers with some other kids in a basement den on the late side of Christmas day, 2012. He didn't feel Alice anymore. Maybe satisfied by the music or low murmur of conversation, she'd moved on. She'd been attentive up there, though. Arien noted that. There was something about her...

"How did you and Bonnie meet?"

"We met at Timberline," Denver said. "She was skiing for Sandy; I was there with some buds from Madras."

"You were busy looking for Ryan White," Bonnie said.

Denver shyly grinned, "I heard he was on the mountain."

Bonnie giggled. "It was a rumor. You believed it."

"Well, Brad told me White was a guest at the Lodge. Why shouldn't I believe him? He worked the front desk that day!"

Arien noted the name, keeping with his habit of not wanting to be known for stupid questions.

A woman was singing now. Her song was instantly iconic, a fresh, yet timeless cowboy-bluegrass thing that sounded so cool. Arien liked it. "Who's this, now?" he asked.

"Gillian Welch," Denver said, picking up the remote to read off its small digital screen.

"What is that, the radio?"

"No, streaming," Salem said. "It's Dad's favorite channel."

"Streaming?"

"It's off the Net, Arien." Denver appeared to be puzzled.

Arien said, "Oh, yeah, of course."

Gillian sang *that's the way that it goes, that's the way...*

"Hello Boys – I need someone up here," Alice called from upstairs.

Arien stood up fast enough to get a look from Denver, not expressing anything so much as watching.

"I'll get it," Arien said.

Of course Buster followed him up, and another bark-at-will broadside ensued at the top of the stairs. Arien had to restrain Buster again while Alice got her pups to settle down enough to reintroduce them. She showed not the slightest irritation with it, though, appearing genuinely pleased with the addition of the bigger critter. Arien resolved there to make an effort to like the especially small dachshunds, or at least not to dislike them so much. It was only fair. They just seemed so ridiculous, but they were kind-a cute and the lady, magnanimous.

"Son, this garbage needs to go out," Alice told him. "My back isn't so good and it's a little heavy. Go that way into the garage. You'll see the cans in there against the wall."

"Sure," Arien answered, and he set about it.

When he returned, Arien saw a plastic bag waiting on the edge of the kitchen canister. He knotted the edge of the bag as they did at Youth Promise to make a secure liner and he efficiently handed it to Alice, who stuck it under the sink. As the dishwasher was already open, he next began to remove stuff and sort it on the counter as Alice put it away in the cabinets and drawers.

"Are you in school, Son?"

"No, Ma'am. It got, uh, interrupted."

"Do you think about going back?"

"Not much," he considered. "I got-a do what's most important as quick as I can. I could get interrupted again."

Alice seemed to take that in. She curled a finger on her chin, thinking. She finally spoke, "You don't have anybody, do you, Son?"

"Oh no, I have family, up the road there," Arien said, feeling suddenly confused.

"Do they know you're coming? Have you called them today to wish them a Merry Christmas?"

He blushed. She was too kind to snow. He lowered his head. From there he was able to rest it on her shoulder when she came over to hug him.

"I hope you don't mind this," she said.

He exhaled slowly to stifle the wave of emotion welling up. She was strong and solid.

"There," Alice soothed, "just be yourself, Arien. You're doing fine. It will be okay." She stepped back with an encouraging smile.

Arien smiled back, putting his hands together at his breast with a slight bow, as the Hippies used to do at greetings and partings. "*Namaste,*" he softly said to her.

He slept that night in the basement den, rolling-out his bag on one of the couches. It was pretty luxurious. Denver said it was okay to have the music playing as long as he kept it low, and that was great. For a long time he laid awake listening and thinking a lot. He liked Alice. She was really cool. It was funny how a thread of Indian People wove through his affairs since the road trip to Woodstock. Why was that? Other than certainly appearing Native American – Wasco, Denver had said – Alice was like anybody else's mom. Her house was like anybody else's house. There was even a picture of Jesus on the wall. It was a small one set in among a bunch of family photographs matted together in a single large frame. But still – She was there for him. She seemed tuned in. That was pretty special.

Arien noted Denver and Bonnie went upstairs together for the night. Maybe Denver's parents were easy. Den and Bonnie were both still in high school. Perhaps it was a new ethic for the era, or just a different way in this family, or maybe nothing. He couldn't know for sure. He didn't follow them up.

Denver said he wanted to see his dad tomorrow. He'd also spoken with a few of his bros on the phone. They talked about getting together. He wanted Arien to meet them. Arien wasn't sure how much exposure he should allow himself. It felt pretty rad to just let things happen like this as it carried him on the current of his will. It was all too easy, though. He could fall into it and maybe let something bad happen.

Arien was reluctantly pulled from a dream by banter on the steps. He opened his eyes to see Buster watching a couple of kids come down with Denver, Bonnie, and Salem.

"Hey, Bros, this is Arien," Denver hollered. "Wake up, Arien. Meet some bros. This is Wes." Denver was a step ahead, and struck a boy in the stomach with a pointing hand. It appeared to be deliberate. At least Wes took it that way and they suddenly slapped at each other really quick, thrusting, parrying, and jumping back like they'd had some practice.

"Hi, Arien," Wes greeted with a deadpan face, blocking and then landing a quick whack at Denver's ear. Wes looked to be Native American, too, or maybe Hispanic. His eyes were nearly Asian, and his complexion, with a somewhat oval chin, was darker. He had long black hair parted in the middle, held back in a pony tail like Salem's. He was agile, throwing energy to spare and looking like he would easily win the tussle, but then both boys stopped to suck some sharp, grinning breaths together as if on cue by whatever director shared their bodies.

The other fellow was Evan, who moved out of Wes's way, nodded, and rolled his hand in a little wave as he offered his name. A few brown curls hung below a dark stocking cap like the one on Denver's head. He also wore a long-sleeve Rugby shirt and cargo shorts dropped below the knees.

Arien sat up a bit self-consciously, not wanting to look like himself, while the sleeping bag falling around his waist only revealed more of him to a veritable nest of homies who were obviously joined at the hip.

"Has this man broke out the bowl for you yet?" Wes asked.

Arien shyly grinned. "Not today."

"It's not happening in the house," Denver said, pushing against Wes's chest with both hands.

Wes slapped him away and it looked like they were about to get into it again, but Buster roused himself to stand squarely between them with prancing front feet and a wagging tail. He yapped once.

"He wants to play!" Wes exclaimed.

Get dressed, Arien. Mom's making breakfast," Denver said.

Everybody sat around the big dining room table in a large, open room. The chair reserved for Dad was soon filled with Cyrus, a sharp-eyed, middle-aged man in a blue shirt with a Madras Fire patch on the sleeve, and the name, Roundtree over the pocket. Cyrus had a good head of barely gray-singed hair, conservatively cut, and parted on the side. He appeared totally comfortable with Denver's friends, like they were all members of his family who had always been there, though he provided Arien an unsettling look when he first sat down, kind-a staring, or locking on, but then seeming to put it away as he passed the towering stack of pancakes around from Salem to Bonnie. Then, the look revisited when Arien was introduced.

"Oh, oh, Wow," the man said, under his breath.

"What's that, Cyrus?" his wife asked, putting a napkin on her lap.

"Um, pass the sausage, Alice,"

Arien could see her drop the question, reaching for the platter, instead. He struggled to feel easy. Be cool, he told himself, taking it from her, and passing to Bonnie. If this guy's not cool... He was so glad he wasn't stoned or his face might have gone red by now.

"There was a wicked wipe-out back in Idaho, Dad," Denver said. "Arien saw it." He applied butter over the top of his pancakes, stirring it to a glistening yellow swirl.

Arien jumped right in. "We missed it by a snowflake," he said.

"I heard about that. Pretty bad. You were lucky." Cyrus sipped his coffee, peering over the top of it.

"Were you hitching?" Salem asked.

"Uh, kind-a, yeah."

"Where did you meet Denver?" Alice asked.

"At the truck stop outside of Boise. It was after the wrecks, and the Interstate was closed." Arien was hungry. The hotcakes were awesome. He looked at them after having a taste, wondering what was going to happen.

"You said last night you're going to Sandy, too," she commented, looking around. "What a coincidence!"

"That's right," Cyrus mused to Bonnie. "You're from Sandy, aren't you?"

She nodded, with a mouthful of food.

"Actually, I'm going to Portland," Arien submitted, "pretty soon." That was awkward, but sweet Jesus... "And Seattle after that."

"When are you going to Sandy?" Wes asked Denver.

"No rush, but me and Bonnie want to do Portland for New Years. Why don't you bros come with us?"

"See if I can," Evan said.

Wes smiled, and he poked his thumb in the air with, "You can count me in."

"You keep it safe, Son, and no drinking and driving that truck."

"Oh, yeah, Dad. No way am I going to wreck my truck."

"Well, it's your truck. You worked for it. I'm just not coming to bail you out-a jail. Got it?"

"Sure, Dad. No way."

"Can I go, Dad?" Salem asked.

"Let's double back on that *no way*." He smiled.

"Ohhhhh..."

Alice was already smirking at her younger son with a raised eyebrow. She apparently didn't need to add anything.

"No," Cyrus added, "way."

The boy's disappointment was palpable.

Cyrus gazed squarely at Arien again. "Alice told me you have a dog."

"Yes Sir."

"He gets along okay with our little guys?"

"We're working on it," Arien said.

"Would you like more sausage, Arien?" Alice asked.

"Sure, Thanks!"

Arien helped himself to another patty and set to cutting it up. He had to focus to keep it together. Though there was no sense of danger in the room, a feeling of rising internal pressure made him uncomfortable. He knew it was vital he not succumb to it, though he realized he was teetering when Bonnie said something, and then Evan, but it didn't register. They probably spoke to each other. There was laughter. Wes was talking now...

Be cool. Be cool... "Huh?"

"More coffee, Arien?" It was Wes. He actually stood at Arien's shoulder with the server.

"Yes, I'd like some." Wow. He'd zoned. Wes was just over there, working on his breakfast! The coffee was bland after the dense stuff Dr. Blake – and Andy – served up. There was caffeine in it, however, and Arien hoped a few good gulps would help return him to the table.

"I have to go back to the station a couple of hours, then I'm home for a few days," Cyrus said quietly to his wife. "But I'll be on call. We're short-handed this week."

"I'm not surprised," she said. "Were you busy?"

"Not really. Chimney fire, but we got it early. There was a wreck. Everybody was okay. I'm not counting the false-alarm. Thanks for the cookies by the way. Everybody liked them."

Alice nodded, smiling.

Cyrus pushed back his chair, deliberately stood to pat Alice on the side of her head, and then take his unfinished plate toward the kitchen. "It was nice to meet you, Arien," he said.

"Merry Christmas, Cyrus!" Evan told him.

"Yeah, same here," Wes added, along with concurring sentiments from Bonnie and Arien, who gauged a certain tension from the man. Something was up. He was masking it.

"Same to you all. Enjoy the rest of your meal. I have to be going."

Alice appeared surprised. "You can't even finish your breakfast?" she asked.

Surely, it was a dissonant vibe. Arien could feel it, like damp sheets against a bare body. Cyrus was a good man. He evidently allowed Denver and Salem a lot of latitude, and it was clear they loved him. Impulsively, Arien got up from the table also, to follow Cyrus. What am I doing? He must have worn it, because everyone else's eyes chased after until finding their limit at the reach of the wall.

Cyrus stood by the counter, looking out the window over the sink. He still held his plate in hand. He appeared surprised to have Arien follow him in.

"I know this is a big deal, and I'm just a kid," Arien heard himself say. "But you have to believe me, it's not what you think!"

"Son, I'm sorry. I saw the nationwide bulletin that's gone out to all agencies, even the Fire Department!" He spread his hands. And, you're in my house! You're right here in my house!"

"It worked out Denver was headed in the same direction as me," Arien said, with a wisp of a grin.

"Your family must be a class act." Cyrus shoved his free hand in a pocket. "It's really unusual for the FBI to make a statement to the national press about a missing kid." He set his dish in the sink. "It was right on the damn front page of *USA Today* – *Where is the Hundred-Thousand Dollar Boy!*" he squeezed-out. "That went around last night at the station. We talked about what we'd do with the money." He shook his head in wonder.

Arien audibly sucked his breath in. His head spun. "I haven't been abducted, Mr. Roundtree, really. Can't you see that?"

Cyrus appeared confused. "The notice says a previously reported abduction was likely a hoax. You're probably a runaway. That's it then, isn't it?"

"Oh God!" Arien sighed, hands burying his face. He sank onto a stool against the wall.

"Why don't you want to go home, Boy?"

Arien nodded inwardly.

"I can't say it. You won't believe me, and with all that money, who would want to believe me?" he quietly said. Jesus! He thought. He might become utterly terrified.

The hand came out of the pocket. Fingers tapped the countertop. "So, uh, what happens now?" But Cyrus' expression and demeanor had perceptibly changed. His eyebrows drew together.

Arien sensed the dead air that followed him into the hole. This was a very tricky place. He hardly understood it, but he'd had experience with what it did. Even now, both Denver and his mom entered the kitchen together, and were drawn up short by the energy there, remaining silent, wondering.

"Denver, leave Mom and I alone with Arien for a moment, okay?"

"Dad, is --?" The boy was very surprised. He hesitated, but Dad's stare invited compliance.

"Go!" was all else he needed.

The remaining three hung awkwardly in the room.

Alice folded her arms. "So," she said, breaking a pregnant silence, "are you going to turn him in?"

"Alice!" Cyrus exclaimed. His jaw dropped. "You knew all along?"

Arien lowered his hands to look at her. What's this?

"Oh, c'mon, it's all over the TV and the Internet." She spat that like it was so beneath her. "We don't need the money, Cyrus."

"Alice, it isn't about the money."

Denver's mom shot a glance at Arien. "Can't you feel him?" she pressed. "This poor boy is terrified, and he's all alone. Don't you think there must be a reason why?" Will you make him to go back to whatever that is?"

"Oh, wow, Lady, you're awesome!" Arien cried out. "Fuckin' A!"

She cocked her head at him, glancing off his glee, "And there'll be no swearing in this house, Mister!"

15 – The greatest rock concert in the world

He was about as out of the woods as a lost hiker in snow-bound wilderness. While it may have distracted a metaphorical cornered grizzly, Alice's intervention did not provide a way forward. Arien knew his Christmas rest stop was fraught with peril. A fat purse was now invested in finding him. The media was spinning sensational myths. He was a prodigy, he could be pathological, and his mysterious patrician parents were richer than Midas. He had a page on Facebook already said to have had more hits than dollars for info leading to his whereabouts.

There were Arien Grove sightings from everywhere. One purported to place him on the Paris Metro, and another, with the dog at a cheap hotel in Cancun. All this from an incredible kitchen confrontation! Alice informed him that the moment she'd recognized him, which was shortly after his arrival, she Googled (whatever that was) his name the first time she could get away, and the hits kept on coming. Alice said she was extremely surprised none of the boys hadn't seen any of this yet, or if they had, didn't make the connection with Arien right under their noses.

He was often pictured with his dog. This was terrible. He was sorry to have taken Buster along now, because he'd come to love the dog. Was that beneath the rage he presently raced to suppress? God Damn it! No! Not again! It hurt so much. The festering scab was still so fresh and tender. I hate it, I hate it! Everyone I've ever loved has been taken from me!

Reacting to the anger, Buster actually barked at him as they jogged around the track at Madras high school. Wow. There was no Garmin thing for navigating this gift, if that's what it was. But, couldn't recent events have gone down some other way? It was probable the dog that helped him walk off the base, and stood to fight with him at a freeway entrance ramp, may now have outlasted his usefulness.

The kids went out for a spin after breakfast. Arien told Denver's folks he could handle it. Cyrus didn't want to let him leave and return again to the house. He was pretty freaked-out. But Arien asked Cyrus for some time to think, and guessed Cyrus would sit on it because it was Alice's wish. It was clear she had some pull in that house. The unmentioned elephant was not if but when somebody would recognize him, or a new friend needing a hundred grand would rationalize his betrayal as a well-meaning thing to do.

The coat came off. He was sweating. He looked from the far side of the track about a hundred yards to the back corner of the school complex, near its rear driveway. Bonnie was on her butt, laughing, and Denver held a football the boys were just tossing. It looked like he was trying to get her to eat it.

"C'mon, throw it, Dork!" Salem yelled, running while Evan and Wes stood by in varying poses of readiness. They were doing their thing, and they allowed the sulky guy to do his. His silence after the closed meeting with Denver and Salem's parents put them off some. No doubt it made the two brothers uneasy, yet extremely curious.

Arien turned away, regarding his hand and the scar at the edge of his fist, a nasty mark rage had made. For what, he asked himself; nothing much, though maybe he could say that about the whole cursed trip. And then Buster lunged playfully, planting his front paws on Arien's chest, nearly knocking him over.

"Get down, damn it!" Arien growled, pushing the dog back hard. Buster fell away to look back blankly, his spine slightly curved in the manner of his landing. Arien took a few steps and sank to his knees. Buster warily approached to tentatively lick the hands covering the boy's face. "Oh, Buster, I'm so sorry," Arien sobbed into the darkness of his palms, "but you've got-a go, Boy. I can't take you with me anymore!"

The tormenting pain used to make him so crazy he didn't care. He'd run away from yet another foster home shortly before turning sixteen to live for months on Portland's downtown streets, and now he tumbled into vivid splashes of the memories, panhandling, petty theft and a few ugly things he could rationalize then for a pulsing spigot of money, buying and selling bud, and meaner chemistry until he was betrayed by an undercover cop, sent to McLaren, and ultimately remanded to Youth Promise. The review itself was painful, but he was transitioning to the other side again where he could objectively see.

He'd barely begun sticking a needle in his arm and was immediately seduced with the marvelous suspension of pain in its soft, euphoric blanket. Holy God, how wonderful! He was lucky, maybe, in retrospect, having been ripped away from that sweet, retching demon in the nick of time! He could see that now, after the impossible thing that happened – *Maybe once in a thousand years or so,* Jamie Sun, the hippie wizard in San Francisco once told him.

His friend, Kevin didn't wake up, after all. They'd shot it together. He'd never told anybody that. Kevin was even younger than he was, and small for his age. Arien felt protective. When he found the boy cold and still where they crashed in a damp warehouse basement, the only thing that seemed right was to take a broken handled shovel to dig Kevin's grave. Arien carried the supple body through subsequent hours of downtown darkness in an amazing, Herculean dance with a police car, ending in victory at a rose bed on the west bank of the Willamette. Kevin never wanted to go home. Arien would see to it that he never did. With blistered hands, and blind with tears, he laid that boy in and covered him up, and managed in the twilight dawn to restore the site as it was, replanting a small rose bush, and refurbishing the bark chips on top. Kevin was probably still there, forever young, floating painlessly in his soft, euphoric blanket.

Buster whined now.

"Stop it!"

Buster wouldn't stop. His worming sound was louder and drew deeper into Arien's awareness. He was about to make a breakthrough. The veil was ready to part, maybe to return to the eye of a bird, or a Para-glider over a cataract of raging, tumbling waters, or the thin, cobalt sheen on the planet's crown where the stars beyond are sharper than the sharpest endurable pain in the abyss of the single eye.

He removed his hands to see his new friends sitting in a quiet circle, watching.

"What?" he asked.

"Buster wouldn't let any of us touch you," Denver said.

"We saw a shooting star!" Bonnie declared. "In broad daylight!"

"Yeah, that's legit," Salem enthusiastically added. "It was right there." He pointed directly over their heads, describing a southerly trajectory.

Arien felt fairly numb. He didn't know what to think and surely not what to say. He sat cross-legged with Buster's head in his lap. He sucked in a long breath.

Denver pulled-out his glass pipe and filled the bowl with herb from a small plastic jar with a screw cap. He twisted around, scanning the gray, wintry campus at the back of the school for a sign of anyone who might see them.

"You're a knarly dude," Wes joined, and Evan nodded in agreement.

The term invited a grin, though still too deeply imbedded to reach the surface of Arien's face. There must have been a glow about him, though, discerning the brightness reflected in their eyes. He accepted the bowl, lighting it with the Bic Denver always passed with it. It was cool to see the familiar utilitarian thing, unchanged since 1990.

"Great Jane, Dude," Arien praised, taking a hit.

"That's the medical," Denver agreed. "These buds have a cool name, too" he added, generally, "White Goddess."

Denver's young brother mouthed the words with evident delight, and this time the buried grin made it to the surface of the strange boy they regarded. Arien passed it to Wes, who reached for the pipe while its contents still tickled his lungs and shot its welcome rush into his head. "I wish my friend Otter could have tried this."

"Did he die?" Salem asked.

"I don't know. When I last saw him... we was high on peyote at the greatest rock concert in the world."

"Wow, cool," Bonnie exclaimed. "Where was that?"

"Oh, back east," Arien told her.

"The greatest rock concert in the world was Woodstock," Wes mused, hitting the pipe, and sounding a tad contradictory.

"Right on," Arien said.

"Believe it," Wes added.

"You're still talking Woodstock, forty-three years later," Arien noted.

"I wish I had a time machine. I want to go to Woodstock," Wes summarily declared. He looked a little lost.

He really means it, Arien marveled.

"Well, Wes, I sure wish you had one, too, because I'd go back there right now with you."

"Can I come?" Salem asked.

"No way," Denver said, and that made everyone laugh.

"Do you like my dog?" he calmly asked later that afternoon in the back yard. It was a rhetorical question because it was plain that Salem did like Buster. They were playing a game the dog started by romping and jumping this way and that, which got Salem jerking around, stomping his feet, waving his arms, skipping, lurching from side to side, and they ended up basically dancing together. Arien thought it was pretty cool. He'd never seen Buster so worked-up and obviously having fun.

Salem stopped for breath before the dog ever did, and he answered the question with a nod and a smile. "This pup could play soccer," he said after a pause. "He just needs to keep his mind on the ball."

"Do you think you could keep him for me for a while?"

"Oh, I don't know, Bro," Salem demurred, wrinkling his face. "He's your dog, Dude. Why would you do that?"

Buster stood with his tongue hanging, looking from one to the other young lad in the yard.

"Salem, you don't know it yet, but you will…" Arien opened, sensing some reckoning in the proverbial wind. "Dude, you're talkin' to somebody at the top of the Government's seriously wanted list." He allowed that a moment to settle. Salem merely cocked his head and squinted back at Arien, waiting for more. "I'd say there's a real good chance they're going to find me, and when they do, I'd feel a lot better knowing Buster's safe." It was hard not to tear-up saying this, so Arien concentrated to fix his expression, earnestly.

Salem pushed at the thin snow with the toe of his shoe. "I – I guess I'd have to ask Mom and Dad." Salem said, taking a deep breath. "Wow, this for real?"

"Just ask your Mom and Dad. They'll tell you. It's for real."

"What for, Arien? What'd you do?" He reached to scratch Buster on his head.

Just then, Denver burst out the back door in his T-shirt with Bonnie right behind. Both looked really upset. "Jesus!" Denver cried, like the house was on fire, "I just got the craziest phone call from Evan! It's, it's unfucking-believable!"

"It's true," Arien calmly said.

"What? True? It is?"

"It's true."

"Oh my God, Dude! Holy fuck! Holy, holy fuck!"

Bonnie's mouth opened like she was caroling, then she reached for a cigarette from her coat pocket. She couldn't find her light, so waved it at Denver.

"What for, Arien?" Salem pressed, to a higher octave, shock doubling over his face.

"One hundred-thousand dollars!" Denver intoned. "Wow."

"Huh?" Salem popped-out. "Did you steal it?"

Arien said, "Damn it. What's Evan going to do?"

"Who knows? I told him to shut up. It had to be a mistake."

Buster came by close now, to lean against Arien's pant leg. Arien guessed it would take a trick to pry him away now, a trick for the both of them.

"What did you do, Arien?" Salem insisted, his voice reaching even higher.

Denver lit Bonnie's smoke. She took several quick drags as if to catch up.

Now Alice came out of the house, her bare arms contrasting with the white surfaces of the yard, a lady with a nice tan. She folded them, maybe waiting for one of the kids to speak or to gauge the situation.

Car doors were heard slamming out front. Arien jerked involuntarily, but remained where he stood, tensing along with everyone else, though more so, and then shedding it as Wes and Evan eventually came through the house. Whew! That was quite a rush. Be cool, he instructed himself.

"Arien," Evan greeted, "Shit! Did you know you're on the tube, Dude?"

And Wes said, "Bro, this is so cool!" He actually wore a grin, flashing his teeth.

"Alright, Everyone, calm down," Alice said. "Let's go inside and talk about this." She led everyone to the basement landing and directed them down to the den. "I'm going to call your father, Denver, see what's keeping him," she told her son.

For Arien, it was dreamlike to be sweeping fingers over the semi-gloss brown surface of faux-wood paneling above the railing. Alongside, Buster carefully negotiated the descending angle and the press of people.

This dog has glued himself to me. He wondered what he needed to do to take charge. He wondered if he could. It was getting hard to cope. He didn't take a seat but stood by a curio cabinet with a few small northwest Indian carvings. One was a model wooden dugout canoe about eighteen inches long. It was fancifully painted in abstract designs depicting fish, birds and sea mammals, primarily in black and white, and it had an impressive set of eyes on the bow. Another was a jar-figurine that was mostly a broad face with widely-set eyes. There were also beaded works, a child's pair of moccasins, and a small drawstring, deerskin bag bearing a simple cross-quartered circle design that struck home. Near to that was a woven-grass basket containing pinecones, shells, and some smooth, river rocks of various pastel shades.

Alice's display was grounding. It made him think of Mother Shongo. He revisited their meeting at the barbeque with the Seneca back in Salamanca. It was in July. What was that she said to him? *And for what is to come, as long as you can be connected to the Mystery, the life that is within you and without you, the oneness of all things, it will be as the life ring is to the man on a sinking ship.* Wow, this ship was foundering. The oneness of all things... The oneness...

"Arien, Arien, what did you do to get you in trouble?" Salem asked again, before anyone else could speak.

"Were you abused, Son?" Alice had just come down the stairs. Her voice was objective but kindly. "Is that why you ran? – Because it seems you left so much behind."

"If you only knew," he barely said, and then raising his voice for everyone, "I had a good friend, an old friend, and he was helping me until I was uh, *rescued*." He spit that last word like curse. "They came swooping down in helicopters and soldiers came out and found me on the hill. I don't know how they found out about me, you know? High-tech shit. They really meant to have me. I wasn't rescued at all. I was kidnapped by a colonel in the Army. They tried to get me to sign up. I don't have any ID, you see, so I could be old enough. They were going to fix it, Mrs. Roundtree. I was going to serve my country by..." He gazed at her curios, fixing on the circle over the beaded bag in there.

"What are you looking at, Arien?"

"I see the Circle, Mrs. Roundtree. I see the Tree People in the Circle, and the four races are there. There's Red Father, and Black Mother, White Daughter, and Yellow Son. We were all together at Woodstock, and we made the Celestial Ship, and we were transported to the morning." He looked up to see a room of rapt attention. "Who knows where else we might have gone," he continued, finding an ounce of strength in his own story, "It was just a little taste, Mrs. Roundtree, and now, I guess, I have a hunger... But then I got zapped again." He looked at Salem, holding up two fingers. "It was the second time. The first time I was running, yes. I was running from a group home and something terrible happened, an accident... That was in 1990. Well," he said, taking a melodramatic breath, "I got zapped," Arien looked right into Salem as if he was the only person there, "and that brought me here, forty-three years later. So, I guess, that's why they want me. They won't leave me alone. They'll stop at nothing. They lied about the kidnapping, and they lied about my parents. I don't have any parents. My father died in Viet Nam in 1973, the year I was born, and my mother died with Grandma in a car crash. That's the truth. That's what I did.

That's all I did. But there's more. I was in love. Oh, fuck, I..." As his vision blurred he looked down again into the cabinet.

Arien didn't realize Cyrus was there now, too. When Arien saw him he guessed Cyrus might have caught some if not most of what was said. Was it enough? Was it too much? But this was interrupted by a faint, though growing vibration that made the hair on the back of his neck stand up, a staccato chopping that could only have one source. "Do you hear that?" he said to Alice and Cyrus.

"No," Cyrus answered, and Alice concurred.

"I don't hear anything," Denver said, though he straightened himself on the couch, and the others became more attentive as well, perhaps along with Arien's concentration. But then it was louder, coming closer.

"Well that's just–" Cyrus began to say.

"Shit!" Arien forced through his teeth, "How? Did any of you call them?"

The confusion seemed genuine, and everyone's apparent sincerity was backed-up by the way they'd followed his story. Otherwise, there was no way to tell.

Buster's ears perked up.

"Quick!" Alice jumped. "Come upstairs with me!"

"Alice! What are you doing?" Cyrus protested.

"It's them," Arien said with a doomed look. They're almost here."

"It's just a helicopter, Arien," Wes said, though the chill of doubt already circulated.

"It's them!" He was following her up the stairs.

"Go back," Alice said. "Get your stuff. Bring everything you brought with you!"

Arien did that. He grabbed his coat, sleeping bag and day pack and rushed up the stairs after her, with Buster, and everyone else at his heels.

"Everybody, up here!" Alice ordered, almost as an afterthought.

"What are you doing, Alice?" Cyrus called, running after her.

Alice turned to face him while everyone clustered, breathlessly around her in the hall near the top of the stairs. "Do you have a plan, Cyrus? Does anyone have a plan? Well, I do, and, thank goodness you came back here with your car," she said aside to Wes. "Look, we have two cars in the garage, Denver has his truck, and Wes' is outside. We will get in all of them and drive away in every direction!"

"But what if it's just some helicopter?" Cyrus protested.

167

"So what? It's a fire drill. You, of all people, should be familiar with those! We know what this boy is up against and anything less won't do."

Arien could hardly believe it. Alice was totally awesome! He could see the shock on her husband's face, and even her boys appeared to be quite impressed. Her certainty this was not 'just a helicopter' made it especially wonderful.

"This might work," he said, with an excited grin. And so the contrast of thrill and elation could not have been greater against the utter implosion of confidence attending a heart-stopping sight of four black SUVs pulling up to the curb the moment Alice raised her garage door.

Alice looked out with an unbelieving shake of her head.

Arien felt like he could faint. His head seemed to float unattached over his shoulders. He leaned against the frame of the door and managed to connect with Alice. "Thank you," he said. "Thank you so much, Mrs. Roundtree."

But now the sight in the road, the front yard, and the short driveway assumed unlikely proportions as a veritable troop of men in black overcoats, some of them with automatic rifles, fanned-out to completely surround the house. It appeared to take all of two minutes, with soulless efficiency. There was only a moment to scan the faces of his friends, reaching deeply, to where any mask would surely be exposed. Someone had to have made the call, right? But the sure sign of duplicity was missing from every face. The only evidence to meet his eye was honest distress and bewilderment's helpless anticipation. There was also a measure of awe in their reflections. A kid with a crazy story that Denver picked up on the highway was somehow vindicated by the show of force. This wasn't the local police, or even the FBI.

16 – I thought Chinese would be a good mix

Now, in the throes of a monstrous violation, Arien was way too stunned to sleep. He'd drawn his bare knees as close to his chest as possible, wrapping arms around them to save whatever warmth his body made. The sticky feel of a plain rubbery cot against his side was hardly better than nothing at all. His feet were cold. He was hungry. Sweet Jesus, it wasn't right! How could this be real? *It's all maya, Brother,* Otter had said. Was this maya, too?

Fuck, fuck, fuck! All the way to this frightful place the bastards wouldn't speak to him. They'd put handcuffs on him with chains to his ankles, in front of everybody. What he especially resented was the way they treated everyone, pushing them back without a shred of respect. They'd zapped Cyrus with a crazy item like a Star Trek phaser set on stun. It threw him to the floor when he tried to step in and protect his wife. And when Buster lunged he'd met the same terrible fate. Everyone was shouting, men barking orders, his friends crying out, his beloved dog-friend trembling on the floor like he'd been hit by a car. It was terrible! He could cry now. He didn't want to show them that before, even as they tore him away from Buster. It was just another bullet to his heart.

What did they do with everybody? He'd seen police brutality in Berkeley, but how would they explain this? What country was this? What could possibly have happened while he was away?

He was in the back seat of a car with a hood over his head for what seemed like forever. He was in a helicopter for a long time as well, and then another vehicle, a van perhaps, boxy, with nothing to absorb the sound of the motor and the tires on the road, and the surrounding traffic, some bits of jangling chain, and his own breathing.

The van took him here. He could see nothing. And they'd cut off his clothes with the cuffs and chains still attached, like he was the creature of Frankenstein, ignoring his protests as they might a lamb about to be slaughtered for meat, and they only removed the hood when he was inside this cold, bare cell with one tensor light throwing a spot on the cot, its frame bolted to the floor. The entire gray-colored room – floor, walls, ceiling –

was an eight-foot square box. There was a steel toilet in a corner without a seat or a lid, a steel sink next to it with a single, spring-handle faucet, a small mirror centered over the sink, and a vent up near the ceiling. That was it.

Sweet Jesus, I can't believe it! How am I going to get out of this? What could I have done different? How did they know? If such thoughts were whips he would have been a quivering mass of gore. The only company was his breath. It went on and on like that for what seemed an impossibly long time.

He was too stunned to sleep. He maneuvered himself off of the cot to shuffle over to a corner where he sank down near to the cold, hard floor, squatting to keep from actually touching it, but the walls were cold, too, and the stupid chains. Why were they still on him? Why? Where could he possibly run? Why was he naked like an animal? And he thought he'd known despair. He thought he'd known the blackness and the terror of no one to be near him, no one to listen.

Time had basically stopped. He was ravenous. His mind was sure to unravel. He was startled by a loud report from outside of his door. It sounded like a shot. What the...? He could hear muffled shouts. It was confusing. What was going on? Was he being rescued? He trembled with anticipation and frazzled nerves.

That came to nothing. It grew quiet. It was too quiet. It went on like that for so long until his knees ached. He simply had to straighten his legs out. Oh God! The floor was so cold! He began to shiver uncontrollably. He listened to his teeth chatter. That never happened before. They really chattered like a tank tracking along on a cobblestone street.

"Please help me!" he screamed, "Help me! What did I do? Let me go! Please!" He screamed louder than ever before in his life, as if volume would validate his sincerity, and shedding all dignity, cried like a baby until his throat became hoarse and he fell into a place of dull numbness encased in a shell of utter exhaustion, sorrow and despair. He felt it. He owned it. It vibrated through his body to permeate every part. He was one with it, interminably, for it went on and on. He feared for his life. He could die of exposure like this!

That was when Arien heard a muffled scream from outside his door. The bastards are mocking me! It tickled his anger on a mountain of soul-shredding rage. He wanted to kill that bastard, scratch his face away, and wrap these chains around his fucking neck! But the shouts and confusing noise returned. It sounded like a struggle. What was happening?

Arien tried to concentrate through his trembling. He heard the snap of the latch. He listened past the chattering teeth, and from a recess of observation watched the door swing open.

"Nevin, stop it!" someone shouted. "Do not go in there!" A soldier in military fatigues struggled to enter. It was almost comical. A man behind him was grabbing the guy's arm in a furious attempt to pull him back outside.

"God damn it! This is crazy! He's just a kid!" the soldier yelled.

"Nevin, it's an order. Stop, or I'll have to shoot you!"

Punches were traded. They grappled with each other, falling to the floor. It was unbelievable. Arien became so absorbed with this display his trembling ceased. What could account for this behavior?

"Oh my God!" he exclaimed aloud in a sudden burst of illumination. Wow. The thread he yanked was beginning to unravel a whole, marvelous cloth. He now recalled his moment with Denver, Bonnie, Salem, Wes, and Evan behind the school, and the solstice circle with Dr. Blake at the vortex, and with Patrick and Marley in the desert... And, further back, to the road trip with his beautiful friends from Oregon, and the Tree Tribe, they'd met in Montana. Wow. He was in such awe of it, this divine energy that, as best he could figure, came from the center of Everything! His cheeks glistened with tears, not now tears of sorrow and despair, but of realization! Yes, he may yet have been alone, but now he had all of the company in the world!

Arien looked up to see the two soldiers staring at him. "I'm so sorry!" the one who'd tried to come in said to him. His face glistened with tears as well.

"Bring me a blanket right now!"

After sleeping for many hours, Arien awakened to a familiar face among a small cluster of soldiers.

"Jesus Christ!" Colonel Griffin shouted. He looked really mad. "The fucking idiots!" He personally came over to the cot. "I regret this, Arien, but I had no control over it." He held out a small key. "They took you away from me when you ran, but now that they've bungled it so bad... Here, if you're still wearing chains you can remove them."

Arien first regarded the man, taking him in before silently holding out his hands from under a blanket with his hollow, unblinking green eyes. It would have been difficult to release them himself. His wrists were cuffed too closely together. Colonel Griffin inserted and turned the key, then handed it to the boy who sat up to reach down to his ankles. Freed, they were sore, and ringed in red. It's not that they were too tight, but they would get yanked every time he raised his arms, or tried to get more comfortable. This was so bogus! Ah, now he could scratch and touch places he hadn't been able to reach. It had been incredibly frustrating. There was no way to touch his back. Just scratching the top of his head without having to take a fetal position was fantastic.

"Is my dog okay? What have they done with him?"

"I'll look into it."

"How about my friends? They were kind to me."

Griffin took a deep breath.

"I'll look into it."

The other men merely hung there, awaiting orders, listening, faces riveted to Arien.

"I need clothes."

"Of course, but maybe you'll want a shower, first."

"And I'm so hungry I could eat those guys." Two of them actually stepped back when Arien pointed at them, but he was in no mood to appreciate the humor in it.

"They told me it's been three days since you've had a meal," Griffin said.

"I thought it was forever."

"Have you had enough to drink?"

"I drank from the faucet over there. Where am I?"

"Outside of Pendleton. Come on, Arien, let's go. I'll show you where the shower is.

Nice touch, Arien considered. He cracked a wan smile in spite of himself, as he picked up the chopsticks on the table.

"Your doctor says to take it easy," Griffin said. "I thought Chinese would be a good mix and easy to break a fast on." But Arien was already shoveling beef with broccoli over steamed rice into his tummy.

It was absolutely delicious!

Griffin appeared to be impressed with the boy's nimble use of his sticks. "Slow down. Count the chews," he advised.

That and momentary indigestion accomplished it.

Griffin spread a napkin on his lap and pushed the plastic lid from his plate aside.

"So this never was very voluntary, was it?"

"Let me be perfectly honest, Arien, you are a highly valuable national resource requiring security. It's possible all the hullabaloo got somebody squeaking, as often happens with this kind of thing."

"I see the newspaper," Arien groused. "Hundred-thousand-dollar boy gets kidnapped by the US Army."

"You are astute, but I assure you that will not happen." Griffin handled his chop sticks well, but it appeared he had to think about it. "No, I'm concerned about other governments. By now, there may be more than one foreign agency actively looking for you."

Arien realized the irony of his destiny had him locked to a path like a rail car, whether subtle or overt; he wondered if it made any difference. 1969 seemed like paradise in retrospect. There, his direction proceeded naturally, among community, and he was coming into his own. This was starkly different, though a menace stalked him there as well.

He shivered. Mrs. Penny Waterson, one of his foster moms, used to say death passed over when that happened.

"So, what now?" Arien was almost afraid to ask, though he had to know.

Griffin waited to swallow. "There are two approaches. You've just seen one of them, the White Coats. To them, you're a fascinating monkey. They couldn't wait to wire you up and plug it in, but they didn't want to risk your going off someplace lost forever, so they were going to begin with pieces of you," he paused for effect, "maybe hair, perhaps a bit of flesh..."

Arien's face went white. "Holy shit," he whispered. "Well, why did they try to kill me?"

"Break you, not kill you, Arien. You terrify them, a lot like the people that were afraid a black hole would be created with the neutron collider experiment that would end-up eating the world. But" – Griffin chuckled – "you went ballistic on them. The suits started asking questions. I'm sure you heard it, and I was warned not to tell you about this, but fuck 'em, the ass holes, that was one of your guards put a bullet into his skull, and you saw the other one, crying like a little... he's washed up. The investment in that man is totally wasted. It would have been better if he'd shot himself, too."

Arien's appetite returned. This was fascinating. "So, what if I walk away again?"

"You won't, now that you know there are consequences. True, you have this interesting ability to find friends, but then you risk them as well, because you can't resist being yourself, can you? Think, if they remove me from project command again I will be done for, and the White Coats will always be waiting in the wings." He leveled a serious gaze at the boy. "My bet is you will not only cooperate but join in. It's your best shot at freedom, because you will be empowered along the way. That's my strategy, anyway. I happen to think we get more if the goose realizes its potential than if we cut it open to see where the gold comes from. You're not a monster. You're a kid, right?"

Arien actually considered that. He finished his meal and was fairly satisfied, but his heart was sorely troubled. His recent experience had been absolutely terrible. It had taken him to the edge of his sanity with more recklessness than any drug he'd ever consumed. He was full of resentment and imagined it would fester. And, he'd had goals of his own that helped keep him going. For now a full stomach's narcotic effect with his psychic exhaustion conspired to wipe him out. He yawned.

"I want to sleep," he said.

Arien had been given a small, efficiency apartment in the Officer's Quarter, a reserved part of a rectangular compound of barracks with a central dining hall, where he'd had his dinner with the colonel. It resembled various facilities an army base might have. Except for him, Colonel Griffin, a maintenance man who rode around in a golf cart, known as the EV, and a small troop of soldiers, the installation was strangely devoid of people. It was surrounded by a tall, electrified chain-link fence with razor wire on top (The "Live Voltage" lamps at intervals around its perimeter were unlit), and it was situated in the middle of a vast wheat field, now stubbly, crushed, and brown-dusted-white with winter, rolling over hills and valleys in all directions, perfectly isolating the camp and exaggerating the scale of the wide-open sky. He wondered about this place and what it was for. Griffin mentioned something about a FEMA camp, but that made no sense. The immediate reality was he was in no position to run anywhere because the compound's three gates were all shut and though the guardhouses were empty, he knew the gates were under surveillance. Though he may have been invested with the idea of free will, the evident reality was he would be staying put.

His first few days consisted of regular sessions with a couple of men who were introduced to him as doctors. They were very intense and personal as they probed him with every conceivable question to achieve, they explained, as complete a picture of him as possible. Though always on task they were pleasant, and he generally cooperated. When he didn't, insisting on being told what happened to his friends and his dog, Griffin apologized for the delay and asked for patience so sincerely, Arien gave in.

They also took hair and a blood sample. He was told it was for making a map of his genome. He wasn't sure what that was about. Colonel Griffin was always present, and accommodating as possible. He waved off the sessions as necessary preliminaries desired by his superiors and constituents. He had to keep them happy, he said, if he was to remain in charge.

Griffin also gave Arien an ankle bracelet with a device about the size of a small square of chocolate attached to it. It had a top that slid back when pressed along each side. It concealed a button to press if he ever needed help. This was a very curious thing. Why would he ever need help? It begged the question, what kind of help? When Arien imagined aloud it was really something to track him with, Colonel Griffin said, no that was installed with the Chinese dinner. Of course Arien questioned that. "It's a powder," Griffin explained, "Totally hush. The chips embed themselves in the intestinal wall where they're powered by chemical reaction, and their random quantity and configuration constitutes a unique electronic signature that broadcasts indefinitely. You will never go anywhere we can't find you." That simple revelation was easily as instantly eviscerating as his capture. Arien was now as lost as a soul in Hell. He had been transferred from one kind of imprisonment to another where he imagined the only remaining option of escape would be death.

Arien spent free time between the gymnasium, which came with a hot tub, sauna and a collection of basic work-out machines, and a broad garden area of about an acre that had been set aside in the northwest corner of the compound. It lay fallow, with weedy stalks and a few twiggy plants making it resemble a miniature grove of trees in their resting season. Arien liked coming here to be alone with his thoughts and for communion with the life around him, such as it was. He drew from the sky and the land and an occasional bird. Though he was very lonely for a close friend, he felt it less intensely here.

You will never go anywhere we can't find you echoed in his brain. It was scary, it was painful and it had to be unconstitutional, right? He mentioned that at breakfast. Hadn't his capture and treatment, and imprisonment against his will been illegal?

"There is nothing illegal when it comes to national security," Griffin answered. "That's the reality. Get used to it."

"Well, who decides what's national security?"

"Listen, Arien, I'm not going to bullshit you," Griffin retorted. "You are living proof of what has been theorized by only a few of the physicists, and a way to test the relevant hypotheses of all the rest. There's no telling what there is to learn about this, and what can be made from it."

"That sounds dangerous as Hell, to me."

"Exactly, Arien."

That's what the man said, that's just what he said, "Exactly..." Did Griffin realize? Weren't the people he served merely the other hand of who had so frightfully mistreated him? Arien never said that but he thought it. It was brutality, wasn't it? What was the value in serving such a system? He imagined that issue would have to be postponed for now. There was so much more to learn about this strange, authoritarian future where people seemed to go about their business as if everything was perfectly peachy when what he experienced was as creepy as his worst nightmare. How did it ever happen?

When he asked Griffin how they found him, he said it was a program that zeroed in on him.

"A program?"

"Yes, it's a computer program that establishes certain parameters around key words, your name, for a perfectly good example. It listens in, using patterns to sort it and narrow the search. Think of the game, Twenty Questions."

"You mean like, the over telephones?"

"Exactly."

"Oh, Dude! Isn't it illegal to listen to phone conversations?"

"Ah, it all depends on what we're listening for. National security, you know." He winked when he said that.

"How does it work?"

"Super computers, Arien. They're far ahead of what most people realize. That's a national security issue, too, you understand."

"But how?"

"They use logarithms, probability theory, and statistical analysis. That narrows it down to a likely and manageable number the spooks can physically scan." Almost as an afterthought he added, "It's specific. Most people have nothing to worry about because it's impossible for real people to actually listen in to everyone's conversations."

"I see..."

So, that made it okay? Wasn't the fact that such a system existed, and was actually being used, awfully scary? He sat on the ground wrapping his arms around the knees of the army fatigue pants he wore, and stared into the broad, gray sky where the thought dangled like a wisp of moisture. It smelled like it might rain or even snow. A lone bird flapped its way in a straight, westward direction. In Arien's daydream it was headed for Sandy. It would come first to Mount Hood and probably fly around the southern side, following the ribbon of highway as it switch-backed down steeply forested slopes to where it descended in a beeline toward the quirky, misty city at the confluence of distant rivers. He imagined it keenly, until he couldn't be sure if it was his imagination or he really saw it.

There were the little villages of varying sizes latching onto the road as it rose and fell, but mostly fell in elevation all the way to Sandy. The road divided there, sectioning the town into three parts, north of it, south of it, and the block-wide strip in the middle.

She had to be there someplace. Maybe she knew I was coming. She would have seen my face in the news like a ghost from the past and she awaited me, but maybe now I will never come. They will always know where I am! He didn't want to cry. He picked a rock out of the dirt and threw it. "Take this shit and go with the rock," he said, along the lines of stuff Andy and Hawthorne used to do. Oh God, that was such a sweet time!

At least nobody turned him in. He was a little ashamed for having thought that, but it was a near certainty Evan's frantic phone call to Denver's house had set his capture in motion. Just a phone call wherein his name was mentioned! If only he'd known. But he could not have known. Perhaps Griffin really was a friend. Cooperation would bring empowerment and that would... He could fantasize, anyway. Maybe he would beat them by joining them.

"Look, I'm only a lowly colonel still trying to reassemble the team," Griffin said, clipping his words to save breath on a jog together around the perimeter track. They weren't bursting for any finish line, but it was a brutal distance. Arien wished he hadn't made an earlier crack about old men in uniform. The guy must have been made of spring steel. Arien was only pushing himself now to save face, as he was past ready to drop-out. He'd asked about his friends again to take his mind off the pain in his side that always seemed to attend long runs. He was more of a sprinter than a jogger.

"What do you want, Colonel?" Arien's winded words sounded sloppy by his own standard, and it made him self-conscious.

"Good question, Young Fellow. Let's turn that around. What would be *your* goal?"

Arien had to concentrate to override the debilitating pain. "Try to find out how I did it?"

"You know, your friend, Mr. Newell wasn't all that cooperative, especially regarding where you might be going, or the associations between the two of you forty-three years ago, or the calculations he relied on to await you, but he did tell me about the celestial ship."

Oh Jesus, Andy…

"It's not for bullies," Arien huffed-out.

"I'll give you that." His eyes narrowed. "Arien, you're still human, or at least I'm inclined to believe you are, so don't go making something too special of yourself. You can bleed and die just like everyone else."

Arien couldn't go another step. He stopped suddenly, folding his body with hands on knees, gasping for fully-measured, deep breathing. "My side hurts," he allowed, as Griffin doubled back to him.

"Jesus, Kid, you're soft. You make a bag of marshmallows come off like the Rock of Gibraltar."

That struck Arien funny. He would have laughed if he'd owned the wind.

Griffin read him correctly, though. "You're amused?" he derided. It's pitiful! That's what it is, pitiful." After an audible click of his tongue, he turned away to continue on down the track.

Arien shaded his eyes with a hand to watch Griffin's steady jog diminish into sunlit-afternoon distance. He wondered if he were being taken for a fool, but he admired Griffin's no BS approach, his plausible directness, and now he was impressed with the man's condition, for an old dude. The boy really wished his own performance could have been better.

Griffin was his usual self over dinner. They ate in a private section of the staff dining room reserved for officers. There, Arien had the opportunity to become reacquainted with the colonel's adjutant, Lt. Jaffrey. He learned the young officer, whose blond hair was just long enough on top to part on the side, only graduated West Point a year earlier. He was an obviously fit and shiny young man who exuded intelligence and competence. His drawback, to Arien at least, was his personal reserve. Where Griffin appeared to be open and at ease, Jaffrey maintained a firewall that allowed only an efficient and businesslike attitude to filter through. It seemed unnatural. Arien saw him the day before briefly in the gym, and hoped to open a connection with him, but Jaffrey collected his towel and water bottle to slip out the opposite door. Was it deliberate avoidance?

"Hi," Arien said, locking on to Jaffrey after acknowledging the colonel's greeting.

Jaffrey nodded politely, but kept his lips together, taking his plain, white, cloth napkin and setting it properly on his lap.

"What's your name?"

"Jaffrey."

A soldier came out of the kitchen with a tray that he set on a bus stand by their table. He went about removing lids from plates.

"I know that," Arien teased. What's your first name?"

"Derik," the young man allowed.

Arien noted Griffin's curious observance of the exchange. Jaffrey had not been present for a meal with them before. It introduced a new dynamic.

"Where you from, Derik?"

"Henrico County, west of Richmond, Virginia," he said, reaching for his water, and pointedly looking at it instead of Arien.

"Did you grow up there?"

"Yes."

"I grew up in Portland, was born in Berkeley, though."

"Yes."

Chicken, mashed potatoes and string beans were set down. Arien dug in before the butter or gravy was passed.

"I hope you don't mind my choice of menu," the colonel offered.

"Go for it, Dude," Arien said, "but hold the powder."

"As you wish," Griffin said.

"What would you like to drink, Sir?" the soldier asked.

"Beers all around, Gentlemen?"

"Sure," Arien agreed. It reminded him of the plane ride from New York State.

"Where's my friend, Andy?"

"Since you ask, I'm working on getting him invited here," Griffin said.

"Oh wow!" Arien enthused, his spirits considerably buoyed. "For real, Colonel?"

"For real."

"Wow. How cool! Oh, oh, Dude. Wow." His eyes brimmed over with happiness. Oh, what a roller coaster this experience was! He set his fork down, too moved to take another bite.

Jaffrey brought a hand to his face, shooting a glance to the Colonel, who benevolently smiled. "Mr. Jaffrey, I have a favor to ask you."

The soldier from the kitchen returned with three bottles of Budweiser. He quietly set them down and left.

"Yes, Sir?"

"This boy is soft as a set of pillows. I know you keep up with your conditioning wherever we happen to be. I want you to take him under your wing, see what can be done with a seventeen year-old."

Jaffrey appeared to be completely taken by surprise. "Sir," he protested, "please, may I decline the honor?"

"No, Lieutenant," Griffin calmly replied. "Your engagement with this issue would be highly appreciated."

"Why not ask Sergeant Munoz, Sir?"

"I'll forget you asked that if you promise me you'll do a good job."

"I – I'll do a good job, Sir."

"Excellent. Are you okay with it, Arien?"

"Sure, Colonel," Arien agreed, with a trace of a smile. "Sir?"

"Yes?"

"Is there a computer on the base I could use?"

"What for?" Colonel Griffin cocked his head.

"The Internet, Sir."

"What do you know about the Internet, Arien?"

"Well, there's Facebook, and I-Tunes, and news and stuff. It'd be rad to check it out."

Griffin was working on a chicken thigh. He set it down. "We'll have to work on that. I need to know you can be trusted not to fill your head with bomb-making information in a quest for revolution. In the meantime, the flat screen in your room will be getting movie channels."

"Wow! Awesome!"

"Work on him, Lieutenant. I want him falling asleep watching good movies so he forgets all about the Internet."

That elicited a barely-stifled grimace from Lieutenant Derik Jaffrey and a deeper smile out of the boy at the Officer's Table.

Arien had been up since six, and even with scrambled eggs and bacon, and two cups of coffee down, he still felt groggy when he met the lieutenant at their agreed-upon time of 8 AM.

"I went to bed late last night," he said, in place of Good Morning after making eye contact.

Jaffrey seemed uncomfortable. He shifted on his feet in a gray sweat shirt and shorts just outside the entrance to the gym. The temperature had to be down in the upper thirties. With the damp air, it made a small cloud of exhaled breath collect around his head. But Arien read the young man's discomfort as psychic, not physical.

"We need to start with lights out at 10 PM," Jaffrey said. "Building your body requires proper rest."

"Yeah," Arien disdainfully agreed.

"You're not dressed right," Jaffrey continued. "The fatigue jacket and pants have got to go."

Arien summarily pulled the jacket off and dropped it to the frosty ground. Then, he untied the tennis shoes he wore so he could pull off his pants. He left that on the ground, too. He put his shoes back on, and stood there defiantly in the army boxer shorts that along with a variety of clothes fitting him were found neatly folded on shelves in the bedroom closet of his apartment.

Jaffrey regarded the kid with an unreadable assessment. "Let's go!" he ordered, beginning to jog in place.

Arien followed suit.

"Get your knees up. Hold you arms like this." He hung his arms loosely with his hands seeming to dangle off the ends, and then he moved away at a moderate pace.

Arien hustled to run alongside. They headed down a lane that was perpendicular to the border fence and the twenty feet or so of open, hard-packed pea gravel that defined its right of way. The only sound was feet crackling the surface. The chill air bit his legs and seeped through the hooded, olive-green US ARMY sweat shirt he wore. He strove to blend with the chill while concentrating on the workings of breath, muscles, and driving will, and he attempted to roll his gait to offset the likely, eventual side pain.

"Why were you up late?" Jaffrey asked.

"Rad movies, Dude."

The lieutenant allowed a smirk to betray his humanity. Arien admired the way Jaffrey moved, like a coiled spring. He was graceful, beautiful, in a way that contrasted favorably with the laid-back beauty of hippie dudes, like Otter.

"How old are you, Derik?" Arien asked as they came to the fence and made a ninety-degree turn to the right, to run along side of it. His effort stoked his furnace, making the temperature more tolerable. It almost felt silky against his legs. This was rad.

"I'll be twenty-four next month."

Wow, about Otter's age, and lovely Aspen, Hawthorne, Willow... Andy was a year or two older, but in there. This was another way to be. Rather interesting – a life on a career path.

"You have a girlfriend?"

"Not any more."

"What happened?"

"The job."

"Huh?"

"Half the time I can't say where I am. The other half, I'm a thousand miles away."

"Wow. Is it worth it?"

Jaffrey didn't answer.

"Is it worth it?"

"It's interesting. The colonel is great to work for. He's really connected. I've met all kinds of people, and been places I never thought I'd be."

"Like where?"

"Moscow, Beijing, Bern, Berlin, Paris, New York State, Tucson, DC, Pendleton." He actually grinned as he ended there. "And that was just in the last year."

"Have you ever got high, Dude?"

"Uh-uh."

"You need to get high, sometime."

"Not likely."

"What are you afraid of?" Arien realized they'd been running along and he was still free of side pain. Cool. He pushed the thought out of his mind else he jinx himself.

"It doesn't interest me."

"Not that," Arien phrased it. "You're afraid – of me, aren't you?"

Jaffrey cleared his throat, and spit off to the side. "Fuck you," he said.

"You remind me of my dad a little," Arien went on, un-phased. "He hated hippies. Straight arrow. He died in Viet Nam, you know."

The lieutenant didn't answer, but he did pick up the pace, which made it more difficult to converse.

Arien was thinking they'd gone a little far to make it back without losing his wind. At the faster pace the familiar body pain began to threaten in his lower-right side. Damn it! It was irritating. He didn't want to wus-out now. He worked at ignoring it.

"What are you afraid of, Derik?" he called. He visualized throwing the rock with a bad thought, but saw it aimed at plate glass. Still, the reaction was greater than he expected.

Lieutenant Derik Jaffrey turned on him like a whirlwind, throwing his hands out as Arien ran right into them. The action crossed a punch with a grapple. Seams tore in Arien's sweatshirt as his head vaulted forward, and Jaffrey lifted him right off of the ground, to throw him down, hard on the tightly-packed pebbles, and stand over him, huffing. "Don't fuck with me, you little shit! It's not going to happen!" he growled.

Arien gasped, winded by the concussion of his fall. But he knew he'd struck it out of the park when he smiled, as soon as he could, and it was a smile broad enough to flash his teeth. "Give me what you got, Soldier Boy!" he taunted.

What does a rib cage have to do with the ability to see? But the kick to his side was blinding. Arien discovered the connection in the awesome spear of pain. His body twisted and curled around it. It was beautiful! It was much better than smashing a puny little fist into barbed wire.

"Ahhhhhhhhhhhhhh!!!!!!!!!!" he roared, and it was a roar like a lion's. "I'm still alive, Soldier Boy!" he screamed. From where he lay on the ground he watched as Derik sank down next to him, elbows on knees, to cover his face with his hands.

"Who's the prisoner now?"

"Shut up, Kid. Please. Please shut up."

Was it worth it? The long, uneven, return walk punched him with every step. He had to breathe shallow. They didn't need words. Jaffrey sweated, though his exertion didn't warrant it at all. His solicitous walk alongside was enough.

They went into the gym where Jaffrey told Arien to sit on the first thing he could, which happened to be a sloping sit up bench. Arien closed his eyes to blend with a throb of pain, while apprehending the interior layout from the ka-clack of the door, and its subtle echo on the broad walls and windows inside. The room could have swallowed a hundred people but they were the only ones in there.

"Lift up your shirt."

Arien rolled it up on that side to reveal a keen, red blot over his curve of ribs.

"Fuck me. I'm so fucked," the young lieutenant rued. "I think I broke a rib or two."

"No, uh, I did, Derik." Arien smiled and winced in tandem.

The Woodstock Paradigm

"Shit! I don't know what got into me."

"I did."

That met with a readable stare, but it carried mixed messages that could have been variously explained.

"You are to be commended," Arien said, pleased to have found such imposing words. He allowed the shirt to drop back down. "You did promise to do good job." His chuckle was necessarily shallow, and a grimace or two escaped him.

"Jesus! What did you do, try to escape?" Griffin cracked when Arien shuffled into the colonel's Spartan office with his lieutenant close behind. There was an oak desk in there that had a sheet of Lucite on top, a computer keyboard and monitor sat on one side, a curved-neck desk lamp, and a land line telephone. Against one wall was a pair of old-style, oak, U-back office chairs, a pair of metal filing cabinets on the opposite wall, and a second door besides the entry, to a restroom. A window with blinds was behind the desk. That was it.

"Yes, I did, but Derik the Brave intercepted."

The colonel appeared to appreciate Arien's response. "Get it off," he ordered, flipping his finger around.

The boy did that, slowly, gritting his teeth.

"Can you hold you arms over your head?"

"Maybe he should have an X-ray," Jaffrey suggested.

"Up here! Hold 'em up. Touch my hand." He held a hand up over Arien's head.

Arien clenched his teeth, but managed to tap Griffin's hand. He practically had to hold his breath.

"Keep 'em there." He lightly pressed on the affected area.

"Ow, ow."

"Keep 'em up!" He stepped around behind to take hold of Arien by the wrists and slowly, he pulled the arms back, arching the boy's spine.

"Oh, God, that hurts so good!" Arien hissed, feeling the man's fingers trace the curve of his ribs, pushing against them slightly, probing.

"These two may be cracked, but they're holding," the colonel observed. "You're good. But we want to watch for swelling. So far, it's only bruised on the surface. No knobs, no weird shapes. You're good. Uh, let me know if there's any change in your breathing or irritation down under that."

He turned to his adjutant. "Okay, let's debrief," he said.

"I was horsing around in the gym and fell backwards," Arien interjected.

184

Griffin looked at him.

"And I hit it, uh, against a weight machine."

"Are you quite finished?"

Arien nodded the affirmative.

The colonel returned his gaze to Jaffrey.

"Sir, I, uh, we had an altercation, Sir."

"And?" Colonel Griffin half sat off the edge of his desk, keeping his hands at his sides. It was disarming.

"I kicked him, Sir."

"While he was on the ground?"

"Yes Sir."

"That becomes you, Lieutenant."

Jaffrey's face flushed crimson.

"Arien."

"Yes?"

"I'm doing my best, and I've leveled with you. Don't ever lie to me again; even to save this man's neck, is that clear?"

"Yes Sir," Arien responded, unconsciously straightening up.

"Your movies are pulled and your beer privilege is revoked until further notice. Now, go to your apartment and stay there until tomorrow. Is that clear?"

"Sir?"

"Yes?"

"I'm sorry."

"Very good. You are both dismissed."

Jaffrey hesitated.

"Yes?"

"Is that all, Sir?"

"You are dismissed, Lieutenant."

17 – Oh, sweet Mother and Father

Arien was bored to extinction. There was nothing to do. He couldn't exactly do push ups, and it didn't even feel good to touch his body. A sunny day taunted him with its untimely break in the week's gray trend. A scheduled meeting with a physicist and a theoretical mathematician was cancelled, which spoke volumes about Griffin's seemingly unfettered ability to orchestrate the particulars of his command. There were some writing materials here and a few magazines but they had been removed by Corporal Donnal, a gangly red-headed soldier Arien had seen around. Donnal explained the colonel wanted him to think about what he'd done without any distractions. Wow.

What did I do? He lounged on his bed like he was pinned by a twelve-foot four-by-four balanced upright on the side of his chest. Jaffrey's consequence was a moment's embarrassment. Was that right? Could there be anything in the Army's rulebook that permitted such behavior from an officer? What did this suggest about Colonel Griffin? Maybe Griffin oversaw a picture too broad for Arien to wrap his mind around, which made him seem god-like, in some respects. If it was a normal world, say, and the colonel was one of Arien's teachers in school, wouldn't he be standing head and shoulders above the rest? The dude was amazing!

Arien grasped his responsibility, however. He knew how he could get inside of people with his feelings and emotions. It wasn't quite pure manipulation because everyone works through a contact high in their own way, but when he'd added his own frustrated thoughts to the mix, his 'elimination' as it were, it invited Derik's rage. Was this a misuse of his talent? Didn't it work as he'd suspected it would – but perhaps too well? Could the guile of ancient demons, Frustration, Anger, and Resentment take everyone near along with him to the Dark Side?

He was grateful to Andy for supplying this line of reasoning to his repertoire. Andy once told him the ancient psychology was a 'pseudo-science' called demonology. He recalled an awesome conversation they'd had in Medicine Bow where the Tree Clan had their camp. For his example he told Arien to think of a drunk, "...you see somebody in your head, right?

And... that's basically the same guy everywhere; that drunken guy is the same in every country. We all recognize his face." And he also said, "It's extremely hard to outsmart them and get your balance back if they ever get hold of you."

He really found himself thinking about this stuff, which obtusely reminded him of an older consideration of luck. Did this apply here? He was a captive, after all, but he could have been remanded to another version of Hell instead of Colonel Griffin. The attempt to 'break him,' as Griffin contended, turned-out to be problematical, but what if Griffin wasn't available to try again? Try what? This was mind-bending.

What did they want from him? What made him so valuable he could not be permitted to find his own way? Was civilization everywhere like this? Someone was always taking charge, and owning everything, and forcing people by whatever means to do it their way.

What was it about Woodstock? Was it about the performances of rock stars? Was it about just being – here, now? Or, was it energy uncorked by a perfect storm of unique conditions that freed a mythic genie? Did the particular assembly of officiates who made up the Circle of the Tree Clan require a Woodstock to make it happen?

There was a tap at his door.

"Yeah?" he called out.

It wasn't locked, but the knob turned one way, and then the other before the door slowly swung open. It was Derik Jaffrey. He was strange, not his usual direct, businesslike self, but hesitant. "Can I come in?" he asked.

"I'm not going to stand in your way, Derik. You've got a killer kick."

An uncertain smile flickered over Jaffrey's face. He stood there, looking a little out-of-place in his sharp Class B outfit, beret, trench coat, and broad, yellow ribboned pants.

"Sit down, Dude." Arien motioned to the swivel chair by a small writing desk in his room. He pulled himself up against the backboard of his bed. He still wore the shorts he ran in that morning, a white T-shirt and sox.

Jaffrey took the chair, sitting ramrod straight at first, but then easing against the back support, and spreading his elbows on the armrests, as if ordering himself to sit 'at ease.'

"Uh, the colonel doesn't know I'm here," he opened, pushing a shiny-black shoe out from under the coat.

"So?"

"This is new for me, Arien. You're a civilian, technically a guest, not a prisoner, so, I suppose me being here doesn't qualify as unauthorized fraternization..." He dangled his sentence.

"Sounds like bogus elimination, Dude. What's this about?"

The boy's tone counter intuitively put Jaffrey more at ease. "Something happened back there," he said.

"Yeah?" Arien pulled a knee up and rested an arm on top. It was painful but he overruled any reaction to it. He wanted to model relaxed and ready to listen.

"Look, Kid, I'm a guy, you know? I'm not a monster. I used to hang with my friends, just like you, but I made a commitment, and my duty is to my country."

Arien blurted the pulse of a laugh with a short blast of breath, and shook his head. "Jesus," he marveled.

Jaffrey blushed, coiled and uncoiled his fists, and took a deep breath. "You know, I'm sorry. I feel like shit. I lost control. This, this whole thing can't be easy for you. I sincerely apologize."

That felt pretty good. Even though Arien protectively tempered his glow, when he held out his hand Jaffrey got out of the chair to gratefully take it.

Jaffrey appeared momentarily confused when the offered palm was pulled back and then fist-tapped to his knuckles. But he wasn't a total dork. He clearly got it. His smile was genuinely glad. "You're a beautiful kid," he said, lingering as Arien's glowing warmth intensified.

Arien knew he was still playing with fire.

Derik dropped his nearest hand on the teenager's stretched-out foreleg and gave it a squeeze. By itself, it was innocent enough but he blushed again. "I – I better get going," he said, in a wavering tone. "If I don't see you later, uh, Happy New Year, Kid."

"Oh, fuck," Arien whispered to himself when the lieutenant was gone. He wished me Happy New Year! "Jesus, it's, it's New Year's Eve!" he said aloud to the empty room. "He likes me, poor bastard, and it's going to eat him for breakfast."

Arien didn't sleep well, being entangled in a recurrent dream where he was hopelessly lost in a crowded, foreign city, and he'd become separated from Buster. He blamed himself, and awoke more than once sick with worry over the dog. The worst part was he could do absolutely nothing about it, and awakening was no relief. In another dream, he was in a traffic accident with his sweet, young, topless mother. The pain in his side was from the collision. Covered with Woodstock mud, he was hauled away in an ambulance screaming, "You have to go back for my mom!" So, Arien was out of his bed before the light of morning began to reveal the world.

Movement brought yesterday's injury into focus, though he was mobile and functional. He peeled his T-shirt off in stages, one arm at a time, and stood in front of the mirror in the bathroom to check out the bright purple shiner. He tapped it lightly with his fingers. There was some swelling. Though a spontaneous deep breath was rebuked, Arien could inflate his lungs near to capacity, slowly. Not too bad.

His thoughts turned to the unexpected encounter with Derik. Arien naturally connected it with Andy. But that was different. Andy wasn't responsible for anything other than himself. This guy risked too much. No wonder Derik had been so guarded! There are so many kinds of pain, and they all hurt. It would have been something to ask Cypriano about if he only could. And, he considered, what would Otter say? Andy, now, would be a Godsend. Like, he needed this! The anxiety strung him so tightly he feared he would snap.

The sun was higher by the time Arien made his way from his apartment down the broad avenue from the barracks to the big, empty cafeteria and the officer's mess. There, he came upon a most unexpected thing; Derik and Colonel Griffin were already seated, but the sweetest little puppy ever was romping around Colonel Griffin's outstretched hand. "Happy New Year, Arien!" the colonel greeted, and Jaffrey's hopeful expression seconded the motion.

As soon as the gamboling ball of fur was aware of Arien, it made a clumsy, floppy beeline to him. "Aw," Arien cooed, carefully scooping it up in his arms. It wiggled, licking his lips while he kissed and hugged it in return.

"Where'd he come from?"

"Oh, I ran into him on a run to Pendleton yesterday afternoon. I brought him back with me because I thought you could use a friend, Arien."

It took no time at all. His torrent of grief came like a rupture of the dam over Johnstown. He collapsed as his limbs gave way. "Buster, Buster!" he wailed. The most curious thing was the puppy whelped right along, screaming and crying out, trembling; a puddle of piss formed under its legs.

"I'm sorry Arien," Griffin said.

"Oh, my God, Kid, please stop!" the lieutenant called out.

"What happened?" Arien cried, his chest so suddenly crushed under turbulent currents and leagues of sorrow, he was losing his ability to breathe. The puppy threw itself against his face, whelping, and licking at his tears. And he knew that was the lieutenant who sat down by him, taking his shuddering body in his lap to cradle his head and stroke his hair.

"It's okay, Kid," the lieutenant soothed. "It's okay." He actually dropped tears of his own. Arien knew because he felt their splatter on his hair, and then Derik planted a kiss right on his forehead.

But Arien really wasn't breathing. He could distantly hear Derik yell something to that effect, and vaguely feel the young man's scuttle to alter position where he could come to press down hard on Arien's chest, again and again.

"One, two, three, four..." the colonel counted.

Arien knew he was in the infirmary. He'd seen it before on a short tour they'd had. His first sight was blowing sleet outside hitting the window and the next was the face of an old man sitting in a chair pulled up next to his bed. Then he could feel the hand grasping his. "Oh rad!" he sighed, flickering a tired smile. "It's so good to see you, Andy!" Tears again, damn it! He thought, with exasperation. His image of Andy grew blurry.

"Oh, Lad," Andy said with a misty-eyed chuckle, "Griffin must be at his wit's end for them to come get me the way they did!" He sounded happy and that really helped. "Here," he added, setting the puppy down on the bed. It ran right for Arien's face, and it coaxed a giggle out of him.

"He said if it didn't stop crying he was going to shoot it."

"They're not going to do that, Puppy. They wouldn't dare!" The pup jumped happily onto Arien's chest, which revealed such sensitivity it made him jerk. "Oh, fuck! What the... It's so sore!"

"Your angel was here, Arien," Andy told him. "Griffin said he thought for a moment you were running away for good."

"Ha!" He distracted the puppy to his side where it playfully tried to bite his fingers. "Have you had the Chinese dinner yet?"

"Can't say that I have, why?"

Arien smirked. "Oh, then I won't say, Andy. It's a matter of national stupid security."

"I'll bet it is."

"Yeah, really! It's this powder that's really some kind of chips. They put it in your food, but you never know. It sticks in your intestines and broadcasts a signal they can track you with."

"Oh my!" Andy grew sober, evidently contemplating the issue.

"Where have you been?"

"Until yesterday, I was still in Arizona," he said, leaning in his chair. "It really got obtuse when they put me in a glorified cell. They wouldn't even let me make that call to a lawyer."

"That's nothing, Dude. The bastards! I got a dungeon! It's right here on this base, too, or camp, or whatever the Hell it is."

"I know. The colonel told me about that unfortunate bit of stupid bungling."

"Our Buster's gone," Arien sighed.

"Yes. Very sad. I loved that dog. Buster was a good, reliable, intelligent friend. But Griffin made a good call with this puppy here."

"Nothing's going to take Buster's place."

The pup was getting more rambunctious. He had a cute growl aimed at Arien's hand. He was diving and biting at it.

"No, I agree, and nothing should. But the pup will help fill a hole that's there, regardless."

"What's his name?"

"That's your call, Arien."

"He's a cute little guy."

"He likes you."

"Everybody likes me," Arien sadly said.

Andy took a deep breath. "Speaking of which, Colonel Griffin's a very interesting man. One of the things we discussed was his, uh, somewhat compromised adjutant."

"Wow. What'd he say?" Arien scooted up, the better to flip his hand about for a puppy toy.

"He said his lieutenant lost it when you passed-out. He cried like a baby, cuddled and kissed you. A soldier might as well stick a gun to his head, he said." Andy chuckled, rolling his hands together. But, get this, Arien, then he tells me, he must have lost it, too, because he decided the hapless lieutenant would certainly die for you, and that might be useful.

"Radical," Arien marveled. "Did he tell you about this?" He pulled his T-shirt up to expose the big blotch of purple on his side, only to see the other one plastered in the center of his chest!

"Oh my, no. He didn't get into the particulars, but did suggest something had gone down. Of course I thought maybe you let him suck you off." Andy winked, affecting a devious grin.

"Not yet," Arien responded, returning it.

"Ah, sweet milk of the beloved," Andy sighed. "In all these years, I've never forgotten it."

Arien studied him. Had he changed, gotten bolder? Maybe there's something about old men that doesn't care. It's another wavelength. I'll probably never be that old.

"Nine times, you little stud. You came nine times!"

"Andy?"

"Yes?"

"Shut up."

Andy chuckled again. He did appear to be in a very good mood. He fidgeted a lot. His hands were busy, folding, entwining fingers, twiddling thumbs.

Do old people usually do this?

"What's he going to do?"

"That's just it, he's undecided. He actually asked my advice on the matter. He presumes a lot of us, I think."

"The dude's really smart, Andy."

"No doubt. We chatted a bit. He's leaning to letting it play out. He understands just the right balance of respect, and love, he said – if that's what it takes, with devotion to duty on the part of people working with you will be the best approach. You have to be insulated like plutonium in a reactor, though. Those are the very words he used. Assembling the right team will be difficult." Andy opened his hands expressively. "Amazing, really; the poor adjutant's expendable, I guess, and that's all part of the risk in his strategy. He said he's only begun to gauge the breadth of your potential." Andy leaned forward. "But it's tricky going. A mistake could jeopardize the whole program. You are in great danger, my Beloved Boy."

"Dude, I'm so glad you're here!" Arien knew his tears drove the point forward.

Andy, all radiant, stood, leaned over and embraced him.

After Arien's close call, he got word Griffin decided his own background training as a medic and first-responder inadequate to meet all possible emergencies, so the Army sent a doctor to be on the staff. Captain McMillan, a slender, light-brown-haired man of about thirty, was an intern who arrived ahead of his security clearance for this assignment. He was therefore not allowed to be alone with Arien, although he was not privy to that directive. Lieutenant Jaffrey told Arien that, asking the boy for his sake not to see the doctor without letting him know.

It was Arien's release day from the infirmary. The doctor wanted him to walk everywhere while being guided by his pain threshold and energy level, instead of using the EV, which Griffin offered for the duration of his convalescence. He was given Ibuprofen for discomfort and told to limit them to no more than four at one time, preferably in the morning and evening. Arien summarily dunked eight, hoping to catch a buzz. McMillan otherwise gave Arien a good bill of health, considering the accumulation of violence to his body, and that lent his alleged physical shut-down, from McMillan's perspective, a level of mystery. Arien couldn't respond to that. It was understandable enough to him.

"I can make my heart stop anytime I want," he asserted, not at all admitting he'd been slammed with grief.

"That's ridiculous," the doctor scoffed.

Lieutenant Jaffrey was there, having been assigned to monitor Arien's last check-up, and to accompany him to breakfast. "Yeah, he is prone to exaggeration, Sir," he said, jumping up from a chair he'd taken. "Come on, Arien, let's go." He put his hand on the boy's arm.

"Fuck you, Derik!" Arien spat, jerking away. "I can prove it."

"Ha!" the captain derided. "I'd like to see that!"

"Please, Sir, beg your pardon, but we have to go now." Lieutenant Jaffrey appealed, the color draining from his already light-complexioned face.

"No, Lieutenant, sit back down. This boy is going to perform for us."

"I'm sorry, Sir, I'm under orders to—"

"You will sit down right now and be quiet, or you will leave my office! I'm your superior as well as this boy's doctor, and I find the issue relevant to understanding his condition."

Arien sat on the examination bench. He had to take several deep breaths to calm himself. There was no way he was going to let some bozo defy his truth. When he caught the relevant thread within himself it invited his defiant smile. Touch this, you ass! He pointed to the center of his chest. His smile remained as he fell into the hole, allowing breath to escape. Rolling his eyes up, he already apprehended a gathering resonance in the concussion of distant breakers on the beaches of the world. He barely felt the cool pressure of the stethoscope as his heart's rhythm retreated, lub - dub, lub - dub, lub...

McMillan's smug expression was summarily confounded.

"My God!" he blurted, moving the chest piece in his fingers quickly under the boy's shirt, from one place to another, as if expecting to find a heart beating here, if not over there. Then he took a flabbergasted step back, still listening.

Poor Jaffrey, his face flushed, visibly sweated.

"This is no exaggeration!" Captain McMillan declared, with a note of alarm.

Arien's thought, *Blessings Be*, hung in his inner sky like a soaring bird. I am free! Oh, sweet Mother and Father of All, I am free!

They told him later a smile remained on his face the entire time he was away. Arien also appreciated how lucky he was Andy was around for that little escapade. He was close enough to arrive, literally running, bursting into the infirmary all out of breath on the one hand, yet able to prevent an overly invasive response to the situation on the other. Nobody called him, either. He just knew. "Don't touch him! Let him be!" he cried, just as McMillan was about to apply the defibrillator.

Lieutenant Jaffrey was a wreck at that point. He'd walked out of the building exactly when McMillan was beginning to poke and tap at the boy who had utterly suspended his personal animation. When he returned with Colonel Griffin, Andy was already there, and the colonel was famously concerned for yet another unanticipated situation. "It's good you called me when you did, Lieutenant," he guardedly said, but the sinews of his neck were drawn out with his clenching jaw.

Then he addressed the doctor,

"Captain McMillan."

"Sir."

"You may know I requested a Major Lundquist, from Ft. Campbell, who was not available."

"I did not know that, Colonel."

"Well, what matters is you're not familiar with this case and you need to bring yourself up to speed with the briefing you were posted before your transfer. I can see that hasn't happened."

"I have not received the briefing, Sir."

"Sir," Lieutenant Jaffrey interjected, "It may be because the captain arrived before his security clearance."

"What's going on here?" McMillan asked. He turned to the boy near him who was still sitting erect off the side of the examination bench. McMillan took a penlight out of his pocket and shined it in one of Arien's eyes. Only the whites could be seen under the half-closed eyelids. "He's catatonic!"

"He's gone into deep meditation," Andy said with a satisfied look. "He's had no education in this. I know he's done it a few times before. Now he's figured out how to do it easily, on demand. It's magnificent! He's a natural."

"And, he's classified," Colonel Griffin said to the doctor.

A side of Arien could hear and see all of this, though it was such a very small part of him it didn't matter. What mattered was the plight of his friends. He looked for them with his inner eye, a beam of light in the great, dark abyss. He already knew the universe existed within his being. The Knowing was there. He only had to see them from the inside. So far, Arien's connection through trauma was established, though he was loath to face it. He took it as a terror that stalked him. He recalled leaving San Francisco with Tina, Otter, Andy, and Jeff. They were originally returning to Portland to pick up Blue Star, who was left behind to settle affairs while they delivered him to the Bay Area to meet the dad he'd never known. The plan was to scoop Blue up for their run to the mythic concert in August. Well, it didn't happen that way. Hearing about a friend being brutally slain is horrific enough, but to be there, to feel it from the inside as it were, that was a different animal. Otter remarked at one point they travelled with a boy seer. It was small consolation.

Then he remembered something attributed to John Lennon by a wrung-out Viet Nam Vet he'd met on the streets, *Life is something that happens to you while you're busy making other plans.* That could just as easily be Death, yes? It came to mind at the time, though he couldn't recall if he'd said so or not. No matter. Better not to play with other people's deep shit. Let them say their piece and take what you need. It was a grain of wisdom beyond his years, perhaps, but he wasn't stupid, and that also helped him survive.

Now he returned to the infirmary of this strange installation in Oregon. The resting muscle quivered with the lick of his will. He entered through a cacophony of blood sucking and pushing with the roar of mighty breakers on the beaches of the world. Lub-dub, lub-dub... His eyes opened in an oddly sorrowful but also compassionate light.

"Wow," Lieutenant Jaffrey said, seeming to summarize McMillan's opinion as well. The doctor's eyebrows and cant of his hand asked permission to use the stethoscope one more time.

"Namasté," Andy warmly greeted.

Griffin appeared troubled. He regarded the boy with an otherwise unreadable face.

"Normal," McMillan reported.

"It's hard to believe they're still not home," Arien dropped, stepping into a spring of indignation. "Why are you holding everyone?" He could see the colonel's initial surprise turn to confusion, slide into retreat, but then, ultimate regrouping. Arien caught himself too late, suspecting he'd just made an important mistake.

"I agree," the colonel answered, grasping hands behind his back. "That whole approach stinks."

"What is he referring to?" the captain asked.

"I don't know if I believe you," Arien retorted.

"Let's take this outside."

"Let's just take it, Dude. What's going on? You have to tell me, now!"

"Oh, my!" Andy exclaimed.

"Yes, Andy. It's not just you. They haven't let anyone go!" Arien slid off the bench. "You've known this all along, Colonel. I'm sure you have. It sucks. Do you get it – how much it sucks?"

"I may be back on the mission, Arien, but some things take time."

"You've still got everybody who helped him?" Andy asked. "You can do that?"

"They harbored an underage boy, a runaway. No new laws had to be enacted. But let me make it perfectly clear, it was not my decision! I counseled everyone be set free immediately. I'm sure most would be quiet. No one would believe such a story anyway; at least nobody that mattered."

"How do you know about this?" Jaffrey asked Arien, obviously impressed.

"How many people are we talking about?" Andy asked.

Arien held his tongue.

"Do you know?" Griffin coaxed.

"I can guess."

"Good grief!" Andy spat. "The longer innocent people are held the deeper the hole you're digging!"

"They're not so innocent. They aided and abetted him."

"You're an asshole," Arien calmly observed.

"This is not a game, Young Fellow. I need you to be patient, especially now. If we're going to resolve any of this we'll have to work together. Please try to see that. You need to trust me." Griffin sounded sincere.

"What's your reason for holding these people?" Andy pressed.

"That's classified."

"Shall I leave the room?" McMillan asked.

"Don't bother. It's still classified," the colonel repeated.

18 – The true jewel

"We've hardly had time to talk," Andy said when Arien was released from the infirmary. They were headed to the officer's quarter. "You have to wonder if we're dealing with Machiavelli."

"Who's that?"

"He was–"

"Wait," Arien interrupted. "Let's go this way. I want to show you where I like to go to be alone."   His chest still felt soundly pounded from the colonel's CPR, so he walked slow and consciously.

"Is it far?"

"I'll be okay, Andy."

They went a good distance, crossing either a parking lot or a parade ground large enough to land a plane. A helicopter rested in a marked-out area to the south center. A small hangar and non-descript sheet-metal buildings stood nearby. Everything was quiet and closed-up, seeming lonely under the wide-open gray sky. A few snowflakes floated down.

Arien spoke quietly to the pavement. "If you look, you'll see cameras all over the place, Andy. Maybe they're listening, too. I didn't want to be around any buildings."

"Hmmm..., you think they're bugged, huh? I guess it's certainly possible."

"I didn't want to go there," Arien rued. "But this shit with the friends I've made, putting them through a bummer," he recounted, throwing out a word from the old days; "It makes me think I need to shut up once in awhile."

"You know, that's an impressive analysis, Arien."

"Poor Denver and Bonnie had a shitty New Years because of me." He was sick at heart thinking about it. "Damn it!"

"Don't beat yourself up. It wasn't your fault."

"Colonel Griffin learned something new today," the boy continued. "It was too easy. I need to make him work for it, or at least have something to trade if I ever need it."

Andy was contemplative. His hands went in his pockets. He looked like a rumpled professor with a bulky sweater under a tweed sport jacket, like they'd found him some second-hand clothes to suit his personality. He hadn't shaved in a few days and the gray shadow was on his jaw and cheeks. "I'd say you learned something new today as well," he said, with a kindly smile.

At length they passed through an animal gate, and beyond its quarter-acre enclosure, another gate opening to the big, ragged field.

"What did they tell you?" Arien asked, carefully swinging it open. He wondered when the Ibuprofen would ever kick in, and considered the uncomfortable proposition it already had.

"Pretty much what I see here," Andy answered.

"And?"

"Griffin said he needed me. This is longer than... Are you okay?"

"I'm hangin'. It's not far from here. Did he give you anything?"

"What do you mean? Oh! That reminds me... He did give me this." Andy reached in a flapped-pocket of his jacket and pulled out a shiny object strung on a leather thong, like a boot lace.

"Oh my God, Andy! I thought that was gone!" Arien exclaimed, joyfully taking the silver Om that was offered. He'd discovered it missing after they'd cut off his clothes and left him in chains in that frightful room. It was a terrible blow, but it fell in and got lost with all the other blows that terrible day. This really meant a lot. Oh, for the highs and lows of his ride!

"Where did you get that, anyway – at Woodstock?"

"No, your friend, Michael gave it to me when we left Page Street."

"But I don't–"

"You weren't with us yet. Otter turned us around and we picked you up on the way. Don't you remember? That was so bitchin', Andy."

Andrew shrugged.

"The sound of everything," Arien whispered, hanging the sacred letter back around his neck. He raised and kissed it, releasing a short, giddy laugh.

"Oh, Michael!" Andrew sighed. "Wow. I forgot him. I wonder where he is now."

"Really."

"He could be dead," the old man mused.

"Or, alive and prospering," Arien hoped aloud. Then he said, "So, did he give you – did he offer you anything?"

"Griffin?"

"No, Machovelli."

Andy smiled. "Machiavelli," he corrected. "Yes, I suppose he did. He offered to clue me in for my help."

"Dude, it's snowing!"

The light stuff that had been drifting down thickened to big, fluffy flakes, suddenly dense enough to white everything out.

"Oh my, we could get lost out here in this," Andrew realized.

"I wonder if the chips in my gut would tell them we died out here."

"You're funny, Arien."

"They would find my body, though, unless you had time to burn it, first."

"And scatter the ashes?"

"Yeah," the boy agreed, with a *got ya* laugh meant for Colonel Griffin. Then he asked, "For your help with what?" And he watched while Andrew pondered the question.

Arien awoke well before the sound of reveille from the speaker on his living area wall. He didn't bother to get out of bed. Another morning of Buster not licking his face instigated a good choking sob. It's funny how a dog can worm its way into your heart. Buster surely had. The puppy cried right along with him and it appeared they shared a thing or two. Arien had him in a large cardboard box so he wouldn't have the run of the place all night and leave a mess, but his insistent whelping got the little critter invited to bed. He licked at Arien's wet cheeks now, so Arien grabbed him on an impulse and licked him back, from his nose to the top of his furry, tan head. Gross, he thought, but funny. He'd never licked a puppy before. He could really smell it. His tongue was delighted with the squirmy little life it stroked. Wow. Crazy. The little guy was so cute!

Ignoring reveille sent another, inevitable invitation finally answered by a tap on his door. It might be Andy, but he knew it wasn't before Lieutenant Jaffrey entered.

"Did you join the Navy?" Arien asked, checking out Jaffrey's white outfit.

"Good morning, Arien," Jaffrey opened. "No, it's battle dress white, for snow."

"What's up?"

"You're not. Tell you what, though, you've got to cut it out." Jaffrey came over to sit on the side of the bed. "I've been feeling sad for no reason except you." His hand found a wet spot on the blanket. "Puppy needs to go out," he added.

"Aretha Franklin said, 'It's too late, Baby, it's too late.' Arien recalled the line from his time in the Haight, though he wasn't sure about the song. He tried to smile.

"How's your body?"

"Sore."

"How am I supposed to toughen you up like that?"

"It'll have to wait, I guess." Arien scooted up and scratched the puppy on his lap with both hands. "Tell me what happened to Buster?"

"I don't know. I wasn't there."

Arien nodded, noting the young lieutenant regarded him rather intently. "You need a girlfriend," Arien admonished.

"You don't know what I need." Jaffrey looked away when he said that.

"I'm all ears, Dude." Arien folded his arms just below the contrast of silver Om and bruising, but the puppy seemed distracted, and then focused into crying.

"He's hungry."

"His chow's in your kitchen cabinet."

"Thanks Derik." But it wasn't so easy. Arien slept in the buff, and though hippies were laid-back enough about nakedness to be proud of it, Derik was no hippie. He was a lieutenant in the United States Army. Fuck it. The dude wasn't getting up. Arien got out the other side of the bed and went for the chow. He turned to see the lieutenant looking away. That was strange, because a certain tension in the air tightened like a string. Be cool, he told himself. It's a test. The dude is older. Can I be a man around him?

The puppy flopped onto the floor after Arien, to race behind.

"You're a beautiful kid," Jaffrey said. He returned his gaze and now firmly riveted his eyes.

"You told me that before." Arien yanked the little can's tab and lid back, dumped it into a cereal bowl from the shelf and set it down for the hungry pup. Then, he went to the box for its water bowl, and considered what to do next. He thought about breathing. An exhale was letting go. The very idea made him feel dizzy in the head. I like girls, but I've been horny as fuck... When I wasn't crying...

"Wow, that's the coolest tattoo. Mind if I see it?"

The boy looked down at his near graphically-perfect, butterfly-shaped birthmark that appeared to alight on the border of his pubic hair, knowing it was hard to miss, even from across a room.

The eyes were there, the hunger. A handsome, powerful young man in white stood and set out toward him along with a rush of blood to his head.

But then there was a knock at the door!

A silent laugh spread over Arien's face. Jaffrey appeared suddenly stricken, eliciting a now audible laugh from the boy. That was another kind of rush, like the heady one that assumes power to abuse. He simply walked to the door and opened it. "Yes?"

"Oh, Arien, I see you're not dressed," Andy keenly observed in the entrance, "And I'm pleased to see so much more of you today!"

Arien reached out and let Andy grip him in a bear hug. It felt great, really. His heart soared.

Andy's eyes were rimmed with wet when they finally moved apart.

Arien stepped back with a wholesome grin. By now Andy saw the lieutenant standing in the room. He nodded to him. "Good morning Lieutenant."

"Good morning Mr. Newell."

"I'm not uh–"

"Oh no," Jaffrey too-cheerfully replied.

"Good, well, I wanted to see how you were doing, Lad. You didn't join us for breakfast."

Arien made his way to the closet for fresh boxers on the shelf, then pulled on the Universal Camouflage Pattern fatigue pants he'd left on the floor last night. He still had to move consciously with his sore chest, but discerned a flexibility that boded well. "I needed my beauty rest," he said.

"I'll see you later, Arien,"

"Later, Derik."

"That was interesting," Andy commented when Jaffrey was gone.

Arien pulled on a T, and got into the lose-fitting shirt matching his camo pants. The shirt had no patches or name tag. "It makes me doubt the room is bugged," he ventured to say, buttoning it. "If it was..." his thought dangled, "he would know, right?"

"Oh, well, then, what did he say?" Andy sat in one of four black, fiber-batted, folding chairs flanking low end tables in the living area. Besides the bed, desk, and desk chair, a folding table and four metal folding chairs in the kitchenette, these comprised the furnishings. The floor was unpainted, polished and sealed concrete. The bare walls were off-white. It was very simple though not unpleasant because the light was good. There were two big, double-paned windows that opened and a plastic-bubble skylight as well.

"He said what he was feeling – or at least he started to." Arien picked the puppy up to sit with it in his lap. "He told me I was beautiful."

"Not what you would expect," Andrew mused.

"No, Dude, not like soldiers in the movies."

Andrew smiled.

"I thought about what you said yesterday," Arien continued, petting the little critter. It yawned.

"Oh?"

"And what you didn't..."

"Like what?"

"Did you promise anything?"

"To be truthful," Andy said, "but you had to promise that, too, right?"

"And what did he promise you?"

"Well, first of all, you – and I, are considered guests. The brutality you experienced was unfortunate, as was my own detention. He made that clear. It was bad. He put it like, well, we're moving past that; we're stepping up for our country now."

"Are we free, then?"

"Theoretically, but we have a job to do. We can't just walk away."

Arien took a deep breath.

"Are you being totally truthful with me, Andy?"

Andy appeared hurt.

"Of course."

"This whole thing... this, this *job to do*!" He spoke the words like a tainted flavor. "Tell me, what do you think they want from us?"

"Certainly, Arien. What do you want to know?"

The teenager huffed, looking away.

"The project is plainly working with you on the physics of moving through time," Andrew hastened to say, "helping set up experiments, providing you with a familiar friend to be a liaison between you and the colonel." Almost as an afterthought Andrew added, "He's also expressed an interest in the phenomenon of the Celestial Ship, which you already know concerns me very much."

"Holy fuck!" Arien said.

"I don't understand."

"You don't?" Arien shook his head in wonder. "Did you tell him how you knew when I would return?" Arien asked, wondering what else was given away.

"I only knew you would be back. At least I had faith that I knew. I didn't calculate the timing, Arien. Mother Shongo, Cypriano, and Ellison did, though it was, all in all, a pretty broad guess. We were very lucky Buster wanted to go outside when he did, or I'd say we would have found your frozen body in the morning. You know, he was usually down for the count by that hour. This is exactly what I told Colonel Griffin; no more, no less." He folded his hands on his lap. "Oh, and Arien, he did mention a perfectly fascinating happening from the lab." The old man leaned forward as if to whisper. "A small sample of your blood was subjected to an electrical current, and it disappeared, right along with the slide it was on. He said it disappeared into thin air!"

Arien was confused. It was difficult to accept Andy's apparent unselfconscious enthusiasm, if not collaboration with the *project*. It was weird. Was it because he was invited to play? Had he changed that much? Wasn't the man still his brother? The favored idea of taking refuge in his friend, his brother, found itself taking an unexpected turn. Yikes! The young lieutenant assigned to him only added another distraction.

What if Griffin is actually listening to all this?

"They did it again, and again, too," Andrew went on. "And every time they got the same amazing result." His eyes sparkled in an animated face.

"I don't get it, Andy," Arien said.

"What don't you get? The goal hasn't changed at all. The means may have... So what? We'll just have to make the adjustment."

Arien's train of thought begged for a second opinion. He could always close-up like a clam. He could play hard-to-get, or be difficult. He considered it for the appointment Griffin made at the infirmary. The so-called doctors who had visited early-on were there again. They were too quiet and focused. It was creepy. They drew too much blood. It left him tired. If either of them bothered to thank him he didn't hear it. Griffin apologized. Arien wondered if official apoligizer was listed in his job title. Maybe it was his middle name.

He liked the steak dinner he was served at mess. He used the opportunity to ask again about his friends.

He'd confided to Andrew earlier, "They have six from Arizona, including Cassie. Andy, I saw Cassie before I split Tucson!"

"Oh, Arien, that's fantastic!" Andrew had said.

"Well, I saw Alice, first, and then the others. You would like her, Andy." He asked Andrew to promise to keep this news to himself.

His old friend went on to inquire, "So, they're holding this woman, her husband, her two sons, and two of their friends?"

"Yes."

"That's amazing."

"It's not right."

"It's incredible that you know it!"

He supposed it was, though it hadn't been the reason for bringing it up. Were they even on the same page? Andrew only wanted to know more about how he did it, and everything he could recall from the experience. "Was it your will to go to them?" (Yes) "Did they know you were with them?" (Alice did) "Were you aware of the passing time?" (No) "Do you know where they are?" (I couldn't give you directions but I could probably find them)... Arien would much rather have come up with a strategy to get out of the situation.

"We might have some movement in this area," the colonel replied, slicing into a steak so raw it could have quivered under the knife. "I'm sure they're ready to get back to their lives."

Duh! What do you think? The really hard part was Arien knew what they were feeling, and it wasn't nice. He tried to make a connection, but only Alice was quiet enough to hear him, if that was the right word. He had to admit achieving a better understanding of his connection with Cypriano, the Tohono elder who used to speak to him like a radio – again, for want of a better word. Sure, it was *telepathic*, but the term doesn't really explain anything. If he was to be honest with himself, he had to accept Andrew's intense interest was not to be insensitive. And Arien knew for it to be effective, Magic had to be well-informed.

"Where's Derik?" Arien asked. The lieutenant was notably absent.

"He's having dinner served at his quarters," Griffin said.

"He is?" This was curious.

"Yes, Arien, I hope you don't mind."

The young guest shrugged, connecting with the old fellow next to him. He noticed Griffin ate with his fork in the left hand, cutting with his right, and not putting the knife down at all except when taking a break, when he would lean back in the chair with his wineglass, holding it close to his lips, taking a sip or two, then trading the glass to take the knife again. The approach either eliminated unnecessary steps or streamlined what had to happen. He was focused, efficiently demolishing his meal.

It followed that a different soldier served this evening. About to refill the colonel's wineglass, Griffin told him to set up a glass for Arien. "Your privileges are reinstated. You gave at the office." It was a Cabernet the colonel recommended when he opened it himself, earlier.

"No thanks," Arien said. This was striking out into new territory. He could have used a buzz. "I'll have coffee," he said instead.

"As you will," Griffin remarked.

Arien caught Andy's gaze over his glass, raised to drink. Andy used the moment to salute him with it.

"Andy, do you have any real coffee?" he said, smirking as the soldier filled his cup.

Andrew smiled. "No, Arien. I haven't been shopping much."

"Oh?" Griffin remarked, do you drink something special, Mr. Newell?"

"Dark French Roast, Colonel."

"Yes, I'm familiar with it. I like it. It's a treat. It seems easier to go along in the Army, though. It's one less thing to think about."

"I suppose so," Andrew agreed.

"I'll order it for you. Do you grind it yourself?"

"Thank you, Colonel. Yes. I usually grind up a supply that's good for a few days."

"And you use an espresso-maker?"

"I do."

"Do you know what we're talking about, Private?"

The soldier was about to leave the room with the glass coffee server.

"Yes, Sir," he answered.

"See to it on the requisition."

"Yes, Sir."

"How about some babes, Colonel?" Arien quipped with a grin. "I could sure use a babe to do a movie with."

He thought about it afterwards in bed while the puppy slept against his ear. Did he really care if he met any babes? When he asked the question the colonel looked at him like a pestered teacher. He wondered how the soldiers carried on as they did. Most of the time they didn't do much; it must have been terribly boring.

Andy came over after dinner. They'd watched a movie together that totally blew him away. According to the announcement thanking customers for their patience, it was broadcast on a recently restored satellite channel. He noted *Titanic* premiered in 1997 which already made it an old movie. Curious, but now over one hundred years had passed since the ship went down. Maybe he was sunk as well. He understood Rose. He got it. He felt like she had to have felt. He knew the true jewel wasn't the one she'd dropped in the water; it was the one she carried in her heart to the future.

Kate Winslet – wow, such an awesome babe! He didn't remember her from the world he'd grown up in. She would have been pretty young in 1990.

"Oh, Arien, there you go," Andy told him. "You're pretty high maintenance, you know it? No wonder Griffin pulled me out of Limbo to help him in Arien Hell." That made Arien laugh, and it helped get Andy to his own quarters on a high note, the better for the both of them. The dude might have been old but he was far from dead.

He went on to consider Derik Jaffrey. The guy messed-up twice. Three times would be the charm. Maybe Griffin had had enough and intervened. If that were so it was too bad in a way. He was getting likable...

Arien's reflections were interrupted by something that was not the same as a moment before. He wasn't sure what it was. It piqued his interest sufficiently to get him out of bed. He peeked through the blinds. Weird, it was the lights. The lights in the camp's lanes may have been kept dim at night but they were always on. Everything had gone dark! He saw stars bright in the canopy of Heaven over the black silhouettes of low-lying rooftops. There wasn't a light on anywhere. He thought he heard muffled voices next, that soon went silent. Very strange.

From there he slipped into that place that could frighten him out of his proverbial box, the stomach-wrenching, out-of-balance effect of another sympathetic psychic experience. He was startled first, and then fell into a brief terror of incapacitation, being unable to pull a wholesome breath of air for a strange chemical smell, to lose a mighty struggle with loss of consciousness, and then snapping back into himself there, gasping on the floor. He knew the intent of the mingling of forces and wills, adrenaline, fear...

"Oh fuck!" he whispered to the darkness, heart pounding, scrambling to find his clothes, and when he heard his door open he could have pissed himself. He was saved the indignity with Jaffrey's sharp whisper cutting through the blindness, "Arien, Arien?"

"I'm here!"

"Come with me, quick!"

Arien only managed to locate his pants in the darkness, and saved space in his awareness to be grateful for that. He was skipping into them as they reached the back door.

"Got him, Colonel!" Jaffrey reported. "We're headed your way."

Arien assumed the lieutenant had a two-way.

Going outside was like a cold swim. His bare feet stung on the snow-dusted pavement, but the shots reporting from somewhere else in the complex kept his attention riveted to the moment. In the starlight and sliver of moon he gathered Jaffrey was leading toward the camp garden. They stopped, crouching by the side of a dormitory as laser beams floated in the alley between other buildings and the lane ahead. It was followed by more shots, and a crashing, door-busting sound coming from behind them. It was very close behind them.

"Ready?" Jaffrey whispered.

"Yeah."

"Stay low! Now!"

They scurried across the alley, to crouch by the next building, and then dash at a full run. Arien was pretty fast barefoot, his feet grabbing at deepening snow as they moved away from buildings into the more open area where rested the silhouette of the big bird. He was so pumped he barely noticed the wash of cold air over his skin or the recent assault on his body. It was bracing, only enhanced his speed, and completely overruled any pain.

Loud popping indicated a different projectile that landed, spun and hissed around them.

"The chopper!" Jaffrey hissed. "Hold your breath! It's gas! Rev her up, Colonel!" he added.

As the bird's blades squealed into motion the side door opened. Now automatic weapons fire sounded, concentrating on the fore-section of the craft and a few bullets sparked, popped and twanged against the spinning rotor stem and tail blades. It was as if whoever was firing could see the target clear as day. This was followed by the loud rattle of a machine gun from the craft itself as it reluctantly lifted off, swaying this way and that.

"Oh! Fuckin' awesome!" Arien cried out, falling onto the floor. He actually laughed aloud with excitement.

"Get it up! Get it up!" Colonel Griffin's voice commanded from the cockpit.

"Ice, Sir."

Fuck! Arien helplessly realized. The puppy! I never even named that puppy!

The craft swayed wildly as bullets continued to ping against it, but the incoming strikes tapered off as it climbed higher. As Arien's eyes adjusted to the dim red light illuminating the cargo area he saw Andy, to his great relief, sitting belted on a bench that ran along the sides, with only two other soldiers on the opposite side, besides the lieutenant, who was already pulling his coat off. He handed it over as Arien crawled on all fours to clamber up with the others on the seat.

"Glad you could make the flight, my friend," Andrew quipped.

"Yo, Dude," Arien breathlessly greeted. "Should I ask?" he added, wrapping himself in the warm coat. Oh, how his feet smarted now! Crossing his legs, he rubbed the numb toes of one and then the other with bare, cold hands.

In a moment Jaffrey had his shoes off. He pulled off his socks and handed them to the boy.

"Put 'em on," he said.

Arien didn't argue. They were so warm they tingled on his feet. "Thanks, Derik!"

"What should you ask?" Jaffrey replied, taking Arien's question while slipping his boots back on.

"Who was that?" Arien didn't ask *what* it was, or *why,* because he guessed it well enough, but who would dare take on the United States Army – right here in Oregon, no less! It was all in the intensity of his voice. It was so unbelievably crazy!

"Good question, Arien. We were ready, though. We saw 'em coming. But we weren't ready enough to hold the camp. They really knew their way around."

They must have seen it coming, with Jaffrey and the others in battle dress and helmets. Arien thought Jaffrey looked so young in that outfit.

"I'd say," a soldier across from them flatly agreed. "We left some good men back there."

Jaffrey's face concurred with the soldier. It also revealed his shock and disappointment, though there was evident relief in having escaped with the prize. It all hung with his cloud of breath in the cold, rattling cab.

For that matter, the swaying bird didn't sound or feel quite right. Arien had been in one twice before and this was different. Arien guessed they weren't out of it yet, though they sank into the silence of private thoughts, and Arien, his physical discomfort, as their craft pitched forward into the night.

"Right, Colonel," Jaffrey said to his mouthpiece after some time had elapsed. It awakened Arien from a fitful nap under the motor's dunning concussion. "We're going to have to make an emergency landing," he said soon after. "We're losing altitude."

As if the craft had ears, it sputtered, swayed, and dropped like a steel box from the sky. Arien's heart lodged in his throat. He gasped, bracing himself. The machine caught air again, swaying wildly though slowing its descent, before taking a final, more terrifying plunge to a violent shuddering, shearing of metal rotors caught up with solid, rapid banging, ear-splitting interference. The moment seemed oddly prolonged before the chopper finally came to a hard stop with a powerful, crackling, crunching **woomph**.

They came to rest at a thirty-degree list and twenty degree pitch of absolute stillness. There was only the dim red light in the cab. At once, everyone stirred in an awkward assessment of life and limb. For Arien, all was good! Thank God! "Wow!" he cried aloud, with a rush of elation. "That was fucking awesome!"

"We all here?"

"Here, Lieutenant," a soldier concurred.

"Here!" another said.

"For a moment there..." Andrew began to say.

Colonel Griffin materialized in the cockpit entry. He held himself oddly, like he'd been hurt. Steadying himself, he said, "Are you good to go, Arien?"

"Yes, Sir."

"Jaffrey?"

"Good to go, Sir."

"We're going with Plan C, Lieutenant."

"Are you alright, Sir?" a soldier behind Griffin asked. Arien guessed he was the pilot.

"Good enough to wait for help," he answered.

"Plan C, Sir?"

"I believe we made a secure distress call, but just in case we didn't..." He paused, his plan obviously evolving on the fly, "Arien, you and the lieutenant are getting out of here. You take the lead, is that understood? Find the nearest friends and hang tight, the two of you." He paused again, obviously catching the dubious smirk Arien threw at him. "Don't worry, I promise they won't get arrested," he said, with an ironic smile.

"I don't understand, Sir," Jaffrey protested.

"Where's your shoes?" the colonel asked.

"At my quarters, Colonel," Arien answered.

"What size?"

"Ten, Sir."

"Sound off, Gentleman! I want your shoe size, now!"

The closest among them was a ten-and-a-half. Private Bursaw was summarily ordered to give up his boots.

"Jaffrey," Griffin continued, "These are my orders: You and the boy will get to the highway, find a way past your uniform, but retain the sidearm. Latch yourself to that boy and keep him safe. You'll be his friend or his older brother, understand? You are travelling together. Take your lead from him, you will be on his turf now, and fit in. Lay low. Use your wits.

"Make no effort to contact me. We'll find you when I can get a handle on what the fuck just happened back there, and we know it's all clear. Do you understand, Lieutenant?"

"Yes, Sir," Jaffrey squeaked, with a perfectly baffled look.

"What about Andy?" Arien asked.

"I was getting to that. Do you know anyone in Oregon, Mr. Newell?"

"I have a few contacts."

"As soon as we're out of this you'll make your way separately. You can make a plan to check in with each-other later.

"Pioneer Square," Arien said. "Two weeks?"

"That's about right," Andrew added, with obvious relief.

"Alright, Arien, wear a bag over your head, for God's sake! And if we pick him up sooner, Mr. Newell, we'll look for you there." Then Griffin asked Arien, "Do I need to tell you to not use your own name?"

"No, Sir." Arien chuckled.

"Sir?"

"Yes, Lieutenant?"

"What if you don't show?"

"Arien here is very good at what he does, and since he was captured once, I'm betting it will be a lot harder for that to happen a second time. You may have to drop out with him, *Mister* Jaffrey, uh, *Jones.* Go AWOL, you understand? It may never be safe for you to report for duty again."

"Good God!" Andrew exclaimed.

Jaffrey swallowed, like a man about to be lynched.

Arien could hardly believe what he'd just heard. Plan C – Holy Hell! He could only imagine what was whirling around his classified young head. This had to be a truly desperate response to the problem at hand. His respect for Griffin soared higher than ever. It was stratospheric!

"You are my colonel!" he proudly declared.

"Compliment understood," Griffin briskly replied.

Arien, struggling to remain upright on the pitched and slanted deck, lurched over to embrace Andrew, and feel again the awesome rush of synching hearts. "Later, Dude," he sincerely affirmed, swallowing a surge of panic with yet another, disorienting separation on the shore of an unknown sea.

With some difficulty, Private Bursaw and another soldier managed to slide the door partway open, allowing a fir tree branch to flick inside out of darkness with a small pile of powder snow that sparkled like grains of red sugar in the dim light.

"I'll be with you, Arien." Andrew intensely said.

"You will, Old Brother. And I'll be with you. Please stay well!"

19 – I could pass for a student

His jump to a target fixed in a flashlight's beam freed a boy's flying *whoop* on the way down, where he lost his balance socking into a deep pillow of snow. He rolled, partly with the momentum, and also to get out of Jaffrey's way, though his chest and the ribs of his side sharply protested. Together they tumbled. Arien came to a steep stop in a nest of snowy branches. Snow had gotten inside the coat. It really smarted against his skin. He opened the coat to brush it off his bare chest in a vocal shiver that would have worked as well on crawling spiders, while reeling with a hammering, thoracic rebuke. He found the silver OM, *the sound of everything,* and lifting it to his lips, kissed it. "Where are you now, Michael?" he said to the darkness. "Look where I am!"

"What?"

"How are they going to find the colonel?"

"GPS," Jaffrey said.

Arien had gotten stuck up to his waist in bottomless powder. It crossed his mind they could die there.

"Move it!" Jaffrey ordered, grabbing Arien's collar, though he struggled enough himself.

It took an enormous effort, worse than any dream where the monster gained inexorably against leaden legs. The slope favored them as they relentlessly fought their way further down, tripping, rolling, swimming, thrashing, getting slapped by bowers of snow, falling – Arien fell last against a straight ridge of crusty snow with silhouettes of dark trees, straight and tall, and the splash of stars in a parting of low clouds above them. This was next eclipsed by a bright light attended with the sound of a passing motor. Struggling up over the barrier, Arien and Jaffrey slid a longer way on the other side to come again to rest on the hard-packed, white tracks of a road. Arien watched tail lights disappearing over a rise, and to the right, an amazing, hulking mountain peak soared up over the treetops so steeply and so high it appeared it would pounce upon them with all of its hulking, dim-white massiveness.

"Mega radical!" Arien hooted, overriding his keen discomfort.

"This must be twenty-six. That's the south face of Hood," Jaffrey declared.

"I know!" Arien exclaimed, laughing between gritting teeth, flapping, and shaking snow out from under the coat again. "Jesus! I feel like you kicked me all over again, Dude. My tummy feels like a fish on ice, and I don't think I have any fingers left!"

"Traffic may not be friendly," Jaffrey considered.

"Let me handle that, Derik," Arien told him.

Another vehicle was already announced by its moving field of light. Arien stepped more into the road, allowing his coat to hang open and reveal he still had no shirt on under it. He stuck out his thumb, wincing into the blinding glare. Sudden braking stopped the car sideways about sixty feet farther in the middle of the road. It was an SUV with a stack of snowboards on top.

"Way cool!" Arien cried. "C'mon, Derik!"

Arien's shit-eating grin caught Jaffrey's unapologetic stare. There was no need to say anything. Arien knew that well-enough. The cup of steaming-hot cider, liberally laced with spicy rum was perfectly delicious, and the crackling logs of the woodstove, its door wide open over a raised-stone hearth could hardly have been more welcome.

"Here, Alex," Jerrod said, passing Arien a long-sleeved T proclaiming, *Windells* between the shoulders. Arien held it up. "The funnest place on earth!" he read.

"It'll do," Jerrod agreed, eyeing the boy's bruises. Jerrod was a tall, dark-haired young man. He had a good build and a confident air. "How long were you two out there like that?"

"It was less than an hour, wouldn't you say, Derik?"

"Uh, yeah."

"That so sucks for the guy to kick you out of a car up here like that! You must have really pissed him off," one of Jerrod's buddies, light-brown-eyed Cody, declared. Cody shared the couch with Keith, who had to move his cup away because it was steaming up his glasses. The two of them appeared similarly athletic. Keith sported shoulder-length, wavy, red hair. Cody sipped at his cider. They were all pretty relaxed. Nice guys evidently intrigued with their unexpected guests.

"Well, he burned us and I guess I couldn't let it go," Arien indignantly answered.

"So he burned you again," Keith concluded, with a knowing smirk.

"We're glad you guys came along," Jaffrey said.

"So, where's the babes?" Arien asked.

"This is Mountain Boys' weekend out," Jerrod said, "We've been doing it every year since seventh grade. The rules are no babes."

"Crazy. Why's that?" Arien wondered.

"Jerrod just broke up with his girl, you see, and me and Keith didn't have one," Cody explained.

"We had to be strong and support our bro in his time of need," Keith added, with a straight face.

Jerrod put more wood on the fire, messing with it, because the log was almost too long for the opening. It caught pretty quickly in an embrace of greedy flames.

Jaffrey fidgeted. He seemed uncomfortable. "What's next, Ar-Alex?"

Arien wondered if he would have to trot out the 'high maintenance' line Andy served him at the base. "We could hitch down the mountain tomorrow," he answered, rubbing his hands together. They still tingled a little, but were feeling a lot better. He leaned into the section of L-shaped couch closest to the woodstove; stretching his feet out over a coffee table a foot away from the raised, stone platform the stove sat on, in no hurry to go anywhere. The vibe from their hosts was no push to go, so much the better. He soon surrendered to the rum and his exhaustion.

Arien was awakened from a long sleep with the door bursting open. He caught the lieutenant's alarm. Where he was, on the couch he could see Derik's hand come to rest on the handle of the M1911, against his back in the seam of his pants. The first of four guys, who like their hosts, appeared to be in their later teens, pushed into the cabin with a surprised look. All of them wore snow suits. Derik backed up to sit on the couch in front of Arien who was lying across it, so the newcomers wouldn't see the pistol.

"Oh, hey, Dude, where's the bros?" a kid with bright red scarf hanging over his matched jacket and rip-stop pants, asked.

"Oh, yeah, if you're looking for Jerrod, Cody and Keith," Jaffrey answered. "They said to send you up to Timberline.

Arien blinked and yawned as eyes fell on him. "Hi, he said, "I'm Alex." He felt comfortable with his father's name. It was beginning to be okay to remember him now. He sat up, pushing the blanket aside.

One of the young men headed off to the bathroom dividing the mud room entry door facing the kitchen and an alcove of the living area. Arien could hear the splashing.

"Close the door, Bitch. I don't want to see your dick," the first boy said.

"Eat me," the pisser called out.

The last guy in remarked about having seen the sauna. He wore a big, oversize, floppy white-knit cap that looked like it could be pulled down over his shoulders. "I can't wait to hit that," he announced. "I'm Jim." He was a brown-eyed boy with three plain rings piercing the rim of each ear.

"Dave," another one introduced. Dave set a large ice cooler on the floor, and stretched a little, like he'd carried it for awhile. Dave was a big fellow, short, stocky, strong-looking, his dark hair parted with bangs covering his forehead.

"Kenny," the boy with the scarf added. Kenny stood about 6' tall. His curly-blonde hair dangled nearly in locks under an olive-green snow cap with ear flaps. His blue eyes sparkled under the brim. "The bitch in the bathroom is James."

"Eat me, Pussy!"

"I'm Derik."

Everyone waved and nodded in their various ways. Derik stood to shake with Jim, who stepped forward extending his hand. It made Arien hold his breath to see if the gun would fall out, but it didn't.

James came out, zipping up his pants and pulling his snow pants up. He reached out, too, but then quickly retracted his hand to look at it, and wiped it on the front of his thermal vest. He smiled, offering his other hand instead. His straight, light-brown hair was maybe longer than Kenny's. His eyes had a gray cast.

"I'll pass. You're good intentions are acknowledged," Derik crisply said, sounding to Arien a little like Colonel Griffin.

That threw smiles and snickers around while Arien stuffed his right hand in the T-shirt he'd been given. "I'll shake," he offered, reaching around Derik. It coaxed a few laughs.

"Shit, did you run into a tree?" James asked, noticing Arien's bruises.

"It felt like a cement truck," Arien said.

"C'mon, Dudes." Kenny ushered buddies out with his hands. "We can chit-chat later. Don't drink all the beer, Dudes."

"Thanks for the delivery," Arien said, warmly appreciating *dude* was still in circulation.

"Come find us!" James invited.

"Thanks, but I think this guy needs to rest up," Derik said.

"Leave him!" Jim offered.

"Love him and leave him!" Kenny added.

And then they were gone, making the cabin suddenly feel empty.

"Damn," Derik said, walking to one of the solid-glass-pane doors on two outside walls of the building. There was a little snow-draped balcony off of each one. He stepped out, leaving the door open a crack. A lot of cold air came in.

"Maybe we can trade our Army duds with these dudes," Arien said when Derik came back inside.

"You think so?"

"Sure. Your whites are cool, but they make you look too straight with that haircut."

Derik repositioned the pistol and put on his loose-fitting fatigue shirt to cover it. "That was close," he mused.

"Do we have any money, Derik? I had a few hundred dollars before I got caught, but…"

"I can't believe this shit!" Derik entwined his fingers on top of his head, tensing and flexing his upper body. His non answer came across like one.

"Join my club," Arien said like an oath. "I've got more shit not to believe than you ever had."

"What are we going to do? I was trained to deal with all sorts of situations, but never anything like this!"

"I can get money," Arien said.

"How?"

"Go to Portland and turn some tricks," Arien seriously considered, though he blanched at the idea. Curious, in a way it had been easier to rationalize such behavior in his earlier life on the streets, although he never actually did it. He came close once, but took the money up front and ran at the last minute. He'd been beaten nearly to death by a boyfriend his mother had. The creep tried hard to have his way, but he'd fought back with such a fury the guy had to be satisfied with nearly killing him, instead. It wasn't her fault, but at the time Arien felt betrayed by her, too, because it was she who invited him into their apartment. The first and only man to actually touch his body sexually was Andy, first in Medicine Bow, and later in Ohio. He accepted it was special, because Andy was a beautiful dude devoted to him with an all-consuming passion, though this wasn't who Arien knew himself to be. He was in love with Tina. That was well-established. Had it been that long ago?

But his new shadow, Derik Jaffrey bristled. "You can forget that," he swore. "Anything with a dick will have to get past me, first."

"Then maybe we could rob them," Arien said.

217

"Jesus, Kid, you want to get us caught? Besides, that's a pretty stupid idea."

"Sometimes, Brother, ya got-a do what you got-a do." Though he believed it true, it didn't sound right. It came to Arien that surely, he'd evolved past that place.

As if reflecting the conclusion, Derik looked at him, shaking his head. He pulled a smart phone out of his pocket. "This needs a charge – but it's just as well. I'll see if I can borrow a call. I've got a friend from The Academy... Yeah. That would be a start," he considered.

"You think one of these dudes has a phone?"

"Everybody has a phone, Arien."

Arien's body hurt that day so he didn't go anywhere. Derik found a cabinet with a DVD player behind its set of unfinished-wood doors, and got a movie going. He picked it out of a tall stack of DVDs, and cried, "Arien, you're not going to believe the title of this movie!" The way he said that was unlike him. Arien invited a "Try me," but when told the flick was *'Taking Woodstock,'* it actually seemed unbelievable. He watched it while Derik explored the cabin, which had a bedroom on the main floor, and two bedrooms and another bathroom up a very steep set of stairs, and then Derik brought firewood in and kept the woodstove going.

"Wow. I guess I didn't know it went down like that," Arien said, transfixed, and into the scene where Michael Lang and his backers were in the farmhouse with Max Yasgur haggling over the price to rent the land. "I saw those guys," he added, not caring if Derik listened or not. "I saw Michael on his motorcycle. This guy looks a lot like him. I talked to him, Derik! They were still building the stage. It was awesome. And I saw Yasgur up there. So rad. He praised our peaceful gathering. It was special you know? So many people. Jesus, it could be done, Derik. If you need proof, you have to go to Woodstock." Arien's eyes misted.

Derik was listening while rummaging in the kitchen. He was transfixed as well, but not with the movie. "Hope these people don't mind we help ourselves," he said, passing Arien a peanut butter sandwich.

"Oh, Dude!" Arien praised. He was very hungry by then, but hadn't wanted to say anything that might pressure his strange case for a friend who followed the sandwich with a glass of water.

"What happened?" he mused aloud. "I know and I don't. But it was so awesome, Dude. It was so fucking awesome." He resisted an inclination to cry. It was homesickness, plain and simple. How he missed his beautiful

Tree friends, his steady, unflappable babe, and that awesome place, that amazing moment. He wanted to smell it again, to take in the wood smoke and Mary Jane and the mass of young bodies in the humid air. He laughed to himself, remembering the portable toilets. Yes, he pined; I would smell that again, too, gladly! He grinned, in spite of himself.

Watching 'Taking Woodstock,' Arien let Derik sit next to him, and allowed a muscled arm around his shoulders. Derik leaned and snuggled into him. It felt good. It comforted, and he was in the mood for comfort from whatever quarter. Their heads rested together. He could feel their hearts find a rhythm between them. Oh God! What am I going to do? He was almost afraid to turn his head and see the crimson mirage of desire flicker beside him. Indeed, Derik's face was flushed and pink. He pulled heavy breaths, but he also carried an air of excruciating satisfaction. His eyes were closed. He practically swooned with it. There was a certain subtle, lusty scent about him, too. Arien's nose was keen. But plainly, this strong young man put him first, ahead of his own desire, which no doubt screamed holy Hell, for he made no move beyond this comforting embrace. Arien relaxed. He trusted, accepting the comfort offered while crying inside for the wonder of the human condition.

It was a sweet story, authentically filmed. How rad was that?

Arien loved the acid scene with Elliot and the hippie couple in the VW Bus. They got it on together. It reminded him of the time he dropped with his friends in Portland, before heading south to the Bay Area. He got to tell his dad about that. Wonder of wonders. A little acid would have been welcome now.

"Ohhhhhh..." Derik sighed.

"What?" But Arien knew well enough.

"I hope you don't mind me so..."

"No."

"They might return," Derik realized.

Arien's intuition informed him otherwise, but he hesitated to say. He knew it would beckon to cross an invisible but electrically-charged line from mere duty and friendship. Derik was no kid. He might have been if he'd attended a conventional college. No, Derik was a competent man who had already achieved something in his young life, though he'd definitely hit a wall.

"Don't fall in love with me, Derik. Be my brother, Dude. Love me, sure. But, Dude..."

"It's too late, Arien." Now it was Derik's eyes misting.

Arien could feel the young officer's heart tumble to a painful place.

"There were so many good-looking guys at The Academy, you know? Beautiful guys. It doesn't get any better than that. I learned to handle it, though," Derik explained. "It was such a relief when 'Don't Ask, Don't Tell' was repealed, but I still didn't come out to the world. I didn't let it happen in the open. Oh, I turned a trick or two here and there, I'm no robot, and there were some heart throbs among my buddies, but I didn't let it beat me, and over four years I was basically a good cadet. My career came first. I kept the grades up, and fell into Intelligence. It was exciting stuff."

Arien listened quietly. Derik's story was causing him to miss the end of the movie, but the only interruption in the thread, and it was a short one, was seeing some obtuse connection to missing the end of the actual event, itself. Oh, sweet Jesus!

"Getting assigned to Griffin's staff," Derik continued, "was like a gift from God Almighty, all wrapped-up with a pretty bow on top. I couldn't believe my good fortune. The buzz was if you wanted *the* cutting-edge, classified assignment, you worked for Griffin. The man has friends in the Senate, too, Arien, through connections with his family." He paused for a moment. "But then... You know, kid, I don't think I was ever as afraid of an assignment at school, or a big exam, as I was afraid of you after getting you sloshed on the jet to Tucson. At first, I'm thinking, who's this goofball kid the colonel sees fit to ply with alcohol? That is so outside the box!"

"Uh huh," Arien commented, being present.

"But before I knew it, all I could think about was the goofball kid. I kept seeing your face, like a mobeus loop. It was scary. I've never been in battle, Arien, but I can't imagine being more scared for my life than I was then. I can't believe I'm even telling you this shit."

"I'm sure. It was easier to kick my ribs in."

"Exactly!"

"I'm so sorry," Arien said.

"What are you sorry about? You didn't ask for this. It's me who should be sorry." Derik retrieved his arm and moved away a bit to face the boy, but kept his leg firmly against Arien's, like the toddler unable to remove a finger from the light-socket.

"My old friend, Andy, he fell in love with me, Derik, and he never fell out of it. He waited over forty years for me, Dude. That's a long time, and I get that he's never been able to love anybody else. Isn't that a good reason to be sorry?"

Derik took a deep breath.

"Who attacked us?" Arien glanced, needing air.

"Great question. Get this, Arien, we got word from Santorri, still at Davis Monthan, you may remember him, that base security was breached."

"How?"

"Oh, it's all satellite. We barely got this one back on, too, while you were on the run. Nobody has to be at the gate to watch it anymore than they have to be there to shoot it up. Anyway, we had about 6 minutes warning. Not much. Griffin's fast. What a mind he has. He had the likely breach-points, and enemy offense program, the manpower assessment, and a resistance and retreat-escape plan ready in that time, and that was after getting out of bed! He's got to be among the best we have." Jaffrey's face waxed with admiration.

"So, who was it?"

"I'm getting to that. One of Griffin's house rules is taking nothing for granted, and I mean nothing. So when we moved the operation to Camp NW6 he didn't trust the existing security system because he didn't install it. If you didn't make it, how do you account for what can go wrong with it?"

"Good call," Arien said, seeing where this was going.

"Yeah it was. Well, what do you expect from an officer who wrote a protocol on tactics? He used it, of course, but he also deployed our own system, monitored by Captain Santorri, in Tucson. Well, when the camp system failed it provided a clue. We can't be sure. We'll have to prove it, but they knew about you, and where you were, and they knew how to take down security. That narrows it to two possible operations units in the service, which seems unlikely to have become so compromised, other than having a mole, and the defense contractor responsible for Number 6. Griffin told me, with enough time he'll get to the bottom of it. Whoever it was, their plan was good. They came very close. They just didn't account for Griffin."

"Wow!"

That bought a little space. Arien watched the movie all over again, fast-forwarding to scenes he missed, or revisiting other parts of the story. He liked Billy, the damaged Viet Nam vet who is only healed though a catharsis of joy at Woodstock. He felt like that, but it was complicated. By the time he got to Salamanca he was a new Arien, though he would never have considered Woodstock anti-climatic because it healed his own terrible trauma, as well. Now, the Trees' grand spiritual experiment could proceed. Now, they could manifest an ancient North-American prophecy. Good God! He was impressed that it actually interested Colonel Griffin.

He liked the way it ended, too. When Elliot left town at the festival's close, he didn't care about the money. He did it for his soul. He could hear the words of the song that lady folksinger wrote: *He came across a child of God; he was walking along the road...* They went out like so many bursting puff-ball, Para-trooping seeds in the blessed wind, and they would never be the same.

What snippets of world news he saw vehemently denied it. He saw Derik patiently return to the movie while watching him, too. Even he could see the country was eating itself from the inside-out in an ongoing war. It just went on and on. What for? When he left 1990 the country was at war with Iraq. In 1969 the country was in the middle of a terrible war in Viet Nam, and now, in 2013, there was war in Afghanistan and nasty scrapping with Iran. Was this going to be the norm now until the end of history? Arien made no effort to distort it. His eyes were open. This is very *heavy*, as they said in 1969.

And the dude looking at me has it bad. It wasn't craven. He wasn't leeching. It was beautiful to feel, really, because its excruciating intensity, purity, and sincerity were easily gathered, as was its tragic hopelessness. From somewhere in his abyss issued this dream image of a beautiful, naked child, bound with silk cord upon a cold slab of marble with channels leading away so his, or her – Arien couldn't tell which – blood could be gathered to quench the relentless thirst of a cruel, pitiless god. Derik got up at one point to go to the bathroom but Arien heard nothing splashing in the bowl, or a flushing, even though the door was closed. It happened to be at a quiet point in the sound track. He was gone just long enough, and when he returned, he spread out over the couch with his weary head nestled into the back cushion and against Arien's hip, and there he fell asleep. He trusted, too.

About dark all seven snow boarders returned to their cabin in time for a welcome surprise. Derik and Arien had found hamburger, but it didn't seem enough to feed everybody, so they mixed a lot of the rolls in after baking the crumbs crispy, chopped-up celery and onions, and added that to it along with some ketchup, and a couple of eggs all found in the refrigerator, and it got stuck in the oven in the nick of time to pull it off. The hungry guys couldn't have been more grateful, which of course complimented Arien's attitude, Thank You. At Woodstock they called it Stone Soup because it begins with a stone in the bottom of the pot, and then everybody chips in whatever they have, even if it's only their constructive energy.

Derik borrowed a phone to reach a friend he told them would help out, while Arien frankly explained they had no money and nowhere to go until they got some money to go there. In the meantime, he wanted to find people in Sandy.

"Who you looking for, Alex?" Jerrod asked, scraping up the last of the meat loaf.

"Um, a girl, Bonnie McCloud, and a guy named, Danner, I uh, forgot his last name."

"Does he go to Sandy High?" Cody asked.

"Holy shit! Did you say, Bonnie McCloud?" Jerrod cried.

"Yeah, I did."

"Oh, Dude! Well you're not going to find her, Bro." Jerrod was serious. "We thought she was skipping classes or something but after awhile word got around she disappeared over the Holidays, along with her boyfriend, a boarder from Madras. Denver, you know, Denver Roundtree," he said, indicating at a few of the guys who either still held their plates or were sipping beers.

"Oh yeah, wow, Dude, crazy, sketchy shit," Dave excitedly added. "Roundtree's whole family disappeared, too! They're saying they all got abducted by space aliens! A neighbor swore it was men in black. They ran one story on channel 2 and that was it. There was nothing else about it. It's got everybody scratching."

"Spooky," Kenny said.

"Yeah, it is," Dave added. "Her best friend, Sharon said Bonnie's mom is freaked. She called the station for follow-up, and they said they're not doing a story on Bonnie McCloud at this time, and she got nothing from the police."

Derik returned, and passed James his smart phone where he sat at the table while James joined, "Roundtree? I know that dude. Good all-around boarder. He's been in some of the competitions, catches knarly air."

"Small world," Arien said, connecting with Derik who seemed to grow anxious.

"There's a Danner at Sandy. He's in my Oceanic Science class," Cody resumed. "That's his first name."

"Yeah."

"Do you know his last name?"

"No," Arien answered, "but I'll bet that's him. I've never met another Danner."

James pecked at his smart phone, and soon announced, "Well, there's 173 David Danners, and 206 Robert Danners, and 154 John..."

"It's his first name, Tweek Nut," Cody corrected.

And James said, "Eat me, Stool."

Arien laughed. "Not many Danners," he affirmed.

Derik scooped another beer out of the cooler and drifted over to stand by Arien at the bar separating the kitchen counter from the crowded dining area.

"You're amazing," he confidentially praised, easing back into the flow. "No matter what happens to you, you wind up where you need to be. We debriefed your friend, Andrew Newell, pretty thoroughly. Even though I was told to take his stories seriously, there's still a part of me that has to see it to believe it. Well, it's pretty amazing, Kid."

"That's why I'm in charge, Derik."

Derik laughed, spraying out some beer. "Shit! If Papa could see me now!" he marveled. "You know, I'd never live it down at the reunion! How do you do it?"

"It's magic." Arien replied. He grinned.

"I will say it's a lot more interesting to study you at your game than holed-up in some FEMA camp."

"Uh..., yeah," Arien heartily agreed.

"Exsqueeze me," James said, stepping up to the bar with a sparkle in his eyes. He pushed between Arien and Derik to set a plastic sandwich bag stuffed full of dried little thingies with dark, orange-brown heads and pale, squiggly stems. "What say we proceed to the next course," he invited.

"Oh wow!" Arien exclaimed. "The last time I had something like this was at Woodstock!"

James shot a precious glance at him, "I know *exactly* what you mean," he quipped, winking. He slapped Arien on the back, crying, "I'm down with this boy!"

"Just keep your pissy fingers out of there until I've had some," Jerrod said, laughing while cutting in to see.

"You should have said that sooner. I soaked 'em in piss before I dried them."

"Now he'll have extra," Cody said.

James spilled the bag out over the bar top. "Everybody down?" he asked to a chorus of yeses and yeahs, while pulling the pile into a thick line, then dividing it up into portions, sorting and distributing heads and stems as he worked.

"None for me, Thanks," Derik said.

"You might like it, Derik," Arien suggested, though he privately wondered if it actually was a good idea.

"You're not a nark, are you?" Keith asked Derik.

"I'll vouch for him," Arien said. "He's on leave from the Army."

"Hey," Derik softly warned, as if Arien slipped up.

Arien's tightening lip and shaking head replied otherwise.

"But we are the world's policeman," Jim said.

"I'll stay sober, Thanks," Derik said.

"Then you're the designated driver," Jerrod joked, scooping a pile of the mushrooms up in his fingers. He made a funny face when he stuck it all in his mouth.

"Dudes, be sure and chew them good. Mix 'em with your saliva," James instructed.

"My friends made a tea with them," Arien told James, focusing on a modest heap and scraping it into his hand. He decided to go for it, open to whatever wonders lay in store. "This is for you, Otter," he wistfully said.

Everyone piled their clothes in the downstairs bedroom. Arien hadn't time to find his underwear when he had to run for it. Along with a colorful, insulating intoxication lending his feet a sensation of walking on air, he noted these kids may have been laid-back, but they weren't hippies. Five of the dudes actually brought bathing suits. The other two wore their boxers. Hippies would have gone into a sauna naked, girls included, as naturally as walking. It wasn't a problem, though, since there were plenty of towels. He wrapped one around his middle to step outside, and for the second time in the same day he was barefoot in the snow. The contrast of realities was startling. Maybe that's why Derik was reluctant to try it out. He told Arien somebody needed to keep watch.

There wasn't a lot of space in there. It had two sets of parallel cedar benches, stepped high and low. Since it didn't feel very hot Arien sat next to the stove, which used electric elements that worked off a timer. Jerrod said, "I don't think it's on, Alex. Crank it up," which Arien figured out how to do when he found the knob. He could see the element below a cover of cinder stones begin to glow a bright orange-red.

The others crowded in, high and low. The little building was probably designed for three-to-five people, so it was tight. Someone's legs touched against his shoulders. Arien could see well enough until the outdoor light blinked off, and they were now enclosed by a rich, blanketing darkness. He could feel the lives pressed in there with him, their energy, and the gravity of their bodies.

"Here, don't spill it!" Cody advised, passing a kitchen pot full of liquid. "Pour some on."

Arien did, sending up a cloud of rolling steam with a hint of orange oil, hissing and spitting. It sounded like a dragon deep in his ears. Waves of heat with swirling colors followed, mixing in the air. It must have been too much for somebody. He had to get up and go out. Arien wrapped his mind around who was left inside, subtracting Jim. Pretty rad. I know it's Jim! It made him giggle, and then he felt that giddiness among them all.

"Wow, this is fun!" Kenny said.

"I'm high!" Dave admitted.

Arien understood he had to keep it light. When his thoughts drifted to his brother and sister Trees, he batted them away. It hurt some to have to do that. So, the next time they imposed their memories in the halls of his wandering mind, Arien placed them in the Circle. There they could all be together where the recollection was joyous in a space that is occupied forever.

"I smell sage," Dave said.

"Is that what that is?" Cody asked.

"Nice touch," Jerrod commented.

"She's always there," Arien softly said. "She always was there, and she always will be."

"Yeah!" Keith rapturously agreed.

"Who?" Dave asked.

"My girl," Arien said.

"She's hot!" James quipped.

"Yeah," Kenny concurred, with a giggle.

"I'm hot!" Arien said. He was right next to the stove, after all.

"More water!" Jerrod ordered.

"You are pretty hot," Keith admitted. "No way I'm letting you anywhere near my babe."

Chuckles went around along with more spitting and hiss.

"He likes you," James said.

"That's not what I meant," Keith retorted.

"He's a fag," James said.

"You're a toad."

"Eat me!"

"Toads are poisonous," Cody warned.

Arien shook his head in the darkness. These dudes were too goofy. "More water!" Jerrod said.

"Jesus, the only skin isn't cooked is under my feet," Arien cried, with sweat running into his eyes like he'd been sitting in the shower.

Then Jerrod said, "If you get dizzy, get out in the snow and cool it off." And Arien was compelled to do just that.

It was very quiet outside in the white-mantled woods. A weight sat in his stomach from dinner, reminding of the more physical dimension mushrooms have over LSD. He arrived early for his body's lecture on *Psilocybe mexicana,* and how they're best ingested on an empty stomach. Oops. I'll have to get a handle on this, he thought. It could get ugly. He stretched as best he could, yet impeded with body pain, taking as much air as possible, kneading the nausea with his thought to work it into the exhale, adding, mixing, and removing to dissipate in a focused process of internal gymnastics.

That was much better than ignoring it, because it was there, heavy, leaden, and dissonant, while light snowflakes also peppered his steaming shoulders with the tiny kisses of wet, fairy lips. How sweet the steam rising off of him, like a kirlian photograph, suggesting his body was a finite form dissolving into the atmosphere along with its leaping heart, a soaring spirit, his dancing prayer, the towel flapping at his thighs, his feet in the soft, embracing snow, working through it, digesting it, transforming it as the pure power migrated outward to his extremities, and his focus sharpened while growing more luminous.

He veritably swam now in the air of the mountain in the waning light of a fat crescent moon's ever-so-brief peek through briefly breaking clouds, exaggerated in this world of white, as fingers of cold air grasped warm palms in a gradual exchange of yin and yang to a balanced imperative, to stasis, to the entwining of mental paths with the paths between the rocks and the forest cloak of the living mountain. "WyEast, WyEast, WyEast..." he addressed the silence. Where have I heard that before? "I know that is your name. See me, for I have come. Know me, I am Arien Grove. I come from the Circle of Light and I bring word of a song of Joy from the flight of the Celestial Ship, with the love of my brothers and sisters, and I cannot forget them, and I will not forget them. They are forever in my heart."

Oh, damn tears again, he thought, with buried laughter, as he apprehended the gravity of bodies drawing near. The sauna was emptying out and the boys from there drifted over to silently watch and listen.

But the energy, the force, if you will, began to fill him; he reached for a hand, and joined another, who then led to all of them holding hands in a circle in the snow.

"Wow! What is this?" James asked.

"Good shrooms!" Kenny waxed.

"God, do you feel that?" Jerrod wondered.

As clouds again swallowed the moonlight, the fine snowfall rolled into a denser flurry. It was perfect. Arien felt perfect, too. He was well above his physical discomfort, and now the blend of temperature between human body and the ambient air was both sharp with contrast and as refreshing as a summer day's cool swim. "Om with me," he gently, yet confidently said, and knowing it was time by the queue of the rhythm of his heart, and the certainly audible song of the invisible stars, he launched a note pitched higher than the usual deep Om, that the others either matched, or complimented one-by-one, until their young bodies rang like tuning forks into the forest's silence. And lo! The snowflakes around their circle brightened, as if glowing with phosphorescence!

Derik ran out of the cabin, apparently attracted by the unusual glow outside, and the energy. Arien knew the contact high would take him, and draw him near. But reaching for Jim, who was still inside, he had to back off. The poor fellow was spilling his guts out in the upstairs bathroom.

He is not ready.

"Holy shit!" Keith cried.

"Do it again!" Arien commanded. "Don't stop!" And he called to Derik. "Come, join us!"

"No, Alex!" the young officer protested.

"Take my hand, Derik!" Arien could see he was afraid.

Derik approached, but he didn't take Arien's hand. He took hold of his wrist. It was strange. It wasn't right. He held it very tightly, and implored, "Alex, there's more to this than you know. Please listen. You've got to take it easy. Don't get too into it, now!"

"What?" Jerrod called. His tone came out affronted with the impertinent interruption. Everyone was getting into the beautiful energy and the cool psycho-technics.

"Yeah," several others seconded.

"Who is this guy?" Cody sneered.

Derik's vibe did jangle it, but Arien could see his sincerity. There had to be a reason. Was it worthy enough? "I'm going back in the sauna," he calmly said, with a real hard stare meant for Derik. He slowly exhaled, to balance himself. This wasn't anything he had to think about. Love had been a good teacher.

The others quietly followed him right back in there.

"What was that all about?" Jerrod asked, as the outdoor light went out and the sauna was again wrapped in darkness.

"We need more water," Dave said.

"Go get some," Cody said.

Dave didn't move. Everyone was listening.

Arien said, "That was cool, huh?" which was answered with a few, "Oh yeahs!"

"Did you see that glow in the air!" Cody exclaimed.

"It reminds me of St. Elmo's fire," Keith joined.

"What's that?" Arien asked.

"Oh, it's like a light that comes from electricity in the air," Keith explained. "Sailors told about seeing it in the clouds or when their masts glowed with it in the old days."

"Yeah, but like we were – we were making it!" Cody added.

"Damnedest thing." It was Jerrod's voice. "I was down with that, too."

"Got-a say, I thought the Om was lame," James admitted, "but, you're right, it did feel good." He laughed rather loudly. James was sitting next to Arien on the low bench. He leaned in, with softly probing words, "That was you, wasn't it?"

Arien hadn't much experience with saunas. He let himself get too hot for too long so when he finally got out of there he was dizzy and nauseous. It took awhile to recover. Derik had him drinking water and his body kept him quiet, which was essentially a continuation of what went on in the sauna. He'd set the tone with a meditation in there, while simultaneously achieving a grasp of how to disconnect. He knew it would take practice, but it was encouraging to hope he could reclaim some expectation of public anonymity with a mechanism of distraction, at least partly describable as setting up a series of mental mirrors in his proximity. He had to credit the 'shroom' high for his counter-intuitive discovery. It worked practically though it was only partly effective around the dudes who were in close proximity, maybe because that particular place with its limited distractions encouraged more personal-consciousness or introspection. He wondered, intuiting the potential for greater effectiveness in crowds. What of a place where a lot of things were happening, like a shopping mall, or – a school, why not?

He'd never answered James' question, either, not knowing what to answer, though he understood a non-answer still amounted to one.

Arien was still only wearing a towel while Derik's eyes caressed him. He'd had to take the washcloth sopping with very cold tap water Derik pushed up under his hair to the back of his neck because it was entirely too sensual. The guys in there must surely have noticed the buff young man who quietly attended to Arien like a devoted private nurse, since personal adjutant would not have entered their frame of reference. It was like he'd been substituted for Colonel Griffin. It wasn't quite clinging but it required some balance.

"Why did you stop me out there?" Arien asked.

"I should have had time to formulate an answer by now, but..." Derik leaned back into loose cushions of the L-shaped couch with his hands behind his head.

Arien waited patiently. He stared straight ahead, absently focused on Kenny, Keith, Jim, who had rejoined everyone, and James playing Blackjack at the table.

"We're out-a beer," Jerrod called from the bar counter. "Rum n' Coke, Arien?"

"Sure."

"Derik?"

"Good, Thanks. There's–"

"That's, you're good, or yes, you want one?"

"I'll have one, thanks," he replied, then turned to confidentially tell Arien, "I reached a buddy from The Academy. He's going to front us some cash."

"So, tell me," Arien said. "I did what you asked. You owe me a reason."

Derik took a deep breath. "Colonel Griffin and I discussed it several times, Arien. There're two reasons: One, is a real possibility you'll conjure that ship, go away, and not come back."

"Did Griffin really believe that?" This was amazing. Just how much did Griffin know about the phenomenon?

Jerrod arrived with two rum and Cokes. He gave one to Arien and joined him on the couch with the other. "Cody has yours," he told Derik, which was presently validated. Cody set the drinks on the sturdy, wide coffee table and went to the entertainment cabinet to rummage among the CDs. Dave sat at the table, but positioned his chair to face the couch.

"Well, it was a considered possibility," Derik conversationally replied.

"What's the other one? Arien asked, knowing full-well the guys around them now listened.

"No." Derik said, tightening his lips. "Not yet."

"You mean, not now."

"Whatever."

"Great word," Jerrod said, absently pulling the hem of the damp basketball shorts he'd worn in the sauna down over his knees. "My mom hates it."

That provoked chuckles.

Arien knew Derik scoped-out the guys, though he didn't appear to. He'd had to have had enough practice to call it an art-form by now. Arien wondered how he would be among a room full of babes. He imagined he'd be with one before the night was over. No one put their clothes back on yet. It was an easy bonding thing among this group of buds. The hardwood floor felt terrific under his feet. The fire was stoked. The space was nice and warm, and now tunes were cranked. Arien didn't recognize what he was hearing. It was a Hip-hop sound including Rock n' Roll riffs that competed with a roar of losers from the table as somebody threw down their winning hand.

"The shrooms are wearing off," Jerrod reported.

"Alcohol brings them down," Cody said.

"That's true," Arien agreed, hanging his toes off the coffee table's edge.

"When was the first time you did them?" Derik asked.

"Oh, fifteen, I guess."

"Alex says you're in the Army?" Jerrod said to Derik.

"Yeah."

"He's a lieutenant," Arien said. "West Point grad."

"Wow."

"You're on leave?"

"Yeah." Derik looked uncomfortable. His private glance told Arien he'd rather have had another story to go by.

"I thought you were a cop," Cody admitted.

Arien smiled. Derik should get it, he imagined. One of the things he brought out of Berkeley was the closer a lie to the truth, the easier it is to maintain. He'd made that connection with the American History they taught in school, when his own experience testified to a lot being left out, going beyond distortion into a shadowy world of reality's alternative versions. Maybe this was a skill Army officers didn't need because their relationships went down other roads.

Jerrod did an unexpected thing. Arien had set his drink down, and for a moment his hand was on the couch. Jerrod, sitting there, picked it up, grasping it in his two hands. "Wow," he rhapsodized. This is knarly. You don't mind, do you?"

"What are you doing, Jerrod?" Dave asked, from where he sat by the table.

Arien could feel the energy flowing to his host.

"Come here, Dave. Check it out for yourself."

"Oh, stop it." Arien protested, pulling his hand away, but his tone was not unkind. He wouldn't overrule his empathy.

Jerrod looked at Arien like good stone rush. "I thought it was the mushrooms," he said.

Dave did come over. He worked his way partly around the coffee table. "Mind if I shake your hand?" he said to Arien.

Derik appeared to be watching with great interest.

Arien smirked, but reached out shyly while also reaching inwardly for detachment. It wasn't easy. He was in a mellow space. The drink was zoning him out. He didn't get there before Dave could say, "You're right, Keith. Don't let your babe anywhere near this dude."

Dave squeezed-in on the couch, rather than go back to his chair. "Weird," he added.

Arien laughed, in spite of himself, thinking, I need the Tree Family staff!

"So, uh, Cody–"

Cody waited for Arien to continue.

"You said you have a class with Danner, at Sandy High?"

"Yeah, Bro, how do you know him?"

"Lost cousin."

"And you don't know his last name?"

"We didn't know his dad."

Cody nodded.

"When do you go back to school?"

"Monday."

"Can I go with you?"

Cody grinned widely. "Crazy, Dude..."

"Oh, my gosh, no way, Alex!" Derik exclaimed, with considerable alarm.

"Yeah, why not? I could pass for a student, right?" Arien continued, ignoring the roadblock.

"You'd pass easy for a Junior, if not a Senior," Cody agreed. "They'll call you out in class, though."

"Oh, Please!" Derik's complexion went ashen.

"Not if I'm transferring," Arien said, thinking it through on the fly.

"What's your friend getting so bent about?" Jerrod asked, apparently amused.

"I can't imagine," Arien said. He winked at Derik, who became too distressed to merely sit there. He got up with a groan, and headed for the nearest balcony door.

James quickly said, "I'm out," and got up from the table to take Derik's spot on the couch. He pushed back into the cushions as Derik had. "What's going on over here," he opened, reaching over the coffee table's corner to pick up Arien's drink and summarily swallow some.

"I'm still stoned. This is fucking crazy," Jerrod said. "It's like a feel-good movie only there's no movie."

"Dude, that's my drink," Arien reminded James, who took another swallow, and still held it.

"Yeah, go make your own!" Jerrod joined.

"It wouldn't be as good as this one," James said.

About mid-morning of the next day, Sunday, as the cabin's contents spilled-out for the slopes, Arien and Derik hiked out the short distance from the cabin on the ski trail access to 26, which they crossed to the Government Camp Loop Road.

"I need socks," Derik said. He wore a rip-stop parka he'd traded with Cody for.

Arien was back in a hoodie Jerrod gave him in the morning, and he let Arien borrow a bulky sweater that could be worn over it. "I like this sweater a lot, or I'd give it to you, too," he'd said. It was good to have something he could retreat into, or people here would no doubt be scoping him out. They were headed for the post office in no particular hurry. They would see where it was. Derik told Arien he thought it would be reasonably safe to have the money sent express mail to himself via General Delivery, that simply showing his ID would not fire rockets and alert anyone of their whereabouts. The hardest thing was having to wait for tomorrow.

The other issue regarding tomorrow loomed like a stalking bear. Eventually, it came crashing through the metaphorical bushes. "You're not going to school tomorrow," Derik measured out, stepping around a large, icy mound of graded snow in his way.

"I need to do this."

"Arien, it's insane. I can't let you do it."

"Did you forget I'm in charge?" Arien asked.

"But that's irresponsible."

"Dude, somebody has to call it. I need to do it. It's the whole reason I'm here. I want to see my family. Can't you get with that?"

It was interesting coming to this place in his head. There were stoners in 1969 that saw reality as coming through places in the head. It was probably an acid thing. In only a few months among them, Arien came to understand their frame of reference, though he was no anthropologist. Most of the hippies, especially the core, defined 'conscious' as having another, distinct quality from mere intelligent functioning in a world of action and reaction, which was really no more conscious than the behavior of other animals, built as they are upon a structure for reproduction and survival, though seeming more complex. How it all fits together of course remains puzzling, mystifying, but "it" appears to be doing the same thing, though on a whole other scale. According to Andy, the Buddhists appeared to know this, and the Hindus, and the Alchemists, too.

Derik helped him clarify a few things.

"You owe me one," Arien reminded. "I dropped the OM because you asked me to." Arien stopped his stride a moment for a car turning onto the Loop road, but didn't step back though the car came real close. He used it to focus his fear like a blade and swing it at Derik. "You said one of the reasons was you thought I could go away and never come back. What is the other?"

A warning issued from the car's horn. Arien didn't flinch, not taking into account the frozen roadway made for treacherous driving. The car came so close it brushed against his sweater as he nonchalantly turned away from the side-view mirror in perfect time. He took that too, slinging it into Derik, all in the same whipping rhythm.

It could have been a combination of Arien's ballistics with simple conditioning in Griffin's method, but Derik went right there, practically blowing it out under the pressure, "The other reason is extraterrestrial," he confessed.

20 – "Holy fuck!"

"I'm not the best source of information on this issue, Arien," Derik said later. "I still don't know if I really believe it or not, myself, you know? But who am I to question Colonel Griffin?"

They'd returned to the cabin. The bruising over Arien's chest and lower ribs had improved a lot, but the flinching and unnatural compensation while balancing on slick surfaces around Govy had drained him. It felt good to hang and play CDs.

Arien was fascinated by the extraterrestrial question, though. What could ET possibly have to do with it? Derik was tight-lipped all day, but Arien was patient. He suspected it was an awkward subject for Derik, and his reticence was more from that than out of duty or honor, which proved to be true. He waited for the right moment, keeping time with the day's rhythm before springing the question, "Did Griffin talk about extraterrestrials?"

"Some." Derik straddled one of the chairs from the table. He had it turned around backwards, resting his arms on the back.

Arien lay on the couch nearest the stove, gazing at the pine-board ceiling. "So, what did he say, Dude?"

"He told me they like to think they're in charge, but there are a lot of variables."

"What did he mean by that?" This conversation was pretty rad!

"There's at least three races, and they have different agendas."

Arien giggled.

"Wow," he gushed. This was a totally unexpected source for such 'far out' information! "How does it work?"

"Good question. If I knew I'd be in charge." Derik stood, joining his hands at his back. Arien could see wheels turning. "They appear to validate the multi-verse theory in physics."

"The what?"

Derik paced. "I expected surprises when I was assigned to Colonel Griffin..." he ruminated. "The multi-verse is a universe with multiple dimensions. They've discovered how to navigate inter-dimensionally."

"Wow," Arien said, again. "I have something to do with this, huh?"

"Absolutely. Your experience implies an organic connection. You may have been an accident, but one with awesome potential for the human race. Griffin told me once he put it up there with the discovery of fire, which was surely an accident, too. Yeah, machines can fit into the equation to one degree or another, but…

"Time and space are inextricably linked. That was Einstein's contribution."

Arien giggled again. "That's so rad," he said. "You take me places, like Andy used to do."

"Oh, and you take me, too," Derik sighed. "I've got to go for a walk."

"Later," Arien said, watching Derik abruptly pick up the parka he'd left over a chair.

"Oh God," Arien said, barely aloud, his mind already changing the subject. He chastised himself for not revisiting Alice after discovering he could communicate with her, even though conditions hadn't exactly been right. He'd thought he could do it in his sleep, but discovered it didn't work that way. If he recalled her in a dream she was still left behind there on waking. Had they spoken at all? There was no way to remember. He sat up, folding his legs, and resting his back against the cushion, he slowly exhaled. His heartbeat slowed. Alice, Alice… He visualized her kind face, the sound of her voice, and the sense of her energy. He could hear the rushing wave of sound in his ears now, surfing it with his consciousness to fall on the subtle, flat-lined beach of physical disconnection, stillness, and expanded awareness, where thoughts appeared and vanished like clouds on a most distant horizon, the curve of his brow, the curve of the earth, and the static, infinite potential.

Hey.

Arien?

How are you?

Oh! Great! Oh, it's so fine to have you here with me. You know? We're all together again.

Are you home?

Not yet, but we're all together, all of us. I've met your friends from Tucson! He saw flicking images of their faces in his mind, similar to his own, but from a different place. Crazy! *They're here, too.*

Arien inwardly laughed with delight. Oh, that's awesome! But, what's going on?

Aha! I felt that!

An Army colonel arranged it. He is a nice man. He said it was for our safety. We've been moved to a National Guard base near Salem. It's been quite a party, but we've been concerned about you. Are you alright?

Yeah, I'm okay. Tell everyone I'm okay. Tell them I'm sorry. Tell Cyrus. Tell Patrick and Marley, Zanna, Cindy, Cassie and Jason, River, Wendy, and Free I am so sorry.

River? Wendy? Free? There's no one here with those names.

Ah, good. God, that's great! At least...

Everyone understands, Arien. Of course it has been difficult. We know it's not your fault. We may have been in the wrong place at the wrong – but, not even; we have all been touched by you.

Some more than others, Arien thought, with a chuckle.

What's that?

On, nothing, Alice. I'm so glad we met!

Me, too! There's got to be a reason. I believe this will all come out well, especially now. We are all together!

This had to be the best news since ice cream. Arien felt an enormous rush of relief and excitement, almost too much to maintain the connection. Wow. Way cool, way cool. Thanks, Colonel Griffin! What are you doing, anyway? But it felt right.

When the bus passed the high school on Bluff Road Arien said, "Hey, Cody, where we going? Didn't we just miss our stop?" Arien had barely swiped the foggy glass after an interminable droning and quiet ride to see a sign proclaiming, "Sandy High School."

Cody yawned. "No, Bro, we go to the new school now, on Bell, just up a ways."

"Get with it, Alex," Jerrod said, catching Cody's yawn. "This is the 21st Century."

Why would anyone even talk like that? Arien wondered. Is that the way they normally talk, or does some part of them know? He was glad when the door opened to empty the bus. Incredibly, he'd gotten past the driver who was preoccupied with a smart phone on his lap for the critical moment of the ungodly hour he and Cody, Jerrod, and Kenny, along with a couple of other kids boarded at the Chevron Station in Government Camp. The Mountain boys were prepared with a transferring-student story if the new boy was stopped by the driver, though Keith was dubious he would be allowed to ride while Jerrod expected no problem at all. Everyone except James, who was on suspension for a 'my bad' transgression, were variously awaiting each other in the parking lot at school. The rest of them lived along one of the two other Mountain Villages routes.

But now here he was out in the cool, damp open, being guided along with the stream of kids passing into the edifying halls of a cutting-edge architectural gem. Arien didn't have to be a student to get it. It spoke volumes. Wow. He had no idea schools could look like this! It was humbling.

He was grateful for the help and generosity of his new friends. Everybody had gotten behind the fun idea of sneaking him into their school. Cody and Keith even drove down to their homes in Rhododendron and Welches for clothes Arien could pick through. He spent the night at the cabin with Jerrod, whose parents owned it, and Cody, who brought what he needed for the next day. Keith had to return home to spend the night before a school day. The other boys went home, too, though Kenny, who lived in 'Govy,' briefly returned with socks and underwear for Derik as well as Arien to borrow, and a package of hair dye.

Derik, of course, remained at the cabin. He expected money at the post office. Otherwise, there was nothing for him to do but lay low. It was difficult getting him to agree with letting Arien out of his sight, but he was squashed between an irresistible force and the immovable object, especially seeing Arien's new friends rally around him. Wasn't this part of the magic Colonel Griffin expected? At least that's how Arien interpreted it.

Arien wanted to make stalking his grandson appear to be a practical joke. He dyed his hair black and pulled it back in a pony tail. Arien told them his cousin probably wouldn't recognize him, anyway, because he hadn't seen him in years, but he wanted to be sure. Arien liked the way it looked, submitting his features in sharp contrast. He didn't worry about the sandy fuzz on his face because it hadn't grown much beyond appearing. Sure, his face resembled the picture he'd seen on TV, but he had reason to believe it wouldn't be on anyone's mind. Some time had passed, and in a sense he'd be hiding out in plain sight.

Cody motioned to Arien and his friends and they split off from the stream of kids entering the building from the buses. He said he needed to pick up a form, so they walked around the complex, with its Cascadian façade, and busy parking lots wrapping around it to their right. At length, they went into the wide lobby. Arien had never seen a school that looked like this before. The impressive entrance led over a two-tone, gray and tan tile floor, lustrous in the winter morning's dingy light. It resembled a shopping mall, with glass-walled administrative offices looking like so many trendy shops, where soaring wood-tone panels depicted the iconic mountain in all its breathless reach; inviting the focused spirit of all who entered, while tickling his brain as it soaked up girls.

Wow, I've been away, he realized, his eyes tasting candy long denied. He stumbled into one while looking at another. It might have been embarrassing, but she smiled when he stopped to pick up the posters she'd dropped.

The boys waited. "Come on, Alex," Cody coaxed. Cody had taken on the tricky task of shepherding Arien through his classes. Danner shared one of them, after all.

"Sorry," Arien said to the girl. He liked her loose, black dress and the horizontally-striped long sleeved stretch shirt and tights she wore beneath it. She was shapely, pretty. Jesus! His trip to high school suddenly reminded him of other possibilities to his highly anticipated experience. Here the lobby was swirling with a mass of arriving kids and this girl was the only person he saw.

Of course he hadn't slept the night before, he was sure, until two minutes before the moment Jerrod yelled to get ready at way dark-thirty in the morning. He didn't believe he would have been so clumsy if he'd caught more Zs. It didn't matter, though.

"My name's Alex," he introduced, playfully touching the back of her hand as it clutched the stuff she carried.

She smiled again.

"Hi, Alex," she said, then she turned to be swept away with the throng.

"Pull your hoodie back," Cody said. "No hats or hoodies up in school." They'd gone a little ways down the corridor when Jerrod pointed, "This way," to the left, as he guided Arien into a wide cafeteria, with the ubiquitous skylights.

"Not going to class?"

"Breakfast, Alex," Keith said.

"I don't have any money, Dude." Arien pointed at the checkout station up ahead.

"We got it," Jerrod told him.

Arien went for the unopened, one-serving box of cornflakes in a bowl behind the counter, a container of milk, a banana, and a small box of raisins along with a croissant, with pads of butter. "Cool," he said, "Thanks, Dudes. I hadn't thought about what I would eat today."

The space filled up fast, but the Mountain Boys' spot was already held by Jim. He munched on an apple as Arien, Cody, Keith, Kenny and Dave sat around the oval-shaped table with a white laminated top and round, attached, individual seating. A couple of girls joined them. They seemed to hover with Kenny and Jerrod, who introduced Arien to Amanda and Julie.

"Where you from Alex?"

"Oh, I moved here from Berkeley," he said.

Jerrod's eyes rolled. "You know those California people," he teased, "moving up here and ruining our state."

"Yes, I plan to totally destroy it," Arien admitted.

"What will you do to it?" Julie asked. Julie was a rusty-brown-haired girl, with a tan, Hispanic face. She had a lovely smile and big, luscious brown eyes Arien was sure had captured his reflection.

Wow. It's going to be harder than I thought! And then he laughed to himself thinking of how he'd phrased that in his mind.

"I'm going to give it back to the Indians," he answered her.

"We could use more Californians like you, then," Kenny praised.

"I'd like to see that, too," Keith agreed.

Amanda's brown hair was cut short like a boy's. She wore a cool sweater that hung down below the beltline, a gray denim skirt and dark tights that matched the sweater. She wore glasses in a thin, black plastic frame, giving her a studious appearance. Arien liked her button nose. She seemed to turn away when he looked at her. Was she being coy?

It was neat hanging with these dudes. Arien relaxed into scanning the broad, day-lit room, bordered by booths that gave it restaurant flair. He knew students were checking him out. He offered a new face. So he returned the favor. He noticed clothes hadn't changed that much, some of the shoes, maybe, but the technology sure had. A lot of people had buds in their ears, some tapped at phones, and others hunkered over laptops. In fact, Keith had one.

Another girl came over to the table. She stood by Cody. There was nowhere else to sit down. Arien ripped off the top of the cereal box, pouring its contents in his bowl.

"Is that him?" she said.

"Yes," Cody answered. "Alex, this is Sharon, Bonnie's friend."

Arien's heart did a little flip hearing that.

"Hey," he greeted, concentrating on opening the milk container.

"Cody told me you were looking for Bonnie," she said. "How do you know her?"

"I travelled with Bonnie and Denver out of Idaho. She told me she went to Sandy. I thought it'd be cool if I ran into her here." He cut the banana up over his bowl with a plastic knife, and then dumped the raisins in.

"Oh..." Sharon said with a sigh.

"Yeah," Arien said. "They clued me in. I'm sorry." He nearly choked-up saying that. Regaining his balance, he dove into breakfast, yet realized she'd received a little shot of his empathy, and appreciated it. She was really missing her friend.

Sharon said, "Thanks!"

"Yeah. It really sucks."

Everyone appeared to be in agreement. Bonnie's disappearance was a scary, inexplicable thing. Arien shook his head in wonder. These were Bonnie's friends at school! His life was so full of coincidences. It was one thing to know everything is connected and yet another to experience so blatantly.

"This guy's amazing," Jerrod told her and the other girls as well. "We did shrooms at the cabin and Alex here led us in a hippy OM and, Jesus, the snow over our heads lit up like a ball o' fire!"

"It's the truth," Cody said. "He's really Gandalf in disguise."

"Uh huh," Jim agreed, with the last of a muffin in his mouth.

Kenny had one, too. He nodded while he carefully peeled the paper off the bottom, sliced it in half and buttered it.

Sharon wore a plain blue blouse under an open sweater. Arien couldn't be sure if she was wearing a bra. It seemed she wasn't. He fantasized if she'd open the sweater just a little more he could probably tell. He masked his flickering smile with a spoonful of corn flakes. *My mind's gone to dick since I walked in this place!*

Funny, Amanda made eye contact with him now. She looked away again, but the connection was made. He knew she liked him.

The boy from Berkeley barely finished breakfast when a buzzer cracked the air.

"It's time to go to class," Cody said.

Arien was fairly blown away with the building, tagging alongside Cody to the Forest Wing like a child at the mall with mom. He stopped in the center of the near two-story foyer of the Mountain Wing, first, to review its great rectangular, colored panels depicting etched scenes from Oregon's iconic volcano.

"Wow," he said. All around the building soared with walls of glass and daylight, views to wild-planted courtyards, neat little accents such as pine columns defining study areas. It was really sharp! The halls were ringed above the lockers with a strip of cork where school flyers, personal messages, and photos were posted. Cody stopped at one of the lockers to toss his book bag in it.

The classroom Cody ushered Arien into faced the hallway study area with a pony wall under glass. The opposite side sported windows over a park-like view, including the lower-level Water Wing; the front and rear, light-tan-colored walls didn't even bother with blackboards. The rear wall was covered with shoulder-high cork-like panels. There were a couple of rectangular whiteboards up front flanking a video screen. The broad room, like everything around here, had high ceilings. The teacher, a man, noticed Arien instantly.

Cody whispered, "It's up to you now, Alex. There's a desk over by the window."

"Thanks, Dude." Arien made his way over to the trapezoidal desk, pushing his chair back, suddenly feeling a bit overwhelmed. He hadn't known what to expect, least of all his own reaction to the strangeness. He could feel eyeballs bouncing off his personal field. He was so anxious to look around. He couldn't just yet. He saw his hands sliding over the smooth, faux-wood grain, and burnt-umber-toned desktop surface as he settled into his seat.

The teacher, likely in his 30s, was casually dressed in slacks, a cardigan sweater and blue sport shirt with an open collar. He wore running shoes. He didn't seem too intimidating. When everyone was in their seats he visited an open laptop on a combination lectern-table to tap at its keyboard. "I see Lee and Sam are not here," he commented over the screen. His words carried everywhere in the room. It was then Arien noticed what had to be a microphone clipped to his sweater. It was tiny. There were no wires. Wow, nothing had wires anymore! Keith's laptop worked without wires, too, just like the I-Pads, and all the phones did. It was pretty trippy.

The teacher opened his laptop's screen further back to see it from a fully standing position. He looked at Arien and then back to the screen. "I see we have someone new here today."

"Yes, Sir! I'm Alex, Alex, uh, Newell."

"And you are sure you belong in this room?"

"Hm, yes, Sir. I'm sure."

"I'm not sure, Mr. Lex," a boy's voice said, which prompted some laughter.

"I'm not, either, Mr. Holland, so please don't feel uniquely confused." Lex smirked. "Very good, Alex," he resumed. "Please see me after class, okay?"

Arien nodded. By now everybody had a good look at him. He closed his eyes. Be cool, he told himself.

"Okay, in preparation for our quiz on Thursday, let's review where we were yesterday," Lex began. He spoke in a quiet voice clearly heard everywhere. "We discussed direct interference in the process of degrading marine environments, which, like degrading terrestrial environments, eventually affects everyone's quality of life. Janet, can you give an example of the type of direct interference we're referring to?"

"Um, restoring coral reefs?"

"Good, well, what was the approach that related to restoring coral reefs?"

Arien finally began to scan the room. He had to be here. Cody said Danner was in this class.

"Yes, Karen?"

"Researchers spend a lot of time under water."

"Indeed. Without that underwater time, the data necessary to understanding what is happening, or what can be done about it can't be assembled, experiments can't be designed to test theories, and we might as well study something else." He paused. "Come on, where did we take this, Friday? Anybody?"

Jesus. There are two or three kids it could be... Arien thought it would be easy to spot him. But now... Maybe I'm trying too hard. Arien focused on Mr. Lex.

"I think the subject was manipulating diversity to restore the reefs," A boy offered.

"Yes! Good. One approach was manipulating herbivore diversity, through re-introduction or restoration of natural species or... Anyone?"

"Getting rid of anything that doesn't belong there?" Arien posed. It helped catch Cody's eye. Arien shrugged at him, turning up his palms, mouthing the words, where is he?

Cody wrinkled his brow.

Mr. Lex smiled. "Well, good – Alex, uh, Alex Newell, you said? I'm glad you could jump into this. What is he talking about? What's an example of an undesirable species in this instance?"

"You want a species?" a girl inquired.

"Not exactly, it's more a type of species. I'm looking for a definition." He looked around the room expectantly.

"Predators."

Cody's eyebrows were raised now. He pointed at the back of the boy near the front of the class who had just spoken. He mouthed the words, *Holland, Danner Holland.*

"That's good, Danner. One of the ways we could manipulate herbivore diversity, with a consideration to restoring the symbiotic relationships of a natural underwater environment, is to limit predators, and of course, any species, such as invasive species that are not natural to the particular ecosystem."

The kid's short-cut, curly hair was dark, almost black, and not what Arien would have expected. Well, there had to be a daddy involved... As Arien stared at the back of his head, the boy turned around, meeting his gaze. He had blue eyes. Arien could tell by the way they caught the light and flashed it from all the way over there. Otherwise, he didn't ring any bells or blow whistles. He could have been anybody.

Arien nodded in acknowledgement, but Danner Holland simply returned his attention to the teacher as Mr. Lex's lesson segued into an Oceanography video.

"Alex, would you drop the blinds by you, please?

As Arien complied, Lex picked up a remote and pointed at the short-throw projector mounted up on the center of the wall, over the screen. The lights dimmed, and an interesting documentary about divers working out of Aquarius Reef Base, 'the world's only undersea research station,' ensued. Arien was vaguely surprised there could be just one such laboratory this far into the future, considering the apparent importance of its work. Hadn't he just heard Mr. Lex report how dire the state of the world's ocean ecosystems had become? But the overriding issue was finding Tina. The boy up front there had to be the key.

Cody waited in the hall for Arien after the buzzer sounded. "Thanks, Cody. You go ahead," Arien told him. "I'm not going to let Danner out of my sight for the rest of the day." He had to think fast because Danner was already coming out of the classroom. Arien remembered he'd promised to see the teacher after class. No time for that.

"Okay, Alex, good luck!" Cody wished, with a conspiratorial smile.

"Wait up, Danner!" Arien called, running after him. Danner wasted no time trekking down the hallway. He slowed with a 'who, me?' face, but did not stop.

"What?" he asked, when Arien caught up.

"I'm in your next class. You can show me where it is."

Danner was a good-looking kid but he didn't seem to be very gregarious. He accepted the hanger-on matter-of-factly, asking no questions but continuing on his way. He seemed totally straight. His clothes were old-fashioned preppy, even by 1990 standards. He wore a collared shirt with a bow tie and a light-tan, V-neck sweater-vest that Arien considered lame, slacks, and conservative, brown walking shoes. He stood about six feet tall, maybe a hair over Arien. He moved gracefully.

"What's with those clothes, Dude?" Arien couldn't help asking.

Just then another kid dressed essentially the same way waved as he walked by.

"Hey, Danner," he called, and Danner said, "Hey!" Then he answered the question. "Oh, it's team day. We have a game tonight."

A girl joined them as they turned down a flight of stairs, slowing for a group of laughing boys chasing past to the landing after each other.

Danner said, "Hey."

She was a blonde girl whose hair was braided around her head like a Scandinavian princess, but what startled Arien were her impossible, aqua-marine blue eyes. Arien might have thought they were fake but she obviously could see. Besides the crazy eye color, she wore a T-shirt, a paint-splattered, wrinkled one at that, and a pair of faded blue jeans. "Who's this?" she said, with a flirting smile.

"Ar-Alex," Arien stumbled. "Jesus, Babe, I've never seen eyes like yours."

She giggled. "That's because my mom's an elf."

"She takes some getting used to," Danner confided.

The downstairs hall continued to dazzle the visitor with its bold design. Arien could see up two stories of windows and the planted landscape between the wings outside. They passed another inviting study area with narrow, peeled-pine columns that defined it from the open hallway, and presented its spacious area with a more personal dimension. Clusters of couches faced each other here and there. Classrooms and project spaces similarly wrapped it, two center classrooms and one on each side. Again, thick glass distributed daylight into all the rooms and everywhere else. It really was a beautiful school.

Downstairs, passing the fir tree-etched glass face of the spacious library, they arrived at another wing, similar in general design to the previous one, but the theme had changed. Arien passed etchings of a kayaker, a fly fisherman, geese, and a diver up at the top in the glass and tiles. It was blowing him away. It was easy to see how such a space invited dedication. He felt a bit unequal to it. His life had made a mess of school. Everything around him seemed like a reach beyond a dreamlike past that couldn't help much here. The graceful, stimulating building began to evoke unhappy contrasts that were sharply amplified in the next class.

Danner and the girl – Arien never got her name – summarily dropped him as they went on to their seats. He missed the support he'd had with Cody, and began to believe he was in over his head.

A big woman with a serious demeanor ambled over to him as Arien was scoping out a spot among other students where a small group of desks had been pushed together into a semi-circular table. "Who are you?" she asked directly.

"Alex Newell, Ma'am, I'm a transfer from California."

"Do you have your schedule from the office, Alex?"

"Uh, no. I must have set it down someplace, but I think I'm supposed to be here."

"Come," she said, curling her index finger in the roll of her wrist. Arien followed her to a table in the corner where her laptop was. "Newell, you said?"

"Yes."

She pecked the keyboard while squinting at the screen. "Hmmmm... Well, maybe it hasn't been entered yet. In either case it's unlikely because this class is closed." She looked at Arien dubiously. It crossed his mind the game was already undone.

"Take your seats, quietly!" she said to a rising volume in the room.

"We did lose somebody, so it's possible..." she unexpectedly debated. "It's just that I should have been told but, well, maybe it was an oversight." Her look was unreadable. "Take Stew's desk for now. He's not coming back."

"Okay."

"We'll resolve this."

"Okay."

"Do you have your book?"

"No, Ma'am, not yet," Arien answered as he settled at a table near the center of the room by a handsome set of umber-stained built in cabinets.

"We're reading, "The Great Gatsby." I'll give you a requisition for the depository so you can get one today. You have some catching up to do, Alex." She turned away.

"What class is this?" Arien whispered.

"Advanced American Lit," the boy next to him warily said.

"Arien's response to that was, "Oh Fuck."

There was little to do now but listen as the teacher launched into a class review of the current chapter.

"What is going on here?" she thundered. It startled Arien. He'd imagined it was because a few students were talking among themselves, but a boy answered her with "Lavish parties for rich people, Mrs. Nielsen."

"Is it about the parties?"

"Not really," a girl answered.

Danner raised his hand.

"Yes, Danner," Nielsen invited.

"I get the impression things are not what they seem, and Nick doesn't buy it, either."

"Anything else?"

"Yeah," he continued, "It's not just about Gatsby, is it? It's about America in the 1920s. It was full of hope for the future. There was all this wealth. But there's another side to it."

"Yes, Holly." Mrs. Nielsen pointed at the girl who hadn't told Arien her name.

"Gatsby didn't make his money legally. He seems to be wasting it."

"Is it all for show?" Mrs. Nielsen generally asked.

Several voices said, "No."

"It's got to be about a girl," Arien courageously groused. He meant it as a joke, but it also seemed right. Girls were certainly a big part of his awareness here so far. He was used to stopping in the right place at the right time by flowing with the rhythm of his heart. It hadn't let him down before. He had perfect faith in it.

Mrs. Nielsen, pacing, reached a bit behind her, pointing a finger at Arien. "Of course!" she exclaimed. "Remember the green light on the other side of the water? It's Daisy, it's Gatsby's love for her, and beyond that, what? Anyone?"

Arien thought he knew. He wasn't accessing the word, so he settled for, "His soul," and Danner chased it with, "The yearning in his soul," and Mrs. Nielsen said, "Very good!" all in quick succession.

This isn't so bad, Arien thought, enjoying being involved. He caught a quick study from Holly and knew he scored with Danner, too. For that matter a few other kids in the class were checking him out. He took a breath to break the connection. It wasn't easy because Holly was a cutie. There was something else. While Arien hadn't decided if he liked Danner, he couldn't help but take a certain pride in him. The dude was smart and had done the work. He didn't have to fake it.

The class went on like this, squeezing every drop out of Chapter 4. Arien backed off any further participation. He hadn't read the book, after all. He tried to listen to what was being said but finally had to fight just to stay awake. By the time the buzzer rang he was ready to alter the game plan. That was settled on the way out the door when he asked Danner what his next class was and Danner told him, "Pre-Calculus."

He followed to see where it was and decided it was okay to wait outside in the study area where a couple of other students were lounging on the floor reading and quietly chatting. He watched Holly give Danner a hug before he went in. Holly noticed Arien as she was ready to continue on her way. She came over to him.

"Where you going next?" she asked.

It gave Arien a thrill to be licked by her eyes. This one's a fox!

"Nowhere," he told her.

Holly laughed. "Is this a free period?"

Arien liked her laugh. "You got-a tell me something, Babe."

"What, **Babe?**" she returned, hitting the word hard.

"Why aren't your eyes in some lab? I can't believe that crazy color!"

Holly giggled. "Do you like the color?"

"Fuck yeah, I do! They're awesome."

One of the kids on the floor overheard this. "You dork!" he chided. "You've never seen 'em before?" Another boy and a girl looked up to see what Arien would say.

"Why are you calling me a dork? I've never seen eyes that color before, have you?" Arien began to feel foolish but he couldn't understand why.

The boy said, "They're contacts, Stupid."

Arien shot the boy a look to kill. He was sorely tempted to kick him, but stepped away instead, fully recognizing what a terrible time and place it was to get into a fight. To enshrine the awareness, he spied a gray-haired cop with a modest goatee and moustache in full uniform, walking towards them with another adult and a student along the corridor. Arien moved nonchalantly so his back was to the officer as he approached. Perhaps the energy intimidated the kid on the floor with an order of self-awareness because he renewed his attention to the book in his lap.

Holly grinned. "You should see the red ones," she said. "My mom hates them."

"God!" Arien exclaimed, with some relief. "I am a dork!"

"That's okay," she said. "At least you're not in denial. That's a first step to finding the cure."

"Yeah, I suppose so," he said, thinking how hot she was in that artsy T-shirt. It acted like an invitation to visualize her lithe body under it. A part of him would have heard a reprimand from his better angel for going there so easily but her own sly angel batted it right back, effectively teasing his hunger with a tantalizing scent. Oh, so way rad!

"You don't have anything to do now, do you?" she asked, confidentially as the buzzer rang out again.

"Uh, no, not really, other than..."

"Come on," she invited, "I'll show you my photographs."

Arien, nodded in ready agreement, and followed Holly along the blue-tiled corridor to the lower level of the Water Wing where they ducked into a large, currently unoccupied room to the right of the stairs. It was obviously an art room, with broad tables under rolls of paper, stacks of poster board, paper cutters, and bristling cans of brushes. Projects at various stages of completion covered other surfaces. There were a few standing easels, too. A good section of space on the right-facing wall had a couple of oil paintings, but mostly showcased an area of framed black and white photographs, many blown up to an imposing poster size. Holly stopped there, waving her hand at them. They were all rather striking, professional-looking landscapes and natural settings, either in deep contrasts of light and dark, or diffused with shadow, though all of them revealed a great deal of play on texture. There was one of Mount Hood, with a startling shot including glacier, crevasse and cauliflower rock face that elicited a "Wow! You had to be right there!"

"I used an old Pantex. It's film, not digital. It almost killed me," she said, with a proud twinkle. "I didn't have the right lens, so I had to get up to it. All the while the other people on the climb were yelling at me." She grinned.

Arien sighed, both for Holly's moxie and the way she stuck her index finger between her teeth after she told him that. This babe sizzled.

Her eyes locked with his. "Um, the ceramic room's this way – if it's open," she said.

Now sure of her energy, he sucked a breath behind a furious hormonal rush to his extremities. It truly resembled the proverbial gust of wind, and it was strong enough to blow his rational mind to the next county. He had to shove his hand in a pocket to conceal what was happening as they entered another, angular space to the right of a set of doors evacuating the lower corridor. She flicked on the lights, revealing long tables over a cement floor, with turning wheels inside. Arien hardly noticed any of that. His mind was already lost in the notes of an ancient set of hollow reeds. They practically chased one-another's last few steps into a big closet at the far end of the studio. It had an air compressor connected to two-inch steel pipes that ran up the double-story wall to the left of the door, a set of likely exterior doors on the adjacent wall, a floor drain, a small table, and stacked boxes of moist clay on the floor. She swung the door shut as their bodies tangled in a feverish embrace.

Crazy, insane... Arien thought, with a complex recipe of giddy euphoria and awkward imbalance. He was depleted, light-headed, and unable to grasp the corners of specific considerations beyond a vague sense he surely smelled funny. His T-shirt was damp. His lips felt bruised. He saw his disheveled hair in a restroom mirror, and wet it down in a sink that required trial and error to operate, finally getting the water running as long as he held his hands under the faucet.

A boy walked in as Arien was drying it best he could with a wad of paper towels. It wasn't easy. His hair was longer than ever now, touching his back between the shoulder blades. The kid docked himself to a urinal but watched over his shoulder as Arien stuffed the dye-smeared wad into the waste receptacle, removed his shirt and wet even more of the unbleached paper – it quickly broke down – to sponge his upper body. The kid might have thought the green-eyed, sandy-haired boy was a bit off.

Stepping out of line-of-sight, Arien, opened his pants, pushed his briefs down and washed his clammy privates, too. Before he could zip it, the fellow was passing to the other sink.

"There's showers in the locker room," the boy said.

"I'm good." But Arien really wasn't sure. A part of him felt like a robber. What am I saving for Tina? But, wasn't that a ridiculous idea? When passion was spent, and the two of them were still breathing heavily into each-others mouths and churning into the sweat, the tangled hair, press and tingle of their bodies, and lingering physical connection, Arien expressed his primal and universal male call of completion, of conquest, with a euphoric giggle, which she appeared to share with him, and he whispered to her, "I thought maybe you were Danner's girl."

It really blew him away when she answered, "Well, yes, I guess I am."

And he answered, "Holy fuck!" but that was awkward, considering.

Holly raised her eyebrows, affecting an otherwise blank expression. "I've got to go to my next class," she said, and that was that.

Now what? He was more presentable, outwardly at least, and alone again in the restroom. Arien had to push himself out of there. His high school escapade was not as easy as he first thought. Sure, he was full of himself for getting off, but its uncomfortable dimension rankled, and he had no idea where to go, next. There was yet a trace of Holly about him. If he saw Danner now, could he look that boy in the eye?

The next period buzzer sounded. He'd lost track of Danner. He needed a guide – Cody, Keith, anyone... As the corridors filled with students, Arien saw another student passing by in a retro preppie outfit complete with the v-neck sweater-vest, and bow tie. He impulsively tapped him to ask, "What time's the game tonight?"

"Seven," the kid said, angling his head while pointing at a flyer that just happened to be pinned to the corkboard strip right above them, The banner read, " RESCHEDULED! PIONEER BASKETBALL MONDAY – SANDY vs. REX PUTNAM – DON'T MISS IT!"

Arien smirked as the boy smartly winked, and moved on. He guessed he'd essentially accomplished the mission here. He knew he would have to return for the game. The problem was what to do with the rest of the day?

"Hiya, Alex!"

Arien was relieved to see Kenny's curly, blond head in the stream of students.

"Yo, Dude!" Arien stepped along with him. "Where you headed?"

"I've got History."

"Can I tag along?"

"Sure." Kenny grinned. "How's it going so far?"

"Crazy."

"Did you see Danner?"

"Yeah. He'll be at the game tonight. I want to go." Arien caught a glimpse of Holly up ahead. He didn't know if she saw him. Strange. She disappeared into a restroom.

"What will you do, hang in Sandy?"

"Maybe I can get a ride back from the mountain."

Arien and Kenny waved at Jim, who was going the other way. Jim returned an inclusive grin. "Like our school so far?"

"It's knarly, Dude," Arien chased, as Jim wove away from them among the moving stream.

"That's a lot of trips," Kenny said.

"I promised Derik I'd be on the bus after school."

"What is it with him? Is he your boyfriend?"

"I wish it were that simple."

"In here." Kenny indicated the room with an ushering hand.

This classroom had its desks arranged in a horseshoe. Arien waited until the next buzzer rang before claiming a seat between two girls. One had to remove some books from the empty chair, and did so with exaggerated remonstrance and a sisterly smile that served as a welcome. Arien nodded his thanks.

The teacher, a middle-weight man about forty in a striped business shirt and slacks, walked down the center of the horseshoe to stop before Arien's desk. Before he could say anything a student came up to him, saying, "Mr. Fowler, I didn't get my report finished last night. Can I have one more day?"

"If you care about your grade, Louis, you can give it to me tomorrow, but you have to give it to me tomorrow."

"Thanks, Mr. Fowler! I will! I really will!"

"Yeah," he said, with a likely grin he steered to the new boy. "And who's this, visiting us today?"

"Oh, yeah, Hi," Arien said, swiping his hand in a short wave. "I'm Alex Newell."

"Okay, that's a good start. Do you have your schedule, Alex?" After he said that his connection became more focused. The nuance was subtle. "Have you been in one of my classes before?" he asked, before Arien could answer.

The guy looked familiar to Arien, as well. Arien slowly exhaled. He had to be relaxed. He knew it was perilous to find a where and when if they existed. He pictured the delicate electro-chemical intention splay out over interlaced neurons in his brain, seeking clues among the memories, and knowing the same thing was happening in the other. *Sheesh!* Think of something else!

"Uh, no, Sir, not possible. I'm here from California."

"Hmmm..." Fowler mused. "Get me your schedule."

"I'll have it tomorrow, Sir. I misplaced it this morning."

"Okay, okay," Fowler said in a louder voice to the class – his microphone wasn't on. He awaited conversation and background noise to subside. "Last time we left off with the growing involvement in Viet Nam in the mid 1960s. Can anybody tell us how this affected the culture of the times?"

'The anti-war movement," somebody said.

"Yes, exactly! Why?" the teacher continued, "Why isn't that happening now? The United States still has troops in Afghanistan, advisors in Iraq, a possibility of involvement in the Syrian civil war, and there have been fist-fights with Iran that has oil so high it's killing us. Where are the protests?"

"The draft," Arien said.

"Yes." Fowler nodded to Arien, and shot a finger in the air. "When everyone has participation hanging over their heads, like a sword of Damocles, they pay attention." He stopped to let his point sink in. "Is this a good thing?"

Arien heard himself say, "Yes!" What am I doing? "It's so different now," he continued. "It seems people had more of a grip in the '60s. And the kids were finding out pigs did what they wanted because their parents let them, they were too busy making and buying stuff. They bought a line of crap and didn't ask questions. A lot of them were pigs, too, looking under rocks for communists while they ate the world for breakfast and paid for it with bullets while they pretended not to see. But the kids took to the streets. It was *their* lives at stake in Viet Nam. Nobody was listening. Life Magazine didn't get it. People got mad at them. But they were telling the truth! They called the General, 'Waste-more-land.' Ha! They should have stayed mad at the pigs, because they could stop it then, and they did.

"I don't think you can stop it anymore." His voice rang with sincerity and conviction, his recollection so present he could still smell the tear gas. When Arien paused he had everyone's attention. He inwardly winced. I have to quit rattling the chain! – But I'm no coward! If I don't say it, who will? He sucked a few breaths and rallied just as Mr. Fowler was about to speak.

"The draft was a brake connected to the people. You don't have brakes anymore. The free ride ain't free, Dudes. The Pig is your king, you're in his wagon, and he's taking you away down a scary, curvy road."

The room was totally quiet. And then Kenny started clapping, a few others joined in, 'yeahs' were heard, and feet thumped on the textured flooring.

"No offense, Alex," the teacher said, "But you don't remind me of anybody, after all."

Arien got it at lunch over an open face sloppy Joe and a decent selection of greens from the salad bar. When he caught up with Kenny on his way out of Mr. Fowler's class, and Kenny said, "Let's hit the food," another teacher, a woman, squeezed by to give Fowler something. He happened to be just inside the doorway when she said, "Here it is, Dan." It stuck in Arien's head. It was like his brain digested it while his stomach did a similar thing with lunch. Dan... Dan... Dan Fowler... Dan Fowler! The Joe got stuck in his throat and he coughed it up.

"Take it easy, Bro," Jerrod advised, in good humor, thumping him on the back.

Arien wanted to scream it out. It was fantastic! There was no way. He had to swallow it and be content it didn't come to him earlier, in the classroom. I won't tell Derik I knew this guy in 1990 at Youth Promise, in Portland, he thought. The straw might break him.

"So, how's your day been going?" Jerrod asked, tossing an empty chocolate milk container into a nearby refuse can.

"Not bad, I got laid," Arien said with an accomplished grin.

Jerrod and Kenny laughed. Sharon juicily rolled her eyes, and Amanda lowered her glasses to focus at Arien expressively over the rims. Jim was the only other Mountain Boy there. He'd looked away like he didn't hear it. Dave had gone back for a spoon. Cody, they told him earlier, had lunch next period.

"You're knarly!" Kenny said. He pointed at Arien to drive it home.

Arien knew they, with the possible exception of Amanda, didn't take his announcement seriously and he was perfectly okay with that.

"You saw the dude?" Jerrod asked.

"Danner? Yes, in first period." He dipped a piece of broccoli in the puddle of ranch dressing on his plastic tray, licked it off, and dipped it again.

"Did he recognize you?"

"No," he said, munching, and looking around, sweeping the room carefully for the source of a strong tap off the back of his head. "I'm going to his game tonight." There was nothing. He was sure someone had been staring at him. It was not the light drag of fingers on the scalp that generally scanning eyeballs expressed, but more akin to pressure, abrupt, strong, serious attention, and then totally gone. He shook his head, momentarily flailing his hair. Yes. The room may have been full with the murmur of students but someone else was surely there.

Curious, there was no discomfort or body-sense of alarm. He resisted the temptation to look again, though the first time probably gave his awareness away. Be cool! Was it anything to do with Holly? Nah, if she were in the Commons he would have seen her. Was it more sinister, and he, or she was really good at masking it? Probably not...

Dave resumed his place at the table, and tore into a little plastic cup of custard.

"What's up?" Jerrod asked, seeming concerned.

People next to me are so hip to my changes! Arien's idea of how easily everything could run out of control was nearly overwhelming. "Dudes, don't look now. Somebody's checking me out and they don't want me to know they know me. Watch behind me, okay? But do it like a spy, not like you're looking. Maybe you'll see who it is."

Jerrod sat across from Arien, and was well-positioned to do it. "Oops. You think they'll blow your cover, n' get you kicked out?" He grinned with vicarious excitement.

"No, it's probably a kid, but it's too weird. I can't think of a kid would know me and not come right over and say, Hi" Arien was being honest, and was glad he could be, grateful for how he attracted the friends he needed, and recognizing he was only as alone as the dissonance his periodic, mulish-grief could get away with. Though that ran deeper than the moment's adventure, the adventure engaged him. It felt right. It held him together.

Amanda said, "Boy, you're sensitive. I may have seen someone."

"Cool."

"I don't remember seeing her before."

So, it's a girl. Hmmm...

Who you talking about? Jerrod asked.

"The dark girl over in the corner," Amanda said. "She's sitting by herself under the banner."

"A Black girl?" Arien was stymied. Who would that be?

"I see her," Jerrod announced, without moving his head. "She's not Black. She looks Mexican."

Dave was on that side of the table, too. "Have you seen her before?" he said to Jerrod.

"No." Jerrod turned his palms up, wrinkling his face. "I don't know how you could go to school all year and not recognize everybody," he answered. "Maybe she's transferring, too." He smiled at his little joke.

"Oh, there's lots of kids I wouldn't know if I saw them somewhere else," Sharon considered, twisting around to see.

"That really has me curious," Arien said, still resisting the temptation to do the same. "What's she wearing? What's her hair like?"

"It's kind-a straight, long and shiny, pulled back. Maybe she's an Indian, or Middle Eastern. All I can see is a red... or whatever," Amanda said.

"And she was checkin' me out?"

Amanda answered, "I saw her looking at our table. I thought it was me."

"So, who's going to the game tonight?" Arien's question was answered with a few shrugs.

"I've seen Danner play," Sharon recalled. "He's good."

"You mean he's good-looking?" Dave asked.

"The Sandy Post loves his picture," Jim said, fingering an earring. "He played killer golf last summer."

The period buzzer blared, rendering sudden, chaotic commotion from the murmurs and rustlings of lunch, though sounds' sharp edges were somewhat absorbed in the open architecture. Arien stood, spun around, and quick as he was, saw no one answering the description of the dark girl among the mass of students headed for the corridor.

He sat with Cody on the interminable school bus to The Mountain. It smelled like ripe kids and steamy breath, and unlike the morning dirge, it was animated with a garrulous jazz of young voices and the motor's droning-trombone song. He watched the blur of passing cars, and tall fir trunks of thickening forest, in deepening snow, through a clouded window as they climbed, and thought back on the rest of the day. He'd waited for Cody in the Commons. He'd eaten a carrot cake slowly to fill the time while Cody demolished a sandwich, and begun to question his sanity when he surely spied a dark girl's eyes drilling into him from the stairwell. It couldn't have been his imagination! He'd gotten up quickly, streaking after her flash of red garment.

Maybe the splayed hand of the teacher or whoever happened to be there slowed him just enough, but even though he'd bounded down after reaching the stairs, taking two at-a-time, she was lost to him. He was sure if she were in the expansive lower level he would have seen her. She would have had to sprint to avoid his scanning eyes. He'd hurried from the tall and broad wall of exterior doors and windows to the opposite corridor. An adult came out from the Career Center and was about to speak to him when he turned on his heel and headed back.

"You thinking of that girl again?"

"What girl?" he answered Cody. "You said she was Mexican, maybe?"

"I don't know. We couldn't tell. A lot of girls were checkin' you out. What's so special about–?"

"I don't know." He interrupted, snapping it out like a rubber band.

Jerrod turned to fold his arms on the seat back and face them. "She was new to me. You said she knew you?"

"Oh!" Cody pronounced. "Well, that's all I was asking." He got up to stand in the isle as the bus came to a stop.

"Later, Cody!" Jerrod said.

"See you tomorrow."

"Maybe." Arien answered.

The bus remained parked, idling while the driver got out to chain up.

The rest of the day he'd accompanied Cody to his afternoon classes. Informal Geometry wasn't too bad. The teacher gave him a book to take home. Right. He told her Cody promised to help him with it. Ha! Advanced Automotive Tech was a trip. Arien was not much of a mechanic. Even though he'd watched while a group of Cody's classmates got a balky motor to hum on a stand, he had no idea how they accomplished the miraculous feat. It seemed most of it had been done on a computer. Personal Finance was a joke. There was a loud kid who appeared to be a can shy of a six-pack in there. He kept asking the same question, and wouldn't pay attention to an adult sitting next to him who obviously knew the answer. He wanted it from the teacher but the teacher had moved on. This scene stretched into a three-way test of wills effectively ending their lesson well before the buzzer wrapped up the day, and then this goofy boy bolted for the door with his heavy-set adult shadow slamming into a chair in her hurry to keep up with him. Arien's eyes toasted the moment with several smirking kids, and it made him feel included.

And now he laughed out loud on the exuberant bus. They'd reached the first switch-back, and were decelerating for the turn.

"What's funny?" Kenny, who had taken Cody's seat next to Arien, asked. He was ripping open a granola bar.

"I got laid today!" Arien announced, with a bemused smirk. He couldn't stand sitting on that, and it nicely covered its inherent cringe-factor about who she was, to bandy.

"Shut up!" Jerrod yelled. "You said that at lunch. Say it again and I might start to believe it, and if I start to believe it I might have to kill you!"

"Who with?" Kenny probed.

"No way," Arien said. "If you open the barn, the horse gets out; if I open my mouth the secret's out." He smiled after his ditty.

"Whoa, wait a minute, Bro, I can keep a secret!"

""He's yankin' our tits," Jerrod scoffed.

"Where?" Kenny chased.

"Where's your tits?"

Kenny playfully punched Arien in the shoulder. "No fucker, where'd you fuck her?"

"In school."

"Dude!" Jerrod cried, balling his fists.

"Is this where a kid gets beat to shit?" Arien teased.

"This is where a kid gets killed!"

"Where in school?" Kenny demanded.

"Ceramics, I think, a closet in the corner."

"No soft bed?" Jerrod followed.

"No soft bed, just hot sex."

"Oh, God! That can't be! If that were true *I'd* die." Jerrod said.

"Holy fuck!" Kenny sighed.

"Well, I don't know how holy. It depends on your religion, I guess."

21 – Maggie had a little boy

Of course Derik was waiting at the Chevron Station. He wore a snow suit with a solid purple cap pulled over his ears. He could have been any young guy on Govy's main street. Arien hesitated to know if relief, irritation, or a mix of them would rule his greeting.

Derik did appear worried. "It's been a long day," he admitted, when Arien got off the bus to swipe palms and bump fists with him.

The guy's not a total stooge, Arien thought, knowing how much he admired Derik's cool demeanor under fire while effecting their escape.

"Did you get your money?"

"See you later!" Kenny parted, walking away.

"Yeah, come on over!" Jerrod called after.

"Later, Dude." Arien waved.

"Right, Bro!"

"Uh, yes, I got it," Derik said.

"Good. You're buying our tickets to the game tonight."

Derik rolled his eyes. "How we getting there?" he asked.

"You want to go?" Jerrod said, walking along a shoveled pathway between four-foot walls of snow to the frozen road with them. I left my car in Kenny's driveway so the plow wouldn't bury it. We'll go to the cabin and scare up grub, relax a bit, and then go get the car. Maybe Kenny will come with us, too. You'll have to buy the gas, though. It's about empty."

The game had already started by the time they got there. Parking in a private driveway was the right idea, but it didn't stop the plowman from pushing a wall of snow off the road, blocking the car in, and it took extra time to dig it out. Then, a tractor-trailer rig became mired on 26 just down from Government Camp. That backed up traffic in both directions, causing people to slow and stop where they should have kept moving to avoid getting stuck. A light snowfall reduced visibility, too, which didn't help, either. So...

Arien already had a glimpse of the gym, but it was amazing to be there for a game. It looked for all the world like a venue for professional sports. The gallery on one side, its lofty ceiling, and the great width of the space with its indoor track circling above the cascading bleachers, made spectators as well as players take a happening in Gym A seriously. Easily eight hundred people were there, and duly amped. Sandy had just missed a shot, eliciting a sonorous groan from the majority. The announcer called an air ball though Arien saw Rex Putnam's defender barely graze it enough to deflect as it left the player's hands.

Derik bought Kenny and Jerrod a hot chocolate from the concession. Arien got a slice of pepperoni pizza and a bottle of water. After that, they made their way to the first isle into the stands and found a space six rows up where the four of them could sit together. Arien chomped on his pizza while looking for Danner, eventually spotting him among a row of white tank-topped kids on the sidelines. Holly was right behind him, whispering in his ear. Crazy babe. She was so hot. Arien's face pinkly flushed, thinking about her with a stifled rush like a galloping horse running headlong into a fence. Danner smiled, returning his attention to the floor. Where would this go if he knew?

The buzzer rang, marking the end of first quarter, while the band took up a boisterous, razzy tune, sounding a bit loose around the edges before getting swallowed in the cavernous space. Arien watched as the coach pointed at Danner, who jumped from his seat to smack palms with a retiring player, and quickly lock into a hands-on-shoulders huddle among the four other active teammates.

Arien refocused his attention to Holly. As best he could make out over the heads of his diagonal view to her, she seemed totally relaxed, talking with an older woman with blonde hair beside her. He couldn't help wondering if Holly fucked any other boys in that closet, not that it mattered much to him. If all girls held such secrets, wouldn't it make them more like boys? Arien, however, recognized a level of responsibility. He could tell himself he hadn't known Holly and his grandson were more than friends, but he had suspected.

They'd fed each-other's passion! This was no doubt a girl who did what she pleased. He'd allowed himself to be fired-up with the proximity of so many hot babes in this place. He told himself he had to watch that stuff.

Now the woman by Holly clearly shouted, "Go Danner!" as the buzzer rang out and the teams hustled back to their starting positions on the floor. She'd said that with a ringing familiarity that could only mean one thing, and Arien's heart leapt like a bullfrog into a throat way too narrow to let it through. "Holy shit!" he gasped, even though he'd had all day to get ready for such a moment.

"What's that?" Derik asked, leaning in.

"Arienne," he haltingly answered, as if the name would wake a fickle goddess. "That has to be Arienne."

Derik followed with, "So, that was your girlfriend, or...?" But then he nervously laughed. "Oh..."

"Yeah, *oh*," Arien echoed, feeling his body tremble.

Jerrod was sitting on Arien's other side. "She must be your aunt, then, huh?" he probed.

That was reasonable, Arien thought. He'd told them Danner was his cousin.

Kenny honed-in, too, though he sat to the right of Derik and missed the gist of the conversation.

"So what's next?" Derik matter-of-factly asked.

Rex Putnam missed a three-pointer their player, 43 scrambled for, and then missed another shot by the teammate who scooped the ball before it blew out of bounds. Then, Danner very aggressively turned another recovery but he couldn't prevent a great layup and score. The buzzer sounded and the scoreboard lit up with an 18 for Rex Putnam, to Sandy's 7. Another general moan coursed among the spectators, countered with a lively cheer among a gaggle of kids and parents on the opposite side. A group of cheerleaders in Rex Putnam's green and white uniforms belted-out a short yell of support.

"See if we could follow them home," Arien said, uncertainly, seeing a flash of red garment on the far side bleachers and feeling the rake of unknown eyes. She looked exactly the same as she did in the lunchroom. She didn't seem to care a wit for the game, any more a tree the clash of rutting bucks. She was oddly familiar. Where have I seen her before? He searched backwards, all the way to Tucson. Should I tell Derik? Why doesn't she just come over and say, hello?

Now Rex Putnam missed a layup, was blocked by a Sandy player, and the ball rebounded to Sandy, bearing a rush to the other basket and a successful two-pointer. The score flashed, Sandy, 9, and it perceptibly kicked the energy higher. Sandy was scrambling to fight back through a set of rebounds over the near court, and tricky passing. Now Danner passed the ball. The receiver jumped like a trap, and the ball flew, cleanly through the basket. Sandy 11.

Rex Putnam's turnover was stolen by Danner who flashed back to the net with a pounding, slippery dribble and executed a great layup. Sandy 13.

"The kid can play," Derik said.

Arien wondered if Derik had his gun in the school. Probably. His mind bounced from floor to hoop. He wanted to get closer to Arienne. He carefully studied her physical proximity. It was pretty dense right there behind the team's bench where a person had to camp before the crowd arrived. Holly twisted in her seat, and at one point seemed to notice him, but her gaze returned to the floor. It smarted a little bit. Well, maybe she didn't see me.

There was pounding in the stands. Rex Putnam fouled. Now Danner had the ball for a free throw. He let go a great, high-arcing shot that slipped through the hoop like a gold watch in a storm drain. Cheers rippled up and down. Rex Putnam Kingsman, 18, Sandy Pioneers, 14.

Arien chomped at the bit. He started to get up once, twice, but sat back again, rocking, working into the rhythm that had served him so well.

"What are you doing?" Derik asked him.

Rex Putnam turned it over pretty quick. Sandy passed and dunked it, bumping the board to 16, and more rippling cheers.

"I got to get closer."

"No, Ari–" Derik nipped the name, but laid his hand on Arien's shoulder to restrain him.

Rex Putnam had a fast player, a little guy who was all over the court, who made up for what he lacked in height with speed and agility. But his effort now, what anyone would have rated a hundred and ten-percent, ran into one of those moments when the defense gels like an impenetrable wall and he fouled.

The kid who made the free throw for Sandy missed as Arien moved to stand up a third time, finally completing the motion.

Derik looked up at him with a pointing finger.

The ball rebounded into a noisy, deck-beating scramble to the other side, but the Rex Putnam player missed his layup.

"I'll be okay," Arien told him, taking his bottle of water, stepping sideways in front of Derik and Kenny, into the isle.

Sandy took the rebound to the net but the kid missed his layup. The Kingsman were fighting hard to hold the Pioneers with a strong defense, which evidentially served them well in the first quarter, but an offensive rebound retained the ball for a good layup which tied the score with tumultuous clatter and cheering from the stands. It was perfect. Arien stepped down one, two, three levels as a man sitting diagonally behind the blonde woman stood with a cell phone pressed tightly to his ear. Arien came to the next level and waited for the man to make his way out, so he could move in front of people about to resume their seats, and there he was, looking over the shoulders of Holly, and certainly Arienne on the bleacher in front of him!

Oh my God! He studied the tip of her ear and the strands of hair around it. She was animated, leaning forward, the visible corner of her cheek pulled back with an anxious grin.

Rex Putnam fouled.

Sandy's free throw was a good shot, even with the thumping racket the visitors raised to distract him, and Sandy pulled ahead, 19 to 18.

Rex Putnam called a timeout, and a choppy murmur of conversation rose over the stands as one team melted away to a huddle on the far side and the other drifted to stand around, chat with their teammates on the bench, or make various contact with friends and family in the bleachers. Danner stopped between two seated teammates. He pulled up his tank top to wipe sweat off his forehead, briefly exposing his tummy. Then he smiled at the woman and Holly beside her.

"You're going to win this one, Danner?"

"Yeah Mom," he assured her, half looking away with a modest tilt to his shoulder and a happy grin. His eye caught Arien's behind them.

Danner looked thirsty. Arien quietly thrust his half full water bottle between the females in front. The kid on the floor hesitated for the barest millisecond before nodding as Holly turned in wide-eyed recognition. "Hi," she said, flashing an insecure smile. She accepted the bottle to pass to Danner between the boys on the bench. Arien watched Danner pensively screw the cap off. He took a few quick swallows before draining it all. His mother briefly twisted to see Arien before returning her gaze to the court.

The buzzer blared, resuming the game with the ball drumming off the floor. Arien leaned back in slow motion, exhaling like a man on a wire. Be cool, he told himself, syncing his heart with the beating ball in a purely coincidental way.

Holly cranked herself around again. "How long have you been here?" she asked, over the consternate wave of Sandy's missed jump shot.

The little guy in green had the ball again and beat it down the court until running into a jam, where he passed it forward to a kid with a clean shot to the hoop. He must have flinched at the site of three defenders rushing him, letting go of the ball with just a little too much force, to bounce it off the backboard.

"Not long." He could see her checking out his desert-tan fatigue boots. She impulsively squeezed his leg, above a boot, and then faced forward.

Nice. She's got the moxie. He liked that word. He'd heard it somewhere. Foxy Moxie, that's who Holly was.

Arienne turned to look at him again. Her wheels were turning but it wasn't about anything earth-shattering. Arien could tell that much. He trusted his ability to read vibes and intuit their meaning. It smacked of his proximity; her son knew him, Holly knew him even better and she didn't.

The turnover to Danner ran a foul. There was an "Aw!" from the bleachers that only deepened as the ball flew away to the basket, blasting out a great, long shot that boosted Rex Putnam's score to 21.

A good assist to Danner repeated the feat for Sandy. He jumped and the ball was a blur to the hoop, tying the score again to a roar of approval. Danner was smoking. The ball was barely in Kingsman hands when he swooped in and stole it, passing to a teammate by the basket, but the tall boy missed his layup.

Then Sandy took an offensive rebound to the hoop, giving the Pioneers, 23, and the Kingsman, 21.

Now, the little guy for the other team had the ball. It beat on the floor with focused intensity in his capable hands before finding its way through the basket. Rex Putnam 24, Sandy 23. Tight and close. There were "Aws" and foot-pounding and a few happy yells on the other side.

A missed jump shot by Sandy came off the hoop like a magnet opposed it. To Arien, the shooter tried too hard, and moved too quickly. That could be me, he considered. I've got to hold on to the rhythm, stay in sync and not buckle under the pressure. He was having trouble keeping his heart where it belonged. It felt like it wanted to wander around his chest to a variation of beats.

This lady is my daughter!

The Kingsman missed his turn, too, zinging the ball off the top of the board.

The defensive rebound was Sandy's. Danner streaked to the other side of the court. He was open. He was already turning when the ball came to him, catching it at his side, looking casual and whirling upward like a propeller, and the way he laid that ball in the hoop was so beautiful there was a delirious roar in the stands that any kid could take to his elder days. The buzzer sounded at Sandy's 25 to Rex Putnam's 24.

While the band straggled-out to a jazzy tune with identity issues, Danner ambled over between fist bumps and hand slaps among teammates. He wore a straight face but his body was all smiles, fluid, almost dancing.

The coach, a tall, light-haired man with a kindly demeanor, approached to confer with him.

Arien, watching, glowed with vicarious triumph. It came from a new place of approximate ownership, a sympathetic string. He didn't understand it, but it was okay. He let it flow. He couldn't be sure if that's what made her turn to face him yet again.

She seemed to mine for words, eventually commenting over the background racket, "I'm surprised he took that water,"

"Germs?" Arien modestly responded.

"No," she said, apparently amused, "He hates bottled water."

"How could you hate water?"

Holly had turned some, and was listening.

"It's not the water, it's the bottles." The woman nodded her head, pushing the point forward.

"What's wrong with the bottles?"

Holly joined, "They clog up the environment. They go to the landfills and will never go away. They're bad."

"Oh." Arien digested that. It made perfect sense. "I'll get a canteen," he said.

"Now you're talking," Arienne agreed.

"But you've got a problem," Arien said.

"Excuse me?"

"Yeah, look around. There's all sorts of bottles and cans going on. That one has apple juice, that one's... Let's see... Yeah, ice tea, and..." Arien studied her. She was a little heavier than average. Her hair was wavy, like his, but the same color yellow as Tina's and she had Tina's big blue eyes. He wondered how he compared with her, guessing he could probably pass more for her son than Danner who likely resembled his dad.

"At lunch they had these soft juice boxes," he continued, taken with their perfectly surreal first conversation. "You stick a plastic straw through the top. I'll bet a big pile of those will be around for billions, too, right? There must be hundreds that come out of this schoolhouse every day."

"You have to start somewhere," Holly offered. "And maybe you missed it; there's recycling stations all over the place.

"You should talk to Danner about it," Arienne said, turning half-way toward the court.

The phrase that came to mind was pissing in the wind, but Arien didn't say it. He thought instead about one of Otter's remarks about the revolution, and how it's waged in a dude's heart. Wow, Otter, what would you think of this stuff, the water bottles and soft plastic juice boxes, the gadgets, and the bastards working for the government?

Danner was looking at Holly, easy with himself, wiping his forehead again with the edge of his glossy-white, bright-red-bordered tank, innocently smiling at her, ignoring a buddy calling to him on the court. This exposed another hurt. Arien was sorry for him though it was too delicious to be wrong. He guessed if he could do it again, he would, though that kind of honesty will brutalize a self-image. He saw Danner catch the peculiar energy from an eye's corner where he was, loitering on the court among his teammates before they disappeared into the locker room.

His body still hurt. It wasn't much of a distraction in the first part of the day, getting it on with this girl, here. Whatever he brought in there only gave it more of an edge. He couldn't imagine being more turned-on. While his bruising healed he was finding it harder to wake up in the morning and get out of bed than it was to run himself through the day as a care-free young boy, but it was catching him now. It hurt at the top of his breath, and to twist and turn. He thought about standing, maybe going to the top of the bleachers to lean back against the wall.

"How do you know Danner?" Arienne asked, in a conversational tone.

"He's in two of my classes."

"Which ones?"

"Oceanic Science, and American Lit. He's real smart." Arien could see she liked hearing that.

"Yeah, he takes after his father."

"Is he here?"

"He was here, last time I looked," she said with a chuckle. "He was sitting right there, and God knows where he is, now!"

When she pointed at him he laughed, surprised. The guy answering the cell phone! Arien tried to remember what he looked like but it hadn't stuck. Then he went for the name Cassie told him. It started with a B... Danner's father is here! Imagine! Grasping the concept, Arien barely averted a descent into melancholy, triggered by the contrast with his own life; this lucky boy! What might I have been if my father had lived? And, that man was Arienne's husband, a real husband. What was that? Would I have liked the dude?

While the band hammered on a brassy show tune, and conversation rippled up and down around him, Arien considered what he'd missed. But he was still a boy, having sown so much while scratching at the beginning of his adult life. It was too strange. He noted his daughter's lock on his face, nothing too cosmic there, trying perhaps to figure him out or place him in some category. He caught Holly glancing at him and then away a few times. What could have been going on in her impulsive heart?

Both teams raced out to the floor again from separate doorways on either side of the set of bleachers Arien occupied. The lockers, showers and team rooms were behind the wall where the dark girl had positioned herself. Rex Putnam's players continued across the floor to wait on the other side where they mostly stood, warming up. Supporters for both teams cheered. The band's base and snare drums pounded a beat like a basketball on the shiny-new wood floor. The cheerleaders danced and posed. All was gearing up for the tight game's last acts.

Third Quarter began with the buzzer. Danner had the ball and let it go just as quickly in a three-point bid. Hitting the rim, it lingered there, tantalizingly close, but it fell away rather than in. A Pioneer caught the offensive rebound to recoup momentum with a two-point layup to the crashing, shimmering accompaniment of the band's set of cymbals, and a horn that could have come from a New Year's party. Sandy, 27, Rex Putnam, 24.

A Kingsman had the ball now – barely. Stolen by a Pioneer, it was fouled by Rex Putnam.

The teams lined up for the free throws. Arien, exhaling to lean forward, whispered near Arienne's ear, "How's Tina?" That was insane, I know, he told himself.

She turned around with a hint of annoyance. "What?" she said, wrinkling her nose.

"Your mom." Arien could see Tina in that wrinkle. It was like finding a jewel in a pile of pebbles, having seen a flash and then confirming its identity with a closer look. His jaw unconsciously dropped for an inaudible vocalization.

Arienne's blue eyes widened, connecting. "Oh, she's fine," she said, then turned away to watch the ball slip into the hoop, a rattle and distracting chant from the Away team's contingent notwithstanding. Sandy's score skipped to 28. When the shooter got the ball again he bounced it once, it came up to him as his hands flailed out to repeat the demonstration. Sandy 29, Rex Putnam 24. People cheered the points, but not like they applauded those 3-point shots.

Arienne didn't see Sandy force a foul, and Rex Putnam miss a jump shot. She'd turned to face Arien again. "How do you know Mom?"

An offensive rebound to a Kingsman went astray at the basket, and Sandy got the ball. Feet slapped the floor like fat, spattering raindrops as the teams folded together in a fast-frame wrestling dance; Rex Putnam was growing frantic to retrieve control of the game. Their quick little guy stole the turnover. It was fouled by a Pioneer.

Rex Putnam again had the ball, but the Kingsman's 3-point shot was a rim-bouncer. An "Aw" could be heard on the far side. The funky horn sounded again. There were some catcalls in the Sandy crowd.

"We met awhile back," he said.

Holly listened, half-turning her head into the words.

The rebound was passed to a Sandy player with a good sight on the basket. He jumped and it found its way. Sandy 31, Rex Putnam, 24. There was a lot of noise with that one. Arien said, "What?"

"What's your name," the blond woman repeated. "Who are you?"

Now the Kingsman missed a 3-pointer to rebound a ball subsequently returned to them. The little guy got it, found some space, and pierced it perfectly, sending it home. Their score bounced to 27.

"I'm Alex. I used to live on Derby Street, in Berkeley." Arien wanted to reach out to shake her hand, at least, but couldn't bring himself to do it. He didn't want to lose it in a place like this.

Arienne focused, questioning, attempting to make a connection. She tilted her head, crossing a leg so it was easier to look up over her shoulder at the intense, long-haired boy.

Sandy took the ball falling through the basket, and tossed it to safety, only to have it return for a missed 3-point shot that died among flailing arms right after the rebound. Then a foul was called on the tall, thin Pioneer.

The little fellow had the ball. He moved like a crouching rabbit, dribbling so low to the deck, weaving from one hand to the other, angling this way and that; even Arien listened for its unlikely jackhammer pulse to end while a couple of hundred spectators held their breath, but it flew out impossibly from under two defenders struggling with such concentration to block it, one of them tumbled head-over-heels while the other ran into Danner and knocked him down just as the net ate the ball, to bite Sandy's heels with 30 points. There were cheers everywhere. That kid was a star!

The game recaptured Arienne's attention, and her father for a moment forgot both his physical and emotional discomforts. He took the opportunity to scan the other side for the girl in red. No sign of her, but... He turned around, startled to see her behind him, up at the top, nine rows directly behind Derik, Kenny, and Jerrod. She leaned against the wall exactly where he'd intended to go! Arien tried to conceal his surprise, nodding at Derik and friends, in a glancing connection, mouthing-the-words, "Cool game, huh?" to distract anyone from turning around. Looking forward, he wondered, why did I do that? Do I have a reason to be afraid of her, or to shield her?

Danner owned the ball after a few seconds of evident pain, uneasy on his legs, but now he jumped for a two-point score. There were more rippling cheers as people remembered who they rooted for. Sandy 33, Rex Putnam 30.

A kingsman fouled and Danner was in position for the turnover. Danner was perhaps six, or six-one in height, not particularly tall, but he appeared tall just then, leaping as he did for the basket and scoring two more points for Sandy.

Rex Putnam called a 30-second timeout, and the Pioneers likewise hustled together for a word. The horn in the stands blew impatiently while the band raked a fragment of brassy number over the bleachers.

"Great job, Danner!" Arienne called, catching his glance at the buzzer.

In a moment, Rex Putnam's little star had the ball in the air for 3 points and some wild screaming from the visitors out of Milwaukie. Their team again nipped Sandy's heels. The kid's return to position along the 3-point line stood for his victory lap. Arien imagined the dude was so effective not only because he was good, but he was unlikely. Danner was also good, but bore the disadvantage of appearing to be so from the get-go.

Danner had the ball. He performed a quick dribble from hand-to-hand and passed it to the tall boy who nicely laid it up. Sandy, 37, Rex Putnam, 33.

A fast scramble to the other side nailed a basket for Rex Putnam, now scoring 35, and then returning, Danner attempted a layup that went south. People just watched, glued to the action. This game was so intense; to look away risked regrettable omissions.

The rebound by another Sandy player, who might have pushed himself too hard, missed a jump shot. He retrieved his ball and tried again, and missed that one, too. Then the ball went dead into a defensive rebound, stuck in a corner of waving arms, as the buzzer marked the end of the 3rd quarter, and the band struck up a contest with the Kingsman's cheer leaders.

Arien leaned forward a second time to ask a question, but Arienne angled toward Holly. "What are you doing after the game?"

"I've got homework." It was like he wasn't there.

He tried again. "How was it growing up?"

She looked at him with a baffled expression, and Holly did the same, but he pressed on. It wouldn't have been much easier if he'd whipped himself to say, "Please, Arienne, I really want to know what it was like for Tina's baby girl." There, he'd said it, he'd said her name! The murmurs of conversation, the raucous music, and the odd acoustics in the yawning space divided a deep, unseen ballast from an obvious expression of his sincerity. The words, of course, hardly matched it, but his feelings surely did, and Arienne fell into a studied silence she appeared to clear with a shake of her hair and an ironic smile.

"You really want to know that?"

"Yeah, Babe."

"Oh?" Her eyebrows went up. "It's Babe, is it?"

"I really want to know," he said, resting before inhaling again, prostrate before her adult woman's roll of attitude. He worried he might pass out. He could feel Derik's stare boring into him from above, and he gathered Holly's curiosity was eating an indulgent treat. He nearly laughed, thinking of the dark girl in red, whom he knew still sat where he'd intended to repair himself, the very spot, no less!

"Oh, it was okay, I guess. Mom was a hippie," Arienne answered, looking askance at him as in, alright, I'll play along...

"Let's see," he chased, "How long were you in Virginia?"

"I don't remember Virginia," she said, obviously impressed, "but I do remember little bits of Vermont, bits of kindergarten, first grade at Hardwick Elementary, a summer around Caspian Lake in Greensboro. Mom was pretty poor in those days. Our family was the kids she lived with, barely older than this." She waved her hand generally at the gym.

"Do you remember Oak?"

"Oh my God. What did you say your name was again?"

"Alex, from Derby Street" – and they both said – "in Berkeley" – at the same time.

"I remember that much," she said, sharing an apologetic chuckle.

"So, do you remember him?"

"Oh my, yes! Only, he was Uncle Oak." She smiled with amazement. "He lived in an old farmhouse with a few others on Wheel Lock Mountain. How do you know about this?"

"I heard stories."

"You are a very strange young man, Alex."

"I guess. So, when did you come back to Oregon?"

"Well, I never came back to Oregon," she corrected. "I'd never been here before we moved here the first time." She tilted her head again. "Are you alright?"

"I'm okay," he said, but he was beginning to feel dizzy.

"We lived at my grandma's house in Marin before we came here. I was about eleven..." Arienne paused, and then she said, "Wow. Derby Street..."

"Yeah?"

"Mom had a good friend that lived on Derby Street! My God! That was so long ago!"

"She did? Who was that?" Arien rallied. He was beginning to smell a vein beyond dirt in the hole he was digging. Jesus, he trembled, this is so rad!

"Ma..., Ma–"

"Maggie."

"Wow, yeah, that's right, Kid! You're something else!" Arienne had now turned entirely on the bench, sitting sideways on it with her knees drawn up in the slacks she wore, and her arms around them. Holly had to make more room for her on the bench.

"Maggie had a little boy, a cute kid about seven or eight," Arienne continued, pulling on the thread. "He had a big mop of hair and an unusual name: Arien. It's easy to remember it because it was my father's name, too. Funny, you know? I was named after my father, you know, because–"

"You were born on his birthday."

"What are you asking me about this, for, Young Fellow? You already know all about it."

"No, I don't, really. Please don't stop."

Arienne bounced a look off of Holly.

The buzzer rang out and the concussion of the ball and primal utterances on the court assailed Arien's ears.

"I only met him today," Holly explained, loudly enough to be heard, but with an exaggerated shrug.

Sandy fouled before anyone could shoot. That was quickly followed by a great, scrambling layup for Rex Putnam. The board lit up the tie score at 37. There was pounding everywhere in the stands. Feet and hands on benches, the line of chanting, gyrating girls, the crazy horn, and the snare drum all noted the score, and expressed an exuberant measure of excitement. It looked for a moment like Rex Putnam would regain the upper hand.

"I played with Maggie's kid in the park. I don't remember it much. I remember the trees were very beautiful, and they smelled good, kind-a like menthol or lemon." She lightly scratched her chin. "We collected those little seed pods or whatever they are."

Arien had to concentrate to hear her. "Eucalyptus," he helped, struck with a new recollection of a pretty blonde woman and her older child who occasionally visited his Momma at Grandma's house on Derby Street. It was the seed pods that brought it back. It was such a wonderful, carefree time. Funny, he'd never made the connection before.

"Oh, and get this," she exclaimed: "My grandfather's name was Alex! Wow. Are you any relation to us?"

"Yes," he admitted.

"Oh my goodness! This is really the most amazing... Mom's going to flip out when she hears about this!"

He sighed. "I expect she will," he said.

Now here was a whole new mystery. How did Tina come to know my mom? Arien wrestled with that one. He guessed it was Woodstock. It had to be, because they were both there. Wow. Talk about coincidences! It brought him down a notch to realize cosmic doings didn't only happen to him, though his trip to the restroom before the game's fourth quarter got going defied him to produce its equal in his experience.

He'd managed to get himself up in time for another synchronistic exchange of place with Danner's father. There he was, waiting to reclaim his seat in the bleachers, having only just returned the moment Arien stood. The dude was likely as tall as, or taller than Danner. His salt-and-pepper hair, cut short, looked right, having likely once been totally dark and curly, and Danner had his dad's intense blue eyes. Arien was taken slightly off balance to see him, but he nodded at the man. He assumed his conversation with Arienne would continue. Now he knew it would not and worried the chance to lock-in his connection with her was being blown.

There was nothing to do but proceed. Derik, watching from above, must have caught the wrong vibe from Arien's expression and was shortly on his way down. Arien's attempt to wave him off didn't work. Derik's vibe resisted with attitude, while up at the top the girl in red was gone. Arien asked himself, how does she get around like that?

It began in the corridor with the strangest sensation, falling and flying, and tumbling head over heels while his ears sort-of screamed. Arien was sure of opening into a parallel awareness, as if dreaming awake, while holding both views in the same eye. It got him dizzy, off-balance, and he barely made it to the men's room.

There was a brilliant flash; surely a bolt of lightning to witness the girl in the red shawl (or... was it a blanket, a cape?), who now assumed the appearance of a human eclipse with a brilliant corona. The mighty concussion of thunder should have leveled the building. It blew him out of his box. He fell into a deep, smothering darkness with ever more distant flashes, booms, answering reports, and their concussions over his field of awareness. He barely sensed feet collide into his body just as the building's illumination returned to eyes lined in a lingering day-glow green, and his physical field received a distant, roaring wave of spectator voices from the gym.

They sat each other up in the invisible ozone redolence. Arien's adrenaline laugh met with a very perplexed Derik Jaffrey. "I'm sorry! I didn't expect to find you on the floor!" he said, and chased that with, "What's that smell?"

Arien wondered if it killed her. "It's Star Wars," he answered, flexing into the ongoing rush. He laughed again, with a crazy edge to it, shaking his head. They were both on the floor with legs sprawled-out this way and that and Derik had already reached out to Arien's shoulders, which Arien returned like a greeting friend.

"There must have been an electrical short in the building," Derik considered as they helped each other up. "I couldn't see a thing. Did I hurt you?"

"No, Dude, I'm good."

Derik looked uncertain. "Arien, is there anything going on I should know about?"

"Uh, no, Derik. Not yet, anyway."

How dizzy he was after that. They barely exited the men's room when he had to sit down on the floor of the corridor with his stomach all set to heave. He leaned back against the wall, feeling cold and sweaty. Derik patiently sat with him, mostly quiet with inquiring eyes. Arien shut them out with a forearm on his knees. He couldn't begin to explain. It was deferred, anyway, by Arienne. He saw her first in his mind's eye and risked an upward glance to catch her come out the nearer doors to the gym across the hall.

She appeared a bit agitated, but it changed to relief when she saw him on the floor after searching first one way and them the other in the wide corridor. "Oh, there you are, Young Man," she declared. "I thought you'd left."

"I almost did," he said, trying unsuccessfully to disguise his discomfort.

273

"Are you okay, Son?" She came over to squat down by him, exchanging glances with Derik, who maintained a relaxed countenance as if they'd been having a private conference in the hall.

"Upset stomach," Arien said. "It might have been the pizza."

She called me, Son! Ha!

"That's too bad. Maybe they have something at the concession."

"Like what?"

"A soda, or I could ask what they've got."

There was a roar, with catcalls from the gym and stamping in the bleachers.

"It's okay, Thanks. I'm already feeling better. Besides, you're missing the game."

"They were disputing points," she informed. "The ball was headed for the hoop, but when the lights went out nobody saw it go in." She smiled, playfully.

Arien looked up at her, waiting.

"You're a relative..." she led.

He subtly nodded, getting a curious vibe from Derik.

"You've got my attention, Kid.

22 – The sight of that big 45

They were stopped at the Dairy Queen on their way through Sandy, with Jerrod and Kenny up front. Arien's head swirled like an inside-out version of the chocolate cone Jerrod passed him from the driver's window. He had to concentrate to lick the cool, sweet stuff all around so it wouldn't run down the side, while two memories struggled to claim the same moment in time, very strange.

"That was a damn good game!" Jerrod praised. "I'm glad we came."

"Yeah," Kenny chimed.

"Me, too," Arien sincerely agreed.

Derik inquired in a low voice, "You said something back there..."

"What's that?" Arien allowed himself to be seduced by the soft cone's sweet charms.

"Star Wars."

"I did?"

The radio came on up front. Arien recognized the song immediately. The lilting rhythm framed Bono's plaintive wail, *You have to cry without weeping, talk without speaking, scream without raising your voice...*

"Come on, please don't fuck with me. It was when the lights came on. The way you said that..." Derik poked his butterscotch sundae's plastic spoon into Arien's arm.

Arien looked out the window. They passed a group of people standing in front of the Gateway Pub smoking cigarettes in a sleety-drizzle that sparkled like shooting stars around the light from the sign under the pub's marquee. He wanted to retreat with thoughts over his hardly digested experience. It teetered toward the dubious. He'd heard about acid flashbacks and wondered if it might have been something like that, though its clear memory lingered and he knew better.

"You're not my only guardian, Derik."

He contemplated the closing metaphor of Bono's song, *running to stand still*. That could be me. God, he mused, that song's older now than all the time I've been alive.

"For real?"

Arien smiled. He said, "What's real?" and felt Derik's attention firmly press against the side of his head. "What am I supposed to say?"

"Who else?"

"I think I've seen her before."

"Where?"

"Arizona," he said, realizing he'd informed himself at the same time as Derik. She didn't look quite the same, but the vibe was spot-on, and that might have been what threw him because it was so unlikely.

"So what's your plan?" Jerrod asked over his shoulder. They'd left Sandy behind over the slosh of deepening sleet in the road. It was too dark to see anywhere but up front in the headlights, and visibility there was limited by streaking precipitation splattering the windshield and holding on like translucent bird drops. The wipers barely kept up. Jerrod sensibly slowed the car. "Are you coming back to school with us tomorrow?"

"Good question," Derik commented.

"I don't know. When you wake me in the morning I'll know. But I think I got what I went for, and then some."

"I'd say," Jerrod agreed.

"Yeah, you got laid, right?" Kenny added.

"What's this, you, you got laid at school?" Derik probed.

Arien nodded.

"You did?"

"Cross my heart." But it was Derik's heart he crossed, with a rusty blade. Arien knew it as soon as the words left his lips. "Sorry, Bro," he said. Damn it. Why must I feel this shit?

"So, Alex, did Danner recognize you?" Jerrod asked.

"No."

"Did his mom?" Kenny followed. "I mean, you rapped with her."

"Yeah," he said, because in a way, she had, though he'd made it rather easy. He wondered what she would tell Tina. How soon would they talk? What would Tina say? Oh, the white-water rush these thoughts were riding on! He reached for the card Arienne handed him out in the hall, anchoring her spontaneous invitation to dinner when he was still too nauseous to do more than thank her. He waved it up like a trophy for Kenny to see, but his friend already returned to looking ahead. The sky was throwing patches of white-and-flaky, and more of it as they drove. It blinded in the light of oncoming cars. Jerrod let up more on the throttle.

"You drive like an old lady," Kenny observed.

"Can you see any road?"

"Are we on a road?"

"We better be or we could eat a tree."

Derik leaned to Arien's ear and quietly asked, "What do you suppose she's like now, Alex?" He set his empty plastic cup on the floor.

"I've a thousand questions, but it comes down to her vibe, huh? Will she even want to see me?"

"Will she blame you for leaving her?"

"Tina doesn't eliminate like that. She's a righteous babe."

Derik was quiet for a moment. "Then she'll want to see you. I know I would," he certainly affirmed.

"Whoa!" Kenny suddenly cried-out.

"Shit, that was close!" Jerrod agreed.

"What?" Derik asked.

"A deer – a deer was right in front of us!" Kenny said.

The idea got Arien tracking along a trail in his head. It led into the darkness of the freezing, sodden woods on either side of the highway. There was life in that invaded, fragmented country. It took many forms, furry, and feathered, sleeping, and awake, having varying degrees of necessity and prerogative, up in the swaying, talking crowns, or down under the earth, or suspended in the rivers and streams with cold, calculating balance, intuiting every nuance of current, pressure, temperature, and odor with the awareness of the eternal now.

The road cutting through it was an anomaly of the treacherous co-existence, like fatty tangles in a demented brain, an impertinent intrusion. Arien could not have felt more out-of-place in Jerrod's blindly-prowling, killer automobile. "We should be walking home," he audibly whispered.

"What did he say?" Jerrod asked.

"He said we should be walking home," Kenney repeated.

"Fuck that."

"We're good people," Arien followed, "but all of us living like this are bad."

"Why, because a deer got in the way?" Jerrod responded.

Funny, how people know where you're coming from when you're high, Arien mused, but they can only answer from their own moment, which cranks-out excuses like perfectly interchangeable parts. This was no back-handed self-stroking boast. Arien knew he was high, because he knew that he knew. Was this a flashback, too? He caught Derik regarding him in the momentary glare of a passing car. It was a look of pure engagement, absorbing some totally new thing. Nope, once again, this was no flashback. It came from who he was, and where he was going.

"We can't all walk. We'd starve," Kenny said.

"That's better," Arien told him. "Jerrod, would you mind turning the car around?"

"What is it, Alex?"

"She's there, Derik."

"Who's there?"

"Alex, you don't have to go to school tomorrow, but I do."

"Please, Jerrod."

The car slowed considerably, finally pulling to the shoulder where Jerrod held the brake in a long moment. The bright red light glowed in the snowflakes beyond the rear window while the wipers muffled smacking spoke from the front. Jerrod huffed with exasperation, leaning forward to rest his head against the wheel.

On impulse, Arien opened the door, hesitating, closing his eyes to block-out the dome light, and feeling for his rhythm; one one-thousand, two one-thousand, three...

"Oh, damn it!" Derik said. "How am I supposed to keep up with this?"

Jerrod sighed.

"Where are you going that can't wait until tomorrow?"

Kenny twisted around to stare at the weird kid in the back seat who was about to get out of the car.

"You're like an accident," he said. "You happened and nothing's the same. Jerrod, who is this guy?"

"It was that circle during the sauna..." Jerrod imagined aloud.

"Forgive me, I can't help it," Arien said, feeling sympathy for their predicament. "I've got to go back."

"To school? They're out-a there by now, Dude, there's–"

"The address on this card," he said. "She's there now. I know it, I just know it."

It seemed to take forever to find the house near the bend on Phelps Road. Neither Kenny or Jerrod knew where it was, so they'd waited at the 7-11 at the first stoplight in town for someone to come along who could give them directions. Everyone urged Arien to call the number on the card, first, but he'd refused.

"I just have to go there, now," he'd told them with convincing certainty.

Their instructions were sketchy, too. Arien was sure when they'd reached the bridge on Bull Run they'd gone too far. "Go back up the hill," he instructed. "We passed it up there."

Jerrod methodically turned the car around to slowly climb the steep, curvy road revealed in the tenuous headlights that bored through a spooky, thickening wall of sleet and snow.

"Good traction," Derik observed.

"Four-wheel drive and studded tires," Jerrod informed him. "You can't live on the mountain without 'em."

"I guess not."

"That's got to be the road, up ahead," Arien exclaimed, leaning forward.

"Damn! I missed it. How the hell did you see that in the back seat?"

"I didn't."

"Your friend, Andy mentioned this," Derik quietly said.

Arien swallowed and held his breath. One one-thousand, two one-thousand, three... Be cool. Be cool, he told himself, holding the reins of his heart close, because he knew it would buck and kick if he didn't.

"He said when you were on the road you always seemed to know where you were going and knew the best places to stop."

The boys up front were silent, but alert, until reaching a tight bend with only enough room for one car to pass.

"Is this right?" Jerrod asked.

"Keep going."

There were lights in windows on the right.

"I can't see any numbers," Jerrod said.

"The mailboxes are getting covered with snow," Kenny agreed. "Pull over, we can wipe one–"

"Not yet. Keep going."

Jerrod said, "Shit."

They passed a couple of more houses and a low, white barn, then drove on until there were fewer dwellings set more away from the road and spaced farther apart. And then they reached one where Arien said to stop. A car was parked there. Steam hovered over its hood in the glare of their lights.

Oh, fuck! He could barely keep it together while their motor hummed, the blower whooshed, headlights drilled a tunnel into the weather, and their wipers counted the time: One one-thousand, two one-thousand, three one-thousand...

He opened his door. They were looking at him in the dome light.

"Stay here," he said. But none of them did. He was doing a poor job of masking his emotion, forgetting to breathe while concentrating too hard on quieting the heaving stallion in his chest. He couldn't be bothered with mere refusals. He knew those poor dudes were attached to him, in thrall of his energy and his mission, full of intense curiosity, and in Derik's case, vigilance. He had to focus as he ascended the wet, slippery lawn in pitch darkness, drawing closer to the front entrance of the house. The door opened with a soft light, and he distinctly heard the words, "Where are you going, Mom?"

"Are you expecting someone, Arienne?" a mature voice said.

The porch light came on, revealing a woman's silhouette on the edge.

"It's some kids," Arienne observed, coming from behind her. "Brett, would you tell Danner I think some of his friends..."

But Arien's feet found the walkway, and he was already stepping into the visible light. When it was full on him the woman at the edge of the porch froze at his approach. He couldn't see her face, but he could feel her well enough.

She said, "Ah," like a dying breath, and she slightly swayed on her feet.

It was all flurries now, big white flakes falling in the halo of illumination to fill the night with deep silence. Derik, Jerrod, and Kenny came up behind and stopped to wait.

Arienne cocked her head, watching, apparently too surprised to say anything as the boy she'd invited to come for a dinner took the last few steps to her mother, who came down off the porch.

He closed those last few feet into a very tight embrace.

"Oh, Tina!" he sobbed. "I'm so sorry! I'm so sorry." With a heaving and pouring of easy tears, he nuzzled into her lightened frame, smelling the side of her damp head until his nose was too stuffed, and then he stroked her lined cheeks, crying. She was so fucking old! She could have been his grandmother!

"There, there," she soothed, swiping tears from under his eyes before entwining her fingers behind his head, to bury them in the wavy hair. "Oh Arien, oh Arien, Sweet Boy, it's okay, it's all okay."

Her voice reached deeply into him, though it sounded off, reedy, like Tina with a cold.

"Arien?" Jerrod queried.

"Arien?" Arienne repeated.

And so there he was, with such an aching stampede in his breast and a spinning head; they fell into a silence occasionally interrupted by Arien's shallow, spastic breaths while snowflakes whitened their shoulders and the tops of their heads, until the man Arien saw at the game filled the doorway to tell the variously gawking onlookers, "Please come inside so we can close the door."

Arien could have been anywhere, or nowhere. He could have floated into the living room, or been carried for all he knew, and he was sitting on a couch almost numbly next to this transformed, diminished old woman with excruciatingly familiar eyes, and expression, and kindness, and understanding. He wished they could be alone. Everyone was staring. Brett stood by a fireplace with a gas flame insert and faux logs. Danner came in, too now, having materialized from somewhere in the house.

"Whoa, what brings *you* here, Dude?"

Arien's emotional cascade turned, just like that, into a bubble of laughter. How easily it changed, for the irony and strangeness of it all. And Tina snickered, also, meeting him perfectly.

"Mom, tell me what's going on!" Arienne firmly demanded.

"Arienne, say hello to your father. This boy is your father!" She stroked the side of his face. "You were named after him, you know, because you were born on his birthday." She rocked back, planting her hand under the boy's chin before grasping his hands.

"Jesus Christ!" Brett exclaimed, "What is this?"

"Oh, *M-o-m*," Arienne practically wailed. "That's impossible!"

"No, Honey, he's come through time, right from Woodstock, isn't that right, Arien?"

Arienne's pallor grew ashen.

"Yeah, just a few weeks ago, Babe." It was so strange to say that to this old lady! "I came here in December. Andy was waiting for me."

"Oh, Andy!" She chuckled, "Who else? How is he doing?"

Arien, though still wearing a face in mourning was already regaining himself. "He's alright, I think, but the last time we were together was when our helicopter crashed into the Mountain."

"No kidding! You were in that?" Jerrod exclaimed. "It was all over the news!"

"You lied to us!" Kenny declared, getting up from the chair he'd planted himself in.

"Come on, Guys," Derik barked. "He had no choice." Then Derik turned to Arien. "I really wish we could have, um..."

"I'm sorry, Derik," Arien said with a shrug. "Cat's out now."

"Wait, you were on the Army helicopter that was in the news the other night?" Brett asked.

Arien nodded.

"This man is Lieutenant Derik Jaffrey," he revealed. His mission is to keep me safe. No one is supposed to know about this or I might become somebody's mad science project."

"No, this is for real?" Danner croaked. "It's a gag, right, Grandma? Tell me it's a gag? You're some dude named Alex, right?"

"Alex." Tina repeated with a smile. "That was your dad's name."

"Oh my God, this can't be!" Arienne squealed.

"Oh but it is, isn't it, Lieutenant?" Tina said, looking squarely at him.

"We're busted," Derik replied.

"Are you armed?"

Arien thought that was a strange thing for Tina to ask.

"Always."

"Can I see it?"

Then Arien got it. Wow! More than anything that could ever have been said, it was the sight of that big 45 that drove the message home. She took it and held it in her hands, turning it this way and that before giving it back to Derik in the stunned silence.

"Peace and love," she distantly mused.

"Some people think he's the most valuable person on the planet, Ma'am."

"I'm not at all surprised, Lieutenant. This one skipped over decades the rest of us had to live." Her words knelled in that room.

Danner's father came to stand near, regarding Arien with the same intense blue eyes Danner had.

"About a month ago you were in the news," he finally pronounced.

Arien yearned for some privacy. Tina seemed to catch that. She gazed at him, sizing him up with an angle to her head.

"Did you color your hair?"

"Yeah." He looked at Kenny, whose lips formed an O. It was Kenny that helped him dye it after snagging a box of his mom's hair color.

"I like it. It's sharp," she said.

Arien's smile was a little glad.

"Right, Brett, I was in the news."

"They said he was a runaway!" Brett declared.

"And they also said his name was Arien," His wife answered. "My God! Remember how I mentioned that? But they said your name was Arien Grove!"

"That's the name the Tree Tribe gave him way back there when I was his age," Tina said.

"No way! You're my grandfather!" Danner realized aloud. He balled his fists and spun around once like the man who won a bet. "They'll *never* believe it!"

"So you won't tell them, unless you want to end the school year early at a government installation," Derik warned. "This is serious, Danner. People have died. Believe it: No one has been allowed to know him and be free to live a normal life. Do you know why our helicopter crashed?"

"Uh, no..." Danner shifted uneasily.

"Anyone?"

There was waiting silence.

"Tell them, Arien."

He considered for a moment, and then said, "Somebody tried to take me by force, right out of a camp where we were with Colonel Griffin. He's with Army Intelligence and Derik here is too, you know. I guess the bullets hit something a chopper needs to fly. We came down in the snow. I'm sure glad you stopped for us, Jerrod!"

"Wow!" Jerrod said.

"So that's what's been going on with them!" Kenny followed. He snickered into a secret joke. "We thought you were gay."

Arien laughed, connecting with Derik, who lowered his head.

Oh, fuck! He was holding her wrinkled, red hand close to his body, feeling her. He wanted to cry again. She was too old. It was too weird. What am I going to do?

"Arien," she whispered, as the others strained to hear her, and her eyes expressed such emotion, "you are even stronger than I remember."

What did she mean? He felt like crap. His life with this lady was stolen! He'd cried in front of everybody! That's strength? Then, for the first time, he looked around the room, absorbing the unlikely group, each falling into their own kind of teary introspection. Sure, it was focused on him, but he grasped the significance of symbols which really boiled down to a predicament about life. It was said among the Tree Tribe, Arien was a natural. Kelsey argued a past-life experience probably bore on this one, while Andy held Arien was gifted to perceive the world from an uncommon altitude. These weren't Arien's words, and he hadn't begun to use them, but he was still learning what they were about.

His grandson was staring. What was going on behind those bright blue eyes? Could there ever be a relationship with him? They came from such different worlds. Arienne looked like she would faint. The room wasn't hot but perspiration dotted her forehead. Her face was flushed.

"You were the little boy I used to play with when we went to Berkeley?" she said, again with a squeal. "Mother, did you always know who he was?"

"I thought things would turn out different," Tina answered. "I wanted to protect you, Arien, but I was terrified of doing anything that could blow our chance to meet in Portland at Blue Star's. I would love to have consulted with Andy about this but we lost touch. I suppose you know about all that, now."

"How'd you meet Maggie?" Arien asked, burning to know the answer.

"Maggie," Tina repeated her name with a sigh. "Even you might find this a bit far-out, Arien." She smiled wistfully. "The day you disappeared, Otter heard an announcement over the PA that somebody was looking for you. When you didn't return to camp, Andy got it real bad that something was wrong, and I thought so, too. I remember it like it was yesterday." Tina squeezed Arien's hand. "We had a Council, and it came up this person who wanted to see you might know something. We followed-up with one of our own the next day, looking for her." Tina's eyes sparkled. "I had no idea who she was, of course."

"Yeah, then what?"

"We hit it off. We liked her, she liked us. She even hung with us for awhile, up in Vermont. Oak named her Maggie Maple." Tina widely grinned. She seemed to have all her teeth, but they were yellowed and looked different, receding gums, wear and tear...

"When Arienne and I stayed with Paul and Janice, in San Francisco – do you remember them, from Page Street?"

Arien guffawed, shook his head, and sniffed mucous that was reaching for his upper lip.

"Oh, God," she said, catching herself with a chuckle. "You probably saw them last week."

"Just about," he agreed.

"Well I couldn't believe it when I ran into her on Market Street one day. Maggie came to the Bay Area the year before to be with her father, who had cancer, and one night out dancing she met a soldier boy named Alex Danner, from Berkeley, and well, the rest is history."

"Holy shit!" Arien whispered, and a pin dropping in that house would have made a very loud noise.

Danner paced in his Grandma's kitchen. Arien sat at the table, nursing a Mirror Pond Pale Ale. It was cold and had a good snappy taste. How cool for Danner to come by! After promising Derik to lay low for a few days, any visitor was welcome, more so this one. Arien had taken Tina up on her invitation for them to stay with her. Of course it was exactly what he expected all along, though it magnified the Devil's charms against the fathoms of the sea, and he now seriously wondered if he could handle it.

"Do you want one?" Arien lifted the bottle.

Danner hesitated, as if not hearing.

"Yeah," he finally said.

Arien pointed to the refrigerator, asking, "Do you know where we can cop some bud?"

"I don't do that."

"Dude," Arien flatly commented.

"I don't want to get kicked off the team."

"Whatever." But Arien smiled. He watched Danner open the bottle with an up-to-date 'church key' that had a beefy plastic handle. He was glad microbrews didn't come in twist tops.

Danner studied him uneasily. He took a sip of beer. "Where's your bodyguard today?"

"He's hangin' in the city at Pioneer Square."

Danner's silent squint posed his question.

"I'm expecting some friends. Any time now they'll be coming there to look for me."

Danner nodded, was still for a moment and then fidgeted in his chair. "What?"

"It's Holly." Danner played with the beer bottle on the table top. "I don't know what's got into her."

"Oh?"

"Well, uh, Holly's my girl."

"Okay."

"Yeah."

"Okay, so?" Arien focused on his breath.

"She asked about you at school today."

"Is that a big deal, Danner?"

"It's not like that, Grandpa – uh, Arien." The dark-haired, blue-eyed boy rubbed his nose and glanced up at the ceiling. A smirk crept over his face. "This is weird," he admitted.

"Yeah, I'm not ready to do *Grandpa*, either." Arien agreed. Good, keep it light, he told himself.

"Well, uh, Arien, she asked me three times today. I didn't want to say anything. I said I didn't know where you were. She told me about your talk with Mom at the game, about how you knew a lot about her. It's got her all fired-up, I guess. It doesn't make sense."

Arien noticed Tina in the doorway with a fresh-scrubbed face. How long had she been there? She wore a bathrobe and her surprisingly full and lengthy gray hair was wrapped in a towel. He still wasn't past the collision of this lady with his bruised reality. He looked for her, the shiny-new adult babe with that scream-sweet, California-blonde, perfect woman-girl's face and creamy-dreamy body she has, and gladly gives to him. The old lady met that like a head-on collision. But she was a great old lady, after all. A bittersweet smile quivered over his lips.

She returned his gaze from an intimate depth. Tina seemed so wise and strong. "Hello Danner," she said, acknowledging the boy. He'd gone silent.

"Hey, Grandma."

"Excuse me, I'll put something on."

Danner nodded, and so did Arien, who feebly recharged the smile. As she retreated there was an intrusive flash of Holly in the closet at school. That girl was a hot, hard, tight little slinky spark, taking him in, swallowing him with firm contractions, and sucking his ecstatic jet into her body's perfect target in a matter of minutes, and then doing it all over again, while Tina awkwardly offered him a spare bedroom with Derik, or a couch in the living room, but he'd stood outside her room, closed his eyes, took a few deep breaths, opened her door and went in to sit on her bed, next to her. She'd accepted that, she'd said, "Get in then, if you want. It'll get cold. I like the window open all night." And that is what he did.

But first, she watched while he took off his clothes, all of them, and he'd made no effort to hide his excitement, though its intensity surprised him and when he climbed under the blankets with her and pressed himself against the length of her, separated by her nightgown, it was an extraordinarily erotic thing for him to have done, right out of a seduction fantasy he'd indulged as a fourteen year-old.

Danner regarded him with an unreadable expression. "She's weird."

"Tina?"

"Holly – uh, Grandma, too."

That was awkward.

"What can I do for you, Danner?"

"I don't know. She was kind-a cold today, except when talking about you. I can't explain it. I don't get it."

Arien chuckled but it didn't come from an easy place. "Tell her I dropped out."

"You're not coming back to school?"

"I was never in school."

Danner appeared confused.

Arien swigged his beer. He sighed.

"What are...?" Danner seemed to struggle. "What are you going to do? You and Grandma...

"I, I didn't sleep much last night." His grimace turned into a yawn. "I already started my essay for Lit. It's not due for two weeks...

"Mom went nuts."

"Arien rolled his eyes. "She wouldn't hug me when I left."

"She doesn't know what you are. At least... that's what she told me after you left."

"She doesn't believe it?"

"Ah, nah, it's not that. She's got a good connection with Grandma. They don't lie to each other." Danner scooted himself up to sit on the kitchen counter. It was an unlikely perch, but he easily alighted there. He nestled the bottle between his legs. "She said she'd never been so sad in her life."

"Hmm..." Arien absorbed that. "Why?"

"I'll major in Psych when I get to college, Arien," he said with a grin.

Arien pretended to shoot him with a make-believe pistol and blow the smoke off his index finger.

"How was your dad?"

Danner laughed. "Pretty bent out of shape, too," he said. "He wants some of your hair."

"For voodoo?"

"Yeah, that's it.

"He'd see it's dyed."

"He kept saying he couldn't believe it, but he really does, I think." Danner looked down at the floor, then at Arien. "I see it. Mom looks like Grandma, but she looks like you, too, and I've never seen Grandma so..."

"Does she have any friends, Danner?"

"Yeah, plenty, I guess." He chuckled. "You know, this is the first time I've ever had a beer at her house." He lit up. "We had whiskey together, once, when I turned thirteen. That was so cool!" He fondly shook his head into the memory. "Mom was so pissed."

"I mean any boyfriends?"

"She's got guy friends, but not like that. I used to ask her what Grandpa was like."

"What'd she say?"

"Oh, you know, she said he was special, he was beautiful, and he was taken before his time." He thought for a moment. "Damn!" he exclaimed, like he'd run into a tree.

"What?"

"I forgot that!"

"What, Danner?"

"At least twice, she said you were from the future! Jeeze, I took that to mean you were, you know, you were a forward-thinking kind-a guy."

Arien thought that was pretty funny. This dude wasn't so bad.

"Hmm, and she never had any boyfriends?"

"No, I don't think so. You'll have to ask her. I'm only seventeen. She's been around longer than that." Danner seemed to have more to say. He fidgeted, sipped beer and looked around the room. When he finally settled on something Arien couldn't be sure if that's what it was.

"Tell me about Woodstock."

"Ouch," Arien said.

"Huh? You didn't like it?"

"One of the Trees drowned on the way. Damn, we were so close. I got over it, I guess. We had a nice memorial for everybody."

"Everybody?"

"Laurel, Tree, and Blue Star, too. He didn't make it, either."

"Sounds rough."

"Yeah."

"So who did you see?"

"Quill, Richie Havens, Joan Baez, Country Joe. I missed Cocker. Santana was awesome. Dude, I danced with my Momma!" Arien's eyes misted over. "I didn't catch the folks on Saturday night; we were doing the Circle, and Sunday, too, *onnacanna*."

"Onnacanna?"

"Onnacanna I wasn't there anymore."

Danner leaned forward on his perch. "Man, what happened?"

Curious, but 'man' was a sixties word... "Dude, I got zapped big-time, lightning, a power line... I don't know for sure, maybe both. It was raining. I was barefoot. It took me right out-a there."

She's been watching me again, he realized. She hovered in the doorway, listening.

"Ellison was sure that's what happened," Tina said, coming in to fill a glass with water at the sink. She smiled at her grandson who acknowledged her with a nod.

Arien focused on the long cotton dress she wore. On a girl it would have looked like a hippie dress, with its low-slung fabric belt and antiquated style. It framed her well. She was a bit thin, but had a respectable figure for an older woman. She'd taken care of herself. Her hair was pulled back in a pony tail. The lines on her face were kindly. Her vibe was full, holding nothing back. She came to sit on the same side of the table as Arien, facing Danner. She shone with a certain unflinching radiance, both sisterly and motherly. This was definitely another dimension of his girl! He was taken by the wonder of it; nobody gets to look that far ahead! He found himself feeling proud of her and loving her all over again.

"Arien, it's not the same," she'd said, when he climbed into her bed last night.

"I know," he told her, boldly wrestling through his trepidation on a firm mat of sorrow, and holding his breath as she reached to delay, and then explore him, and he realized there were some things he knew he could no longer bring himself to do. At first he didn't look at her, which hardly mattered when she pulled the chain on her bedside lamp. He felt her in darkness, sliding on top of her nightgown to stretch himself over her body, making contact with as much of her surface as possible, finding how her firmness had fallen like an old corduroy cushion on a street-found sofa. Mercifully, it was comfortable. And when he kissed her, her textured cheeks were wet with her brave tears.

Now, Danner hovered on the edge of his front-row seat, watching the two of them. His eyes rounded, his mouth opened, and his head swayed, obviously reading something in the thick silence between his grandparents. "Damn!" he allowed.

"It's hard to believe, isn't it, Danner," Tina remarked.

"Uh, I uh, need to get going," Danner abruptly said, draining his beer and slipping off the countertop. The back door was only five feet away. Without another word, he was at it, turning the deadbolt; he slipped out and was away.

"That was strange."

"Not really," Tina said, apparently concerned.

They sat quietly for a spell, where Arien was disturbed by a reluctant insight.

"Babe, I'm a little lost," he admitted.

Tina sighed.

"You have to decide what you want." Her concern dissipated. She now appeared confident and she leveled a steady gaze at him, absently tracing the rim of her glass with her finger.

"I need more time," he said.

"Do you have it, Love?"

"I don't know. Probably not." How could I know that? He could feel the fire recede to his inner space as a distant spark. I've climbed a mountain and look, there's another one!

"Aw," she said, flowing with empathy.

"I'll be okay," he responded, facing it. It felt better to do it that way. "I'm going to have help."

Her gentle laugh issued from a deep place. Arien could tell. He smelled victory in it, without fully knowing what he'd won.

"Wow! Why didn't you tell me you had some herb, Babe?" Arien said, seeing Tina enter the living room with a graceful, blown-glass bong.

"It's for medicine, Arien, not just for smoking until it's gone. As I recall, you were a serious stoner." Her sly grin was special. She set the pretty-colored thing on the coffee table with a small jar of great-looking, gummy bud.

Oh that felt so good. Arien couldn't explain it. Everything was so mixed up yet maybe it would work out. The day with her had been amazing. In the morning when he awoke, he'd hugged her close. Her scent was not sweet as it used to be, to want to lick her like ice cream, but its earthy appeal invited closeness. He knew he could feel her life, her spirit, and he freely shared his own. He found the syncopation of their hearts enveloped in wholeness and held on for as long as he could before his body's needs, nagging for relief and a glass of water, over-rode his bliss. But he returned and she did, too, and he closed his eyes into an embrace that lasted several hours more.

The two of them glowed all day. It was Danner who'd dropped the only wrench in it, but Arien didn't begrudge the boy his perspective. Though probably subconscious, maybe Danner was getting it in stereo. Holly had been indiscrete.

Surely, Tina struggled. She mentioned Danner's abrupt departure when Derik got back from the city and he expressed some gratitude for being kept in the loop. Today, when they'd finally gotten out of bed she'd absently mentioned him, and Arien could tell she found it difficult to let go of. She commented, "He doesn't think it's right."

Arien wasn't sure if he did, either. Why? He asked himself, should years have anything to do with it? Knowing Andy ruled-out gender, why couldn't he blow age away, too? Well, Holly sure was hot. There was that. "We're not all the same and we're not simple," he observed.

Her connection with that carried some admiration. It went down well, like a small achievement offering a glass of lemonade to a thirsty boy. And then she passed a lighter and the bong to him after filling it with a pinch of some very piney bud. His hit was interrupted by a knock at the front door.

"Wait," she said, reaching-out to wrest the bong from his hands before he could touch it with fire, "Let's see who this is, first." She set it under the coffee table, out of sight.

"It's changes," Arien realized aloud, contemplating the lighter he still held. Though, wasn't it a girl's voice that drifted in from outside? His mind's ear surely heard a man's... This was dissonant, somehow un-right. His heart's rhythm picked up without an explanation.

Derik came in from the sewing room-office in the enclosed back porch of Tina's bungalow where he'd been poking around the Internet on her computer. He stood in the hallway, one hand out to hold Arien's attention to whatever would happen next, and the other reached around behind his back.

"I haven't any idea, Honey," he heard Tina say.

Arien was already up, connecting with Derik. They both fell back o the kitchen, behind a solid wood door.

"Who is it?" Derik whispered.

"Damn! That's got to be Holly."

"Who?"

"The babe at school."

Derik's eyes narrowed. "What babe at school?"

"She's – ah, Danner's friend." Arien swallowed. "She was at the game."

"Oh," Derik said, not sounding particularly relieved.

Arien could hear them come into the living room. He blew a, "Fuck," under his breath and moved to the doorway to listen.

"Oh yes, we've met. He's a relative, you know," Tina was saying.

"Yeah, I know, Ms Deacon. He said so to Danner's mom at the game."

Holly called her, Ms Deacon. Arien wrapped his head around that. It was her maiden name in 1969.

There was a pause and then Tina said, "Does Danner know you're here?"

"You won't tell him, will you?"

That bought a space. It was hard to believe she really said that! Tina replied, "My Dear Girl, why choose to keep a secret from Danner?"

Holly's response was unintelligible. Damn! It bit not to have heard what she said!

"Well, I won't bring it up, how's that? But if he asks me, Holly, I'm not going to lie to him."

"Sure, yeah, okay."

"Why's she here, Arien?" Derik whispered.

"Looking for me, I guess."

But now came a soft clicking from the door behind them. Arien's inhale was a deep one.

"Ah!" He turned in time to see the knob on the deadbolt flip while Derik gasped and spun to a crouch, the pistol extended straight out between his hands faster than a card trick.

"Oh shit!" Derik hissed, plainly trembling on the edge of do and don't.

"Put it down, Derik," Arien calmly said. "It's the boss."

23 – I'll never eat Chinese again

Colonel Griffin hardly needed a uniform. Even in civilian clothes he owned the attention. In the dingy light his magnetic scan from the front passenger seat of the mini-van got Arien to look up and make a connection. The colonel's expression was serious, even strained. It drove his mission home. Arien didn't have to be told his inclusion was not required but was given, regardless.

He nodded, and returned to contemplating his hand, goofing on a silly recollection. When Arien was in the eighth grade he had a buddy named Claus who assured him the 'four fingers' would ever remind him how to be a free man. He could still see Claus flipping out a finger for each point, beginning with the pinky, *"Find 'em, feel 'em, fuck 'em, and forget 'em."* He laughed to himself, because Holly was in the van, too, right along with Tina, going – who the hell knew where? Forgetting her was not an option. She sat next to him with a totally dazed look, and her energy was confused, which was no surprise, but Arien thought she scored points with her relative patience so far at being abducted. Maybe she was getting a thrill out of it, or riding on how upset she had been with Tina, and probably Danner, seeing Arien had been in the house all along. He was very grateful Danner wasn't with them now.

Tina sat in the seat behind him, with Derik. She'd put her hand on Arien's shoulder as they started out, which was appreciated. Not that he needed consolation. But it served more to assure him she was along for the ride and likely wouldn't have had it any other way if given the choice. Of course, he thought, that was the Tina he remembered! In their short time together since Monday night he'd managed to fill her in on most of his doings after arriving in Bethel, and accounting for the spaces between the news items she'd seen on television. Maybe that was all she needed. Tina knew him better than anyone.

Griffin only gave Tina fifteen minutes to pull it together, so she'd left a note for Arienne to take whatever she wanted from the refrigerator and to discard the rest; it might be awhile before she returned. He'd seen it on the kitchen table. It had to be the first thing she did! He admired her extraordinary flexibility and preparedness. She had an overnight bag in her office that was already packed. "In case of fire," she'd said. But she grabbed a few extra things Holly might need when Colonel Griffin warned the contractors were on his tail, honing-in on Arien, and people in this house were not safe.

"What? Alex has been here the whole time!" Holly indignantly cried the moment he came in from the kitchen.

Derik hastened to say not to blame Tina, who was only trying to protect her, while Arien practically ignored her.

Alice, I'm sorry I haven't been a very good.... I've been...

Where are you?

In a van with Colonel Griffin. We seem to be headed back toward Sandy.

We're waiting. We're ready, Arien.

What do you mean? But he could feel her excitement. What's with this lady? She was ripped from her home with her husband and her kids because of me, but she's so totally there! For what? Shouldn't I know?

Alice threw an image at him, of Andy and Hawthorne, too. How remarkable to see people he knew through the eyes of another; the same and yet different, in aspects of tone, color, vibe, nuance, or their personal association and reflections on all these things and more! They're...?

Yes.

And Doctor Blake!

Yes... Yes, Cassie, too.

Griffin's stare pulled Arien back into the van.

"What?"

"When did you remove the anklet I gave you?"

"You said it wasn't for tracking me. How do you know I took it off?"

"I told you what it was for. We pinged it Monday night. There was no reply. That told us you weren't wearing it."

"Why Monday night?"

"We were at the game," Holly recalled.

"What happened?" the colonel probed.

"Nothing." Arien returned to his fingers and their adolescent admonitions.

"Were you at the game, Lieutenant?" Griffin's voice was louder.

"Yes, Sir, I was."

"What happened?"

"Arien met with his daughter, Sir."

"Come on, Lieutenant, think! Something happened!"

"His daughter?" Holly's face tightened, and she shook her head.

"A blackout, Sir. That's all."

"No, that's not all. You are mistaken."

"Sandy, or McKinnon, Sir?" the driver asked.

"McKinnon."

"Turning left on Hudson, over," the driver said, and all the vehicles braked.

Voices came from an up-front speaker, "A, check; C, check; D, check;" spoken in succession as their vehicle slid forward on an invisible patch of black ice. The driver lightly tapped the peddle to bring it under control, missing the van in front by a mere whisker. Arien looked up to see they'd passed an intersection to the left, by a shuttered, two-tone wooden store on the corner that was barely visible in the dingy glow of the headlights in the bone chilling, dank and foggy afternoon. The windows were steaming up.

"I don't understand, Sir."

The van began backing up.

"What do you think happened, Colonel?" Arien calmly asked.

"I let you go for a few days and you become a smart ass," Griffin retorted.

"What's he getting at, Arien?" Derik asked. "You didn't seem right when I stumbled into you in the hall, but..."

"His name is Alex," Holly corrected.

"Young Lady, don't make me regret letting you into this car."

The colonel's rebuke made Arien laugh out loud. Though it was likely more than merited, it felt good to release some of the nervous energy.

"What?" she growled.

"Are we going to Arienne's?" Tina asked.

Arien could hear Derik say, "I don't think so, Ma'am," and it sounded so formal.

"Hang in there, Babe," Arien told Holly. "You're doing pretty good so far."

"Somebody has to tell me what's going on!" she squeezed through clenched teeth.

"So, what did I miss at the game?" Derik followed.

"Chrissake, I don't know yet!" Arien huffed. "It was out of this world."

"What do you have, Colonel?" Derik asked.

"He's a colonel?" Holly blurted.

"Only a major electro-magnetic anomaly, that's what," Griffin answered, with a hard stare at the boy. "It registered like a sun spot but it didn't come from the sun; too coincidental to be ignored. I felt we had to move, even if it was premature."

"I'll never eat Chinese again," Arien rued aloud.

The colonel smirked, turned away, and Arien followed his view forward. The rural road was a ghostly tunnel in the monotone blend of fog, bleak snow banks, and tangle of bare roadside trees. It fell steeply, with what seemed like a sheer drop off to the left and then leveled-out before they made a sharp right, where it soon descended again into a series of tight switchback curves.

"Where are we?"

"Arien, this is Lusted Road," Tina answered from behind him. "The bridge over the Sandy River is at the bottom. It eventually runs into Ten Eyck, north of Bull Run and Phelps. Now do you know where you are?"

Ah, the river. It was the river of his vision, running through the deep gorge it carved for itself over and again through volcanic detritus on its way to the Colombia. He remembered seeing the bridge from the sky. Last time, they came to Arienne's from the other end. *Derik's wrong. We're going for Arienne!*

Yikes! Holly grasped the hand that was unable to forget her and her energy travelled right up his arm. She looked straight ahead, not giving herself away to anyone else.

He sighed, catching her scent like an opening gardenia on a balmy breath of humid air, sensing the tsunami of wildly crazy, supercharged attraction this girl had surfed like a champion, *and tell me what else you've got, Little Boy.* Oh my God! Arien nearly said, **ouch**, because he swelled so suddenly, rock-hard into his pants. He needed to adjust himself. It was painful.

Oh no! It mustn't happen like this! Everyone will feel us! So he tried to pull his hand away, but with no better luck than a man holding a live wire in a bath tub.

Sit on it! Sit on it, he told himself, fighting to take charge of his breath and ignore the exquisite juicy seepage already under his zipper. He did say, "Oh, God!" focusing on the hollow sound of the van's tires on the bridge, the Sandy's hush beneath it, their ascent out of its narrow yard, and the lights of a few rural houses in the early twilight.

They didn't go very far after taking a sharp left, but slowed along a wide field, following the van ahead between stone columns and open iron gates.

Behind that was a dark, shake-walled cottage with a single light on in one of the windows. But their caravan continued past the residence on a winding drive that went by a large shop, on the right, and then onto what looked like a long, narrow field between fir and hardwood hedgerows and surrounding woods. The caravan turned right here. Then it was slow-going over grass with a few inches of soft snow on top. Continuing gradually uphill, slipping-out here and there, they passed a dimly lit, closed-up airplane hangar on the left, with a few vehicles parked there, and going on they finally approached the top where a few soldiers with assault rifles stood in the shadows.

Holly would not let go of his hand. Her vibe was fearful now but his balls ached.

"Wow," Arien allowed, pulling the awestruck girl along as he stepped uncomfortably out of the van. Tina and Derik came up resolutely on his other side, where the four of them awaited Griffin, who conferred with his driver. Outside, they chased their wisps of visible breath in the cold, damp air. There, in the last throes of twilight loomed a trim and graceful, twin-prop airplane with a veritable presence like a new species of crouching predator.

Though not a jet, it was similar to the plane he'd ridden before, even to the string of round porthole windows along the side. A darkly-painted underbelly wrapped itself in the shadow of the woods while its light-grey top beckoned to very low clouds in a starless murk. It was parked facing the downhill runway's full length, disappearing into night, with its high tailed, T-top stabilizer backed right up against a rush of branches reaching out of the dense woods behind it.

Derik was right, Arien thought, relieved. They weren't going to Danner's house, after all.

Tina took a deep breath and leveled her eye on him.

His head swam for balance in an awkward eddy. He still held Holly's hand. All in all it seemed right, else she lose it or who knew what; the way she looked at the plane, and him, at Tina, and Derik. So, Arien stood ramrod straight with his chest out just a little. It was better not to buckle. *I'll protect this girl while I guard myself.*

He admonished himself to find authority in the Light. "I give it all to you," he said under his breath, feeling his body, the air, the slumbering earth, and a nearly frozen mist tingling against his cheeks.

Was it worth the wait?

297

"I don't know yet, Babe," he replied to Tina, with a tinge of sadness and even some embarrassment – or was it shame, and it got her wrinkling her brow.

Colonel Griffin finished his conference and all three vehicles moved away from the plane's outstretched wings before two peeled off to drive down opposite edges of the runway.

The plane's entrance was at the rear of the fuselage. Arien and the others followed Colonel Griffin to where a red-headed captain stood by the opening. He saluted.

"Everything's in order, and ready, Sir."

"Very good, Martel. Then let's go."

It had that new car, fresh, top-dollar-plastic smell. That was the first thing to register as Arien stepped up to enter. The second thing was complicated; Arienne, Brett, and Danner were already on the plane.

Their anxious faces locked on Arien, immediately calculating, assessing, wondering, but Danner's jaw dropped to see Holly, who flashed him a glimmer of smile as she moved forward. The seat across from Danner was empty. He reached out to catch her wrist as she moved past it. Her eyes met Arien's for a mere moment. Then she turned away to sit by Danner.

Arien wasn't sure how he felt about that. He knew it would have been bad if she hadn't, but...

He chased after Griffin to the backward-facing aircraft chairs against the cockpit wall. These opposed the center section for four, which were back-to-back. There was seating for eight passengers, in all, with the last two at the rear, facing forward. Their party filled them all. Captain Martel slipped between everyone and entered the cockpit, and Arien could see another officer was up there with him.

"Awesome ride!" Arien exclaimed, wiggling into his seat like a little kid, consciously kicking past the emotional currents swirling in their high-tech little tube. Derik and Tina watched him from the center section. Arien wondered if he could keep it together. *I have so far*, he thought.

"I'm inclined to favor the Beechcraft," Griffin agreed. "The 350s have plenty of oomph and range; they're adaptable and reliable."

You heard me back there, didn't you? Tina said, and Arien realized her words came through the thoughts in his head as if borne on actual words he could hear, as Alice's did, and as Cypriano's had, back in 1969.

"Yes," Arien said aloud to her, trying to avoid feeling the weight the words could carry.

Colonel Griffin curiously scanned him until Martel stuck his head in the open entry of the cockpit. "We're going to rev it up before take-off to be sure we clear the trees."

"Very good, Captain."

The twin turbo motors sprang to life with a quickly-climbing whine, the craft began to vibrate, and the seatbelt light came on over the cockpit door.

"Please buckle-up for take-off," issued from the side console speakers.

What do you think is going to happen?

A reasonable question, was she moving on already?

I'm not sure, but we're going to see everybody.

Who's everybody?

Arien reviewed his inventory of faces.

Oh, Arien, this is amazing! Cassie and her husband... uh...

Jason.

Yes, that's it! And... Is that Andy?

Yes.

Oh, wow. He looks great! And who's this one?

That's Alice. We can do it, too, like you and me.

Wow, really? She knows we're coming?

Yeah, and she's told the others.

So, this is how Cypriano—

Yeah, exactly. He smiled, yet caught the crackling under her thoughts, like a teetering chunk of ice that insinuates an avalanche. Oh fuck. I'm just a kid.

What did you expect?

Can't I ask you that, too?

There was a pregnant blank from her, as in, nothing.

I won't get weepy now. We'll just have to wait and see, Tina. He rolled under her weight of years, and her likely explosive anticipation. How had she borne it so gracefully? But his feelings must amount to something. And then the pressure from the others fell against him also. He knew it, deeper down than most of them could go – at least without some help. He was just too connected whether he liked it or not.

"What are you thinking?" Griffin asked him.

"How high will we be flying?"

"Thirty-five thousand feet," he said, with one eye half closed.

"Then don't bring me down, Colonel. It's a long way to the ground."

It was a long way down in more ways than one. Sure, it was great to be riding in this thing; who could have predicted his life would take him to thirty-five thousand feet for a second time in as many months? But the vibes in the plane weighed upon him. He didn't have any answers for them. He looked forward to seeing Andy again. Maybe Andy would help him to navigate it all.

Arien fixed his gaze on the colonel.

"What?"

"What's the plan?" Arien asked him.

"Do you remember what I said the last time you went there?"

"I don't know."

"Come on, I know you've got more inside your pretty head than flower power." Griffin replied. He folded his hands expectantly.

Arien dutifully recited, "What do I want to do," while noticing the way Derik honed-in on it.

"You found her," the colonel motioned at Tina, who was deep in thought. "What's left?"

The 350 hit turbulence, and produced a dropping sensation before catching itself, as the engines responded with increased power. It was pitch black outside. Arien returned a grin. "Do you remember what I said the last time *you* went there?"

"You don't have a choice," Griffin said, "and the pressure's not going to come from me." He waved his hand at the others. "It's going to come from them."

Wow. This dude was amazing.

"You don't get it." he fended. "I can't make it happen. Everything has to be right." He was no magister, like Andy, but this much he knew.

"We don't have a lot of time, Kid," Griffin said. "You'll just have to make it right, or we all ride the damn break in a little canoe without the proverbial paddle."

Derik sighed. As Arien gauged it, the young officer was resigned to do his duty. But surely he had to wonder what it was.

Tina's vibe was alarmed.

"Doesn't that include you?" she asked.

"It's all or nothing, Ma'am," Griffin answered. "I'm just another chip on the table."

He knew it was possible. It nearly happened at Jerrod's cabin on the mountain.

He watched Tina give him an unreadable look as she unbuckled her seatbelt. She moved carefully in the narrow isle to stand at the rear to initiate a quiet conversation with her family. Soon enough, Holly offered Tina her seat and impulsively came forward to sit while Danner's evident concern and confusion bounced off her back. This was neither what Arien had expected or desired. It made a simple vision of immanent peace and brotherhood complicated. Shouldn't it be easier?

Holly offered him a private smile that might as well have been posted on the Internet. Both Derik and Griffin certainly caught it, because Derik's face grew long, in spite of himself, and Griffin snorted.

His own emotions were complicated, too. Isn't that my family? Shouldn't *I* have gone to talk with them? But it was heady to own Holly like that! It flaunted his wealth. He could have had her right there. He balled his fists with frustration at his limits. He asked himself, is it my age and inexperience, or is this the way things really are and will always be? If the answer was yes to always, it offered a chilling prospect, and that called his empathy like an obedient dog. Damn it! We're such sorry bastards.

Holly shifted her position in the seat. It was a subtle reach.

He smiled weakly. "When are we going to get there?" he asked Griffin, who had reclined his chair.

The colonel's sardonic expression skipped to the twenty-four-hour watch on his wrist.

"It's just over three hours. We've a couple to go, Arien."

"Oh God!"

Griffin closed his eyes.

"Don't fold on me now, Kid. I've bet the farm on you."

He could feel them. It was so strange, hearing the turbo-prop whine in a crazy kind of stereo from where he was inside it, and also in the distance from the hangar that was lit up among hulking shadows of aircraft on the tarmac. Arien guessed they'd returned to Davis Monthan. It had to be Alice. She was there! They were all in there! Holy fuck! This guy was serious!

Arien's heart leapt in a raw clash of joy and concern. They were such cool people. He loved them. In a sense, they were his family, at least as much if not more so than his relatives on the plane, an extension of his circle at Woodstock, who were variations of the twelve people in the world. And who were these others he glimpsed? There were two more, old folks he didn't recognize, but they seemed to know him.

He was glad he'd gotten up in time to stand with his blood kin though, before they landed. It eased the vibe somewhat, or at least his place in it. He knew soon enough Griffin had shared little with these people beyond, "For your safety," and that Arien was a valuable item requiring them to be together for the present. Tina was doing what she could to round things out from her perspective. Arien slid between the chairs in time to overhear, "All these years I've kept him in my heart."

He knew it was too quick. There hadn't been time to pack anything, and they could do nothing but watch it go down like an accident. *Where have I heard that before?* This time the words came from Brent, who also wondered about his rights as a citizen. Arienne worried about the cat. But Danner was going to a darker place. Arien struggled to connect with the kid's sullen eyeballs that kept darting away.

"Dude, I'm sorry!" Arien snapped. But it only served to corral the Holland's unease.

"I'm really having trouble thinking of you as my Dad," Arienne admitted.

"Lighten up, all of you!" Tina said. "Can't you see it's not his fault?"

Oh, Alice, I'm so fucked.

Be strong, Arien. We need you. Andy's told me a lot.

Arien saw the spark of Andy's eye in her stream of thoughts, the pulses of light and feeling flowing from her mind into his, and he appreciated her yearning for the marvelous. She was not like anyone else, except maybe Cypriano, with a little bit of Andy, who concerned him now because... Andy used to call it the Operation. For Andy, that was paramount; the process. But it reflected the value of money to a whore. Back at the FEMA camp Andy revealed his willingness to make arrangements with Griffin for the sake of their mutual goal. It didn't smell right. Arien wasn't sure of his own goal, whatever it was, especially now that he'd found Tina, Tina and—

Tina cocked her head. She appeared to be listening.

Can you hear her?

Who?

Alice.

No. I can't seem to get into your conversation, but I got you were having one with somebody.

And it's blocking you, Arien realized. I can be with you or with her, but not with both of you at the same time.

Interesting.

Arien considered trying a simultaneous communication but was interrupted.

"Please return to your seat and buckle up for landing," the captain announced.

Danner shot a withering look as Arien turned away.

The sound of the plane was louder in Alice's ears. Her excitement was a revelation. She bore the hopes of everyone and their yearning for a change in their prolonged predicament. They trusted her because her family did and because she had been consistent and firm. How do I know that? Oh, so much was borne in this woman's thoughts and feelings, and through the transom of her mind. He rested over her brow like a sunset, and she over his, and together they felt the infinitude of each-other's firmament, like parallel beings with binocular awareness. It was marvelous. He was close to dizzy, intoxicated.

As the hangar loomed closer, the engines' stereo tones from inside and outside the craft played with Arien's head, growing louder to Alice's ears, while their images superimposed and his mind hustled to make sense of it. With closed eyes it was clear, but awkward in the same space with Brent, Arienne, and Danner, who were variously clueless and dissonant. It was a weight on him, limiting his reach, and it returned him to the interior of the plane.

You're not perfect, Arien thought, of Griffin. You can make mistakes.

In a series of elongated minutes and levels of power to the engines, and some incremental turns, they taxied to the hangar. It ultimately swallowed them as its big doors rolled aside and then closed, even before the propellers stopped spinning.

The energy fell upon Arien like a breaking wave. He actually flinched as people clustered around the aircraft in a state of high excitement. When the door opened he could hear their murmurs as Arienne, Brent, Danner, and Tina disembarked, and then Holly, and Derik. Finally, Arien came to the opening with Colonel Griffin behind him. Here, he was met with yet another wave; but this time it carried applause, cheers, cries of wonder, and even astonishment from a few faces of some strange elders who apparently knew him.

Arien saw Dr. Blake – "I had to call in sick, Arien!" Blake exclaimed, and fixed on Hawthorne right away. They tightly embraced, laughing happily together, and from there it was a moving and surreal hug-fest through Cassie – "Wait 'till you see who else is here, you beautiful boy!" her husband, Jason – "It's about time Young Man!" and Patrick – "Where the fuck have you been?" Zanna – she whispered, "You're as hot as ever!" Marley – "Dude!" Cindy kissed him on the lips; a broadly smiling Andy – "Finally we can get to work!" a beaming Alice – "Wow! Your friend, Andrew told me all about Cypriano," with Denver – "Oh Dude, am I happy to see you!" and on through Bonnie – Arien confided, "Sharon misses you a lot," to which she replied, jumping and covering her mouth in surprise, "Oh my God! You met Sharon?" Salem, and even Wes, and Evan, and all appeared to be variously happy and relieved to see him again.

Arien came to an old woman who was all tears, who took hold of his shoulders with outstretched arms and held him, to regard him with wonder and joy.

"Do you know who this is?" Cassie squealed in her old-Cassie voice, as people pressed around.

"Kelsey? Holy Shit," Arien exclaimed, half-guessing, looking into Kelsey's amber eyes, sizing up how her body had changed. She was still that hale, medium build he knew, but she'd morphed subtly away from the pattern of nature's youthful nod to gender. It was funny how that happened, this evident trick of years, trading characteristics until boys and girls became something else as elders, with similar voices, squarer frames, and how they grew to be more alike.

"Crazy, huh?"

"Yes, isn't it? My God! Arien!" her words broke, "It's really you!"

Tina embraced Kelsey, too, when Arien finally let go.

"Oh, Kelsey! I never thought I'd see you again!"

"Tina! Oh my Dear! You look good! You look so good!"

"How did you get here?" Arien implored of Kelsey, and then looked around at all of them, eyes on him, listening. "How...?"

"Arien, you were all over the news," a tall, rather heavy old fellow said. His full head of gray hair was rusty around the edges. He sported a bulbous, red nose, his double chin was shy of a shave, and the man's tummy was well ahead of the rest of him. He had been hanging near Hawthorne, but backed away, watching as Arien greeted and was greeted. But now he came forward. "I Googled Hawthorne, and found him in Jerome, Arizona, and he told me it was true, he really saw you, and you were still exactly the same!"

Arien stared into hazel eyes. "God, this is like a crazy, mixed-up dream, Dude!" Arien couldn't imagine who this guy was. He wavered, not wanting to embarrass the man or himself.

"It's okay, Arien. I know. I've grown to look more successful." He laughed at his little joke. "Do you remember Willow?"

Lying on his back on the lawn behind their barracks, Arien was so deep into his thoughts the words, "I wondered if I should look for you," sounded like a car horn to an absent-minded kid on his bike. He flinched, drawing his knees up, and squinted at Tina, standing above her shadow, her face framed in the blue Arizona sky. But she carefully sat down cross-legged on the grass next to him, not waiting for an answer.

"You didn't have to." His wistful smile was telepathic, not showing over his features.

"Arien—"

"It's okay, Babe."

"No, hear me out."

He waited.

I'm still getting used to this.

I love the privacy.

He chuckled aloud.

Does the, uh, colonel know about this?

I guess. He knows I can do it with Alice. He lucked out. She's kept it together for him.

What do they want? Tina gestured physically at the barracks.

Arien merely recalled glowing snowflakes over his OM with the boys on the mountain, and for good measure added the memory of Derik's interference.

Oh! As if your jump through time wasn't enough!

Arien watched her move over the landscape of her memories, with interest. Tina was delighted to find them suddenly in the complex, illumined, fractal tangle of glowing, shimmering, interlaced mendalas and resonant tones that had to be the real marvel to come out of Woodstock, the secret miracle of inherent, cosmic, creative forces they'd blended with their heart-song, and the yearnings of the race over tens of thousands of grinding, suffering, living and dying years, deep in the honey of the hive, in love with themselves in the moment, and with song, and the magic of the thing, and the sense of living spirit that simply cannot be faked.

Arien smiled inwardly, but brought Tina from there to caution and even alarm. That's what he really wants. That's why we're all here. Can you think of a better reason?

Well, it's totally understandable. It's the most wonderful... Oh...

"Yeah, he's a soldier." Arien said this aloud. He sat up, circling his knees with his arms.

They wouldn't dare!

Ha! But... You know, Tina, I may know something about all this that he never bothered to tell me.

She waited.

The next image he grasped in his mind was the burst of energy that blew the circuits at Sandy High.

"Whoa," she said.

He's sure they need the technology. But we're way not ready for that.

"Star Wars," he said aloud, with a grin.

"Oh, oh wow," she said, her eyes widening.

"Yeah." His chuckle had an edge to it.

And here I come with personal matters!

Thanks. But it all matters. You still own my heart, Girl.

That was like plunging from his raft of stretched animal skin into the Ice Age Sea. Arien suddenly felt so sad and ashamed.

Tina smiled.

"Hey, you're just a kid," she said, feeling her way. "We've been asking you to grow up too fast." *Besides, Arien, she is a cutie!*

God! You're sweet! He swiped at welling eyes with his knuckles.

"That reminds me of something Otter said, once."

"Oh, Otter," was Tina's refrain.

"I wish he was here. I wonder what happened to him."

What did Otter say?

He gave me some rope but wouldn't do entitlement. He was always on me for that shit.

"Hmmmmmmm......."

Arien focused the image for Alice, too. It's just for us to know, he insisted, when he was sure she understood.

"What?" Tina asked, but followed Arien's awareness to where it pointed. Across the lawn was a bench under the shade of a small trellis. It was along the walkway between sections of officer's housing. They could just make out the corner of a bright red garment on the person sitting there. Though her back was to them, Arien, Alice Roundtree, and now Tina knew Someone Else kept watch.

They came for mess in a shell of empty barracks that appeared to have been unused forever. There were cobwebs in the multi-pane, casement windows. It had a stuffy, still air smell blended with grilled burger, French fries, and the murmur of voices bounced from floorboards and bare, white-painted walls, and hung in the space like tangled mobiles suspended from the open collars of the rafters. It was set up with portable tables, and prepared food delivered from elsewhere on the base. When Arien and Tina drifted in for lunch, everyone looked up for some idea of what was going to happen next. The colonel was notably absent, and Derik, once again in a field uniform, didn't know anything.

For that matter Derik hadn't known anything in the morning either, and gave Arien the impression he'd just as soon not. He was different somehow – the uniform, the colonel, the new people, the assignment...

There was a meeting scheduled here for 1300 hours. Arien could only guess its significance. He was nibbling a lone, salty French fry in his fingers, contemplating his opinion for the crowded table when his daughter leaned forward to be visible from the other side of her husband. "I'm sorry, Dad," she opened, "I haven't been very understanding, have I?"

"Is it because my English sucks?"

People in earshot laughed.

Arien was pleased to see a smile crack on Danner's face, temporary though it was. Holly didn't get a chance to sit next to Arien, who saw her try. He was sure Danner saw that, too. She wound up at the other end of the table for her trouble, near neither. Now she kept looking at him.

Arienne daubed her lips with a paper napkin. She warily smiled. "Like I said, you'll take some getting used to."

"He's seventeen," Tina reminded.

"You'll learn to respect your old man," Arien added, but his grin connected. It felt good. He really wanted to know her. Then he fixed his gaze on Andy, who sat across from him, next to Dr. Blake, who had been pumping Andy with questions at every opportunity, like a reporter facing a deadline.

"I can't just make it happen."

"I agree, Arien," Andy said. "What do you need?"

"I don't know, but it's not here."

"Where is it?" Hawthorne asked.

Patrick got up from the long, folding table he occupied with the group from Tucson. He brought his metal chair, setting it behind, to one side of Arien, where he parked himself to listen. It set off a cascade effect, with Alice coming over next to Arien's other side, then Cassie followed suit, and Kelsey, and the others from Tucson, and also the remainder of the group from Madras, all arranged in a horseshoe around Arien's end of the table. They sat quietly attentive.

Arien sighed, visualizing a broad, muddy field with umpteen thousands of kids, frenetic drums and the soaring strain of blended, electric guitars.

Tina covered her eyes, and Alice said, "Woodstock."

"What would Otter say?" Arien posed, half to himself.

"Probably something good, but definitely off the wall," Andy submitted. Hawthorne agreed, with a chuckle.

Tina grinned. "Otter would tell us we're the revolution," she said. "It begins between our ears."

"Yeah," Arien mused, "and I'd drink his peyote tea, and get all fucked up."

"Oh my God," Willow added, "Otter had this liquid acid we did in Medicine Bow."

Arien silently listened. The branding on Arien's brain from that night still sizzled. It was interesting to see Willow go there after so long.

"Jesus! That was the night Tree died." Willow paused. "Well, Otter rolled it out again at the circle we did at Woodstock, but he was already rockin', and it only got to a few of us." Willow smiled wistfully. "I knew I'd never forget that day."

"Yeah, I remember that!" Kelsey exclaimed. "And I remember the first time we dosed that stuff. Arien came down later from Old Rock to tell me Tree was gone. Wow."

"Oh, you guys!" Cassie joined. "You're serious? You did it again at that circle?"

"Yeah, you didn't get any?" Willow asked.

Cassie shook her head. "Don't know if I did. But, would it matter?"

"Contact high," Kelsey said, with a modest giggle.

"I didn't either," Arien admitted.

"I seem to recall you didn't need it," Tina added.

"You're right. Me and Otter were still flyin' on the tea."

"You were really something!" Andy praised. His eyes sparkled with it.

"You were our guide, Andy," Arien countered.

"That's right," Willow agreed.

"What happened there?" Bonnie asked.

"Yeah," Wes joined. "There's a lot of the story we haven't heard!"

"I know, it's all about that, isn't it?" Marley said. "That's why we're here, right?"

"Really?" Jason asked. He'd been standing behind Cassie's chair with a hand on her shoulder. "It isn't about your uh, time travelling, and the government wants to keep it a secret?"

"If it were only about that, there'd be no need for us," Alice said.

"That's right," Dr. Blake agreed. "People say whatever they want all the time about all sorts of things, UFOs, 9-11... As far as I know nobody's been abducted as we have."

"What do you say to that, Lieutenant?" Jason asked Derik.

Derik pushed his tray away, dropping his napkin in it, leaned back in the chair, and folded his arms. "I could say that it's classified," he said with a smirk.

"Derik, don't be a dick," Arien fired. "Dudes, it's about the celestial ship. He thinks we can make one for the United States Army." Arien couldn't read the fixed, but vacant look his comment earned from Andy.

"That's crazy," Tina huffed.

"Jesus!" Hawthorne scoffed.

"There's no way," Willow agreed.

"What's this, celestial ship?" Cyrus asked, obviously carrying the question of many.

"Oh, my!" Alice said with a sigh.

"What, Mom?" Salem asked.

"A fuckin' UFO?" Patrick guessed.

"Does the Army still experiment with LSD?" Hawthorne said, with a chuckle.

"You're right," Willow joined.

"No," Andy said, "he can do it, can't you, Arien?"

"Oh, wow," Dr. Blake said, and the way he did got everyone's attention. "You certainly tweaked my brain at our solstice circle in December, Young Man."

"Is this true, Lieutenant?" Patrick asked. "He can land a UFO?"

"I don't know," Derik answered.

But Arien guessed Derik believed it, or why would he have nipped it, if that's what it was, on the mountain in Oregon? For all that Arien barely grasped it, himself. It took a certain something to meet a moment like that. It hardly seemed relevant. The uncertainty and confusion in this room didn't seem like a good place to start.

Derik looked at his wristwatch. He'd called it a chronometer last night when Arien observed it was the only watch he'd seen on anyone in 2013, where everybody kept time with their cell phones. A blank look came over him. It had to mask some unease. Arien could tell. When Derik made a point of projecting confidence and professionalism even the lesser clue of a blank face could signal a problem. It exceeded the personal stuff.

Arien closed his eyes, thrusting away from the turbulent comfort, such as it was, of these expectant people who for the most part also loved him. Did they ask too much? He let himself slip between their hearts, their yearning and anxiety, to cast himself out beyond the support of land beneath his feet and drawing his arms together, pressing against his sides, and pushing off with the wings he owned in his dreams. Open, his eyes would have caught Derik peek at it again, flipping the edge of a sleeve up just a bit to be sure. But Arien knew something wasn't right. The hair on the nape of his neck rippled as if dragged with the fingers of a hand.

"I don't know where to go from here," he said, focusing suddenly at the uniformed young man with a watch.

Everyone was still in the discussion hanging over the table like cigar smoke, and missed the import of Derik's connecting whisper of what, to Arien, was already old news, "It's 1307."

Alice got it, and then Tina: *Should we be worried?*

Arien shouted, "Quick! Barricade the doors! There's not much time!" Oh my God! This can't work! The shot of adrenaline was too much. His head suddenly felt like it would split right down to his tightening stomach.

"Arien?" Derik called over the sudden clash of startled voices, and chairs scraping over the gray-painted wood floor. "What are you doing?"

"It's up to us, Derik. Believe me! The colonel's not coming!" Arien was already bounding to the front where he grabbed at a collapsible table under the casement window at the left of the door. He pulled and dragged it to block the way. Denver was shortly by his side, then Wes, Evan, and Zanna. Furiously, they piled folding chairs and another table against it.

He knew his energy and the alarm it carried injected itself into them all. He could hear the clatter behind him as people worked at the other end. Oh rad, oh rad, they get it.

Derik drew up, heavily panting.

"This is crazy!" He had drawn his gun and was checking the clip in the handle. "We can't do this! I can't hold this building!" he protested, with a noticeable tremble in his hands. "Anyway, I've heard nothing! I have no orders!"

Arien gazed around him at the windows in the wall. Oh fuck. "Now!" He yelled, "Form a circle!"

Andy wore a face that had surely won the lottery. Well, at least he's here, swiped a grateful thought, as everyone assembled themselves in a wide ring around three of the tables in the center of the room and clumsily reached to join hands.

Oh fuck! Be cool! Be Cool! His heart pounded. He could hear the rushing in his ears. There was barely available breath to Om. He tried a second time, calling, "Focus!" Some of them joined in, with Andy and Dr. Blake the loudest. It felt so weird, so counter-intuitive. It seemed impossible to leverage his overpowering urge to run like the wind. He had to master himself before he could begin to master this circle. He fell backward into the air of his mind, weightless, flailing his arms and hands over the deepest chasm while the hands of the circle held them like sinkers bound to feathers. Mightily he tried, over a distant crashing racket.

"Ooooooooommmmmmmmmmmmmm................"

A bright light flickered to the far sound of blended bells, and utterly deep basso horns.

More joined in. It was almost total. Almost.

There was breaking glass, tumbling metal, and then a few shots, so loud. It intruded over an unaccounted resistance. Why? He could feel the disconnection, like bleeding. He swooned, to fall with his face to the floor among far shouts and cries. Derik was right there on the same gray plain as Arien, not two feet away, connecting for a mere instant. His eyelids were stretched back in utter astonishment and then relaxed as his connection faded into unaccountable dismay and disconnection. He seemed to sigh as a glossy puddle of warm liquid reached out from under him to pool, warm around Arien's cheek. He could smell it, watering his mouth in the creepiest way. The impulse to rear in horror went nowhere. Arien's head only pounded more, and then it all went dark and silent.

He fought awakening, with no wish to go there at all, but it drew him out of oblivion, dragging his broken-wheeled chariot of awareness and its dead horse with the other that was still alive. He strained to lift himself and then knew he was totally restrained on a padded examination bench in only a thin smock, his forehead, wrists and ankles secured, and nothing to see but the square light with a thick lens staring down at him.

"You're awake."

He didn't answer the woman's voice, but closed his eyes against the bright light.

The light was swung away. There was a buzzing sound and half the bench began to lift, raising him to a sitting position. It was cool in this room. His bare feet and limbs were cold.

His mirthless chuckle was ironic. This bitch actually wore a white lab coat like the doctors in a B-grade movie! She was fortyish and fit, her brunette hair swept back under a hairnet, very prim and neat.

He resisted the cacophony of questions and concerns rattling his mind, but stared at her as calmly as he could muster. This can't last, he told himself. I'm stronger than you.

"You're a handsome boy," she said. "I got to examine you thoroughly." She thinly smiled.

"Fuck you, Bitch," he evenly answered.

She lowered her head slightly, but held on to a slightly taunting expression.

"Arien," she said, "this is only a precaution. We don't wish to keep you restrained like this. I just need to be assured you won't try anything stupid. You cannot escape from here, and even if you did, you know we can track you anywhere you go."

Arien had to cradle his sinking heart with pure will to slow its tumble. He imagined she'd feel it and being prepared, ride it with knowledge he'd rather not allow. He scanned the small examination room. On one side of his bench about four feet away was a counter with a sink. On the other was a small table with a laptop computer and chair. The lamp that had been in his face extended down from the ceiling on a flexible boom that could be positioned just about anywhere. He noted that.

"You got me," he said, mustering charm. "I won't try anything stupid. I know you're only doing your job."

"Good," she said. "I want to trust you."

She reached and yanked the fabric restraints on his ankles loose. He looked down at his bare legs, keeping them where they were. All I'm wearing is a stupid green smock! It's embarrassing. What can I do with that? Then she came close, to release a wrist restraint. When she stepped away, he opened the other one himself, and then disarmingly entwined his hands.

"Thanks," he said, adding a bit more charm. He wanted to search in his head for Alice and Tina, but knew he had to remain focused.

The woman in the lab coat went over to the chair and opened the laptop.

"Can I have a drink of water?"

312

"Sure. See the cups there? Help yourself."

Arien slipped off the sticky plastic seat and took a step to the counter, reaching for a paper cup in a wall sconce while turning on the tap. He raised the cup with a grateful gesture as his other hand found the stopper and tweaked it shut. What-the-heck, I got-a go for it, he thought.

She was peering into the screen and then looked at him curiously as the running water began to splash in the sink.

"What's your name?" he asked.

That bought another precious moment. I've got to try!

She drew in a quick breath as Arien reached for the lamp at the end of the boom.

The woman jumped up so fast her chair fell backwards to smack on the floor as she lunged at him, but Arien was faster, plunging the lamp into the sink, splashing its thick glass globe into the stainless bottom with both of his hands.

Arien had been there twice before; galloping into some other Idaho on an ear-splitting screech of steel wheels over shuddering sparks, and an ozone whiff, and then a cast-away, outside-of-his head drift to nowhere, to darkness, and nothing.

24 – Ḥe really wanted an answer

Coming to, the boy began to feel himself, finding his arms pressed tightly against his chest with hands at the chin and his knees drawn up there, too, in a tight package. Slowly, he uncoiled. It was too dark to see. There was also a slight burnt odor at his proximity but the air otherwise smelled moist, sweet and verdant. An owl hooted off somewhere. The examination smock he had been wearing barely hung on him. "Ha!" He felt his nipples through the holes in front. It reminded him of the shirt he gave to Tina when they first met in the spring of 1969. And she wore it for him!

"Oh, Tina where are you?" He had to resist that. No going there now. He'd succeeded, yes? He'd escaped. Maybe they would find him, maybe not. It depends on where I am, he figured, or, *when* I am... He giggled with a shot of anticipation. "I did it! It worked! I did it!" he said aloud, carefully standing on rubber legs.

It was hard to keep balance. His bare feet toughed it over – was it sand, dirt, pebbles, grassy stuff? "Ha!" he cried again, and the sound was soaked up by empty distance. Stars twinkled overhead. Moist air and a deep night conspired to make them as bright as ever, except, of course, when he was out there with them, where their brightness defied his mortal eyes to ever see like that again, and the voice that either was or was not his own (he really didn't know which) brought him to apprehend the wisdom of returning. Oh, that seemed so long ago now. So much had happened since then. Ah, San Francisco, you were good to me. Otter... The Page Street people...

He folded his arms around his torso. "Oh, damn," he said, squatting where he stood, before easing the thin smock he wore under his bare buns to sit on the ground, and coiled himself up again for warmth. The night air was crispy and he barely had a rag between it. So, he dozed and shivered and had to stretch aching knees and rub himself to keep warm all through the night, with the hooting owl, yapping coyotes, and perhaps a poor will for company. It's wild here. I'm outside. Did I go back? Did I go way, way back?

Arien let the stars keep watch. It was the one thing that never appeared to change. He thought about that and what they were, a portion of forever blazing coldly over the people of the earth. And then they faded while a landscape manifested out of darkness in tones of gray with a whiff of wood smoke. Wow. I'm not in Tucson. I thought I'd be there. Maybe I was out longer... Maybe they took me somewhere else?

When there was enough illumination to the ground, he set out stiffly on tender feet in the direction of the smoke and when it began to carry an odor of nourishment it quickened his pace.

Northern Arizona, maybe, he speculated. He recognized junipers, pines, an occasional oak and wondered at the sunrise explosion in glorious gold crowns worn on patches of proud birch standing in bright trunks of fresh-painted white. The birches: Ah... Beautiful! Stunning.

Arien was grateful for the sun. Maybe it would be a warm day. He could hope so. Nice, though a part of him grieved. Oh! Not that again! His last sight of Derik, his friend, his protector who loved him too much... That experience suddenly returned with a suffocating vengeance, stabbing him deeply.

And what could have happened to the others? Why didn't he ask her? Should he be sorry he'd been so impulsive, to escape, yes, but to leave everyone else behind, and to add another crazy mystery to his life? But the Watcher in him reflected a moment that might not be repeated. He went for it. Now he was here. There's at least two of me, he mused. One watches while the other does everything. One's behind the other. Perhaps it's when I confuse that One with something else that I can hear people who can speak to me in their minds. Just a thought. I don't know...

"Wow. Rad." Down in a draw, with a fair creek running a bit below it in a grove of tall cottonwoods, wrapped in clouds of fluttering yellow leaves was a picturesque stone cabin with a sloped, wood-plank roof, perhaps a hunting camp. Or? He trembled with the prospect of being kicked further back in time than he'd ever been before. Crazy.

"I'm getting too old for this," he said, while frightened tears dried over his apprehension. He was awfully hungry now, and bore a powerful thirst as well. It complimented his courage.

"Jesus, I wish I had some decent clothes!"

And I am so fucking cold...

Just when Arien saw the dog it caught the scent of him. It was a medium dog, with a tan, short-haired body, upright ears, curved at the top, and a floppy tail that looked a tad longer than it needed to be. The shape of its head advertised a generic breed. It growled first, then began barking and growing more insistent. There would be no sneaking up to this place.

"Hey, Boy!" Arien gently called, with outstretched hands.

The critter let out a little whine, cocking its head.

Arien crouched.

"Hey, now," he said, with his tender heart out. "Good Boy!"

The dog approached in tentative steps, its raised tail drawing a small circle in the air.

They connected. The dog was won. When the cabin door opened the man who peered out (Was he wearing a skirt?) and, a girl behind him saw a strange boy about fifty yards away, scratching their doggie's ears.

Seeing him relaxed put them at ease. The man (Her father?) hurried out to inspect their visitor. The girl soon followed. For the longest time they merely stood, though it seemed as if they spoke as expressions flashed across their faces and their expressions worked toward a peculiar curiosity.

Finally, words did come forth, were totally unintelligible, and they spoke with a funny accent, too. Whatever. Weird. There was no way to tell what they said.

Arien modeled politeness. When he told them his name, the fellow lifted an eyebrow and it really seemed to alter his demeanor. He said a little more but it sounded like total nonsense.

The man looked to be about forty. He put a hand on his chest, "Arlos," he said, and indicating the girl, "Bessie."

She nodded, smiling.

"Hey, Dude, I'm sorry to come on you like this, but could you spare a little food?"

The man considered this as Arien patted his tummy and pointed into his mouth.

Arlos said something that sounded like an invitation, with a gesture easy enough to follow.

Their clothes appeared homespun; resembling a Western movie, other than the fact that the girl's dress was cut at the knee, and so was his. Could this be the Middle Ages? But if that were so, wouldn't they be Indians?

Very strange.

She was a cutie, maybe fifteen or sixteen. Her skin, a deep tan tone, was smooth as butter and her luxurious, black wavy hair grew long down her back. She was barefoot. He noticed her bare legs were unshaven. He'd thought it looked so hot on a pretty girl ever since meeting Tina, a girl who also spurned razors. She looked at Arien as he might have gazed at a sports car, all wonder at first, and then want. It was pretty cool. He had to struggle with getting turned on right then and there. Funny thing was her father, if that's who he was, didn't seem to mind at all. Arien thought it made the energy kind-a strange.

Likewise, the cabin was primitive. The fire crackled in a wide fireplace, with a smooth stone face, and lacked a mantle. It was obviously well used, having blackened edges. A few pots on the apron were a mix of soot and rust. On a rough plank table was a woven grass basket, and a couple of thick, hollowed boards with a serving of breakfast that resembled oatmeal with nuts and berries in it. It smelled good. When Arien stared at it, the mature man of medium height, with a ruddy coffee complexion and a short beard and mustache with flecks of gray, took another board from the fire apron and scraped out what food remained in one of the pans.

There were wood chips over a dirt floor, having a pleasant cedar odor, but after the long walk to this place even the chips raked at Arien's sore feet. He wasn't used to going so far over rough terrain without shoes. When he sat on a stool they throbbed, and he wondered if his swollen soles would feel better bleeding. Woodstock was grassy and muddy, mostly muddy, and real easy on bare feet. It was not like this. But the still-warm gruel had a hot-granola flavor that was chewy, yet palatable, especially with an appetite.

"Arien," the man repeated, watching him eat.

"Yes."

He reeled out another sentence of gibberish.

Arien shook his head, they were Mexican, maybe? Indian? Black? They spoke a language Arien couldn't recall ever having heard before.

Had that been a question? Arlos seemed to be waiting for an answer.

"Portland."

The fellow blankly stared, said, "Tsahh," and then shrugged.

"Oregon."

The man looked at the girl. They both shook their heads. "Tsahh," she echoed.

"Damn," Arien said under his breath, and thought, either I'm in another country or I've skipped a real long way! It began to worry him.

When the girl spoke it was worse. Her sentences tumbled out like a rock slide, though here and there he thought he recognized a meaning; by what measure or reference he couldn't imagine because it was so foreign and jumbled. But it felt better to speak to them, and Arien determined there was little need to stray from the truth, although he didn't tell them he beleived he came from the future. They listened intently, which he took as politeness. They appeared to be baffled by the word, government and the word, hunted brought a rather plain, off-white tunic out of a large basket with a lid. It looked a lot like a skirt to Arien, the material was coarse, but it was an improvement over the skimpy rag with burn holes in it that he arrived with.

He modestly went to put it on outside. They seemed to laugh at this, simply following after him to watch. "Oh well," he said aloud to himself, slipping out of the tattered smock. "I guess there's no TV."

"Essah TV, weet Arien," Arlos explained with a smile. He proceeded to explain something Arien couldn't understand any better than before, though the vibe was reassuring. He patiently listened until it sounded as if the man repeated himself, and then Arien shrugged.

"Essah TV!" Arlos said again, more emphatically this time.

Whatever that meant... Arlos flashed a note of friendly frustration, meeting Arien's shrug. As soon as Arien had eaten he was invited to follow them outside where they walked away from the house. Bessie stole glances all their way along a yellow leaf-strewn pathway winding among tall cottonwoods by the water's edge. The dog ran on ahead.

They spent the day down in a hollow near the creek in a broad meadow with southern exposure, harvesting vegetables in a rectangular garden plot. It was roughly forty by sixty feet, on surprisingly rich and loamy soil. It was all under a woven wattle cage, high enough to stand up in and stoutly reinforced with lashing. Arien surmised it kept out pests, like deer. The sticks, thinner at top, were spaced widely enough to allow plenty of light. A variety of plants were there, herbs, vegetables, leafy greens. Some had gone to seed.

His hosts easily squatted down at the head of a row to begin their work filling large baskets that were waiting, with few words between them. Arien awkwardly sighed. Was it impatience, and with what? What else was there to do besides freeze his ass? His legs and feet felt just shy of going blue in the crispy air. So he chose a row next to Bessie's where he could watch her lithe body pass among the plants. This girl was hot, seriously dark, shiny and glowing, supple, and soft...

He worked faster to be nearer, and she slowed her pace until they worked alongside, and Bessie crushed an herb between her fingers and held it playfully under Arien's nose for a minty splash at his senses.

Oh my God! That coy smile with a stunning set of teeth! He had to catch his breath. She was so young, but such a rad babe. He glanced away to hide the clenched jaw tension and worried over the animal feelings leaking into his combustible aura where it would surely consume them both. Oh, even Arlos peered at him now and Arien hustled to the task at hand, seeing the man's brief, appreciative nod as way too whisker close. Yikes!

Now she reached from behind with a small spray of slender, violet flowers that tickled his nostrils in a jasmine rush. "Stop it," he said, but his eyes didn't mean it, and the air in his lungs seeped out of him with a breath too heavy to carry.

His mind wandered along the road to Woodstock ... Aspen was a lot older, in her mid-twenties. She played guitar so beautifully. She sang like an angel. How easily this can run off the highway. I loved – love a girl already. Oh, Tina, I could have lived with you forever! What if it had been Aspen instead of Andy that night? Andy had simply sucked him off, again and again and again like some machine milking a cow! He sported a grin as the memory crossed his mind and was surprised to see Bessie's gaze fall on him like a harbor light.

This was another dynamic. Who are these people? What are they all about?

Bessie smiled, too knowingly for her own good, as Arien perceived it. How could she know where he was at? She was still part baby-faced kid.

What seemed most out of place was this: the spray of jasmine flowers in her hand was again among the order of the bountiful plant they came from. Arien could have sworn she'd merely put them back with a brush of her hand!

I must have missed something. But he looked vainly for them lying in the pathway.

His musings broke under a sentence from Arlos Arien was sure he understood. He would go back and soak beans for the evening meal, and there were a few errands to run. How do I know this? It dawned on him his quickening around Bessie must have tuned it in!

Oh my God! Arlos barely turned away and the girl was on him like a ravenous cat. A spotted, amber-colored squash dropped from his basket as they fell into the hay covered aisle.

"No! No!" He tried to push her away, but it had to be the most erotic push of his life. Bessie danced around his arms until their randy fire exploded like colliding stars. How her body collapsed onto his, peeling their tunics away in a shuddering spasm of pleasure, rolling and tussling, and spontaneous laughing, and now it was she looking up at him, with the firm, coffee pectorals of a teenage Aphrodite. It was so pure and powerful, her eyes wide and delighted, and her body was as warm as hot bagels, steaming, smelling delicious, all ready to eat.

"Oh... I've died and gone to Heaven!" he cried, and pressed trembling lips, breast and limbs to hers, and she kissed his misgivings, his trepidation, and his better angel, and she seemed to suck them into herself with her breath and blow them back into him as something transformed and transcendent, beautiful and sweet.

Jesus this baby is high! Arien found his way into her as if Bessie's whole body opened and closed, and she might as well have taken the rest of him inside of her as well.

Taught, ecstatic waves rode out of her now. They splashed back through him and into her again; she dug her fingers into his back, they roared like lions, and Arien just knew their consummation would ignite another life. Holy shit! He knew it! He knew it in his very bones. Tina, she gathered to her, and Aspen. They were having the coupling of gods! It was the first and the best between, all at once. And what he blew into young Bessie Girl took everything he had to give.

Arien could still feel her body when he awoke, but it evaporated in thick, tender grass as he pushed himself up, coming to his senses, warm in his body's impression, and warm on his back under a perfect sun. Hot damn, I must have crashed, big time!

"Huh?" His surprise fell against the curious inspection of a handsome young dude, maybe fourteen, give or take a month, hunkering over him. The boy's wavy, neck-length, sandy hair and green eyes were a striking contrast against skin tanner than life on a tropical beach. It contrasted with a light-blue tunic in that rough homespun of the clothes people here wore.

Arien realized he'd awakened without anything on. His tunic was missing! He was in a meadow, though he recognized its location by the creek. The garden had ceased to exist!

"What...? How?" he asked aloud.

There was a long moment where the boy inspected him with a curious cant to his head. "Diss doan lettin seet – ond naut," he haltingly said, pointing with a grin, and a few other, likewise unintelligible words, but his meaning was fairly clear, even without a telepathic advantage. He bore a striking resemblance to Bessie, come to think of it. He could have been her brother!

"Bessie? Where's Bessie?" Arien sheepishly asked, feeling his way through sitting with drawn knees, or bravely standing, when another strange awareness came to him, the cottonwoods over the creek wore buds of bright green, not yet big enough to block the sunrays but enough to catch the yellow light and loudly glow with it. It was obviously a balmy day, sometime in the spring! This was totally crazy. He watched himself wonder if his head would explode.

"Bessie," the boy repeated under drawn eyebrows. Arien could practically see the wheels turning in the kid's head. He giggled with a familiar recognition, disarming and friendly, rattling out a torrent of foreign words.

Then Arien caught the drift of meaning with the sure ascension of yet another threshold. Wow! I'm getting his thoughts! Maybe all these people were like this! Cypriano, Alice, Tina, Arlos, Bessie, and now... *Bessie is the name of my mother! How do you come to know her name?*

Arien sank under an awful reflection. This was totally out of control. He grasped for any explanation to deflect an unsettling dread; the eternal orphan at his hundredth foster home. Would it change with the hours now, in a time-lapsed detonation to a rootless hell? He decided to stay where he was, seated on the ground. He folded his legs and modestly joined his hands for a scrap of cover.

The teenager appeared confused, evidentially reading the stranger as best he could. *Who are you? Where are you from?*

Maybe the future, maybe not. I don't know, Arien answered, while wondering if he'd actually died and was stuck in an afterlife. He reviewed recent events at the air base and later, in the examination room with that creepy doctor, or whatever she was, and then finally coming to this crazed epoch. What the...?

The boy's eyes widened with the drop of his jaw. He followed that with a fusillade of wonderings; complex questions seeking associations and meanings, all organically and intrinsically linked to his feelings, emotions, senses, even down to the biological consignments of his living and conscious brain! Arien followed him like a bird, soaring high over the country of dreams, memories, and their chemical and emotional associations. They appeared out of darkness to grayscale photo-frame hedgerows bordering fields, red as clay, and hills with sparking, yellow-flashing, snapping branches in the canopy of its tangled forests, and all under a thick, black blanket of sky, before touching down on landmarks where clues and secrets are tucked away; digging, reaching, prying for that mother lode, that gangster's ledger with every conceivable incrimination, but with true empathy, and concern, yet relentlessly fueled with feverous, infectious, shamelessly greedy curiosity.

At first Arien freaked! His natural reflex was to block the veritable assault. The perfectly fascinated boy had sunk to his knees and leaned forward, catlike, knuckles in the grass, leading intensely with his startling green eyes, and they were mere inches from Arien's. This marvelous intrusion was far too intimate for a stranger, yet the stranger was so self-confident, earnest, and true. His eye was single, and through that eye he poured the keenest, searching beam, while Arien reflexively struggled against an unlikely submissive impulse to just let it flow.

No! No! Stop! I'm being raped!

"Ah!" Arien helplessly squeaked, only too conscious of his objective and subjective exposure and melting defenses before the most determined, psychic plundering by a preternaturally beautiful and psychically powerful kid.

He was very familiar, going far, far beyond, "Where have I seen you before?" It was really strange, reminding Arien of the first time with his dad, in Berkeley, in 1969, and they were the same age, and there was this underlying, self-evident thing between them. My God, this kid could be my brother, too!

And now the bird hung midway in the air. It seemed to stop there, defying the physics of moving objects, even objects as light as thoughts.

What is your name? Arien formulated, relieved to know this capacity hadn't been stolen along with his virginity, if it could be called that.

"Arien," the teenager said aloud, *and you are Arien, too, yes?*

Of course Arien's mind turned to Bessie. She was such a nubile kid, barely older than this boy here, and easily as beautiful, soft, and steamy hot as a volcanic spring.

Funny, but coming to respond, Arien realized he was inside of Arien as well, finding his way over the strangest bloody tangle of a landscape, over measureless distances of pulsing convolutions with a storm of thoughts and feelings in scattered flashes of lightning, color and shadow. At least this power, if that's what it was, worked both ways or not at all. And the boy could lean no further, but pressed his forehead against the visitor's, and he unconsciously pursed his lips into a kiss. And then he drew away enough to display his surprise, with a hint of a smile, and he'd grown hot and was blushing. *For all that is holy!*

A giggle erupted suddenly between the two of them. Arien was rock hard, and he knew this slightly younger version that bore his name had a boner, too. And that only compounded his rushing, and its exponentially erotic oscillations. So he pushed to stop him when the teenager leaned into him a second time and tried to turn away as their foreheads ever-so-barely tapped together once more. But he couldn't quite do that. Resistance simply crumbled. This was new, and the reflex to block it was overwhelmed by a morbid, insistent curiosity and the sheer thrill of the ride. He defeated himself, his very bearings slipping out from under his feet like a sand dune.

It was so quiet. Arien could hear the ripple of the creek, and the waft of the lightest, balmy breeze through branches in the cottonwoods. The grass smelled as if it had been cut beneath him, and the tender, early growth had its tender, early sound, like fingers moving through hair.

You are so innocent, so fresh; so eager to know!

For all that is holy!

Please don't touch me.

I don't have to. He laughed, projecting this.

Arien wanted to think of something else, but the boy kept leading him back. He wanted to see it. He wanted to know what it was like!

My mother... Oh, this is so... He groaned.

Arien felt wet, and he knew the boy was, too. He was exultant, panting, gurgling with pleasure and falling into the warmth of an evidently marvelous new experience.

She's still hot, Arien thought, seeing her as she was now in the mind of this unlikely kid.

He really wanted an answer to the mystery of these people. Having self-consciousness forcefully removed, as it were, freed Arien from his seat in the grass. They could have grown up together in the same room. Such a relief! He simply stood and wandered to the bank of the creek where the chill water snapped at his toes. The boy followed with a shit-eating grin stuck to his young face, and Arien spied the lad's glistening testimony, still drooling as he pealed his tunic off.

Jesus! Shouldn't I be grossed-out, maybe freaked-out, or is this one of the most beautiful things I've ever seen?

I didn't even have to touch it! Arien the Younger marveled.

Arien's thought was, you can't fake it on acid. It was like that, very clear and certain, but without any drug.

What is 'acid'? He blithely followed the question with an easy step over Arien's cracked foundations and buckled walls into the deep detritus of a pillaged room. And Arien watched his own thoughts and memories deliver the experience until the kid was satisfied. *Oh. It seems like a tool to do what you can anyway do.*

But it's not so easy without it. Most people I know need it to get there.

Young Arien's stare politely refuted that. *I'm sorry if I may have frightened and offended you. I didn't know. I never knew anyone so, so rusty. You know only other rusty people? You are from a very strange place.*

Was rusty the best word? It did appear to translate what he meant. Arien tried his pressing question again. What is your history (fully recognizing the irony of asking such a question)? It was met with an overwhelming set of images and associations, too many and fleeting to stick in his head. It made him feel illiterate and stupid. Wow. I don't get it.

You're not making any sense, he admitted. He tried a different tack as he waded into the crisp, hurrying water. What year is it?

You don't know?

Arien didn't answer him. The creek wasn't deep, though there was a hollow in the bottom better than a full bath. He eased into that with a slow exhale to distract his cold water reflex. It always worked. He was submerged before the shiver could change his mind, and controlling his breath further, along with a determined movement, maintained the distraction long enough to get with it.

Young Arien studied him while he followed to settle in another, but shallower spot.

I like that. You taught me something new.

No problem.

It's the eleven thousandth, four-hundredth and fifty-second year since the Great Fever, Father. When his thought went there, to that word in Arien's mind, *Father,* his eyes matched the sparkle in the current's ripples against the younger's hair. He rolled his head into gravel just under the water's surface, even though his lips were surely going blue.

Perhaps it's his tears, Arien considered, moved by the very bright inner-light and deep well of joy emanating from this boy.

Oh my, such a long time! The Great Fever? Was that a plague?

Hmmm... Our Mother's Fever. Oh... Oh... You are not from here at all! You are from...

Arien watched the wheels go round in the boy's head as he provided an overview, seeing trace expressions, subtle shadows, and complex emotions flutter over his face.

For all that is –

– Holy, Arien finished, totally fascinated. What is this, this process, unlimited as it appears to be, either by individual bodies or the distance between them? Arien searched frantically for symbols to appoint the pure gush of new concepts. The word, *telepathy* described it about as well as a photograph explained the Grand Canyon. Think Cypriano, and then later, Alice, and then Tina! And, there he'd thought this was a rare thing.

Arien recognized her when she appeared on the bank with a garment hanging over her arm. She looked to be about thirty, and squeaky cute had become a vision of arresting beauty. Her image in the boy's mind had been spot on.

I wondered if I would ever see you here again.

Dazzled, "Wow," was all Arien could say, and he caught the proud smile from their son. Of course he had a box full of questions. Of all he'd ever seen and done, this baffling place and the family in it took the grand prize. Who were these people? What was their country? Where am I in time? Eleven thousandth – what?

Bessie's raven hair reminded Arien of someone...

Young Arien got out of the creek, holding his arms together close to his chest and carefully, gracefully, and without reticence in his mother's proximity, stepped over the rocks. She said, or thought something to him as he picked up his tunic and pulled it over his head. Arien couldn't follow it. He'd run into this before with Alice and Tina, who were not privy to the other's communications. He searched for an analogy. The best he could come up with were different radio stations. There had to be a word for that...

Alright, I'm damn cold, Arien realized, so he followed the younger's example while the two of them watched him with pride and serenity, and in the reflected beauty of a transcendent moment. It moved him, and for some reason it reminded him of Woodstock. Crazy, I never even swam in Flippini's Pond! But he remembered it from the movie and the image worked.

Arien could tell there was a full-fledged conversation going on between the lad and his mother. As she handed over the garment she'd carried to the creek for him, her attention was askance where young Arien worked his hands and expressions along with an occasional sound, a very basic sound, as a baby might make.

Don't you use language? Why, you and Arlos –

For the deaf, yes, we are considerate of others.

Arien laughed.

You are not deaf.

But deaf people can't hear!

And this is not the same thing?

What are you saying? The lad broke in. *You can't speak to us both?*

Not at the same time, no.

Oh, she seemed to say. *This is unusual.*

It's rusty, the young fellow added.

Arien, you're rusty, yes, though her smile seemed to know more than she told.

It was strange walking away with them, *deaf* to their conversation. He worried he might appear stupid.

The modest house where Arlos and Bessie once lived looked very much the same, as did the room where he'd sat on a stool with tenderness to the soles of his feet. Come to think of it, they were still a little sore! Arien never spent enough time there to toughen his feet or recognize the changes in more than a decade, though he felt them. He expected to see the old fellow, so asked about him. Arlos wasn't home.

Arlos has moved on, Bessie's mind forwarded. Her face wore a wispy smile.

He died?

That's not what I meant.

Then, where did he go?

Young Arien chuckled, watching – and reading his young father, who modeled some of his features in white skin, with the keenest interest.

Wow, she has such love in her eyes! Arien wondered if he deserved it.

She settled onto the very same stool she was on, "only yesterday." It was in the corner of what appeared to be whitewashed walls.

Yes, that's different than it was in Arlos' house.

So, where did he move to?

Arlos didn't move to anyplace, Arien. He moved on, out there. She pointed at the ceiling.

Oh... what do you mean? Arien frowned.

The boy's grin faded to empathy.

Wow. He's so beautiful!

We move on because we can, she explained. *Almost everyone has. There are very few of us left here. Some revisit, but do not stay.*

Okay, Arien conveyed, recovering himself. It would be better to move on than be stupid. This instant family thing was very strange, having experienced two versions of it already in his life... It was now, in the confines of the moment, that Arien allowed a glimpse of trepidation over his own "moving on." One moment he'd been with this fantastic young girl and in the next was being recovered by a dark boy, only a couple of years younger, who resembled him very much. Oh, damn! Where was the lightning that time? This is SO out of control!

But then she added, *Arlos was here for our boy while I was away, awaiting my return before his passing.*

I see. Where did you go? He'd clasped his hands together while working on staying focused.

I went looking for you, Arien. You had stolen my little girl heart, she smiled, *and, well,* her smile was an invisible mountain beneath the island in a bottomless sea, *I found you just in time!*

Yeah, I guess you did, he understood, though guessed he'd missed a part of her message.

Whatever young Arien's thoughts were, his, *"This is so cool!"* expression, wide eyes, on the proverbial edge of his chair (though he was standing, swaying, and eagerly rubbing his hands together), came cleanly across.

Holy fuck! The hair on Arien's neck tingled with the rush of his profound surprise. Through a passage to another room he could see it, hanging on the far wall. He got up from where he'd taken a meal once with Arlos and Bessie, and went right for it, both knowing and disbelieving, and with a hammering heart he laid his hand on the heavy, bright red blanket, or – or was it her cloak?

"This can't be!" he protested aloud.

Oh, I wish I could have been there, Father! The boy was practically giddy. He paced and excitedly clasped and unclasped his hands.

Bessie's smile had gone obscure and deep. Arien could feel her against the back of his head. The pictures reeling-out over and across the brow of his mind from hers were from a reality that was very far away, in the desert of Arizona, the gymnasium of a spanky-new high school in Sandy, Oregon, and many other places in between. And he marveled at the awesome power she wielded, defending him against another advanced, but pathological race. Oh, there was so much to learn! These were not simple people at all!

You're still coming of Age, Arien. You were among the first in your time. Eventually you will learn to control it, maybe even as well as our child. It's okay. You will be alright.

As well as Arien! "Oh, my God! This is too awesome! It's way too rad! Oh my God!"

What a funny language! The lad sent to his father. *You're so –*

Primitive? Arien turned around to face him. It was a strange word for him to dig out of his head.

How? He asked of her. How did you go there?

At first, it takes at least two of us. Arlos didn't want me to go, but then he reached for the answer, its rightness, and it came to him, Why not? This was a big thing. So he agreed, and together we manifested the way.

But how? Arien became the question. He had to know! It was perfectly excruciating.

Bessie obviously spoke, and their boy suddenly appeared ready to explode with excitement.

What did she say? Arien could see an important decision was going down.

Arien, do you want to do it with him? He repeated, along with his response, carried in the moment's inscription of his memory, *Oh, Mother! May I?*

Calm yourself, Son, Arien conveyed to him. Take a few breaths.

Now Bessie clapped her hands in glee, and young Arien certainly blushed, for his periphery glowed with a hint of rose, and there was surely an instants' beaming from his eyes in ruby to vermillion and magenta tones, recalling fanning rays of a setting sun piercing the red horizon's flotilla of clouds.

Arien gaped at him. The kid's vibe was so intense, as a force of nature can dazzle the very soul of the observer. "My God!" Arien exclaimed aloud. "Arien, you're my son! Oh, so way mega radical! I can't believe how much I love you! You're so fucking beautiful! I can't believe it!" And I've only met you today!

The fervent wash of emotion was so great it threatened to swamp his boat. A rush so powerful almost reached for the needle that could have remained stuck in his arm. He struggled to hold onto his mind, to stand without sinking to his knees in a whirlpool of joy and sorrow, love, and even oblivion.

This is perfect, Arien, Bessie confided. *Hold onto that.* And she said something to the boy as well. Then, she added, *Quick! We need to go outside while the sun is still high enough!*

A breeze had come up, swaying branches in the treetops, as if from the Effects Department adding a pinch of drama to the occasion. They went on to an open area, away from the cottage, halting between a pair of ancient cottonwoods in a pool of daylight.

Stand shoulder to shoulder with him now, like this, Bessie instructed, and she stepped on one side, to wrap an arm around Arien's waist. *Face the sun, the two of you. Close your eyes. Concentrate on the light and all you see there.*

The boy's vibe was even stronger to hold him. Arien swooned with another rush to his head.

Concentrate!

Arien rallied. The kid was so strong, but he knew he had it, too. Tree knew it, at Medicine Bow; the Stand, Andy, Otter, Tina, and Jeff knew it well enough. All the Tree Family would know it. Arien had something special. And it was no small thing that Bessie drew their concentration, focusing them like a pair of lenses.

The pink glow of a slanting springtime sun from inside eyelids began to do its thing. Perhaps it was the shadow of a branch, or the tiniest blood vessel, but a form seemed to manifest, amorphous at first, and then assumed a slight undulation; a fabric in the gentlest breeze.

"Wow," Arien whispered, which was just enough of a sound to hear its faintest echo. He opened his eyes just as Bessie let go of him and all he saw of her was a ball of brilliant light move away from the two of them inside this thing, arms yet wrapped around each other. Young Arien wore the most beatific expression. They were surrounded everywhere in an interplay of light and pure energy. It had a sound, a vibration pitched above audibility, yet sensed and known by their souls as well as by the tingle in their bodies. And with roaming thought and a spontaneous utterance – the OM Arien instinctively belted out, to join a harmonious blending of the younger's voice – the structure began to assume itself into a recognizable object while reflecting sound in a marvelous interplay of color, and shades of color, and tones of colors beyond description. And there it was, and they were inside of it; sparkling bits of light, delicate silvery, undulating threads to lines and arcs, into an infinitely complex structural design like a ball of huge, interlaced snowflakes, above, around, and below them.

Is it form? Is it energy?

Both. It's both.

The Celestial Ship!

Oh, where do you want to go? The boy was so eager to run with it.

I want to see a real dinosaur! And, oh... Do you think we can visit some other planets?

But first, Arien saw himself in Sedona on that day the world didn't end...

And, oh wait! We have friends and family there, Ari. We need to get them out of a jam, Dude.

www.ingramcontent.com/pod-product-compliance
Lightning Source LLC
Chambersburg PA
CBHW071525260626
47170CB00002B/506